WARNING

This book contains sexually explicit scenes and adult language. It may be considered offensive to some readers. This book is for sale to adults ONLY.

* * * * * * * * * * * * * * * * * *

Please store your files wisely where they cannot be accessed by underage readers.

ISBN-13: 978-1987863673
ISBN-10: 1987863674

Other Books by Carla Coxwell:

<u>Star Bright New Adult Romance Series</u> (This series follows "<u>Fifty Recipes For Disaster New Adult Romance Series</u>")

Torn between her feelings for her agent, Jon, and Rich, a charming bad boy who has ties in the movie industry, Jenny finds herself working through her own past to try to get a grip on her present. As she struggles to learn the lesson that in Hollywood not everyone is what they appear to be, Jenny tries to become a person that she can be proud of. Will she be able to find love and success in Hollywood? Or will she be dragged down by her past forever?

<u>Torrid Exposure New Adult Romance Series</u>

April is finished with school and ready to build a career. Coming from a well-to-do family, she has decided to reboot her life completely. With family scars too deep to mend, April craves a fresh start. But the past is harder to shake than April ever would have imagined. At the center of it all is Bennett, an old family friend who is the heir to a billionaire media mogul company. Bennett and April haven't been able to stand each other since they were kids. But as the world shifts, the two of them discover the past might be the key to their future.

<u>Devil's Advocate BBW MC New Adult Romance Series</u>

When Kristie comes home from college, the last thing she is expecting is her world to be turned upside down by the appearance of her step-brother, Gray. Gray is rash, impulsive and breaks the law. Kristie's mom asks if she can try to befriend Gray, in hopes to get him on the straight and narrow. The plan backfires, however, as Kristie finds herself falling for Gray. Is it possible he feels the same way? The connection between them threatens to tear down everything Kristie has ever held dear.

<u>Obsessed Bounty Hunter Romance Series</u>

Jacqui Schneider couldn't help it. Every time the memories of her family's brutal murder haunted her, she had to escape. The only thing that could replace her sorrow was sex...and lots of it. Depressed and with no goal in sight, Jacqui continued on with her self-deprecating lifestyle until it all changed one day. Uncle Max, an old family friend, appeared unannounced. Jacqui was astonished when Uncle Max revealed a secret to her about her father. From those few words, Jacqui's world turned completely upside down. She really didn't know her own father. In fact, she didn't even know much about Uncle Max, except that he visited them for a few days at a time over the years.

Get the latest update on new releases from the author at:

https://www.carlacoxwell.com/newsletter

This book contains all the stories of the "<u>Fifty Recipes For Disaster New Adult Romance Series</u>"

Book 1

Trying to win a competition for best chef is cut-throat business. Kiara Sands has just won the opportunity of a lifetime. When she arrives at Fission, she has no idea just how much her life is going to change. She's immediately introduced to Jenny Foster and Robbs Martin, her competitors in the cut throat competition. The only thing Kiara finds more distracting than Robbs' hateful attitude is the handsome executive chef, Paul Weston. It doesn't help matters that Paul is quite taken by Kiara, and showers her with more attention than he gives her competitors.

Book 2

Life in the Fission kitchen has become difficult for Chef Kiara Sands. While she tries to focus on her work, the rest of the employees pass their time gossiping about her boyfriend, Executive Chef Paul Weston. Paul isn't making things easy either. His time is consumed with rearranging things for the pending changes in his life. He is pushing most of his workload off on Kiara. Instead of an apprentice, Kiara is acting more like manager in the kitchen. As Kiara and Paul's relationship is tested, a new threat arrives in the form of celebrity chef James O'Toole.

Book 3

Chef Kiara Sands finally feels like she's getting her life back on track. She's arrived in New York City to start her dream job as apprentice to celebrity chef James O'Toole. But just as she settles into her new life, her past comes back to haunt her. Jenny, Paul, and Robbs have all arrived in the city and they each want something from her. Kiara is convinced that her life will be perfect if they would just leave her alone. What she doesn't realize is that an unknown force is working against her, not to ruin her perfect life, but to end her life completely.

Book 4

Kiara learns that her scholarship at *Le Cordon Bleu* has been revoked and no one will tell her why. Her almost boyfriend, Chase Abbott, promises to look into it for her… he also gives Kiara and Jenny a safe place to stay until the police capture Robbs. The attraction between Kiara and Chase rekindles the moment they're reunited but Kiara isn't ready to start a new relationship. The women struggle to put their lives back together and live with the constant fear that Robbs will return. Will the police catch Robbs before he hurts Kiara and Jenny again? Will Kiara finally let down her guard and give in to her feelings for Chase? Or will everything end in disaster?

Fifty Recipes For Disaster New Adult Romance Series

Books One to Four

By Carla Coxwell

Copyright Revelry Publishing 2015

Table of Contents

Book One

Chapter One

"**ALL RIGHT**, chefs, you have ninety seconds to get your food plated and presented. If your dish isn't ready, you will automatically be eliminated."

My cooking instructor, Chef Michelle Lee, walks through the room, examining our stations. My fellow cooking students and I are competing for the chance to enter another competition. The winner of today's cooking challenge will get the chance to compete for a full-time apprenticeship at Fission, one of Austin's hottest restaurants.

I'm not confident in many aspects of my life, but I know I dominate in the kitchen. I begin plating my dish just as Chef Lee approaches my station.

"Your food presents beautifully as usual, Kiara," she tells me with a smile. "If it tastes as good as it looks, you've got this in the bag," she adds with a soft whisper.

The instructors at *Le Cordon Bleu College of Culinary Arts* aren't supposed to show favoritism to their students, but Chef Lee keeps a soft spot for me. Along with being one of my teachers, she's also my faculty adviser, and she knows the unusual circumstances that brought me to the school.

"Time's up," she calls out to the class. "Place your finished plates on the head table."

I walk my plate to the front of the room and place it on top of the placard that holds my student ID number. My classmates follow suit… several of them glare at me after looking at my dish. I am delighted, knowing they're all both jealous and impressed I was able to execute a well-developed *Cioppino* within the given time frame. My rich seafood stew is accompanied by fresh sourdough loaves. I examine my classmates' dishes and feel my chances of winning are good.

"Clear away your stations," Chef Lee directs. "Chef Lawton will be here shortly to judge your plates, and I don't want any evidence of who made what on display when he arrives."

Chef Lawton is the *sous* chef at Fission and the judge of this stage of the apprenticeship competition. I clear my station quickly and then I take a seat at the front of the room. I want to be able to see Chef Lawton's expressions as he tastes each dish.

As I sit nervously in my chair, my classmates finish clearing their stations. I can tell everyone else is just as anxious as I am… we've received plenty of critiques from our instructors but this will be the first time a professional chef from a restaurant will be tasting our food. The door of the classroom opens and a tall man wearing a black chef's jacket enters the room.

"Chef Lawton, it's so lovely to see you," Chef Lee welcomes him. "I can't tell you how excited we are to participate in this competition."

"We're excited as well," Chef Lawton replies. "We're always looking for new, innovative chefs at Fission. I'm looking forward to tasting the dishes and welcoming one of your students into the final leg of the competition. I see that all of the plates are ready. If it's all right with you, I'll get started."

"Of course," Chef Lee agrees.

I try not to hold my breath as I watch Chef Lawton sample each of the plates. I feel encouraged when he reaches mine. Instead of sampling one bite and moving on, he holds the broth in his mouth for a moment, and then tastes each type of seafood in turn. The expression on his face tells me that my stew is perfect, and I say a silent prayer I haven't been out-cooked by any of my classmates.

"First off, I'd like to say this is an impressive display," the seasoned chef begins. "Everything on this table is up to par with the level of skill and talent I expect to see from second-year students. That being said, there is a clear winner. One chef not only executed a delicious dish, but also added a few subtle, original touches that showed innovation and creativity."

Adrenaline rushes through me as he moves to stand behind my dish. "Who created this *Cioppino*?" he asks.

I blush involuntarily as I raise my hand.

"And what is your name, Chef?"

"Kiara Sands," I reply, trying to mask the excitement in my voice.

"Well, Chef Sands, it's an honor to welcome you to the next stage of the competition. I look forward to tasting more of your food as the weeks progress. I am needed back at Fission, but Chef Lee will provide you with the details of your new position." He turns to the rest of the class. "To the rest of you, don't be discouraged. You all provided me with excellent dishes, and you have bright futures ahead of you."

"Thank you, Chef," the class responds in unison.

Chef Lawton makes a quick exit, and Chef Lee takes his place behind the head table. "Excellent work today, class. You're dismissed until tomorrow," she announces. My classmates gather their things and leave the room… I stay behind to talk to Chef Lee.

"Kiara, I'm so proud of you." She beams once we are alone. "As you know, there will be two other chefs competing with you at Fission. You're the only one who's been selected from *Le Cordon Bleu*, and I know you'll represent us well." She moves to her desk and pulls a large package from her bottom drawer. "Here is your apprenticeship packet. You'll receive your Fission jacket when you report for work tomorrow morning. If you have any questions, or just need someone to talk to, you know where to reach me."

"This seems like a wonderful dream, and part of me is afraid that I'll wake up any minute now," I confess.

Chef Lee gives me a maternal smile. "This is a dream, Kiara. It's *your* dream. And you're well on your way to achieving it."

<<◇>>

The information packet Chef Lee presented me with instructs me to be at Fission at 10:00 am. I check my dashboard clock as I pull into the parking lot… 9:40 am. I feel smug, knowing I'm probably the first of the three competitors to arrive. I check my makeup in the rear-view mirror before exiting my car.

Fission is housed in a modern brick building in East Austin, one of the city's burgeoning hipster areas. The area gives off a relaxed, laid-back vibe, but I know the kitchen of Fission will be anything but.

I push open the heavy, solid oak door and am greeted by a pixy-sized hostess with spiked, lavender hair.

"Table for one?" she asks me brightly.

"No," I reply nervously. "My name is Kiara Sands. I'm supposed to start work today."

"Oh! You're one of the newbies!" She says warmly. "I'm Megan. It's a pleasure to meet you. The other two are already here. I'll show you to their table."

Damn it! I'd been so sure I'd make the best impression by arriving first, and here I am, the last of the apprentices to report for our first day.

Megan seems to sense my disappointment. "Don't worry. Paul doesn't give a shit how early people show up. As long as you're here when you're scheduled, you'll be fine. And you haven't missed anything. The other two have just been sitting alone since they got here," she offers reassuringly.

"Thank you for that," I say half-heartedly. As I follow Megan through the restaurant, I'm struck by the eclectic, well-placed décor. All of the tables are made of the same polished oak as the front door. The water goblets on the tabletops are tinted in hues of blue, green, and rose… a selection of art from all around the world adorns the walls. The ambiance is on the right side of the fine line between cozy and overwhelming. The restaurant offers a large main dining room, with smaller, more private rooms on each side.

"This is a beautiful place," I say as Megan leads me toward the back of the main room.

"It is," she agrees. "Paul handled all of the decorating himself. He says that Austin is a melting pot, and he wants all of our customers to feel at home when they dine here."

I'm about to comment on how successfully that goal had been achieved when we arrive at a table occupied by a beautiful blonde woman and a swarthy man with sandy blond hair. A pot of coffee and three cups sit on the table.

"Kiara Sands, this is Jenny Foster and Robbs Martin," Megan introduces us. She checks her watch before speaking again. "It's a quarter to ten, so I imagine that Paul will be out shortly. I suggest you get fully caffeinated and enjoy this time off your feet. It will be the last one for today," she warns with a friendly, knowing tone.

I take a seat in the chair next to Jenny as Megan moves back to the hostess station. "It's a pleasure to meet you both," I offer.

"It's a pleasure to meet you too," Robbs replies. "Congratulations on making it this far in the competition. And I'd like to apologize right now for how thoroughly I'm going to kick both of your asses. This job is mine." He speaks with a blend of arrogance and sarcasm, and I can tell immediately that Robbs and I are not going to get along.

Personal relationships are something I struggle with. In my experience, there's no point in getting close to someone who will inevitably let you down. I prefer to keep my head down and focus on getting my job done. As Chef Lee said yesterday, I have a dream and I'm well on my way to achieving it. I'll be damned if I let Robbs or anyone else get in my way.

"Just ignore Robbs," Jenny advises me. "He thinks that he's God's gift to food... women too, probably." She giggles. "So Kiara, what's your story? Which campus were you plucked from?"

"I'm in my second year at *Le Cordon Bleu*," I answer with pride. In my opinion, *Le Cordon Bleu* is the best culinary school in the area—it's also the hardest to get in to. Jenny seems impressed by my background, but Robbs laughs and dismisses it immediately.

"The *Bleu* is all right, I guess," he snorts, "if you're happy being complacent and doing everything old-school."

"I wasn't aware that being classically trained is a bad thing," I reply shortly. "Tell me, what culinary Mecca do you hail from?"

"*Escoffier*," he answers with a cocky smile. "You know, where all of the innovative, cutting-edge people attend. Three of my instructors were nominated for the James Beard award. So like I said, no hard feelings, but I'm going to kick both of your asses. *Escoffier* specializes in farm-to-table cuisine, so I'm exactly the kind of chef Fission is looking for."

I dismiss his statement with a glare. While the *Auguste Escoffier School of Culinary Arts* is reputed for turning out fantastic chefs, in some culinary circles it's dismissed as a hipster college that prioritizes food trends over basic technique and skill.

I don't feel like debating the merits of my education with Robbs, so I turn to Jenny. "And where do you go?" I ask pleasantly.

"The Art Institute," she replies. "I'm still not positive that cooking is my life's passion. I wanted to go to a college that offers other programs, in case I decided to change my major."

"If you're not sure that you want to be a chef, then what the fuck are you doing here?" Robbs asks hotly. "You should give your spot to someone who knows that this is what they want."

Jenny's green eyes fill with both anger and embarrassment, and I can tell she's fumbling for a response.

"I don't agree with that at all," I say warmly. "What better way to find out if you enjoy working in a real kitchen, than by actually doing it?"

"That's exactly what my instructor said when I won this spot," Jenny says with a nod.

"I see how it's going to be," Robbs interjects with more sarcasm. "The two of you are going to band together in 'sisterhood' and gang up on me."

"That's not how it's going to be at all," a firm voice says from behind me. I turn to see one of the most attractive men I've ever laid my eyes on. He's tall, with broad shoulders, blue eyes, and sandy blond hair. He's also wearing a black chef's jacket, identical to the one Chef Lawton wore when he judged my dish. He holds eye contact with me for several moments before he speaks again.

"This competition will come down to one thing and one thing only... the quality of your food. Only one of you will be named my new apprentice, so ganging up on each other won't serve any purpose. I'm Paul Weston, and I'd like to welcome you to my restaurant." He extends his hand to me.

I respond with a firm handshake and a smile. "I'm Kiara Sands. Thank you for this opportunity."

"You're here because you deserve to be. No thanks are necessary," he assures me.

"Chef Weston, it's an honor to meet you," Jenny gushes as she shakes hands with the executive chef. "I'm Jenny Foster."

"It's nice to meet you, Jenny," he says before turning to Robbs. "And I'm assuming that you're Robert Martin?" he asks while extending his final handshake.

"Just Robbs, Chef Weston," he responds with an air of professionalism. "I admire your talent and your vision. I'm confident I'll be a strategic asset to you."

"That will be for me to decide, Robbs," Chef Weston replies curtly. "Thank you all for being on time. I'm going to start by going over the rules here at Fission, and then we'll tour the building." He signals Megan before taking the final seat at our table.

"First and foremost, while you are here, you will show nothing but absolute respect for the rest of my staff. I take much care in handpicking each and every person who works in this restaurant. If you find yourself doubting the ideas, techniques, or decisions my staff makes, assume *you* are wrong, not them. You will do what you're told, and you will do it quickly, with a positive attitude. Is that understood?"

The three of us nod in unison.

"Fantastic. Now, that being said, I am open to hearing your ideas and opinions. You will discuss those ideas and opinions with me, and only me. If I like what I hear, I'll address it with the rest of the staff. I believe you all met Patrick Lawton, my *sous* chef?"

We all nod again.

"In addition to Patrick, there are seven line chefs working in my kitchen. You will work with each of them in turn, and they will provide me with input on who deserves the apprenticeship."

I shift uncomfortably in my chair as Chef Weston speaks. While there are three of us at the table, it seems as if he's speaking only to me. His eyes remain fixed on mine, and his face reacts to my expressions. *It's because you're the only one who comes from The Bleu. He knows you come from the best training... that's why he's speaking directly to you.* I repeat this over and over in my mind, but there's still a small part of me that suspects Chef Weston is interested in more than my cooking skills. As I try to convince myself that those suspicions are unfounded, Chef Weston continues to speak.

"Fission is open seven days a week, you will work six. You will all work twelve to fourteen hours on Saturdays and Sundays. If that presents a problem for any of you, you should leave now."

"That's not a problem at all," Robbs replies pompously. "In fact, I could pull more hours if you need it, Chef Weston."

"That won't be necessary," Chef Weston replies dismissively. "But your statement brings us to another point of discussion. When we are in the kitchen, you are all to address me and the other staff as 'chef'. Outside of the kitchen, you're welcome to call me Paul. The other chefs and I will provide you with the same courtesy."

"Let me explain my vision behind Fission," Paul continues. "I've always been intrigued by the role food plays in different cultures. After graduating from culinary school, I spent three years traveling the world and learning about exotic ingredients and techniques. When I came home, I opened Fission as a way to showcase what I'd learned and show how those ingredients and techniques can be blended to create food that is both exotic and familiar. There are no rules in my kitchen regarding the types of cuisine you can blend and the types you cannot. I encourage you to use your imaginations and your talent to make the best dishes possible."

"This sounds like my dream job," Robbs interjects. "And I'd like you to know I'm highly skilled in executing farm-to-table menus. I know that's important in today's culinary atmosphere."

God, will he ever stop bragging about himself?

"Robbs, if you're as skilled and knowledgeable as you should be, then you already know the farm-to-table concept is nothing new," Paul answers impatiently. "In many areas of the world, all restaurants are 'farm to table' and families rely on their harvest to feed their customers. While I admire the American chefs who are utilizing that concept in the U.S., I refuse to limit myself and my staff in such a strict way. At Fission, we use as many locally sourced ingredients as possible. All of our beef, lamb, pork, and chicken come from farms in the surrounding area, as well as our seasonal produce. But exotic ingredients are imported from the countries that know how best to grow them. I'm sure a chef of your caliber understands that."

Listening to Paul take down Robbs relaxes me, and I'm comforted to know that the executive chef and I share the same attitude toward food.

"Of course, Paul," Robbs replies in a defeated tone. "This is your restaurant, and I respect your vision."

"Fantastic," Paul continues. "Now that we've covered the cuisine, let me describe what your next twelve weeks will be like. As already stated, you will each work six days a week. During each shift, you will either assist one of the line chefs or you will be assigned other tasks that will help me understand your talents, skills, and visions. Once a week, we will hold a cooking challenge with specific requirements. The winner of each challenge will have their dish featured as a weekend special. High volume, fast-paced kitchens aren't for everyone, so if at any time you feel overwhelmed, you may bow out of the competition. As you're each receiving college credit for your work here, anyone who chooses to bow out will be allowed to continue helping in the kitchen through the end of the semester. Any questions?"

The three of us shake our heads.

"Perfect. We open for lunch in thirty minutes. I'll give you a quick tour of the kitchen, and then your first shift will officially begin. Today you will be shadowing the wait staff."

Robbs appears disappointed by the announcement, while Jenny's face reflects the confusion I feel at the assignment.

"I know what you're thinking." Paul smiles. "This competition is for a spot in the kitchen, so why are you bothering with the servers? I feel too many chefs become complacent in the kitchen. The chef is rarely the person who takes heat from the customers when their order isn't to their liking. I've also witnessed many chefs who believe, unjustly, that their training and skills make them superior to the servers. That is not the case here. Each employee serves a specific purpose. We are a team, and each member of the team is vital to the restaurant's success. During your time here, you will learn to appreciate the roles of each and every one of my employees. Is that understood?" Paul asks the question to all of us but directs his gaze specifically at Robbs.

"Of course," Robbs answers tensely. I can tell the day isn't playing out the way he expected.

Paul rises from the table and the three of us do the same. We follow him through the swinging doors at the back of the room and enter the biggest kitchen I've ever seen. Viking ranges line both horizontal walls, while a line of butcher-block tables cuts the room in half. Five chefs work on the lunch specials, in anticipation of the crowd that's sure to descend at any moment.

"Each member of the kitchen staff works their own station, ovens, and stovetops," Paul explains as we walk to the back of the room. Three-fourths of the back wall is made of stainless steel, and I correctly assume it's the walk-in refrigerator. Paul opens the metal door and gestures inside. "The walk-in is to remain clean and organized at all times. The introductory packet provided by your instructor details the health department codes for food storage. You will be tested on those first thing tomorrow."

Paul shuts the metal door and moves to the wooden one that opens to the other quarter of the space. "This is the pantry," he informs us. "Like the walk-in, it is to remain organized at *all* times. I can't emphasize the importance of this enough. For service to run smoothly, everyone who works here needs to be able to open these doors and go straight to what they need."

"Understood, Chef," I respond.

"Yes, with your *Cordon Bleu* background, I expect you do," he replies with a warm look. Once again, he holds his gaze on me a little longer than necessary.

Robbs visibly tenses beside me. He clears his throat. "Chef, I was told we'd receive our jackets when we arrived this morning?" he asks in an obvious attempt to steer the subject away from my education.

"You will receive your jackets when I decide you've earned them, Chef," Paul answers firmly. He turns to face the rest of the kitchen. "Chefs, gather for just a moment please," he calls out.

There is a clamoring of noise as each of the chefs pull pans off of their stoves and place utensils to the side. They line up in front of us as if they are military officers reporting for inspection.

"Chefs, these are the new up and comers who will be competing for the apprenticeship spot." As Paul introduces us by name, I now feel as if I'm the one being inspected. "Chefs Robbs, Jenny, and Kiara, this is most of the team you'll be working with. They will now introduce themselves and describe their duties."

The portly, bald man standing to the far right takes one step forward. "Welcome to Fission. I'm Chef Michael, and I'm the Roast Chef. I also serve as Butcher. I hope to enjoy working with all of you."

Chef Michael steps back and is followed by Chef Cole the *saucier*, Chef Henry the seafood specialist, Chef Harrison the grill-master, and Chef Jacqueline the fry chef. They each greet us warmly, but with reservation, as if they're sizing us up to determine if we're worthy to be in their kitchen.

"Chef Patrick and his assistant, Chef Carlton, as well as Chef Claire, our *pâtissier*, will arrive for the evening shift," Paul explains. "You will meet them before you leave tonight. If there are no questions, I'll escort you to the server station, where you will receive your shadow assignments."

Chapter Two

I sit alone at a small table in the back of Fission. This is my third day at the restaurant, and the first I'll be allowed to cook. It's Thursday morning, and the first challenge for the weekend special will start in half an hour.

I've discovered I like to come in early and enjoy a pot of coffee before work begins. It gives me time to settle in and feel comfortable in the restaurant I still find a bit intimidating. Over the past two days, I managed to follow all of Paul's instructions and complete the chores assigned to me with a happy disposition. Tuesday, I shadowed Kinley, the head-waitress. I made polite conversation with the customers, carried her trays, and filled her drink orders. When we arrived yesterday, Jenny, Robbs, and I were informed we would be the cleaning crew for the day. Jenny and I bussed tables, washed dishes, and cleaned the bathrooms, all the while maintaining a pleasant, cheerful attitude. Robbs begrudgingly completed the same tasks, letting everyone in the restaurant know by his attitude that he felt he was above doing the scut work.

I hope my positive attitude, especially compared to Robbs' petulant one, is the reason Paul seems drawn to me. Over the last two days, I caught him gazing in my direction several times. He even helped me clean the ladies' room yesterday. He said as the boss, he believes he should never ask an employee to do something he's not willing to do himself. While that's a wonderful philosophy, I still feel like there's more to the attention he's giving me than professional admiration.

As I sip my coffee, I wonder about today's cooking challenge. I am confident in my skills, but I haven't seen Jenny or Robbs cook yet. For all I know, they are better than I am. I check the time on my phone just as Jenny walks through the front door. She sees me sitting at the back table, grabs a coffee mug from behind the bar, and joins me.

"Good morning," she greets me brightly. "Are you ready for the challenge?"

"I hope so," I answer with a nervous grin. "Paul said these challenges will be specific. I wonder what we'll be doing today."

"I don't know. I must say, the way this competition is set up reminds me of all of those cooking shows on television. I keep expecting a cameraman to pop up any second."

"That's exactly what I think!" I agree with a laugh. "I admit, culinary reality TV is one of my few guilty pleasures. I watch all of them."

"Me too!" Jenny replies. "I'd love to be on one someday... or judge one."

"Maybe one day we'll do one together." I don't make friends easily, but I like Jenny. She seems kind, honest, and genuine.

"My parents would just die if I end up on television," Jenny says. "They're incredibly conservative. I was never allowed to watch anything but the public access channels. And even then, they had to approve each show before I watched it."

"That sounds rough," I respond uncomfortably. I know what's coming next, and I dread it.

"What are your parents like?" Jenny asks.

This is a common question, and one I never answer honestly. "They were great," I answer quickly. "But they passed away when I was sixteen. I've been on my own ever since."

"Oh, I'm so sorry to hear that," Jenny quickly replies. She can sense I am uncomfortable and pulls out her cell phone. "I'm going to take advantage of these last few minutes and study."

I know this is her way of giving me some space, and I appreciate it. One thing I said to Jenny was true. I've been on my own since I was sixteen years old. Everything else was a lie. My parents weren't the best people, and they aren't dead... at least, not that I know of. My earliest memories with them are happy ones, but everything changed when I was around nine years old. That's when my father, a once-successful salesman, lost his job at the company he'd been with for twenty years. Instead of picking himself up and finding a new job, my father drowned his depression in drugs and alcohol. And instead of putting her foot down or leaving him, my mother joined him in his addictions.

After their savings ran out, my parents started selling drugs to pay for their habits. Between my ninth and sixteenth birthday, we moved fourteen times. Each new place was smaller and dirtier than the last, and I was usually left to fend for myself. When I was sixteen, I arrived home from school one day to find my parents had moved without me. The note they left behind is still tucked away in a box in a far corner of one of my closets. *Dearest Kiara, You'll be better off without us. One day you'll understand.*

I have no siblings and both sets of my grandparents died before I was born—that note was the end of my family. I shamefully explained my situation to the landlord, and he let me stay in the apartment until I graduated from high school. I worked two jobs to pay the rent and utilities, and I've become quite adept at taking care of myself. I'm not ashamed of my past, but it's not something I like to talk about, and I'm relieved Jenny isn't pushing the subject.

"I hope we're not required to make a dessert," Jenny says from across the table. "I haven't mastered pastries yet."

"I doubt it," I assure her. "The winning dish is going to be one of the weekend specials, so I'm assuming we'll be doing entrees."

"I hope so." She sighs. "I admit, I'm nervous."

"I am too," I agree as I refill each of our coffee mugs.

"If I don't win, I hope you do," Jenny says. "Robbs is a total ass. I wish we could vote him off the island."

"That would make life easier," I reply. As we joke, Robbs walks in the front door. He sees us immediately and joins us at the table.

"Good morning, ladies," he says with an arrogant grin. "Are you ready for the first of those ass kickings I promised you?"

"Sure, Robbs." Jenny smirks. "Give it your best shot. At the end of the day, we'll know who's got what it takes to be here."

"Your trash talking could use some work, Jen." Robbs smirks.

"I'd prefer if you didn't call me Jen, Robert," Jenny retorts.

As they glare at each other, Paul emerges from the kitchen with a pile of black jackets over one arm.

"Good morning," he greets us. "I hope you're all well rested and ready to get to work. There are three open stations in the kitchen. Today's assignment is fairly straightforward. You will each get a full hour to prepare an entrée. You must incorporate Latin cuisine with any other cuisines of your choosing. You're also required to incorporate at least one wood-fired element in your dish. At the end of the hour, you must present five professionally plated portions. Any questions?"

"No," Jenny, Robbs, and I answer in unison.

"Great. I'll be moving around the stations watching you as you work. I'll be judging your techniques as well as your final product." He pulls the jackets off of his arm as he speaks. "Before we step into the kitchen, I thought you all might like one of these." He passes each of us a jacket adorned with the Fission logo and embroidered with our names. We pull them on eagerly, but there is no time to admire them… Paul turns and moves toward the kitchen, and we follow. I know the exact dish I want to make, and I'm raring to get started.

We step into the kitchen, and I see the three stations closest to the back of the room are cleared off for us.

"You'll get quick access to the pantry and walk-in," Paul explains. "Chef Harrison has the grill fired up and ready, and he will taste your dishes today. You will also taste each other's dishes, not as a judge, but so you know what you're up against. Your knives are located at your stations, and your time starts now."

Robbs and Jenny immediately rush to the walk-in, so I head for the pantry. I'm going to make green curry tamales, so I gather mesa, corn husks, curry paste, and an assortment of other Indian spices. I deposit my selections at my station and move to the now unoccupied walk-in. I grab a beautiful piece of lamb, and then return to my station to mix up my marinade. I want to use the grill twice, first to cook my meat and then to sear the outside of my finished tamales. I slice the lamb and toss it into the marinade before starting on my corn mixture.

The aromas of soy and ginger fill the air and I know at least one of my competitors is preparing an Asian-inspired dish. I'm tempted to peek at their progress, but I control the urge. It wouldn't be professional, and I can't spare the time to worry about what anyone else is doing. I finish my corn mixture and then spread it out across the corn husks. Paul comes to my station to observe and

I do my best to pretend he isn't there, despite the fact my pulse races every time he looks at me.

"This is an interesting combination," he says, glancing toward my marinating lamb. "I can't wait to taste it."

"Yes, Chef," I respond without looking up.

He leaves my station, and I decide I need a fresh element for my plate. A glance at the clock tells me I need to get my lamb on the grill, and I do it quickly. Chef Harrison stands watch over the fire to ensure we don't sabotage each other, so I leave the lamb and head back to the walk-in. I consider doing a Mexican street corn with Indian spices, but decide that would be too much corn on one plate. Instead, I grab fresh spinach, tomatoes, and tomatillos. I return to my station and chop the produce. I toss half of the tomatoes and tomatillos into a food processor and add chili and spices. With a quick whirl, my dipping sauce is ready. I can smell my lamb, and I rush to the grill to turn it. The meat is seared perfectly, and I'm happy with the progression of my dish.

I return to my station just as Paul approaches again. "Your knife skills are excellent, Chef," he says with a wink.

My stomach flutters, and all I can do is nod. *This is all part of the game. He's just trying to throw you off balance. Concentrate on the work.*

I whisk up a quick vinaigrette with ginger, garlic, and a touch of black cumin. I retrieve my lamb from the grill, spread it evenly across the corn mixture, and then roll the tamales. Once I place them in the steamer, I return to the walk-in and grab a couple of kefir limes. I grate the zest into my vinaigrette, then slice them and add the juice. The salad is finished and the tamales are steaming, so I finally steal a moment to take in my surroundings.

Robbs is bent over his cutting board, painstakingly rolling out fresh tortillas. Jenny is standing over the grill, and Paul is next to her. They each let out a laugh, and I'm startled by how jealous I feel that Paul finds Jenny so damn amusing. He's your boss, I remind myself. Or at least, he will be, if everything goes right. And the only way to make that happen is to keep my head in the game.

"Fifteen minutes, ladies," Robbs calls out. "I hope you're ready for disappointment."

I turn toward Robbs' station and see he is sweating. I don't know if it's because of the heat in the kitchen or the stress of the competition, but I'm happy to see he's losing his composure a bit. I return to the pantry and select my plates. I grab kidney-shaped bowls for my salad to ensure the vinaigrette doesn't soak into the rest of my food. I return to the kitchen and gently poke one of the tamales. It feels firm, so I use tongs to retrieve them from the steamer basket.

I pause for a moment, trying to decide how I want to present my food. Traditionally, tamales are served in their husks, but that creates quite a mess for the diner, and if there's one thing I hate, it is trash on a plate. I decide to de-husk them, and do so carefully before transferring them to a platter. Paul approaches once more as I make my way to the grill.

"No husks?" he asks. "That's an interesting choice."

"Yes, Chef," I reply nervously. Damn it. I knew I should have left them on. To think, I'm going to be done in by fucking corn husks.

There's nothing I can do about it now, so I continue my dish as planned. I gently place the tamales onto the grill, careful to keep the corn casing intact. I cook them just long enough to get beautiful grill marks on each side, and then quickly return to my station. With four minutes left, I want my plates to be perfect. I transfer the dipping sauce into a squirt bottle and squeeze intricate starburst patterns onto the left side of each of my plates. I place the tamales on top of the sauce, careful to leave at least half of them on the dry portion of the plate. I portion the salad into the bowls, and then set them on the right side of the plates. A few moments after I finish drizzling the vinaigrette over the salad, Paul announces that our time is up.

"Leave your plates at your stations. We're returning to the table at the back of the main dining room," he instructs us. We follow him into the dining room and take our seats. Chef Harrison joins us, and a few moments later, Sydney and James, two of the lunch waiters, appear with our dishes.

"Chefs, before we sample the plates, I'd like you each to briefly describe your dishes," Paul instructs.

I'm not at all surprised when Robbs opens his mouth first. "I've prepared cumin-spiced chicken raviolis with a Parmesan butternut squash sauce," he announces. There's so much pride in his voice that one might believe he raised the chicken himself. But his plate is beautiful, and I despise him for it.

Jenny clears her throat. "My dish is a Korean short-rib taco, with a cabbage jicama slaw," she says quietly.

"And you made the tortillas yourself?" Paul asks.

"Of course." She blushes.

"I made my pasta from scratch," Robbs interrupts eagerly.

"Yes, I know," Paul responds patiently. "There's no premade pasta dough in the kitchen, but there are plenty of corn tortillas." He turns to me. "Kiara, tell us about your dish."

"I made green curry tamales," I say quickly, "with fresh salsa and an Indian-spiced salad."

Robbs snorts at the mention of my salad, and I know he feels that I took the easy way out.

"All right everyone, let's dig in," Paul directs.

We silently sample each of the dishes in turn. Robbs' sauce is well developed, but his pasta is undercooked. I know after one bite that his dish won't be featured on the weekend menu. Jenny's dish, however, is delicious, and mine turned out exactly as I'd hoped. Paul and Harrison seem to agree with me. They finish the tacos and tamales but leave Robbs' pasta practically untouched.

"Robbs, now that you've tasted all of the dishes, I'd like for you to tell me where you went wrong," says Paul.

"The pasta could use a few more minutes in the water," Robbs answers coldly. "But I believe the sauce and the chicken were well seasoned."

"They were well seasoned," Paul agrees. "But that doesn't matter. If one thing is wrong on the plate, the entire plate is ruined. You walked in today overconfident, and that led to being careless with your dish. I suggest you don't make that same mistake next week."

"Yes, Chef," Robbs replies bitterly.

Paul turns to Jenny and me. "Ladies, both of your dishes were exceptional, and I'd be happy to serve either of them to our customers. But this is a competition, and a winner must be chosen. Harrison and I are going to speak in the kitchen for a moment, and then I'll return with our decision."

Paul and Harrison rise from the table and disappear into the kitchen. Robbs, Jenny, and I exchange glances but before we can comment on the challenge, Megan appears at the table with a pitcher of cola and three glasses.

"I know it gets hot in the kitchen," she says cheerfully. "I thought you might be thirsty. How did it go?"

"One of the girls won," Robbs answers harshly. "Paul and Harrison are in the kitchen deciding which one has the best rack... I mean dish."

He's crossed the line. "Are you suggesting our breasts had something to do with our abilities to fully cook our food?" I sneer.

Jenny lets out an involuntary chuckle. "This whole time I thought my skills came from hard work and studying. If I'd known my boobs were doing all of the work, I could have saved a fortune in tuition."

"I know, right?" I agree. "Poor Robbs doesn't stand a chance against our wonder-breasts."

Megan, Jenny, and I giggle while Robbs fumes in his seat. He opens his mouth to retort, but the kitchen doors swing open again and Paul returns to our table.

"Ladies, this was much closer than we'd expected. You both prepared delicious food, so since this was a grilling challenge, we based our decision on who we felt best utilized the cooking method," he announces.

Excitement fills my body. I used the grill twice, so I feel certain that I won the challenge.

"Kiara," Paul continues, "your tamales were delicious, and Harrison and I both enjoyed the fact that you pulled the husks before serving. Leaving them for the diner to remove leads to greasy hands and unnecessary trash on the plate, and it was better to avoid both situations. However, we felt Jenny's barbecued short-ribs best represented the grill. The smokiness of your lamb was overshadowed by the curry, whereas Jenny's sauce served to enhance that smokiness."

Jenny beams, and I offer her a weak smile.

"Congratulations, Chef Foster," Paul says warmly. "As your dish will be featured on this weekend's menu, I need you to walk Chef Harrison through it. He will ensure all of the ingredients are stocked, and you will be assisting him for the next three days."

"Of course, Chef," Jenny answers. "Thank you so much."

Paul nods at her, and she rushes off to the kitchen to find Chef Harrison. "Robbs, as your dish was the least successful, I'd like for you to return to the kitchen and prepare a plate of fresh fettuccini. No sauce is necessary, but I need to be sure you can correctly execute homemade pasta. Once I'm satisfied with your results, you will be handling the prep work for tonight's dishes."

"Yes, Chef," Robbs replies with defeat. He, too, returns to the kitchen, leaving Paul and I alone at the table. I sit quietly, expecting to receive my assignment for the day. Instead, Paul reaches across the table and rests his hand on my forearm.

"Kiara, I want to emphasize that your dish was fantastic," he says warmly, his clear blue eyes steady on my face.

"Thank you, Chef," I reply with a blush.

"Please, Kiara, we're not in the kitchen. Call me Paul."

"Thank you, Paul," I correct myself nervously.

"I watched you carefully during the competition. You have excellent instincts and incredible skill. I think you're going to do very well here." He pauses. "Your tamales made me wish that we could award two winners, but, unfortunately, that's not the case. As your runner-up prize, I'd like to offer you the opportunity to choose the chef you'll be assisting over the weekend. Harrison is already taken, of course, but you can pick among the rest. The list includes me, as I practically live in the kitchen during the weekends," he finished with a suggestive smile.

With his thumb, he traces small circles on my arm and shivers of excitement rush through my body. I pull my arm away before my emotions get the best of me.

"Thank you so much for the opportunity, Paul," I begin. "I look forward to working with you directly, but I think it would be best if I assist Claire this weekend."

"That's an interesting choice," Paul answers with surprise. "May I ask why?"

"Desserts are my weakest area," I explain. "I'd like to watch Claire... learn her tricks and secrets. I feel that's where I need the most help."

"It's admirable that you're aware of your weaknesses. It's even more admirable that you're willing to admit them," says Paul, smiling. "One of your competitors would do well to follow that example."

"Oh, but Robbs doesn't have any weaknesses," I say jokingly. "He was just thrown off because he wasn't able to visit the chicken farm before his main ingredient was slaughtered."

Paul laughs. "You're probably right. The 'full experience' is what the farm-to-table hipsters preach about, isn't it? I admit I was hesitant to even include *Escoffier* in the initial stages of the competition. Like you and Jenny, I was classically trained. But Patrick convinced me to give each of the area's culinary schools a fair chance, and he was impressed by Robbs' initial dish. We'll just wait and see if he can keep up with you girls."

"We're going to give him a run for his money," I assure Paul.

"Yes, I expect you will," he replies with a sly grin. He stands up. "Claire doesn't come in for another couple of hours. You're going to have a long weekend. Because of the demanding brunch menu, Claire stays late on Fridays and Saturdays and comes back at six a.m. on Saturdays and Sundays. Take the rest of today off and practice basic dough recipes and pastry skills. You should also brush up on your pastry bag skills. Claire is sweet, but she doesn't have a lot of patience for teaching."

"Thank you Che—Paul." I stop myself from addressing him formally. "I'll see you tomorrow. If you haven't had a decent plate of pasta by then, I'll be happy to make you one," I add jokingly.

"Thanks, Kiara," he says. "I may hold you to that."

Paul disappears into the kitchen, and I decide to use the restroom before heading home. I am disappointed I lost the competition, but it's overshadowed by the exhilaration I feel after my talk with Paul. There is no longer any doubt in my mind that he is interested in me, and the thought of spending time with him outside of the restaurant is both thrilling and terrifying. I check my makeup in the mirror before locking myself into a stall. My nerves over today's challenge made it hard for me to sleep last night, and I'm looking forward to getting home and crawling back into my bed. I'm just about to exit the stall when I hear the restroom door open and two female voices fill the room. I can't tell who the voices belong to, and I don't want to interrupt their conversation. I decide to remain in the stall until they leave.

"Can I borrow that lip gloss?" the first voice asks.

"Sure, just let me dig it out of my bag," the second voice answers.

"So should we start placing bets on which one of the new girls he's going to fuck first?"

"Charlotte, you're terrible," the second voice scolds. "If anything, we should warn both of them. I'm sick and tired of watching him fuck and dump every woman who walks through the doors."

"His shit didn't work on either of us," Charlotte reminds her friend. "If either of those girls is stupid enough to fuck him, then they deserve what they get."

I feel guilty about eavesdropping, but the women's conversation intrigues me. I wonder who they're talking about, and Charlotte's next statement confirms my worst fears.

"You know, I wouldn't be surprised if one of those girls tries to fuck her way into the apprentice position. You know that's how Claire got the *pâtissier* position. Patrick told me that several more qualified people applied for the job. But Claire spent one night with Paul, and then the next day she was hired."

My heart sinks, and I feel like I'm going to be sick. Just a few moments ago, I was imagining myself falling in love with Paul. Now I am sure he is nothing but a player. *Shake it off. This is for the best. Getting involved with him would just be a distraction, and Jenny and Robbs would resent me for it anyway. I'm going to win this apprenticeship, and I'm going to do it without taking my clothes off.*

"Maybe he'll hire that Robbs guy," says the second voice. "They could be each other's wing men."

"Oh, Amy, be honest. You had your eyes on Robbs since he first walked through the door. You want Paul to hire him so you'll have someone to play with."

"A girl can dream," Amy replies with a giggle. "We'd better get back out there and see if any of our tables are set."

I hear the women leave the restroom, but I remain seated in my stall, absorbing what I just learned about Paul. I decide there are two things I need to do. First, I find a way to shoot down Paul's advances without jeopardizing my position in the competition. Second, I need to warn Jenny about his history as a player. With a new resolve, I leave the restroom and head for home.

Chapter Three

"It doesn't surprise me at all that Paul is a player," Jenny insists. It is Saturday, and the two of us are taking a break between the lunch and dinner rushes at the restaurant. As Paul warned, I've already had a long weekend and it's only half over. This is the first chance to tell Jenny about the conversation I overheard in the restroom.

We sit at a small bistro table in the café down the street from Fission. We'd both agreed we needed a break from Robbs, Paul, and Fission in general.

"It's absolutely disgusting," I tell her. "I feel so awkward working with Claire after hearing how she got her job."

"Does it appear like she knows what she's doing? I can't imagine Paul would put a bad chef in his kitchen, even if she's good in bed."

"She seems perfectly capable," I reply. "And her food is delicious."

"Maybe the gossip is only half right," Jenny suggests. "Maybe she slept with him, but that may not be the reason she was hired. You know how gossip works. It's like a margarita… it should be taken with several grains of salt."

"I don't like salt with mine," I say with an upturned nose.

"Come to think of it, neither do I…" she says, "but the saying still applies. We just need to keep our heads down and focus on our jobs. No good ever comes from sleeping with coworkers anyway. That's not a lesson I need to learn twice."

I can tell Jenny is trying hard to be my friend, but I'm still not quite ready to let my guard down. I've had too many 'friends' who were decent enough at first, but bailed as soon as I let myself be vulnerable with them. When people hear about my past, they become closed off and treat me as if I'm damaged. And as friendly as Jenny seems, at the end of the day she's still my competition. The last thing I want to do is let her know where my weaknesses are.

"You're right," I tell her. "It shouldn't matter if Paul is a player or a saint. He's our boss, and becoming involved with him isn't an option."

Jenny shakes her head. "Chauvinists always assume successful women slept their way to the top. The last thing either of us should do is prove them right. To be honest, I don't care if you beat me or I beat you… as long as Robbs doesn't get the apprenticeship, I'll consider it a win."

"Agreed," I reply. We lift our coffee mugs and toast our mutual dislike of our male competitor. I take a long drink of my coffee and check the time. "The dinner rush will be starting soon. We'd better get back."

As we exit the café, Jenny loops her arm through mine and we walk back to Fission together.

<<◇>>

"I can't fucking believe they picked Kiara," Robbs hisses harshly. The three competitors had just finished the second cooking challenge, and the winner was just announced.

"You're just pissed that you lost again," Jenny insists. "Really, Robbs... you need to lighten up. Quit being such an ass during the challenges and maybe Paul won't feel the need to shoot your dishes down."

"You tasted her sauce, Jenny. It was fucking *broken*! Last week my pasta was slightly underdone, and I had to make the bastard a fresh plate so he'd know I'm not incompetent. And today we both watched little *Miss Cordon Bleu's* sauce separate on our plates, and he made it the goddamn weekend special!"

Jenny furrows her brow. "You do have a point. I know my seafood plate was a flop, but your duck was delicious. And Kiara's sauce did break..."

"He's fucking her, I know he is," Robbs insists. "Or he's trying really hard to. The way he fawns over her all of the time is disgusting. 'What a lovely plate, Chef Kiara,' 'I'm so impressed by your work ethic, Chef Kiara,' 'Let me help you carry those plates, Chef Kiara.' They may as well go at it on the prep table. I'm telling you, Jenny, if she hasn't already opened her legs, she's going to. And then we'll be out on our asses."

"I don't think Kiara would do that," Jenny insists.

"And you formed that opinion because you know her so well?" Robbs snorts. "Aside from where she goes to school, what do we know about her at all?"

"I know as much about her as I know about you," Jenny answers defiantly.

"I'm an open book," Robbs replies. "Ask me anything you want, and I'll give you a straight answer. Then go talk to that brown-haired bitch and see if she does the same. I'm telling you, I'm not going to sit back and lose this job because the boss man wants a hot new piece of tail... and you shouldn't sit back and take this either. You're an amazing chef, Jenny, and you deserve to be recognized for that. Paul's barely spoken to you since you won last week's competition. Not to mention that you're much more attractive than Kiara. I'd think if Paul wanted in anyone's pants, it would be yours."

Jenny blushes. "Thank you... I think," she says. "But I'm still not sure you're right about Paul. I mean, if you are, then we should obviously do something about it... maybe report him to our instructors or something... but until I'm as convinced as you are, I'm not going to do or say anything about it."

"What if I find a way to show you that I'm right?" Robbs asks deviously.

"What are you planning on doing?" Jenny answers with a tone of suspicion.

"Nothing illegal, if that's what you're worried about," he assures her. "But I could create a situation... see how he responds. I don't have an exact plan worked out, but you'll know it when you see it."

"You're going to do something to make her look bad, aren't you?" Jenny asks. "You're bitching about the competition being unfair, and now you're talking about sabotage. What's fair about that?"

"I won't do anything to get her kicked out of the competition. But I'm going to prove that he's showing her favoritism. If I can do that, will you help me do something about it?"

Jenny considers his question for several moments before answering. "IF I see something that makes me believe that Paul is showing Kiara favoritism because of anything other than her food, then yes, I will help you put a stop to it," she says.

Chapter Four

"Kiara, I'm glad you're here early," Paul says as he approaches my usual morning table.

"I take my coffee here in the morning," I explain. "What's up?"

Paul takes a seat at the table and pours coffee into the mug he had carried over with him. "Enrique called about ten minutes ago. His wife went into labor this morning, so he's going to be out for a week or so."

Enrique is in charge of the daily prep work. Paul already told Robbs, Jenny, and I that we will be covering for him after his baby is born, so I know where the conversation is heading.

"Kiara," Paul continues. "I know your dish is the special this weekend, but Cole and Harrison will be executing the majority of it. Since Enrique's leave is starting on our busiest day of the week, I'm hoping you won't mind handling today's prep. You possess the best knife skills, and you work the fastest," he says with that charming smile that makes me want to melt into my chair.

"Whatever you need, Paul," I answer quickly. "I'm flexible."

"Thanks, Kiara. I knew I could count on you. You know, flexibility is an important quality for an apprentice. That will serve you well in this competition."

"Thank you. I enjoy working here, and I'll do anything to earn a permanent place in the kitchen."

"Anything?" he asks with a sly smile.

"Anything, within reason," I answer with a blush.

"I'll keep that in mind." Paul stares at me intently, and I think that he wants to say something else. Before he can speak, I am startled by the sound of a voice clearing behind me. I turn and see Jenny standing with her arms crossed.

"Good morning," she says coldly.

"Good morning," I reply. "Are you all right?" Something is obviously bothering her.

"I'm great... just ready to get to work." She turns to Paul. "What is my assignment for today?" she asks impatiently.

"Well, as you came in second in yesterday's challenge, you get to pick the chef you will assist this weekend. I was just telling Kiara that Enrique's baby is on its way this morning. She'll be handling the prep work, so you're welcome to assist Cole or Harrison, if you'd like to practice your grilling or your sauce skills. Everyone else is available too, of course."

I can see on Jenny's face that she's insulted by the suggestion that she help with my dish. "I'd like to assist you this weekend, Paul," she answers quickly. "You're the best, and I'm here to learn from the best."

"That will be fine, Jenny," he says. "I need to take care of some administrative stuff before I put on my jacket. Why don't you sit down and enjoy a cup of coffee with Kiara? You should be well caffeinated if you're going to keep up with me."

"I can hold my own," Jenny says boldly, "but a cup of coffee sounds good."

"I'll bring you a mug," Paul offers as he stands. Jenny takes Paul's abandoned seat across from me, while he walks over to the bar and fetches a mug for her. He brings it over to the table. "We'll get started in about half an hour," he tells her before heading off to his office.

Jenny stares at me for a minute before speaking. "So, you two were pretty cozy when I got here," she says with an air of accusation.

"We were just talking about covering the prep work. He's getting us to all take turns with it," I explain.

"I thought you felt uncomfortable around him after what you heard in the bathroom last week. But you certainly didn't seem uncomfortable just now."

Her hostility confuses me, and I'm not quite sure how to handle it. "He's our boss, Jenny. I'll talk to him. And I'm starting to think that Amy and Charlotte were exaggerating about him being a ladies' man. Like you said, gossip has a way of taking on a life of its own. I think Paul is just a good guy. And he obviously cares about other chefs, or he'd have never started this competition in the first place," I observe.

"Well, I guess I'll see how much he cares first hand over the weekend," Jenny answers shortly.

"Jenny, I'm sorry I ever said anything to you about what I overheard. Talking about it puts us on the same level as Amy and Charlotte, and we have more important things to do than gossip."

"Uh huh," Jenny replies. "Kiara, I'm sorry for being cranky this morning. I didn't sleep well at all last night. I wasn't happy with my dish yesterday, and I'm still shocked that he awarded me second place. It got me wondering about Paul, and whether or not he's showing us favoritism because we're women."

I laugh. "If he's showing us favoritism over Robbs, it's because we're not pompous pricks."

"You may be right about that," Jenny says. We sit and drink our coffee in silence for a while, and then she speaks again. "I'm going to head into the kitchen. Call me a brownnoser if you like, but I want to get Paul's station set up for him."

"I wouldn't call that brown nosing," I assure her. "I'd call that being proactive. I still need to look over today's prep list. I'd better get in there too."

We clear away our table and then set off for the kitchen.

Chapter Five

"Chef Kiara, we needed those stuffed hens ten minutes ago," Robbs calls out impatiently. I was covering the prep station for four hours, and I'm completely in the weeds. If I'd been thinking more clearly when I planned out my work, I'd have started with those damn hens. Instead, I started with the *mise en place* for everyone's assorted dishes.

"I'll get them to you in ten," I call out. I grab a deep, stainless steel container and set off for the kitchen to retrieve the hens. At least the stuffing is ready. I toss twenty Cornish hens into the container and head back to the prep station. The hens are heavy. I heave the container onto the edge of the station and watch in horror as my cutting board tumbles to the floor, along with most of my day's work.

"Shit!" I scream. Everyone in the kitchen is staring at me... I avert my eyes helplessly and try to fight back my tears.

"What the hell happened here, Chef?" Paul demands as he walks over to the prep station. "I asked you to cover this because I thought you could handle it! Why am I looking at hundreds of dollars of produce and meat lying on my kitchen floor?"

"I'm so sorry Chef," I stammer. "I was just putting the hens on the table... I don't know what happened... I somehow knocked the edge of the cutting board off the side of the table... when I went to set the hens down, everything just came crashing down around me."

"Pay attention to what you're doing!" Paul growls.

"I know, I know. I'm so sorry! I'll fix it, Chef," I insist. I drop to my knees and start picking up the mess I made.

"It's okay, Kiara," Paul says softly. "We're just going to prep as we go." He turns to the rest of the kitchen. "Chef Kiara made a mistake, and I think we all know what that feels like." He takes a deep breath, and I can tell he's trying to come up with a plan for how to deal with my mistake. "Here's what we're going to do," he announces. "We're going to eighty-six my dish tonight. I'll ask the servers to take it off the board. Chef Jenny and I will assist Chef Kiara, and we'll just prep as we go."

The announcement draws sneers from everyone in the room, and none are as hateful as Jenny's. I know she's pissed about helping to fix my mistake, but I don't care. I'm just relieved I wasn't fired.

"Thank you, Chefs," I say almost inaudibly.

Paul puts an arm around me and leans into my ear. "Mistakes happen, Kiara," he whispers gently. "Shake it off, and don't let it affect the rest of your night."

My emotions get the better of me, and I wrap my arms around Paul. He returns my embrace and holds me tightly. "It's okay," he assures me again as he pulls away. "We've got your back."

Jenny approaches the prep station, her arms loaded down with fresh produce.

"I'm so sorry, Jenny," I apologize as she deposits the food onto the cutting boards. "I know this is the last thing you wanted to do tonight."

"Just pay more attention to what you're doing next time," she snaps. "I'm here to learn from professional chefs, not to clean up your messes."

I know there's no point in saying anything else, so I grab a knife and get back to work.

"Are you ready to admit I was right?" Robbs asks Jenny with a satisfied look on his face.

"Yes," Jenny replies angrily. "I can't believe I had to spend the entire night helping that bitch redo her prep. And I can't *believe* the bastard hugged her! If you or I had done that, he'd have chewed us new assholes. But nooooo... poor little Kiara just made a mistake. WE need to help her."

"I'm sorry that what I did ruined your night, Jenny," Robbs says softly. "I didn't mean for you to get mixed up in things. And I know that sliding that board over the edge of the table was a dirty trick, but if she'd been paying attention to what she was doing, she would have noticed it before she ruined all that food."

Jenny nods. "I'm not pissed at you, Robbs," she assures him. "I'm pissed at Kiara... and Paul. If he wanted to help her, he should have done it on his own. He could have transferred me to any other chef in the kitchen."

"And you saw the way Kiara wrapped her arms around him, didn't you?" Robbs asks. "Do you still think she's only interested in him on a professional level?"

Jenny shakes her head. "I overheard them this morning. I didn't have a chance to tell you about it yet, but Kiara told Paul that she's willing to do *anything* to win the apprenticeship. And believe me, when he heard that, he was damn near drooling. It was disgusting."

"Does she know you heard them?"

"Yep. And I made it pretty clear that I thought she was being shady. She insisted they were just talking about work. But she also made it pretty clear that she thinks Paul is a decent guy. It's only a matter of time before they start hooking up. You and I could out cook Julia Child and still not win this contest."

"How far are you willing to go to keep that from happening?" Robbs asks quietly.

"As far as it takes," Jenny answers with determination.

"I enjoyed working with you this weekend," Jenny tells Paul. "Especially today, when we actually got to cook together... your tenderloin was divine."

"I enjoyed it as well," Paul replies politely. "I was impressed by the way you handled yourself in the kitchen, and the credit for the tenderloin belongs more to you than me. Your skills at the roasting station are phenomenal. I may get you to assist Michael next weekend."

"Unless I win Thursday's challenge," she reminds him with a grin.

"Yes, of course," he says. "If you win Thursday's challenge, you'll execute your own dish next weekend."

It's nearly midnight, and the wait-staff have already left for the night. Paul, Jenny, Robbs, and Claire are the only chefs still in the kitchen. Paul and Jenny are cleaning the roasting station, while Claire and Robbs finish wiping down the butcher-block tables.

"Chef, I'm just about finished up for the night," Claire calls from across the room. "The muffin batter is ready. I'm going to wait until morning to bake them off."

"Great, Claire, good work tonight... drive home safely," Paul replies. "Robbs, if you're finished, you can go ahead and leave too. Jenny and I will do a bit more scrubbing, but we're not far behind you."

He turns to Jenny as the other two chefs exit the kitchen. "You can go ahead and leave too, if you'd like," he offers.

"Actually..." Jenny begins slowly. "I was hoping you can help me with something. I'm taking a class next semester on pairings... you know, alcohol and food?"

"Yes, Jenny, I know what pairings mean," Paul says with an indulgent smile.

"Of course you do," she says with a forced blush. "I don't have a good understanding of the process, and I was hoping you might be able to give me some tips. I know it's late... and you probably don't feel like drinking..."

"As it happens, I'm quite skilled at pairings," Paul tells her with a cocky grin. "And I'd be happy to give you a few pointers. If you'll finish up here, I'll hit the walk-in and the bar and set up a tasting area."

"Thank you so much!" Jenny gushes. "I know I'll be a shoe in to ace the class if a chef of your caliber shows me the ropes first."

"You're more than welcome, Jenny," Paul replies. "I'm always happy to help the next generation of chefs. That's the whole point of this competition."

Paul carries a large tray into the walk-in while Jenny continues scrubbing the roasting station. As she finishes up, Paul reappears with an assortment of cheeses, produce, and cold cuts.

"We'll start off simple," he explains as he gestures to the platter in his hand. "It'll be easier to do this at the bar."

Jenny carries her rag to the sink, rinses it, and follows Paul through the swinging kitchen doors.

"Thank you for asking me to do this," Paul says as he sets the platter down and steps behind the bar. "I need to teach all three of you about pairings. We always offer drink suggestions alongside our menu items, but I forgot all about having you guys sample them.”

“I'm excited to learn.” Jenny beams. “I know the basic pairings. You know... champagne with strawberries... white wine with fish, red with beef. But that's where my knowledge ends.”

“Well, why don't you take a bite of a strawberry and then a drink of this?” Paul suggests. He holds out a glass of white wine and Jenny accepts it.

“That's amazing!” Jenny says after sampling the pairing. “After tasting the strawberry, the berry flavor in the wine just pops!”

“Take another sip and tell me what else you taste,” Paul directs.

Jenny complies. “Hmmm... peaches, green apple... and pepper?”

“Impressive,” Paul replies. “You're better at this than you think.” He slices a thin piece of sharp cheddar and pours a splash of red wine into a glass. Jenny reaches for them, but he quickly stops her.

“You need to cleanse your palate between wines,” he explains. He grabs a bottle of Kettle One vodka and pours them each a shot.

“You're right, that does help,” Jenny tells him after downing her shot. She samples the cheese and red wine together. “The crispness of the wine is a welcome contrast to the creaminess of the cheese,” she observes.

Paul pours them each another shot of vodka before pairing prosciutto with a light chardonnay. They continue the process for an hour, with each of them taking a shot between samples.

"I'd like to work on beer pairings next, but I'm afraid I'm already pretty drunk," Jenny teases. She rests her chest on the bar and positions her cleavage directly in Paul's line of vision. He tries not to stare, but he can't help himself.

"We can do beer pairings another night," he suggests. "And next time, we'll use black coffee to cleanse our palates," he adds.

"I know I already thanked you, but I hope you know how much I appreciate this, Paul," Jenny says, dropping her voice to a seductive tone. "I admire you so much." She reaches across the bar and places a hand on top of his. He flinches at first, then opens his fist and caresses her hand with his forefinger.

"Thank you, Jenny. It's always nice to hear that I'm appreciated."

Jenny stares into his eyes. "You know, I'm no expert, but there's always one thing I enjoyed with my alcohol," she says daringly.

He holds eye contact with her as she wraps her hand around one of his fingers and begins stroking it up and down. "Oh yeah? What's that?"

"Sex," she answers boldly.

"Jenny... I don't know if that's the best idea. We work together... I'm your superior." He breathes heavily as she continues stroking his finger.

"I don't see why that matters," she whispers. "I'm not talking about a relationship. Just two people enjoying each other after a long day at work." She rises from her stool and climbs on to the bar, still stroking Paul's finger with her soft hand. "Would that be such a bad thing?"

"Well, when you put it that way," Paul says. "How is a guy to resist?" He wraps her hair in his free hand and pulls her lips to his. They kiss passionately, and Paul climbs onto the bar next to Jenny. "No strings attached?" he says quietly as he pulls her shirt over her head.

"No strings attached," she assures him as her honey blonde hair falls over her shoulders. She wiggles out of her pants while Paul strips off his clothes.

"Do you want to move to a booth?" Paul suggests. "It may be more comfortable."

"I'm fine here," Jenny insists. "I want you to fuck me on this bar, so you'll think of me every time you see it."

"As you wish," Paul replies. He pulls a condom from the pocket of his discarded jeans, opens it, and rolls it over his long, thick cock. He pushes Jenny's legs apart and buries himself inside her.

"Oh, Paul," Jenny moans as he rocks in and out of her. "You feel so amazing." She clenches her pussy muscles around him as he leans down and takes one of her breasts into his mouth.

"You feel pretty amazing yourself," he tells her.

Jenny arches her back, giving him easier access to her erect nipples. "Bite me, lover," she demands.

Paul does as he's told, nibbling each breast in turn as the juices of her satisfaction flow over his cock.

"You like that?" he says gruffly. "Are you coming for me, baby?"

"Yes!" Jenny cries out. "So hard... keep giving it to me, Paul."

Paul jackhammers into her. He isn't ready to come, but he's too drunk to stop himself. "I'm going to come with you, baby," he moans.

"No!" Jenny moans. "Don't stop. I want you to fuck me all night long."

Paul tries to hold back his orgasm, but he loses all control of himself. He explodes in ecstasy and collapses on top of her.

"I'm sorry," he says after a few minutes. "I couldn't stop myself."

"That's all right," Jenny assures him. "That just means you'll have to make it up to me, some other time."

Paul hops off of the bar and helps Jenny to the floor. They dress quietly, and neither of them notices Robbs lurking on the other side of the restaurant.

"Can I call you a cab?" Paul offers.

Jenny shakes her head. "My apartment is only a few blocks away. I walk to work."

"This is a pleasant neighborhood," Paul observes. "How do you afford a place here?"

"We all have our secrets," says Jenny. "I'll see you in the morning?"

"I'll be here." Paul walks Jenny to the door and locks up behind her.

Outside, Jenny reaches into her purse and retrieves her phone. She scrolls down to Robbs' number and calls it.

"Did you get it?" she asks.

"Every last second of it," he tells her. "That was quite a show. I can't wait to play the video for Kiara."

"Just hold on to it for now," Jenny insists. "This is too good to waste. We'll keep our eyes and ears open for the right time to strike."

Chapter Six

"Jenny, are you sure you're all right?" I ask as we clean our stations after the lunch rush. A week has passed since my supreme fuck up at the prep station, and Jenny has been distant with me ever since.

"I'm fine," she insists. "I'm just tired. And I'm frustrated that Robbs won this week. It's only Friday afternoon, and I'm already about to choke on all of his smugness."

"I understand," I assure her, but I don't think she's being completely honest with me. Something strange is going on at Fission. Paul is still shamelessly flirting with me, but he's softened his attitude toward Robbs. And he's been downright short with Jenny. She came in last in this week's competition, even though her lobster was decadent and my prawns were overcooked.

"I'm a little tired myself," I tell her. "Want to walk down to the café with me over our break? I could use a shot of espresso... or five."

"A strong cup of coffee does sound good," she agrees.

We walk into the employee break room to retrieve our purses and find Amy and Charlotte laughing at the table. They silence themselves abruptly when they see us in the doorway, and I see Charlotte shoot Jenny a dirty look.

"Hi, girls," I say kindly, breaking the silence. "We're going to walk to the café for lunch. Would either of you care to join us?"

"No thanks. Our break is almost over," Amy answers for both of them.

Jenny grabs both of our purses and pushes me back through the door.

"What do you think that was about?" I ask.

"Who the hell knows with those two?" Jenny says. "They're probably just talking shit. I swear half of the people in this place act like they're still in high school."

"God, I hated high school," I groan.

"Really?" Jenny asks in surprise. "I thought you'd be in the popular crowd. You have the body of a cheerleader," she says with a tone of resentment.

"Nope," I say, shaking my head. "I was kind of a loner. I never was good with other people... I always preferred to keep my head down and work."

"So you were in the smart group? Hours and hours of studying?"

"Not exactly," I say. I don't feel like revealing my entire past, but I'm compelled to give Jenny a few details, if for no other reason than to get rid of the jealousy she's directing at me. "I worked two jobs while I was in high school. Once my parents were gone, there was no one left to take care of me, so I had to make sure my bills were paid."

"Oh God, Kiara, I didn't realize that," Jenny says apologetically. "Didn't your parents keep life insurance?"

"No, they weren't big on planning for the future. I lost them so unexpectedly. It actually helped to throw myself into work. I was too busy to think about them."

We step into the café and place our orders at the counter. "Want to share a club sandwich?" I ask.

Jenny shakes her head. "I don't have much of an appetite."

She pays for her latte, and I order a macchiato and a slice of vegetarian quiche. We make our way to a small booth and sit down before continuing our conversation.

"Jenny, are you sure you're all right?" I ask again. "If you don't want to talk about it, I completely understand, but you seem a little off this week."

"I was just questioning my decision to compete for the apprenticeship," she confesses.

"But you're so talented!" I argue. "Why would you question yourself? I know that when we started, you weren't sure that being a chef is what you want. Did you find something else you're interested in?"

"No... but, Kiara, you can't tell me you didn't notice the way Paul's been treating me lately," she says softly.

"I did notice," I tell her. "Did something happen? Did he make a pass at you? Oh god, what Amy and Charlotte said that day is true, isn't it?"

Jenny hesitates before answering. "It's nothing like that. I'm just afraid that he's realized I don't belong here... not like you and Robbs."

A waitress arrives with our orders, and we sit quietly until she leaves.

"That's ridiculous," I tell her. "It would be one thing if you'd decided to change your major. But you're incredibly talented, and you deserve to be here. Even more of a right than Robbs, because you're not a douchebag."

Jenny doesn't find my joke funny, which surprises me. Since our first day at Fission, we've bonded over our mutual dislike of Robbs. "Robbs isn't a bad guy," she argues. "He's cocky, but most talented chefs are. And part of his attitude comes from the fact that Paul shows you such obvious favoritism."

Ahh, so that's the problem.

"What favoritism?" I ask with frustration. "Robbs won yesterday, didn't he?"

"Yes..." Jenny agrees. "But you're the only one of us that Paul's nice to. He flirts with you all of the time, Kiara."

"But it's harmless, and I don't reciprocate," I argue. "Is that why you've been so distant toward me lately? Do you think I have something going on with our

BOSS? You know I'd never do that! We talked about it the first time we came here!"

"I don't know what you would or wouldn't do, Kiara," Jenny hisses. "But I'm certain that Paul would take you in a second, if he thought he could."

"He *flirts* with me, that's *all*," I insist. "What do you expect me to do about it?"

Jenny slams her coffee cup down on the table, slides out of the booth, and grabs her purse. "Nothing, Kiara," she says hatefully. "I don't expect you to do a goddamn thing."

She rushes out the door, leaving me alone at the booth.

"You've done a fantastic job today, Kiara," Paul says. "You know, your work ethic is better than any of my employees. I love the way you keep your head down and focus on the tasks at hand."

"Thank you, Chef," I reply shortly. Two days have passed since Jenny and I fought at the café, and she's barely spoken to me since. Paul hasn't noticed the tension between us, but Robbs certainly has. He and Jenny started drinking their coffee together in the mornings and disappearing with each other during our lunch breaks. I catch them sneering at me but pretend not to notice.

"Listen, Enrique was supposed to stay late and clean up tonight, but his baby is colicky and his wife's exhausted. I'd like to let him off early, if you don't mind staying."

"Whatever you need, Chef," I agree.

The restaurant is slow for a Sunday, and three of the chefs were sent home. I spend the rest of the day manning the fry station, while Jenny and Robbs work together on Robbs' scallop kabobs, the dish that won him the latest cooking challenge. I hear them whisper as I work, and I know they're talking about me. Their attitudes make me even more sure of my decision to keep my past a secret from them.

The kitchen closes at eight o'clock on Sundays, and by quarter after, Paul and I are the only ones left in the kitchen.

"I'm going to supervise the front of the house cleanup, if you can get started on the ovens," Paul announces.

"No problem," I agree. I welcome the silence and the solitude. I know Jenny and Robbs are off somewhere talking about the fact that Paul and I are working alone in the kitchen tonight, but I don't care. Fuck them. Robbs is jealous because I'm a better chef than he is. Jenny is jealous of that too, *and* the fact that Paul finds me attractive. She probably just wants him for herself. Hot blondes like her always think they can have any man they want. She probably made a pass at him and got shot down. That would explain why he's been so distant with her... and why the waitresses keep giving her those dirty looks.

"How's it going in here?" Paul's voice startles me. I turn to see that he's just walked in to the kitchen.

"Good," I tell him. "Three ovens are cleaned, with two to go. Then I'll start on the stovetops." My stomach growls loudly as I speak.

"My goodness, Kiara. Have you eaten today?" Paul asks.

"I forgot," I confess with a blush. The truth is that Jenny and Robbs' attitudes had made me lose my appetite.

"Well, we're in the perfect place to do something about that," Paul says. "What sounds good?"

"I'll just eat whatever's left over from dinner service," I answer quickly. "I don't want to make a mess or be any trouble."

"That's ridiculous, Kiara!" Paul insists. "You have a world-renowned chef offering to prepare you whatever you want! You should take advantage. Opportunities like this don't come around every day." He smiles. "What is your absolute favorite thing to eat?"

"*Croque Madame*," I answer sheepishly. "I know it's not fancy, but it's what I like."

"That's one of my favorites too!" Paul exclaims with a broad grin.

"I can work on the béchamel sauce, if you want to grill the sandwiches," I offer.

Paul shakes his head. "You've been working your ass off all day. I'll handle everything." He disappears through the kitchen doors and returns a moment later with a bottle of chilled Zinfandel and two glasses. He pulls a stool over to one of the butcher-block tables and gestures for me to take a seat.

"I'm going to have a glass of wine," he says. "Would you like to join me?" I recognize the brand name and know that the cost of the bottle would cover my electric bill twice.

"I'd love one, thank you," I accept graciously.

Paul pours the wine, then sets off for the walk-in. He emerges with a tray of smoked ham, gruyere, butter, eggs, and cream. "Claire made some *Challah* this morning. Does that sound good to you?"

"*Challah* always sounds good." A warm, relaxed feeling fills my body as I finish my first glass of wine. "Do you mind if I pour another?" I inquire softly.

"Of course not. Pour as much as you like."

"You know," I say as I pour the wine, "I don't usually drink anything this expensive."

Paul laughs. "I remember being a poor college student. Until I opened the restaurant, I never drank the expensive stuff either. The only reason we're drinking it now is because I can write it off."

"The perks of being the boss," I say with a grin.

Paul fires two burners and sets small skillets on top of them to warm. He slices the beautiful loaf of *Challah*, butters one side of each piece, and assembles the sandwiches in the skillets. He fires a third burner, retrieves a saucepan from the rack, and starts on the sauce.

"This is one of the first things I ever learned to make," he tells me. "Well, sort of. Back then, it was just a grilled ham and cheese with Rotel sauce."

"That doesn't sound half bad," I tell him.

"Back then it was delicious," he agrees. "But today, you won't catch me dead near a block of Velveeta."

"Grilled cheese was one of the first things I learned how to make too," I confess. "But I rarely had any ham to add."

"I thought so," Paul says, nodding.

"You thought what?" I ask in confusion.

"That you grew up poor... no, no, I didn't mean that in a bad way," he says quickly when he sees me blush. "I grew up poor too. My father left my mother before I was born. She worked three jobs to make sure my sister and I didn't go without anything we needed. But there wasn't much left over for the things we wanted..." He flips the sandwiches in the skillets. "I was the oldest, so a lot of the cooking and housework fell on me. That's how I learned about fusing different flavors. We were all tired of eating the same stuff over and over again, so I started experimenting. I fell in love with cooking… it was my way of taking care of my family."

I finish my second glass of wine and pour the third as I reply. "I started cooking out of necessity. You're right, I grew up poor. But I didn't have anyone working to take care of me. Both of my parents were alcoholics and addicts. If I hadn't learned to cook, I'd have starved to death."

"You said your parents were addicts... have they recovered?" Paul asks gently.

I can't believe I'm opening up to him, but something about the way he's looking at me makes me feel safe. "I wouldn't know," I answer plainly. "When I was sixteen, I came home from school and they'd moved without me." I tell him about the note that's still hidden away in my closet as he plates the sandwiches, drenches them in sauce, and gingerly lays the fried egg on top.

"I can't imagine what that must have been like for you," he says softly. "Why in the world did you save that note? I'd think that it would be a painful reminder."

"It is," I agree with a nod. "But it also makes me grateful. My life has been far from perfect, but things started looking up for me once I was on my own. It was difficult, of course, keeping a roof over my head and keeping my grades up at the same time. But I shudder to think of where I'd have ended up if my parents had stuck around."

"Wait, you were completely on your own?" he asks in awe. "No aunts or grandparents to help you?"

"No one," I answer sadly. "My grandparents were gone before I was born, and my parents burned every bridge they had during their downward spiral."

"And you were too proud to ask for help," Paul guesses.

"What makes you think that?" I ask.

"The way you carry yourself... the determination you show in the kitchen. It says a lot about your character."

"Thank you, I think," I say, smiling. With a large fork, I pierce the egg and let the yolk gush over the rest of my sandwich. The first bite is heavenly. "This is the most delicious thing I've ever put in my mouth."

"You're just hungry," Paul insists. "I can do much better. Wait until you taste my empanadas."

"So, you're planning on cooking for me again?" I ask.

"I'll cook for you whenever you like," he answers seriously. He's looking at me again, in that way that makes me feel like he's imagining our future together. Suddenly I'm reminded of the hostility I've been getting from my fellow competitors. Emboldened by the wine, I decided to bring up the issue.

"You know, I'm pretty sure Jenny and Robbs have been gossiping about us," I tell him.

"They have?" I can tell that he's not surprised. "What are they saying?"

"I haven't heard anything directly from Robbs, but I know Jenny thinks you've been showing me favoritism... because you're attracted to me."

"Well, Jenny is absolutely right, and absolutely wrong," he says firmly.

"I don't understand. What do you mean?" I ask with a wine-induced giggle.

"I am attracted to you, and you are my favorite. But you're not my favorite *because* I'm attracted to you. You're my favorite because you're the most talented competitor."

"Do you really think so?" I ask. "I only won one of the challenges, and you and I both know the sauce was broken."

"The flavors of that dish were perfect," he says quickly. "And I wouldn't expect a perfect sauce from a second-year culinary student. *Sauciers* spend years perfecting their craft. Ask Cole, if you don't believe me. I do, however, expect second-year students to be able to cook a plate of pasta, which Robbs did not."

"If a man had served you the dishes I prepared, would you think he was the best?" I ask with suspicion.

"You've been listening to the gossip around here," Paul answers with a grin. "Kiara, I made mistakes. I got involved with people I shouldn't have, and some of what you heard about me is probably true. But I'm serious about who I put in my kitchen, and you're the best chef I've seen in years. And, yes, I'd feel the same way if you were a man."

"Thank you," I say with a sigh of relief. We sit silently for several minutes enjoying the food in front of us. "That was delicious," I tell him as I push my empty plate away.

"Thanks," he responds. "I look forward to cooking for you again."

"Paul..." I begin slowly, "a few minutes ago, you mentioned getting involved with people that you shouldn't have. I'm one of three people competing to be your apprentice. Am I not the definition of 'people you shouldn't get involved with'?"

"Yes," he says. "But that doesn't stop me from wanting to be involved with you."

"But it will never be the right time," I argue. "It would be inappropriate now. And if I win the apprenticeship, which I plan on doing, it will be inappropriate then, too."

"Are you attracted to me, Kiara?" he asks. I blush and remain silent. "Come on now," he encourages me, "I laid out all of my cards on the table. You know how I feel. So tell me, do you find me attractive?"

"Of course I do," I confess.

"Do you have many friends, Kiara?" he asks softly.

Again, I feel compelled to be honest with him. "No, I don't have any friends. I thought Jenny and I were getting close, but then something changed."

"So what would the harm be if we spend some time together, just as friends?" he asks. "This may come as a shock to you, but I don't have many friends either... I have employees. But when I'm away from the restaurant, I'm either alone or babysitting my sister's kids. I think it would be a welcome change to be away from here and enjoy some adult conversation."

"Just as friends?" I ask hesitantly.

"Just as friends," he assures me.

"I guess there'd be no harm in that."

"Perfect." He smiles. "Would you like to meet me for dinner tomorrow night? It's your day off, and I know a great little hole in the wall Thai place. Then maybe we could get some coffee after and just talk."

"I'd love to," I answer.

Chapter Seven

I walk through the parking lot of Barton Creek Square, digging for my keys in my purse. I find them at the bottom and push the alert button on my keyless entry remote. I hear the horn of my car blare in the distance and start walking toward the noise. As I walk, I realize that I'd left the mall from a different set of doors than I'd entered. That explains why I lost the damn car. I am filled with relief when I finally set eyes on my twelve-year-old Honda Civic. I climb in and toss my bags in the seat beside me.

Initially, I'd planned on buying a new top to wear for my evening with Paul. But I'd given in to temptation, and with encouragement from a perky sales clerk, I'd purchased an entire outfit, shoes and all. I pull my new emerald green top from its bag, hold it to my face, and study myself in my rear view mirror. As I hoped, the shade of the fabric complements my skin in the natural light as well as it had under those god awful fluorescents.

Suddenly I am overcome with sadness. When I was a little girl, my mother always dressed me in emerald green. "It blends in so beautifully with your dark eyes and hair," she'd always say. I toss the shirt back into the bag and shake off the onslaught of emotions. So she knew what color to dress me in. That doesn't make her a good mother. I'm not missing out on anything, living my life without her.

I pull out of the parking lot and turn right, mindlessly driving toward my apartment. I scold myself for getting emotional over the mother who left me. This always happens before I go out on a date with someone new. I start wondering what my mother would say if she was here. What advice would she give me? Would she curl my hair and tell me stories of the dates she went on when she was my age? I'll never know, so I may as well stop torturing myself.

With no memory of the drive, I pull into my apartment building. It's a small, charming place in an area that was once the trendiest neighborhood in Austin. The crowds have long since moved on, but the buildings have been well maintained and the neighborhood is still safe. Most importantly, there are no drug dealers in my building. I can spot a dealer from a mile away. I know someone on my floor smokes weed because I sometimes smell it in the hallway, but that doesn't bother me. Hell, I toke up myself sometimes when life gets overwhelming.

I ride the elevator to the third floor, unlock my door, and step into my cozy home. My furniture is a collection of thrift store finds that I refinished myself, and my walls are covered in bright, abstract floral paintings. I toss my bags onto the sofa and walk to the bathroom. I need a long, hot shower before I get ready for dinner.

I get the water to the perfect temperature, slink out of my clothes, and step into the tub. The warm water rushes over me, washing away the hurt I feel after thinking about my parents. I decided to focus on the future instead. I let myself fantasize about Paul. As I wash my hair, I imagine us going to the farmers' market on our days off and cooking delicious food together in my kitchen. I wonder what his lips would feel like, pressed against mine, and remember the soft touch of his hand.

Thinking about Paul in this way turns me on, and I decide to indulge myself. I take my handheld shower head from its cradle and sit down in the tub. I lay back, switch the water stream to massage mode, and point it at my clit. As the water dances over me, I imagine it's Paul's tongue providing the sensations. I pinch my nipples with my free hand and soon I'm rewarded with a soft, satisfying orgasm.

Better safe than sorry, I think as I stand back up. I reach for my razor and quickly shave my legs. Satisfied that I'm well groomed, I turn off the water, step out of the shower, and wrap myself in a towel. I hear my phone ringing in the other room, and I rush to answer it before voicemail picks it up.

"Hello?" I ask with a little confusion, because I don't recognize the number displayed on the screen.

"Kiara? It's Jenny."

"Hey, Jenny... is everything all right?" I ask.

"Yes, everything's fine. I just feel awful for the attitude I've been giving you lately. It has nothing to do with you. I just had so much going on lately... I was stressed, and I took it out on the wrong people. I'm so sorry."

"It's all right," I assure her. "I completely understand."

"Thank you, Kiara. Do you think we could get together sometime and talk? I could use a friend right now, and I don't know anyone else right now... I'm always so busy with work and school... I'm sure you understand that, too."

"Absolutely," I agree. "I'm always here if you need to talk. Do you want to meet at the restaurant early in the morning for coffee? Or we could go to the café for lunch again."

"Would you be able to meet me somewhere tonight?" she asks nervously. "I know it's short notice, but I could use someone to talk to."

Shit. "I'm so sorry, Jenny. I already made plans this evening... I'm meeting a friend from culinary school. We're going to practice pastries," I lie. "I'd invite you to join us, but I'm going to her house and I'm not sure how she'd feel about it."

"No, that's okay," Jenny replies quickly. "We can meet for lunch tomorrow."

I'm filled with guilt and quickly backtrack. "Jenny, if you need me, I can cancel."

"I'll be okay," she assures me. "Enjoy your time with your friend, and I'll see you tomorrow."

Robbs is sitting in front of his oversized flat-screen television watching Monday night football when his phone rings. "Did you talk to her?" he answers, after looking at the name on his screen.

"Yes, I just hung up with her," Jenny replies. "I also called the restaurant and asked to speak with Paul. Megan said he's taking the day off. Kiara gave me a lame story about having plans with a girl from her school. I'm almost positive they're meeting up tonight."

"So it's go time?" Robbs has been waiting for this moment since he first shot the video of Jenny and Paul together.

"It's go time," she agrees. "Did you find her address?"

"Yep. I saved the route to her apartment in my GPS. Are you sure you want to do this? Once I show her the video, I can't unshow it. I don't want you to regret it after and whine about how we went too far."

"I'm positive," Jenny assures him. "Take the bitch down a few pegs and I'll do nothing but celebrate."

"How about I call you after?" Robbs suggests. "You can bring your fine ass over here and we can celebrate together."

"You're on."

Chapter Eight

I stand in front of my full-length mirror and examine myself. My new, dark denim skinny jeans make my ass appear plump and firm, and the emerald shirt showcases my 36C breasts perfectly. Since Paul only ever sees my hair up in a bun in the kitchen, I decided to wear it loose around my shoulders for our date.

It's *not* a date, I think, catching myself. It's just two people enjoying a meal together... just like last night, only a different setting. I fasten a silver bracelet around my left wrist and pull my new brown leather boots from their box. As I tug the left one on, my doorbell rings.

What the fuck? I check the time. It's only six o'clock. Paul and I aren't going out until seven-thirty, and the plan is for us to meet at the restaurant.

"Hold on," I call out as I pull the boot back off. I make my way to the door and peek through the peephole. Robbs is on the other side, tapping his foot impatiently. I fling the door open.

"What the hell are you doing here?" I demand.

"Now, now," Robbs chides me. He pushes his way past me and into the apartment. "Is that any way to welcome a guest?"

"The word 'guest' would imply that you'd been invited," I reply harshly. I shut the door behind me as I turn toward him. "I don't recall inviting you, so answer my fucking question. And while you're at it, you can explain how you found out where I live."

"You'd be surprised by what you can learn on the Internet," he answers sharply. "Kiara, I'm here as a friend. There's no need for all of this hostility."

"I have a hard time believing that. Since when the hell have we been friends?"

"I know I'm an ass at the restaurant, but you shouldn't take it personally," Robbs insists. "I do admire your talents in the kitchen, but you're the competition, and I've been treating you accordingly... you know, it's considered good manners to offer your guests something to drink."

"I'm not planning on you being around long enough to finish a drink, but there's some bottled water in the fridge. Help yourself if you want one."

Robbs walks into my kitchen and retrieves a cold bottle. "This is a quaint place you keep here," he comments as he returns to the living room. "Small... but charming." He opens the bottle and takes a drink.

"Cut to the chase, Robbs. Why are you here?" I ask impatiently.

"I'm here because I'm worried about you, Kiara. I see the way Paul looks at you at Fission. And a person would need to be blind and deaf to miss the way he flirts with you. Last night, I noticed you returning those looks. I think you should know what kind of guy you're dealing with."

"Paul may flirt with me, but it's harmless," I insist. "And even if it wasn't, it's none of your business."

"We're competing for a spot as Paul's apprentice, so I feel that it's very much my business," Robbs argues. "And I know things about our boss... things that would make you never want to set foot in the restaurant again, much less flirt with the asshole."

"I know that people at Fission gossip about him, Robbs. There's nothing you can tell me that I haven't already heard. But I don't put much stock in gossip... though I'm not surprised that you do."

"I've heard stories from Amy and Charlotte too, but that's not why I'm here. If you can look me in the eye and honestly say there's no part of you that's tempted to give in to Paul's advances, then I'll leave right now. But if there IS a part of you that's considering being with him... even a small part... then there's something I need to show you."

His last statement got my attention. "Show me...?" I ask slowly.

Robbs pulls his phone from his jeans' pocket. "Show you..."

What the hell. Let him play whatever game he wants and maybe he'll leave. "And what is this earth-shattering video you have for me?"

"I'm glad you ask," Robbs says, smiling sadly. "You're making the right decision. I know you stayed late at the restaurant with Paul last night. Jenny and I had a drink after we finished up, and I left my phone at our booth. I went back a few hours later and saw your car pull out of the parking lot when I drove up."

"We spent a long time cleaning," I explain quickly.

"I'm sure you did," he says, nodding. "That's not why I'm here, though it does make me wonder if I'm too late." He takes another long drink from the bottle and stares at me intently.

"Go on..."

"The front door was unlocked, so I let myself in and grabbed my phone. I hit the head, sat in there for a while and checked the messages I'd missed... logged in to Facebook... you know the drill. Anyway, when I was finished, I opened the bathroom door slowly. I didn't want Paul to know I was there. Frankly, I didn't feel like talking to the bastard. But to my surprise, I stepped into the dining room and found Paul and Jenny at the bar."

"Jenny?" I ask in shock. "What was she doing there?"

"Paul," Robbs answers simply.

My mouth drops in disbelief. This can't be happening. There's no way he slept with Jenny after our dinner last night. "I don't believe you," I tell Robbs.

"I don't imagine you would," he says with a nod, "but you can see if for yourself." He holds his phone out to me. "All you have to do is push play."

A part of me, a big part, doesn't want to see what is on his phone. If I don't see it, it's not real. But curiosity combined with my need to protect myself takes over, and I take the phone from Robbs' hand. I swipe the screen to reveal a still shot of Paul and Jenny at the bar. Paul stands behind it while Jenny perches on a stool.

"You may want to sit down," Robbs warns.

I take a seat on my sofa and push play. I watch Jenny and Paul speak, their hands entwined.

"Is there any audio?" I ask Robbs, desperate to hear the conversation.

He shakes his head and takes a seat beside me. "You won't want to hear it anyway," he assures me.

Jenny moves onto the top of the bar, followed quickly by Paul. My heart breaks as I watch them strip off their clothes and go at it like animals.

"Kiara?" Robbs says softly. "Do you want to turn it off now? I think you've seen enough."

I shake my head without taking my eyes off of the screen. I need to see everything, to know exactly what happened. We watch the rest of the video in silence until, finally, it ends. Robbs puts an arm around me and I'm too upset to shake him off.

"Kiara, I'm so sorry. I know the video is graphic, but I also knew that you had to see it."

"Do either of them know you filmed this?" I ask softly.

"No," he assures me. "After they finished, I ducked down in a booth and hid until Jenny left and Paul went back to the kitchen. Then I snuck out the front door."

"*Why* did you film them?"

"Because what Paul is doing is wrong. I think he needs to be stopped. I knew if I didn't have concrete proof, people would assume that I was accusing him of things because I'm not doing well in the completion. Though I think what I have here proves that I'm not doing well because I don't, shall we say, have the right equipment."

"Thank you for showing this to me, Robbs," I say as I rise to my feet. "If you'll excuse me, I have some phone calls to make."

Jenny paces the floors of her small apartment, waiting for the phone to ring. When it finally does, she answers it quickly. "Is it done?"

"It's done," Robbs informs her. "I think we've seen the last of Kiara. Now get your ass over here so we can celebrate."

<<◇>>

I wake to the sound of my phone ringing. I roll over, see Paul's number on the screen, and silence the call. I check the time on my bedside alarm clock. It's seven-thirty in the morning. I yawn, stretch, and try to hold back my tears as the memories of that video fill my head.

After Robbs left last night, I spent a long time trying to figure out what to do. I wasn't ready to face Paul, so I stood him up and ignored his calls. I know I have to face him, so I retrieve my phone and listen to his messages.

"Kiara, it's a quarter to eight. I'm just wondering where you're at. I've got us a table, call me if you're lost and I'll give you directions. See you soon."

"Kiara, it's eight now, and I'm really starting to worry about you. Please call me back as soon as you get this message."

The next voicemail came through at nine o'clock. "Kiara, I'm incredibly worried about you. If you don't call me back soon, I'm going to start calling the hospitals and police stations."

I'm oddly satisfied to hear the worry in his voice. Let the bastard suffer for a while. I start the fourth message.

"Kiara, I don't know what's going on. I know that you're not at any of the hospitals, but I'm still afraid that something's happened to you. Please, please call me as soon as possible. If you've decided you don't want to spend time with me, that's all right. I'll understand. I just need to know that you're all right."

"You're just worried that I've caught on to your slime ball ways," I scream into my receiver to no one. I click on the message he left a few minutes ago.

"Kiara, this is Paul again. I finally got a hold of Jenny last night, and she said you had plans with a friend from culinary school. Was I confused about our plans? I thought we were meeting for dinner last night, but if I was mistaken, I'm sorry for all of the messages. Call me back, or I'll just see you when you come in to work today."

I can tell by the tone of his voice that he knows damn well he wasn't confused about our plans. He knows I stood him up on purpose, and he's panicked. My phone rings again, and once again I silence it. I know I have to face him, but I want to do it face-to-face. I want him to look me in the eye and admit to what he did.

I roll out of bed and carefully select my clothes for the day. I pull on my new skinny jeans and a tight cowl-necked sweater that accentuates my curves. It's not an outfit I'd work in, but I'm not planning on doing any cooking today.

I ride the elevator downstairs, climb in my car, and drive toward Fission. On my way, I call Chef Lee's office.

"Hello?" she answers on the second ring.

"Good morning, Chef Lee. This is Kiara Sands."

"Hello, Kiara! It's so good to hear from you. I've been wondering how things are going at Fission. Your weekly reports from Chef Weston have been phenomenal. I'm so proud of you! Are you enjoying the experience?"

"That's actually why I'm calling, Chef Lee," I tell her. "I was hoping you have room in your schedule to

meet with me this afternoon. There are some things I'd
like to discuss."

"Let me check..." After a long pause, she returns to
the line. "I can meet with you at three-thirty. Will that
work with your schedule at the restaurant?"

"That will be perfect, thank you," I answer.

"Great, I'll see you then."

I disconnect the call just as I pull into the parking lot
of Fission. It's eight-thirty, and Paul's car is the only one
in the lot. I'm thankful no one else is here. I have a lot to
say and I don't want to be overheard by Amy, Charlotte,
or any of the other nosey, gossiping staff.

I push the front door, and I'm relieved to find it is
unlocked. The dining room is dark and quiet. Any other
time, I'd find the atmosphere peaceful, but this morning
it just seems sad and lonely. I walk into the kitchen and
find Paul sitting on a stool next to the prep station. He
looks up as the door swings shut behind me.

"Kiara, thank God," he says as he rushes toward me.
"I've been so worried. I didn't sleep at all last night." He
wraps his arms around me.

"Don't fucking touch me," I tell him as I escape
from his embrace.

"Kiara, what's wrong?" Confusion fills his face.
"Has something happened? Were you in an accident? I
called over and over again. Have you lost your phone?"

"You know exactly what happened," I answer
hatefully, "and now, so do I."

"What are you talking about? I don't know anything. Did I do something to upset you? Is that why you didn't show last night? If I overstepped, if you feel like us hanging out together is inappropriate, I understand."

"What's inappropriate is that you fucked Jenny on the bar Sunday night," I say firmly.

All of the color drains from his face. "Kiara, I didn't..."

"Save it, there's no point in lying. I didn't come here to listen to your excuses. I just wanted to bring this back," I tell him as I pull my folded Fission chef's jacket from my bag. "I have no interest in being yet another employee you screw and then screw over. Consider this my resignation," I say as I throw the jacket at his face.

He catches it and lays it across the prep table. "Kiara, I don't know what Jenny told you, but it didn't happen the way you think it did. I admit I slept with her. And it was wrong. That was one of the incidents I was talking about when I told you I've made mistakes."

"No, it wasn't," I argue. "You fucked her after I left Sunday. I know you did. What happened, Paul? I didn't drop my pants fast enough for you, so you moved on to Jenny? Did you at least wait until I left the parking lot before you called her, or had you already made plans with her before we had dinner together?"

"That night with Jenny was weeks ago," Paul insists. "It was before I thought I had a chance with you... she asked me to help her study for her pairings class, and we got way too drunk. Things went too far, but it didn't mean anything. You're the one I care about, Kiara."

"I see," I reply angrily. "So Jenny was just a fuck for you. That speaks volumes about your character, Paul."

"I understand if you don't want to spend time with me outside of the restaurant," he says with a sigh, "but please don't quit the program. You deserve to be here, Kiara. And working here would be a big boost for your career. Please don't throw away this opportunity because I made a mistake."

"The winner of this competition will be your new apprentice, and I'd rather light my hair on fire than work for you," I hiss. "I've scheduled a meeting with my faculty adviser at *Cordon Bleu*. Hopefully, I can make up the last month of classes and finish out the rest of this semester. If not, I'll take an incomplete and start over in January. Regardless, I won't be setting foot in this place again."

I turn around, slam the swinging doors open, and step back into the dining room. I glance at the bar and feel like I'm going to be sick.

"Kiara."

I turn and see Paul in the doorway. "Don't follow me," I demand. I rush out of the restaurant and nearly run Jenny over on the sidewalk.

"Good morning..." she greets me awkwardly. "Are you leaving?"

"Yes," I hiss as I walk past her and step into the parking lot.

"Is everything all right? When are you coming back?"

I turn on her. "Everything is fucking perfect, especially for you. After all of that talk in the café about how we shouldn't screw our way to the top, you turn around and do exactly that."

"Look, Kiara... I can explain," she insists.

"I don't need to hear your pathetic explanations. I know exactly what happened. Your 'I'm not sure this is what I want' bullshit was just a line to get me to let my guard down. You're jealous of my cooking skills, and you're jealous Paul found me more attractive than you. You knew that the only way you had a chance in hell of winning the apprenticeship was if you screwed the boss. So you win, Jenny. You can have the job and you can have Paul. You deserve each other, and I deserve better." I turn and walk toward my car.

"Kiara, wait..." she calls out.

I leave the parking lot without looking back.

Chapter Nine

"Kiara, this is quite surprising," Chef Lee says with obvious disappointment. "Out of all of my students, I thought you'd be best suited for this competition. Do you realize how many of your classmates wanted that spot at Fission?"

"I understand, Chef Lee. And I'm sorry," I apologize, "but the environment at Fission is not one I can work in. There's a lot of... internal politics at play."

"Is the environment hostile?" Chef Lee asks. "Should I contact the labor board?"

I shake my head. "There's no need to do that. Nothing going on there is illegal... exactly."

"Kiara, I'd love to help you out, but first you're going to have to tell me the full story. You're obligated to Fission for the next eight weeks, and your semester grade depends on you completing the competition. I may be able to pull some strings, but only if I know the facts of the situation."

"Chef Weston seems more interested in how his female candidates perform outside of the kitchen," I say firmly.

"I see," says Chef Lee, perplexed. "And I assume you're not talking about the front of the house?"

I shake my head. "If I can't make up my work here this semester, I understand. I'll start over in January. But I can't go back to that restaurant."

"Kiara, I don't mean to pry into your personal business, but did you develop a physical relationship with Chef Weston?"

"No, I did *not*."

"But you felt pressured to do so in order to win the apprenticeship?"

"I felt that the events occurring outside of the competition were detrimental to my success. Chef Weston showed obvious favoritism to me, and he made it clear that he was interested in me in a nonprofessional way. That favoritism and interest caused the other competitors to develop hostile attitudes toward me. I can't prove it, but I'm certain my work was sabotaged at least once."

"At some point, you're going to have to learn to work in hostile environments," Chef Lee advises. "Professional kitchens are notorious for drama. I'd have thought you already knew that."

"I understand," I assure her. "But Chef Weston's actions have made me completely uninterested in being his apprentice. I feel that continuing in the competition would be a waste of my time."

Chef Lee stares at me intently and is silent for quite some time. "Very well. I'll need you to write an official statement detailing why you are leaving the competition. You don't have to get specific with the details of Chef Weston's flirtations, but I'll need something for your file."

"I can do that," I agree.

"I must warn you, Kiara, you're going to face some scrutiny from your classmates. You've missed four weeks of class, and most people in that situation would have to take an incomplete for the semester. I'm willing to let you make up the work you've missed, but I can't give you any other special treatment. Midterms are next week… you'll have to have all of your make-up work turned in before then, and you have to take the tests as scheduled."

"Thank you, Chef Lee," I say with relief. "I understand. I'll get started right away, and I'll be prepared for the exams."

"I certainly hope so, Kiara. You're incredibly talented, and I'd hate to see this set your graduation date back. I will email you a list of make-up assignments. You can do the written work online, providing you log in to the system with your webcam on so no one can accuse you of cheating. The practical assignments can be made up during my planning periods."

"Thank you, Chef Lee. I know this is a huge inconvenience to you."

"Wait until after next week's exams to thank me," Chef Lee answers impatiently. "You're incredibly talented, but I confess I'll be surprised if you're able to complete all of your work on time and prepare for your midterms. As your advisor, I must reemphasize that the best thing you could do is set aside your personal issues and complete your time at Fission."

"I understand but I just can't," I tell her again. "I will get all of my work finished on schedule. And as for my exams, it's not like I've taken four weeks off from cooking. I'll surprise you, I promise."

"We'll see, Kiara. We'll see."

"Time's up, pencils down," Chef Lee announces from the front of the classroom. Over the last two hours, my classmates and I have been taking our midterm practical test. I have to admit I wasn't as prepared as I thought I'd be.

"Please step away from your desks and move to your work station," Chef Lee continues. We stand and do as she directed. I arrive at my work station and find an assortment of ingredients spread out on the table.

"This is a three-hour practical exam," Chef Lee explains, "during which time you will complete a variety of dishes that comprise a full-course meal. The salad course will showcase your knife skills, and all dressings must be made from scratch. Following that, you will create all five of the mother sauces. You will reserve a sample of each before taking two sauces of your choosing and turning them into small sauces. Those sauces are to be served with a dish of your choosing, both of which must have meat components. Finally, you will create an ice cream, sorbet, or gelato. Once you've moved on to the next stage of the exam, you may not go back and correct any of the other stages. Your time starts now."

I survey the ingredients that are already at my
station. Everything needed for the mother sauces is
already there. I set pans to warm on my stovetop before
rushing to the walk-in for my salad ingredients. I want
to make a classic Caesar, so I grab romaine, parmesan,
lemons, mustard, and Worcestershire sauce. I stop in the
pantry for anchovies before returning to my station.

I finish the salad quickly and begin on my sauces.
While I work, I consider which sauces I want to use in
my next course. I know most of my classmates will be
tempted to create a simple cream sauce, as it's the least
time consuming. I want my work to stand out, so I
decide my entrée dishes will include beef with a
Bordelaise sauce, which will be created from my
Espagnole, and poached salmon with a *Maltaise* sauce,
which I will make from my *Hollandaise*.

I complete the mother sauces and reserve samples of
them as Chef Lee had instructed. I return to the walk-in
for beef tenderloin, mushrooms, salmon, and asparagus.
I return to my workstation and my heart sinks. My
reserved *Veloute* sauce has broken in its bowl. There's
nothing I can do about it now, I just have to move on
and make sure everything else is perfect.

I glance up at the front of the classroom and see
Chef Lee grading the written exams at her desk. I'll
know whether I've passed or failed before I leave for the
evening. I wasn't as prepared as I should have been for
the written portion of the midterm. That, combined with
my broken *Veloute*, sends anxiety coursing through my
body.

Just keep it together. It's all about the food. I know
what I'm doing. I brown the tenderloin in a hot skillet

and transfer it to the oven. The salmon will only need to cook for a few minutes. I prepare my poaching water, then return to the walk-in once more for my dessert ingredients. I enjoy savory tones in my final course, so I decide to prepare a pink grapefruit and sage sorbet. I gather the ingredients, return to my station, and check my tenderloin. I press it with a gloved finger and can tell it's overcooked.

Damn it! I pull it out of the oven and leave it to rest on my cutting board. I slam the pan down and draw the attention of several of my classmates. "Sorry," I say sheepishly. This isn't going well at all, and a big part of me wants to give up. But if I have a prayer of finishing the semester, I have to complete this midterm. It'll all be over after today. I'll be caught up with everything and start fresh next week. By finals, I'll be kicking everyone's asses again.

The entrée portion of the exam must be completed before I can start on my sorbet, so I slide the salmon into my poaching liquid and add the necessary ingredients to my sauces. While the sauces simmer, I slice the tenderloin. It's still pink in the middle, and I'm slightly encouraged. I let the asparagus steam while I plate my beef dish. Once I'm satisfied with my entrées, I set them aside and move on to my final course.

I make a simple syrup on the stovetop and juice the grapefruits into it. I toss in the sage and let the flavors meld for a few minutes. While the mixture simmers, I glance back at my bowls of mother sauces… everything but the *Veloute* is still intact.

I hear a noise at the front of the room and look up to see Chef Lee leaving her desk. "You have thirty minutes left. As you should all be on the dessert portion of the exam, I'm going to start sampling your other courses."

She walks up to my station and I'm relieved that she is tasting my entrées while they're still hot. I'm also relieved that I'm too busy with my sorbet to watch her reactions to my food. I strain the simple syrup mixture into a glass bowl and transfer it to the ice cream machine at my station. There's nothing left for me to do but wait.

Once again, I wake to the sound of my chiming phone. I've had a restless night, and the noise startles me.

"Hello?"

"Kiara, this is Arabella Lee. I'd like for you to come in to discuss your midterm grade."

"Yes, Chef, of course. Is there a problem?"

"I'd rather discuss it in person, Kiara. Can you be here in an hour? If not, I can meet you at four o'clock, after my advanced pastry class."

"I can be there in an hour," I assure her.

"Thank you, I'll see you then."

The line goes dead, and my heart fills with panic. I know I didn't do well on the written exam, but I'd felt confident about the practical. I jump out of bed and pull on the first set of clothes I find in my unfolded pile of laundry… baggy jeans and a soft, frumpy sweatshirt. I slide my feet into my laceless Converse and examine myself in the mirror. My face is pale, and I have dark circles under my eyes. I dab on some concealer and lip gloss and make my way to the kitchen.

I have no appetite, so I pour myself a glass of orange juice and start a pot of coffee. It will only take me fifteen minutes to drive to the college. I spend twenty minutes pacing the floor and going over the practical exam in my head. I'd tasted all of my dishes, so I know my flavors were well developed. My sorbet was slightly grainy, but it had been delicious all the same.

I glance at my phone and see that it is twenty-five minutes till nine. I pour coffee into a travel mug and head out the door. The drive to the college is uneventful, and I arrive at Chef Lee's office five minutes before our scheduled time. I knock lightly on the door.

"Come in," she calls out.

I open the door and find her sitting behind her desk. She's on the phone, so I wave my greeting.

"Thank you," she says to the person on the other line. "I'll speak with her and get back with you."

"Good morning, Kiara," she greets me as she returns the phone to its cradle. "Thank you for coming in on such short notice."

"Of course, Chef Lee... you said you need to speak with me about my midterm?"

"Yes," she replies, studying me carefully. "How do you feel you did?"

"I know I could have done better on my written exam... and I know my *Veloute* sauce broke. Other than that, I feel like I did all right," I answer.

"And is 'all right' acceptable to you?"

"No," I admit meekly.

"Kiara, you know I have a soft spot for you. But your exam results were quite disappointing."

"I understand," I reply, lowering my head.

"You passed the midterm, but just barely. Your current course grades are so low that it will be next to impossible for you to receive anything but B's and C's on your finals. And while you'll be able to continue on next semester..."

"I'm going to lose my scholarships," I finish the sentence for her.

"Yes, I'm afraid there's only one sure-fire way that you'll be able to retain your financial aid package," she tells me.

"What's that?" I ask quickly. "I'm willing to do whatever it takes, Chef Lee. You've been so understanding about the situation at Fission. I'll do anything you ask."

"I was on the phone with Chef Weston when you arrived," she begins and my heart sinks. I know where this conversation is going. "He takes full responsibility for the actions that led you to leave his competition. He's willing to let you return to Fission. You've only missed six days of work there, which you could easily make up. Is that something you're willing to consider?"

"I don't know..." I hesitate. "May I have some time to think about it?"

"You may have a day or two," Chef Lee agrees. "I understand this isn't what you want, but I'm afraid you may have no other choice... unless, of course, you apply for student loans to pay for the remainder of your education. You need to decide if avoiding the restaurant is worth tens of thousands of dollars to you."

I let out a long sigh. Hearing it put that way makes me see my situation in a new light, but I still can't bear the thought of working in a kitchen with Paul and Jenny. "I'll have my answer to you by tomorrow."

"Take until Monday, if you need to," Chef Lee offers. "If you come to a decision before then, call me on my cell."

"Thank you, Chef Lee," I say as I rise from my seat. "I know I've been a difficult student this semester."

"I just want to see you succeed, Kiara," she says kindly. "Please consider your options carefully."

Chapter Ten

I sit at my desk and stare blankly at the screen of my laptop. It's Saturday night, and I've been researching student loans since I left Chef Lee's office the previous morning. The information I've found is discouraging, but I still can't imagine walking back in to Fission. I feel a pang in my stomach and realize I haven't eaten today, so I walk in to the kitchen and survey the contents of my refrigerator. I decide on scrambled eggs, which I make quickly and eat directly from the skillet. I finish and toss the skillet into my sink as my doorbell chimes.

Who the hell could that be? I remember the last time I had an unexpected visitor. I walk to the door and say a silent prayer that Robbs isn't waiting on the other side again. I look through the peephole and see Jenny. That's even worse.

I decide to pretend I'm not home. I take a seat on my sofa and wait for her to leave.

"Kiara?" she calls out loudly. "I know you're home. Your car is in the parking lot and your neighbor says you haven't left all day. Please let me in. I'm not leaving until you listen to what I have to say."

I stomp over and swing the door open. "What do you want?"

"Can I come in?" Jenny asks with hesitation.

"I think you've already proven you'll do whatever the hell you want," I snap harshly as I move back to the sofa. She steps into the apartment and shuts the door behind her. She stares at me intently before speaking again.

"Are you all right, Kiara?" she asks. "You look awful."

I glance down at my clothes. I'm wearing plaid flannel pajama pants and the same sweatshirt I wore to my meeting with Chef Lee. I know my hair is a mess, and I can't imagine the circles under my eyes have improved since I last checked in the mirror.

"Thank you for the critique of my appearance," I say with a sneer. "If that's all you came for, you can leave now."

"Kiara, don't be ridiculous. I'm sorry. I'm just worried about you."

"I'm sure you are," I reply sarcastically. "You're such a selfless, charitable person. If you're here to check on me, you needn't have bothered, I'm just fine."

"I know you're pissed at me, and you have every right to be," Jenny says softly. "And I know you're in trouble at school. I overheard Paul talking to your instructor yesterday."

"Ah... tell me, were you under Paul when you overheard him? Or do the two of you save that for after hours?"

"I deserved that," Jenny replies anxiously. "But nothing's going on between Paul and me. I came here to explain that video you saw."

"So you know Robbs caught the two of you."

"Kiara... I knew Robbs was filming us that night. I *meant* for Robbs to film us."

"What?"

Tears fill Jenny's eyes. "This is the worst thing I've ever done. It was all Robbs' idea. We were both so jealous of the way Paul treated you, and we thought you'd win the apprenticeship. Robbs convinced me that we had to stop you, that we had to find a way to make you quit."

"Let me get this straight," I interrupt her. "You were afraid I'd sleep with Paul and win the apprenticeship because of it. You resented that idea, so you decided the best way to deal with it was sleeping with him first?"

"I know... looking back now, I can see it was hypocritical and devious. I can't apologize enough for what I did. But it's no reason to sacrifice your education. Come back to the restaurant... please?"

I shake my head. "I don't care what your motivations were. Paul still slept with you. He wined and dined me after work, and then had sex with you as soon as I left."

"That's not what happened, Kiara. That's what I came to tell you."

"I saw the video, Jenny."

"I know, but Robbs lied about *when* it happened. Paul and I had sex way before you started showing interest in him."

The pieces all fall into place in my head, and I begin to understand. "It happened right before he started acting so distant toward you," I say softly.

Jenny nods. "And it was all me, Kiara. I seduced him. I asked him to help me study for a pairings class because I knew the only way I had a chance with him was if he was drunk. I kept the evening going, kept asking for more samples and bigger shots of vodka. And even after all of the booze, I still had to talk him into having sex with me. That's why there's no audio on the video Robbs showed you. We didn't want you to hear me convincing him that it was okay."

"So everything Paul said when I confronted him was true?"

Jenny nods. "It's been awful at Fission since you left. Paul is devastated. He sulks around the kitchen and snaps at everyone who tries to talk to him. And we didn't even have a cooking competition this week. He said his heart just wasn't in it. Please, come back."

I sit silently for a moment, absorbing what I've just learned. "Jenny, I'm glad you came over to explain this. But there are parts that I'm still not understanding. Like why in the world you'd ever join forces with Robbs."

"He got me riled up over the fact that Paul was showing you so much favoritism. At first, I thought he was crazy. But he got me to agree to help him, if he could prove that Paul was unfairly favoring you... that day you were covering the prep station..."

"He's the one who pulled the cutting board over the edge of the table. He's the reason all of the food fell to the floor. He blatantly sabotaged me, and you were okay with that'?"

"I was being selfish." She's sobbing again, and I feel that she's truly sorry for what she did. "I wasn't thinking about the situation being unfair to you. When Paul hugged you after the food fell, then made ME help fix the mistake, I was convinced that Robbs was right... that you'd win the apprenticeship regardless of how well he and I cooked."

"I should have known Robbs was up to something when he showed up here with that video. I came so close to not watching it... I didn't trust him. But he gave me a long speech about his attitude at Fission not being personal, and claimed that he was trying to protect me. I should never have let him through the door."

"He would have made sure you saw the video no matter what," Jenny says gravely. "I'm so sorry... I know I keep saying that, but I want you to understand. Robbs has been even more smug and hateful since you quit. If for no other reason, you should come back to work to kick his ass in the competition."

"How much of this does Paul know?"

"None of it," she admits. "He hasn't asked me how you found out that we slept together. And to his credit, he hasn't taken out any of his frustrations on me specifically. If he did, I'd deserve it. I think he might actually be in love with you, Kiara. If you were ever interested in him at all, you should go talk to him... he's probably still at Fission."

I stand and grab my purse.

"Does this mean that you're coming back to work?" Jenny asks hopefully.

"I don't know. But you're right. I need to talk to him."

I speed all the way to Fission and arrive in record time. With the exception of Paul's black Land Rover, the parking lot is empty. I pull into a spot, jump out of my car, and rush to the front door. As usual, it's unlocked. I let myself in, run through the dining room, and barrel through the kitchen doors. Paul is bent over the sink, scrubbing a saucepan. I clear my throat and he jumps before turning around.

"Kiara?" he asks in surprise. "What are you doing here?"

"Oh, Paul," I cry and throw myself into his arms. "I had to come talk to you. I'm so sorry!"

He holds me tightly and caresses the back of my head. "What's the matter, Kiara?" he asks in a soothing voice. "Is it your midterm? I spoke with Chef Lee yesterday. I told her that you're welcome to come back to work here."

"It's not the midterm," I answer with a sob. "It's everything else. I talked to Jenny. I know I was wrong about when the two of you hooked up. I know you weren't lying when I confronted you that day."

"Thank god," Paul says, holding me even tighter. "I'm so sorry, Kiara, I never should have been with her.

It's you who I've wanted all along. I've been infatuated with you since the moment I saw you sitting at the back table. Your incredible talent in the kitchen just made me want you more. Will you ever be able to forgive me?"

I pull away slightly and look into his clear blue eyes. "I already have."

His eyes light up and a broad smile spreads across his face. He leans down and kisses me softly… his lips on mine feel better than anything I've ever imagined. I open my lips slightly and tease his tongue with mine. Shivers coarse through my body, and I feel as if I'm going to collapse in his arms. I slip my hands down to his chef's jacket… my fingers fumble as I try to undo the first button and he pulls away suddenly.

"We can't do this, not like this," he whispers, still holding me.

"I know," I say, agreeing with a disappointed nod. "If I'm going to rejoin the competition, we can't get involved."

Paul lets out a laugh. "That's not what I'm talking about. Come sit down with me," he says, pulling me toward the group of stools arranged around the prep table. We each take a seat and he continues.

"I'll figure out how to go forward impartially with the competition. That's not why I just stopped you from undressing me," he explains with a sly grin. "I stopped you because I want to do this right. I know you've been through a lot in your life. I know you're hesitant to trust people. And you know I've made more than my share of mistakes with women in the past. I think we should take things slowly. I want to prove myself worthy of you. When we finally make love, I don't want there to be a doubt in your mind about my feelings for you. Does that sound like something you'd be interested in?"

With tears in my eyes, I nod and fall back into his arms.

Chapter Eleven

Jenny and I sit at our usual back table and drink coffee before our shifts start. It's Thursday, my fourth day back at Fission.

"Are you ready for today's challenge?" I ask her.

"I hope so," she replies with a nod. "But as usual, as long as one of us kicks Robbs' ass, I'll be satisfied."

I've been able to forgive Jenny for the part she played in all of the drama, but I'm still having a hard time being civil to Robbs. Every time I see him, I remember the smug look of satisfaction he had on his face after he showed me the video. I still haven't told Paul that his night with Jenny was a set up, and I don't intend to. I also haven't shared with him that Robbs sabotaged my prep work that day. I know it would be an easy way to get Robbs kicked out of the competition, but it will be more satisfying to kick his ass and win the apprenticeship.

"How are things going with Paul?" Jenny asks.

"Perfect," I say. "We still haven't consummated our relationship, and I have to admit that I'm enjoying all of the courting. He opens doors for me, pulls my chair out at tables... I feel like I'm living in a romantic, Victorian-era movie."

"I've never had a man treat me like that," Jenny says.

"You will," I assure her. "You just have to stop discounting yourself. Demand to be treated with respect, and you will be."

Jenny and I have gotten closer over the last week, but I still haven't worked up the courage to ask her the question that's been nagging me. The way Robbs looks at her leads me to believe there was more to their relationship than planning my downfall, but I don't want to bring up a sore subject with her. If anything physical did happen between them, I'm sure it's over now.

"You may have to remind me of that next time I start dating someone," she says.

"I will." I smile. "That's what friends are for."

We each take a long drink of our coffees, and Robbs walks through the front door.

"The asshole has arrived," I tell Jenny. She turns and we watch Robbs pour a cup of coffee behind the bar and take a seat at his own table. His shit talking has stopped completely since I returned. He still sneers at me every chance he gets, but his silence has been a welcome change.

"You know, I heard him talking to Amy yesterday," Jenny tells me. "He called his faculty advisor and reported Paul's relationship with you. He insisted that it gives you an unfair advantage in the competition and asked if there was any legal action that could be taken. His instructor told him to grow a pair and stop complaining."

"That just makes me want to kick his ass even more. He's such a whiny little bitch," I observe. "Paul knew he'd try to pull something like that. He's been trying to come up with a way to make the competition fair."

"After what Robbs and I did to you, it would be fair for us both to be thrown out on our asses," Jenny says.

"Jenny, I told you I forgive you for that. There's no reason for you to keep bringing it up," I remind her.

"You're a better friend than I deserve, Kiara," she says.

"Don't worry. I'm sure I'll fuck up eventually and then you can have a chance to forgive me." I laugh.

Paul walks out of the kitchen and joins us at the table. "Good morning, ladies. Are you ready for today's cooking challenge?"

"We hope so," I reply. I want to kiss him hello so badly, but we agreed to maintain professional behavior when we're at work. I am positive everyone at the restaurant knows that we're seeing each other, but neither of us wants to fuel the gossip flames.

"Robbs, get over here. We're about to get started," Paul calls across the room.

Robbs slinks over. "I don't know why we're even bothering with this anymore. We all know that you're going to choose your girlfriend's dish."

Instead of returning Robbs' snarky attitude, Paul smiles. "I thought you might feel that way, so I won't be judging the competitions anymore. I'll be tasting your plates, of course, but Patrick and Claire will choose the winning dish."

"That's more than fair," Jenny assures him.

Paul turns to Robbs. "You would do well to remember that your attitude will be a factor in the final decision of who will win the apprenticeship."

"Yes, Chef," he answers half-heartedly.

"Excellent," says Paul, smiling. "Now, as I'm sure you realized when I mentioned Claire, we're having a dessert challenge today. I don't care what you make, as long as we don't already have a similar dish on the menu. You will have a full hour, and you must plate six portions. Your time starts now."

Jenny, Robbs, and I jump up and race to the kitchen. I've been expecting a dessert challenge, and I know exactly what I want to make. I race past my cooking station and go straight to the walk-in cooler. I grab eggs, cream, and butter before moving on to the pantry. There I get vanilla beans, flour, baking powder, and lavender buds.

I take my ingredients to my station and set them on the table. I set the oven to preheat, grease six small loaf pans, and shake flour into them. I mix my batter and finish just as the oven beeps to alert me that it's reached my desired temperature. I pour equal amounts of batter into each pan and place them on the top rack of the oven.

I glance at the clock and see that I still have forty minutes left. The cakes need to bake for twenty, and I need to come up with something to serve with them. I go back to the walk-in and survey the contents. I see a bag of Meyer lemons and decide that a frozen custard would be the perfect accompaniment to the cakes. I take three pieces of the fruit back to my station.

I glance in Jenny's direction and see that she seems confident. I can't tell what she's making, but two cartons of eggs sit at her station. I don't care what's going on at Robbs' station, so I don't bother looking his way.

Claire and Patrick are walking around the kitchen, while Paul sits quietly at the prep table. I start my custard base on the stovetop then grate the lemon zest into it. Meyer lemons are sweeter than regular lemons, so I decide to add a little of the juice as well. I let the ingredients simmer just long enough for the sugar to melt. I transfer the mixture to a shallow metal pan and then slide it in to the blast chiller.

I return to my station just as my timer beeps. I slip on two mitts and remove my desserts from the oven. I set them on a cooling rack and go back to the storage shelf for plates. I decide that the small, square plates will be a striking contrast to my round cakes and I take six of them back to my station. I gently turn the cakes out onto the plates and check the time. We have ten minutes left in the challenge, and I have nothing to do.

"There's a lot of waiting around involved with dessert making." Claire says as she approaches my station.

"Yes, Chef," I agree.

Claire moves closer to me and drops her voice. "I'm glad you came back, Kiara. And I want you to know that Paul is a good guy. Don't believe everything you hear around here. Charlotte's cousin applied for the pastry chef position at the same time I did. I know she has the wait-staff convinced that I slept my way into the job, but that couldn't be further from the case. My girlfriend and I have been together for six years," she adds.

"Thank you for telling me," I reply kindly. "And I've learned my lesson about listening to Amy and Charlotte." I wink.

"Good girl. You're going to go far in this field."

Claire moves on to Jenny's station and I once again check the time… we have five minutes left. I walk to the blast chiller, hoping my custard has had time to solidify. The cakes could be served on their own, but I think the addition of the custard will guarantee my win. I retrieve the pan and stop for an ice cream scoop on my way back to my station. I create six perfect spheres of custard, but leave them in the pan. I want to wait until the last possible second to plate them… the last thing I want is for them to melt and make my cakes soggy.

I look in Jenny's direction again. She has six perfect flans plated. I give in to temptation and glance at Robbs' station. He seems flustered, and the plates on his table are empty. He's bent over a large pan, cutting his cake into squares.

"You have sixty seconds," Patrick announces.

I count to thirty and place the custard on my plates.

"Time's up," Claire calls out. "Step away from your stations and move to the dining room."

We all obey and take seats at a round six top. Paul, Claire, and Patrick follow us, each carrying two plates.

"All right, Chefs, explain your dishes," Claire calls out.

Jenny goes first. "Today, I've prepared a maple-infused flan with a bourbon blueberry sauce."

Robbs clears his throat. "My dish is a maraschino chocolate cake, with just a hint of cayenne to keep things interesting."

"I made lavender-vanilla lava cakes with frozen Meyer-lemon custard," I say.

"These all look spectacular," Patrick compliments us. "Let's sample Kiara's dish before the custard melts."

I cut into my cake… the outside feels spongy and the filling oozes over my spoon. I add a touch of the custard and then sample my dish… it's as delicious as I'd hoped it would be. And unlike my failed midterm sorbet, my custard is perfectly creamy.

"This is amazing," Claire says, her mouth still full of cake. The others nod in agreement.

We sample Jenny's flan next, and the moment I taste it, I know I have some serious competition.

"Have you ladies been practicing your desserts?" Patrick asks.

"We practice everything," Jenny answers confidently.

We move on to Robbs' cake. It's dry, and the 'touch' of cayenne sets my mouth on fire. The other chefs reach for their water glasses, and I know that Robbs' dish is definitely in third place.

"This is certainly interesting, Robbs," Claire says as her eyes water. "But I'm afraid you were a little heavy handed with the pepper. I suggest that in the future, you sample your batters before baking."

"Yes, Chef." Robbs' face is red, but I don't know if it's because of the heat of his cake or the embarrassment he feels at Claire's critique.

"If you'll excuse us, we're going to step into the kitchen and decide on a winner," Patrick announces. He and Claire rise from the table while Paul remains behind with us.

"Paul, I'd have no problem if you want to weigh in on their decision," Jenny tells him.

"That's quite all right," Paul says. "I'd hate for anyone to be accused of receiving favoritism. Besides, I trust Patrick and Claire completely... and I don't envy the position you and Kiara have put them in. This is the closest challenge we've had yet."

"Thank you," says Jenny, smiling.

Patrick and Claire return from the kitchen. "Before we announce the winner, I want both of you ladies to know that your dishes were divine," Claire begins. "In fact, I'd like to suggest to Paul that we put both of them on the permanent menu. It's time to change things up a bit, and I'm tired of cooking the same damn stuff all of the time."

"Thank you so much!" Jenny gushes.

"Thank you," Claire says. "Since both dishes were flawless, we based our decision on who successfully executed the most components. This week's winner is Kiara."

Paul smiles brightly at her announcement.

"Thank you so much," I say, beaming. I open my mouth to say more, but Robbs cuts me off.

"Now that the winner has been announced, could I please have my assignment for the day?" he asks Paul. "Or would you like me to go back to the kitchen and prove that I can make a chocolate cake?" he adds sarcastically.

"You know what? I'm in a generous mood today, Robbs," Paul answers. "I'm going to let all three of you decide who you'd like to work with today and throughout the weekend. I'll even let you choose first, Robbs, if the ladies don't have a problem with that."

"It's no problem for me," I reply.

"Me neither," Jenny agrees. "I'd be happy to work with anyone in the kitchen... well, almost anyone." She looks at Robbs.

"I'll work with Harrison then," Robbs says sharply. He pushes his chair away from the table and stomps into the kitchen.

"I'd like to work with Michael, if that's all right with you, Kiara," Jenny says. I suspect that Jenny has a bit of a crush on the Roast Chef, and I tell her that if she wants to work with him it's just fine with me.

"Michael won't be in for another half hour at least," Paul informs her, "which will give you plenty of time to share your flan recipe with Claire... I agree that both of your desserts should be put on our permanent menu."

"Thank you, Paul." Jenny says and turns to me. "Who are you going to work with this weekend? When you're not helping Claire with your dessert, that is?"

"I'm going to work with Cole," I announce. "It's time for me to learn how to make a sauce that won't break," I add.

I smile at Paul before Jenny and I set off for the kitchen to share our dessert recipes with Claire.

"That was some impressive work you did at the restaurant today," Paul tells me. We're sitting on his comfortable, overstuffed leather sofa watching Top Chef. Paul loves culinary reality television as much as I do. It's just one of many things we have in common.

"Thank you, baby," I say.

His doorbell rings, and he jumps up from the couch. "That must be our Chinese food," he says as he crosses the room. We'd both had a long day at work, and we agreed that delivery was our best option for dinner. We haven't discussed whether or not I'm going to spend the night at his place, but it's getting late and I'm hoping that tonight will be 'our night' together.

Paul opens the door, hands the delivery man two twenties, and takes the bags from his hands.

"Oh my god, that smells delicious," I say as Paul deposits the bags on his coffee table. "What goes best with Chinese food, red wine or white?"

"White goes best with what I ordered for us," Paul explains. "But if you're going to drink, then I'm going to insist that you spend the night. I can crash on the couch, if that will make you more comfortable."

"We're both adults," I answer. "I think we can handle sleeping next to each other in the bed."

"I'm not so sure about that," he replies. He walks into his kitchen and retrieves plates, utensils, wine glasses, and a chilled bottle of chardonnay. He sets everything down on the table and returns to his seat next to me while I unpack the food.

"I'm so glad you came back to the restaurant," he tells me as he pours the wine. "We're going to have so much fun working together. And I'll be so glad when I can get rid of Robbs."

I laugh. "Be careful, the way you're talking, someone might think you've already chosen your new apprentice."

"But I'm not making the decisions anymore," he reminds me.

"Then how are you so sure I'm going to win?" I ask.

"Because you're the best," he replies.

I lean in to kiss him but his phone rings and interrupts us.

"God, I hope it's not someone at the restaurant." His frown turns to a smile when he checks his phone. "Hi, Mom," he answers happily.

I feel awkward listening in on his conversation, so I stand. "Bathroom," I whisper. He nods, and I make my escape. I don't actually need to use the restroom, so I check my makeup in the vanity mirror. The dark circles under my eyes have disappeared, and the gauntness is gone from my face. It's amazing what being happy can do for my appearance.

I crack open the bathroom door and listen for Paul's voice. The apartment is silent, so I'm fairly certain he's finished his call. I step back into the living room and see that he's enjoying a crab pot-sticker.

"Is everything all right with your family?" I ask as I return to my seat. "It's awfully late for your mom to be calling."

"She knows I usually work late in the kitchen. She always calls around this time," Paul explains. "And yes, everything's fine. She wanted to know if we were going to be able to make it to Thanksgiving."

"We...?" I ask. "So she knows about us?"

"Of course she does. I tell my mother everything... she even knows about what an ass I was. She's the one who advised me to take things slow with you."

I'm glad that Paul is close to his mother, but I'm not sure that I'm comfortable with her knowing all of the intimate details of our lives. "So what did you tell her... about Thanksgiving? I assumed we'd be working over the holidays."

Paul shakes his head. "I close the restaurant down on Thanksgiving, Christmas, and Easter. I don't feel right asking my employees to be away from their families."

"You have such a kind heart, baby," I tell him as I twist lo mien onto my fork. The food is salty and satisfying, and I chase it with my entire glass of wine.

"Slow down, baby," Paul teases me. "Are you okay? You threw that wine back like something's bothering you."

"I'm just a little jealous, I guess," I admit. "Sometimes I wish my mom was around to give me advice."

"Have you ever thought about trying to find your parents?" Paul asks softly.

I shake my head. "They left me. If they want to see me again, they can find me. For all I know, they're dead."

"I'm sorry, baby. Let's change the subject. It looks like Charlie and Sarah are in the running to win this week's challenge," he says as he gestures to the television.

"I hate Sarah," I say. "I hope Charlie kicks her ass."

We finish our meal in silence while we watch the drama play out before us. As I'd hoped, Charlie wins the competition.

"I'd love to be on one of these shows one day," I confess. "Or maybe one of the networks could shoot a show at Fission!"

"Oh my god, that's the last thing I'd ever want to do," Paul groans. "Think about it, all of the cameramen would get in our way."

"But it would be good for business," I argue playfully.

"Business is just fine." He smiles at me and once again I feel as if I could melt into the chair.

"What are you smiling about?" he asks after several moments.

"You," I answer. "I'm so happy when we're together, Paul. I feel like I'm living in a fairy tale."

"This is no fairy tale," Paul insists. "Fairy tales end. And I don't intend to ever stop making you happy."

I fall into his arms and our lips meet. We kiss softly… I lay down on the couch, pulling Paul on top of me. He runs one hand through my hair while the other grips my ass. I wrap my legs around his waist and lift my pelvis to his… I can feel his growing erection against my hip. I thrust back and forth against it.

He pulls away from me slightly. "Kiara…" he says, "if you keep doing that, I'm not going to be able to control myself."

"What makes you think I want you to control yourself?" I ask in my most seductive voice. "I know you want to take things slowly," I say as I continue rocking my hip back and forth against his throbbing cock. "So we can go as slowly as you'd like."

Paul climbs off of me, stands, and lifts me into his arms. "What are you doing?" I squeal in delight.

"I told you I want to do this right," he explains with a grin. "So I'm taking you to the bedroom." He carries me into his room, and we collapse together onto the bed. I reach for the hem of my T-shirt, and he covers my hand with his.

"Let me," he insists. He lifts the shirt over my head and tosses it to the floor. I sit up, and he reaches behind me and unhooks my bra. "You're so beautiful, Kiara," he tells me as he takes off his own shirt. He rolls onto his side and pulls me down next to him. We kiss passionately, our tongues dancing together as we hold each other close.

I reach for Paul's belt, and he stops me again. "We're taking it slowly... remember?" he whispers into my ear. "I just want to lay here for a minute, and enjoy the feeling of your bare skin against mine."

He kisses me again, and I wrap my arms around his torso. His smooth chest moves against mine as we breathe in unison, and I lose myself in the emotions of the moment. We continue kissing softly for what seems like both a second and a lifetime. Involuntarily, I start pushing my hips into him once more.

"All right," Paul says, grinning as he pulls away from me. "I can take a hint." He loosens his belt and pulls off his jeans before sliding my pants down my legs. I part my legs and reach for his hips, but he has other ideas.

"You know that a good chef always has to taste what he's working with," he whispers before his head disappears between my legs. I feel his tongue lash against my clit, and I cry out in passion.

"Oh, Paul..." I moan. "Oh, baby... just like that." My eyes roll back in my head as he increases the pressure of his tongue. He slips one finger inside me, and it sends me over the edge. My body spasms and explodes in ecstasy. Paul leaves a trail of kisses from my hip to my earlobe.

"Did that feel good, baby?" he asks me coyly.

"So good," I moan happily. "Would you like me to return the favor?"

He shakes his head. "I'm aching to be inside you," he whispers.

"Then let me offer you some relief." I push him onto his back and climb on top of him. As I lower myself onto his throbbing prick, he reaches up and massages my breasts. I slide down onto him and then remain still for a moment as my pussy stretches to accommodate him.

"You're so tight, baby," he moans. "You feel so good."

I slowly begin moving my hips in wide, clockwise circles. I feel his cock hit every inch of me, and my juices start flowing again.

"You're so wet... god, Kiara, you're so perfect." He sits up and bends his knees. I lean back on his legs and plant my feet on the bed behind him. We hold each other tightly and rock together, slowly at first and then with more urgency. The position we're in puts constant pressure on my G-spot, and I know my second orgasm is imminent.

"I'm going to come again," I warn him.

"Come for me, baby," he whispers in my ear. He nibbles my earlobe and I grip his cock tightly with my internal muscles. We come together quietly with heavy breaths.

We remain locked together long after our orgasms subside. Paul stares lovingly into my eyes. "I've never felt this way before," he confesses.

"I feel the same way," I tell him. I feel a cramp in my thigh and I cringe.

"Are you all right?" he asks, his voice full of concern.

"Leg cramp," I explain.

He smiles back at me… we untangle our bodies and fall asleep in each other's arms.

Chapter Twelve

I feel soft lips on my face and wake to find Paul lying next to me. His hair is wet, and he smells like soap and aftershave.

"How long have you been awake?" I ask as I stretch.

"About twenty minutes. Coffee is ready, when you want some."

"You should have woken me up before you took a shower. I'd have joined you." Paul's cleanliness emphasizes the fact that I still smell like a kitchen.

"Why don't you enjoy one on your own?" he suggests. "There's a boutique down the street. I can run out and grab you some fresh clothes."

"You'd do that for me?" I ask.

"Kiara, I'd do anything for you," he says.

"Then that sounds like a plan. But don't spend too much money," I insist.

"My robe is hanging on the bathroom door," he tells me. "If I'm not back by the time you get out, feel free to put it on... or don't," he adds with a seductive grin. He helps me off of the bed and we walk hand in hand down

the hallway. I stop at the bathroom while he continues
on.

Paul's entire apartment is sleek and modern. The
shower is a walk-in, with beautiful glass-blocked walls.
I turn on the hot water and step into the steam, careful
not to let the water touch my skin. My muscles are sore
and the steam helps them relax. After a few minutes, I
add cold water to the hot and let the spray fall over my
body. I am delighted as I survey the products on the
shelf of the shower. Paul has three types of expensive,
salon-brand shampoos but not one bottle of conditioner.
I grab a bottle and wash my hair, knowing that I'm
going to have a hard time brushing out the tangles.

I wonder if it's too soon for me to bring some stuff
over. Conditioner, a curling iron... maybe some
pajamas. Normally, I'd never consider moving stuff in
to a man's home so soon, but I'm certain Paul is
different. He's gone to buy me a new outfit. I don't think
he'll freak out at the sight of my toothbrush.

The water begins to cool so I step out of the shower
and dry myself with a fluffy towel. I eye Paul's Jacuzzi
and decide that we definitely need to have some fun in
it. As I wrap my hair in a towel, Paul's doorbell rings. I
wrap myself in his bathrobe and step into the hallway.
He must have forgotten his key, I think. I'm proved
wrong when I hear the door open.

"Jenny?" I hear him say. "What's wrong?"

"Oh, Paul!" she cries. "I'm so sorry to bother you. I
know it's early, but I didn't know where else to go. I just
got off the phone with my parents, and they won't help

me. They said I've disgraced the family, and they never want to see me again."

"It's okay," he assures her. "Come in and have a seat. Tell me what's happened. What could you have possibly done for your parents to say something like that?"

Part of me wants to join them and offer my friend comfort, but my instincts tell me that that would be a mistake. Instead, I move closer to the living room, but keep myself hidden from their sight.

"It's not something I did, Paul," she sobs. "It's something WE did..."

It's quiet for several moments and dread fills my body.

"You don't mean...?" Paul begins. "But we used protection, Jenny," he says softly.

"I know we did, but I'm knocked up anyway. I've been feeling rotten for the last couple of weeks, but I thought it was just the stress of the job. I haven't been sleeping well either. Last night, I realized my period was late, so I bought a test. I don't want this to be your problem, Paul... I know you're with Kiara, I know that I mean nothing to you..." The rest of her words are lost in her sobs.

"Jenny, I don't mean to sound insensitive, but are you sure the baby is mine?" Paul asks softly. My heart drops to my stomach when I hear the word 'baby'.

"I'm sure," she says, sobbing even louder.

"All right, all right," he says soothingly. "Just calm down. However you want to handle this, I'll help you," he tells her. "Kiara?" he calls out, startling me. "You can come out of the hallway. We all have a lot to talk about."

-To be continued in Book 2-

Book Two

Chapter One

"**HOW LONG** on the spot prawns, Chef Kiara?" Robbs asks me with mock reverence from across the kitchen. Two months have passed since I was awarded the apprentice position at Fission. Paul Weston stayed out of the decision. No one was able to outright accuse him of being biased and giving the job to his girlfriend, but the rumors are swirling. The rumors about how I landed my job are the least of my problems, though. Paul and Jenny's upcoming arrival is what really has everyone talking around here.

Every time I think of that fateful morning at Paul's appointment, I'm overwhelmed with the same sick feeling in the pit of my stomach. When Paul called me out of the hallway that morning, Jenny bawled and apologized over and over again. She even offered to get rid of the baby, but Paul and I were against it. Paul had immediately insisted an abortion wasn't an option. I agreed with him, but I still can't wrap my head around the idea that in roughly six months, my boyfriend will have a child with another woman. This wasn't supposed to happen, and I'm helpless to do anything about it.

When the apprenticeship contest ended, Jenny left Fission. It's easier for me to deal with her now that I don't see her every day. Paul spent a lot of time reassuring me that I'm the woman he loves, but a part of me doesn't trust him. Family is important to Paul… he'll want to be a hands-on type of dad, and being with Jenny would make that possible.

A year ago, I'd have never been in this position. The situation unfolding before me is a perfect example of why I never let anyone through my walls. But there is something about Paul that made me drop my guard. I am in love with him, and if this baby is going to be a part of his life then I guess it'll be a part of mine, too. I just hope Jenny keeps a lid on all of the 'baby mama drama.'

"Chef?" Robbs calls loudly and brings my focus back to the present.

"Prawns will be up in three," I tell him.

Never having to put up with Robbs Martin again was what I'd been most looking forward to at the end of the apprenticeship competition. But two days before the contest was over, Paul's prep cook Ernesto gave his notice. Ernesto and his wife had just given birth, and he'd been offered a better paying job that would allow him more time off with his family. Paul was overwhelmed and had no time or patience to interview for a new hire. Before the results of the competition were announced, he opened the prep cook position for one of the runners up. Jenny had already decided to leave Fission and take some time to decide what she really wants to do. Robbs was awarded the job by default. I'd expected the bitchy attitude he'd had during the contest to carry over into his new job, but so far he's actually been pleasant to work with. He shows up on time, he helps the other chefs once his tasks are finished, and he makes friendly conversation while doing so. I'm enjoying his new work attitude, but I still don't trust him any farther than I can throw him. Robbs already showed me his true colors, and I don't give people second chances... except for Paul, that is.

I pull the prawns from the grill, plate them, and carry them to Robbs' station. He sets them next to the vegetables he's already prepped for tonight's seafood chowder.

"Did you toss the shells and tails into the stock pot?" Robbs asks me, as if I don't know what I'm doing.

"Of course I did," I answer politely. I can't stand the guy, but I'm not going to give him the satisfaction of letting him get to me.

"Thanks, Chef," he says with a fake smile.

I nod at him and return to my station. I'm doing an appetizer special tonight, and I need to get everything prepped. I prefer to do my own knife work, instead of relying on Robbs. *I have plenty of time for prep work. It's kind of hard to be a chef's apprentice when the chef is never here...*

The toll Jenny's pregnancy took on my job was even harder than the toll it was taking on my personal life. Paul is constantly leaving work to go to doctor's appointments or to shop for cribs. Once he left just because Jenny was craving cheese soup from Mamma's Kettle and was too tired to leave her apartment to pick it up. I had a lot of freedom in the kitchen, but I fought for the job to *learn* from Paul, not to cover for him.

I can't let myself drown in frustration. Not when a lot of work needs to be done. I fill three stock pots with water and set them to boil on the stove. To one I add cumin, cinnamon, and chili powder. The second gets saffron and kefir limes, while the third is seasoned with basil and rosemary. The pots begin to boil, so I toss a handful of salt into each, add my rice, and carefully replace the lids. I turn off the burners and turn my attention to my proteins. I'm making a sushi trio inspired by different areas of the world. I want to do a marinated beef tartar for the Latin roll, but I'm still torn between a couple of different fish for the Indian and the Mediterranean. I need to consider our stock of each of the fish, so I set off for the walk-in cooler.

"Chef Kiara?" a voice calls from behind me. I turn and see Megan, one of the hostesses, standing in the kitchen doorway.

"What is it now?" I groan.

"Two things." Megan blushes. "First, Lancing's called, and our order is going to be late by at least three days... their distribution truck is in the shop waiting for a part to arrive."

I exhale loudly… Lancing's is a small, family-owned organic farm. Paul has an exclusive contract with them for beef, lamb, chicken, eggs, and dairy. "I certainly hope you led with the worst of the two. What's the second issue?"

"Chef Weston called, and he's going to be a couple of hours late tonight. I got the Lansing call first, and I told him about it... but... he asked me to tell you to handle it," she finishes sheepishly.

I'm infuriated by the news but I do my best not to show it. "Thank you, Megan. I'll figure something else. Did Chef Weston say what's keeping him this afternoon?"

"No, Chef," Megan replies.

"All right. I'll go over the menu and see what we can cut... though I don't know how we'll get through the weekend without that delivery," I say.

"I'm sorry, Chef... let me know if I can help with anything," Megan says before turning away and returning to the dining room.

I continue on to the walk-in and survey our stock. There is plenty of seafood, so my appetizer dish is covered, but we're running dangerously low on eggs, steaks, and lamb. I grab tubs of tuna and sea bass and return to the kitchen.

"Hey, Chef, I couldn't help but overhear your predicament," Robbs calls out to me as I place the fish on my prep station. "I may have an idea... if you're interested."

"It's noon on Thursday, and we don't have enough food to get through tonight's dinner service, even if we cut half of the menu," I tell him. "If you have an idea, I'd love to hear it."

"Well, it's only a thirty-minute drive to Lansing's," he begins. "We don't have a refrigerated truck, but I have an SUV... and we have all of the catering coolers."

The idea is so simple and brilliant. I can't believe I didn't think of it myself. "I don't know if we can do that... it may be against health department codes or the insurance policy or something..."

Robbs shrugs. "Call Lansing's and ask if we can pick up the order. If they say yes, I'll go get it. If someone says something about it later, we can tell them that since the distributor was all right with it, we assumed we weren't breaking any rules..."

I consider the idea a moment. "You really wouldn't mind picking it up? I can get gas money from petty cash."

"Anything to help," Robbs assures me. "I finished all of my prep work for the dinner service. I can leave as soon as you want."

"Hold that thought." I walk into Paul's office and find the number for Lansing's Farm. I make the call and to my relief, Mr. Lansing has no problem with us picking up the order ourselves. He does caution me that one trip in an SUV might not be enough to haul the entire order. I thank him and return to the kitchen.

"Lansing's has no problem with it, but you won't be able to get everything in one trip. Load half of everything, and Chef Weston can pick up the rest later." I direct Robbs.

"Are you sure? I don't mind making two trips."

"Keeping food stocked isn't our job," I remind him. "We'll do enough to cover for Paul until he gets here, but then it's on him."

"Whatever you say, Chef." Robbs smiles. "I'll head that way right now."

"I think I should go with you," I suggest. "Half of everything may not be the best approach, and I know what we're running low on. Go make us a couple of to-go drinks. I'll get my proteins marinating and meet you up front."

"Coke?" he asks.

"Diet."

Robbs disappears into the dining room while I quickly whisk together three marinades and start soaking my proteins. I'd rather be going to the farm with anyone but Robbs, but he's strong enough to load the order and he has the biggest vehicle. I sigh and silently curse Paul for putting me in this situation.

Chapter Two

"I'm so sorry, Kiara, I couldn't help it," Paul tells me again. It's eight-thirty at night, the kitchen is slammed, and I'm rolling my sushi to order after losing two and a half hours of prep time to the delivery fiasco.

"Yes, I know you're sorry. But your apologies aren't getting my food plated. Either help me or get out of my way," I tell him.

Robbs and I had picked up over half of the food order and returned to the kitchen at three o'clock. I'd expected Paul to be there, but he didn't arrive until almost five. We've been snapping at each other ever since.

"I'm sorry, you're right," Paul mumbles as he takes a rolling mat and spreads it with Indian rice. "You handled the Lancing issue perfectly. You're going to make a great executive chef one day, Kiara. You think on your feet, make quick decisions..."

Robbs clears his throat from his station, to let us know he's listening to our conversation.

"Picking up the order ourselves was Robbs' idea," I tell Paul. "If it was up to me, I'd have let us run out of everything. Maybe then you'll snap back to reality and remember your responsibilities."

"Reality?" Paul snaps back. "I've been dealing with reality all day, Kiara—the reality that my child will be here in six months and will have nowhere to sleep. You know I have to get settled in a bigger place, and today was the only time the realtor could meet with me."

"This kitchen is what's going to pay for your big new place," I remind him. "Keep running things the way you have been and see what kind of home you'll be able to afford."

I know I'm right, but I also know that I'm being a bit harsh on Paul. The truth is that what's bothering me most isn't that he's neglecting the restaurant, but that he's neglecting me. We've been dating for months, and he didn't even stop to consider I might like to give my opinion on potential homes.

I layer chopped tomatoes and sea bass onto the Mediterranean spiced rice and roll it into sushi.

"Kiara," Paul says. "I know you're right. I'm sorry I put the Lancing problem on you. I should have handled it myself. I've been taking advantage of your capabilities. I've been so distracted lately and when something comes up that I know you can handle, I let you. That's not fair, and I promise I'll try to do better. Do you forgive me?" He flashes me a smile that melts my heart.

"Of course I forgive you." I sigh.

He leans down and plants a soft kiss on the top of my head. It's the only public display of affection we share in the kitchen, and none of our coworkers seem to mind.

Paul slices a Latin roll, tops it with the accompanying sauce, and samples a piece. "This is amazing," he says with a grin, his mouth still full. "And it's the perfect dish for Fission... so many flavors, so many cultures... we may add this to the permanent menu."

I laugh. "If you keep this up, we'll be serving more of my recipes than yours."

"I've been thinking maybe it's time to completely revamp the menu," he answers seriously. "Most of the dishes we serve have been around since I opened the place. We can scrap them all and start fresh... create the new dishes together..."

"That would mean a lot of time in the kitchen together." I smile.

"I know. That's the best part of my plan." He grins devilishly. "What do you say?"

"You're the boss," I tease. "If you want me to help you create a new menu, who am I to argue? But let's talk about it later… I'm in the weeds here."

"No problem." Paul reaches for another scoop of Latin rice, but I stop him.

"Please, I can cover this. I just need some space," I tell him.

"Yes, Chef." He says, walking back to his station.

I take a deep breath, center myself, and get to work, focusing only on the food in front of me. I spend thirty minutes rolling sushi to order, and then the early rush dies down. I spend another thirty minutes rolling the rest of the appetizers, in anticipation of the late rush.

"I'm finally finished," I tell Paul as I approach his station. "Can I observe you during the late rush?"

"Of course." He nods. "I'll walk you through the dish a few times, and then we'll see how you handle it on your own."

While Fission has a large, permanent menu, the only dishes Paul cooks himself are the nightly entrée specials. The specials change every day and are always a unique, exciting twist on ethnic staples. Tonight, Paul is making Italian sausage and roasted vegetable pot pies. The meal is rich, heavy, and decadent, the perfect choice to warm you up on a cold February night. The meal is also complicated… everything from the garlic and cheese pie crust to the sausage itself is made from scratch. I watch as Paul mixes a fresh batch of sausage in a stainless steel bowl.

"We're not going to put it in casings," Paul explains, "because we want the meat to soak up as much of the sauce as possible. And also, casings are gross..."

"Chef Weston!" a squealing voice interrupts. We turn and see Charlotte, one of the waitresses, at the front of the kitchen. "You're not going to *believe* who's here!"

"Calm down, Charlotte," Paul says patiently. "Whoever it is, there's no need to make a fool of yourself. Who's here?"

"James *O'Toole*!" she replies shrilly.

I blush with excitement. "James O'Toole?" I ask in disbelief. "As in *Kitchen Wars*, James O'Toole?"

"Yep!" Charlotte nods in delight. "Megan's seating him now. He said that he'd like for the chef to choose his menu."

"Oh... my... god," I say, leaving my mouth agape.

Paul rolls his eyes. "Seriously, ladies, you have to calm down. He's just a guy, the same as any other customer. Charlotte, tell Mr. O'Toole I appreciate his trust, and that his starters will be out shortly. And please, try not to look so star-struck when you speak to him. If I hear that you're hovering over his table, I'll replace you myself."

"Yes, Chef Weston." Charlotte nods, trying to calm herself. She takes a deep breath and calmly returns to the dining room.

"James O'Toole." Robbs whistles. "What are we going to serve him?"

Paul surveys the kitchen and makes the decision with lightning speed. "Starters are the sushi trio and the duck ravioli. For entrées, we'll do the spot prawn enchiladas and the pot pie. Claire, I'll let you decide the desserts," he says to the pastry chef.

"Thank you, Chef." Claire nods.

"All right everyone, get to work. And don't let this distract you from our other orders. James O'Toole isn't the only customer in the dining room… hell, I'm going to comp his meal. Concentrate on the customers who keep the roof over our heads."

"Yes, Chef!" everyone replies in unison.

Paul turns to me. "How much time will you need for your app?"

"Three minutes. It needs to be plated," I tell him.

"All right, go get it done and come back to my station. We'll finish the entrée together."

"Yes, Chef," I reply with a warm smile. I rush to my station, hoping that my excitement doesn't show on my face.

Robbs is nearby, plating his duck ravioli. "I know we're not supposed to act excited, but this is exciting!" he whispers with a grin. "I can't believe Paul chose my dish."

"It's a good dish," I tell him. I still don't trust Robbs, but his idea did save my ass today, and I feel a little warmer toward him.

I slice the sushi rolls and arrange them on a serving dish with their accompanying sides… a lemon and caper sauce for the Mediterranean roll, a sour cream and cilantro sauce for the Latin roll, and green mango chutney for the Indian roll. Next to the unique sauces, I plate the traditional soy sauce, pickled ginger, and wasabi. I'm filled with anxiety at the thought of James O'Toole tasting my food… a glance at Robbs tells me he is the same way. After a few seconds, he catches me staring at him.

"It's going to be fine." He winks. "We've got this."

I nod, smile and rush back to Paul's station.

"I have all of the ingredients ready. I need you to roll and fill the crusts and then pop them into the oven," he tells me. "If you don't mind," he adds, and I know that he's thinking about the fight we'd had earlier. "I'd like to check the plates before they go out to O'Toole. I also need to get out there and introduce myself. It would be rude not to."

"So he's not just any other customer," I tease.

"No, he's not, in the worst possible way," Paul says in frustration.

"What are you talking about? This is James O'Toole! You love his show. We watch it every week!"

"You're star-struck right now, Kiara," he insists. "Yes, we watch the show every week. And every week, we talk about how O'Toole is the worst judge on the panel. He's an ass, Kiara! He's skyrocketed to fame because he's pretty, not because he's talented. And just last week, you pointed out yourself that he obviously favors the attractive female contestants. Now that he's in the other room, you've forgotten all of that and you're going to make a fool of yourself."

"I'm not going to make a fool of myself!" I answer defensively. "I just think it's an honor... that a chef of his notoriety wants to taste our food."

"He wants a free meal, that's all. He probably does this every night. I'm going to shake his hand, serve him a meal, and tomorrow he won't remember my name. Can you cover this? I do need to get out there." He says.

"I got it," I tell him with a comforting grin. He turns to walk away. "Chef Weston?" He turns impatiently and walks back to me. I wrap one arm around his waist and stare into his eyes. "I just want to remind you that *you* are the best chef under this roof tonight. It's a privilege to eat your food, whether James O'Toole recognizes that or not."

A broad grin spreads across Paul's face. He leans down and kisses the top of my head once more and I release him. "Thanks, babe," he says, his eyes bright with satisfaction. He walks through the kitchen with a new skip in his step, and I know he feels better.

Talk about multi-tasking. I'm being a fantastic chef and a fantastic girlfriend, all at the same time. I carefully roll the delicate pie crust dough and spread it into the pie plates. While the crusts blind bake, I cut out the top crusts and check the consistency of the filling. I pull the half-baked crusts from the oven, add eight pieces of sausage as Paul directed, and then cover them with the tomato-based roasted vegetable sauce. I add a generous handful of blended Italian cheeses and carefully place the crust tops and slide the pies into the oven.

Paul walks up as I'm setting the timer. "Did you remember the cheese?"

He's under a lot of stress, so I decide to take his attitude in stride. "Yes, baby, I remembered the cheese." I laugh. "How did it go?"

"Better than I expected," he confesses. "Turns out, he read about the restaurant in an Austin cultural magazine that was left in his hotel room. He seems genuine enough, I guess. He's eating on his own."

"No hot female companion?" I ask in over-exaggerated shock.

Paul chuckles. "Not tonight... unless it's later tonight," he adds with a sly grin.

"Chefs, where are we on the apps for Mr. O'Toole?" Charlotte calls from the kitchen door.

"I'm plating mine now, Charlotte. Wait a second," Robbs answers.

Butterflies fill my stomach, and I pinch myself to make sure it's not a dream. Asshole or not, James O'Toole is a world-recognized culinary personality, and I can't quite believe he's about to taste my food. Paul senses my anxiety and wraps a comforting arm around me.

"It's going to be fine," he says reassuringly. "Your app is fantastic. And as I'm the most talented chef under this roof, I think you should take my word for it." He smiles and I instantly relax.

"If you love it, that's all that matters to me," I tell him with a grin. "Now, we have eight minutes before we can pull the pies. Should we check on the enchiladas?" I suggest.

"Yes, let's taste the apps, too. I know they've already been served to O'Toole, but they're delicious and I'm starving."

My stomach growls, and I realize how hungry I am.

"It sounds like your stomach agrees with me," Paul teases.

"I skipped lunch... I had to run an errand, remember?"

"Oh god, baby, I'm sorry. Let's feed you."

We each eat a portion of the appetizers… we finish our raviolis as Patrick pulls his enchiladas out of the oven.

"Ready for tasting in three minutes, Chef," Patrick tells Paul. Our oven timer chimes from the back of the kitchen.

"Plate two portions and bring them to my station, I have to pull my pies," Paul tells him. I follow Paul to the oven… he retrieves the pies and slides them on to a cooling rack. A few moments pass, and Patrick arrives with his plates.

"They're pretty spectacular, if I do say so myself." Patrick grins.

Paul and I each take a bite, and the flavors fill my mouth with joy.

"These are spectacular, Patrick," I say.

"They are," Paul agrees. "Between these and Kiara's sushi rolls, I'm going to be shown up in my own kitchen." He laughs.

"I've tried your Italian pot pies, man, I think you're safe," Patrick assures him.

"ETA on Mr. O'Toole's entrées?" Charlotte calls out as she returns to the kitchen.

"Entrées up," Paul answers loudly. He gingerly lifts a pie from its tin and transfers it into a shallow bowl. Patrick returns to his station for his plate, which he passes to Charlotte as she walks toward us.

"Mr. O'Toole enjoyed both appetizers," she tells us. "He even said if he has any room left after dessert, he wants another serving of the sushi!" She beams at me.

For a moment, I think I imagined her words.

"Good job, Kiara!" Paul tells me with genuine pride.

"I wasn't sweating it," I joke. "I already had your stamp of approval, after all." I pretend I don't care what James O'Toole thinks, but inside I am bursting with excitement. Charlotte leaves the kitchen with O'Toole's entrées, and Paul places one hand on my shoulder.

"I'm proud of you, Kiara." He smiles.

"Thank you, baby... watching *Kitchen Wars* will never be quite the same."

No, I don't think it will," he agrees. "Do we have any open tickets?"

"Not a one. I don't think anyone in the dining room is going to give up their tables until our celebrity guest leaves," I tell him.

"You're probably right. So, since we have some free time, would you like to sit down and share one of these pot pies with me?"

"I'd love to," I agree.

Paul carries two stools to his prep station, while I plate the second pot pie. I grab two forks and meet him at the butcher block table. As I take my first bite, the kitchen doors open and Charlotte steps through the door with James O'Toole.

"Excuse me, Chefs," Charlotte announces loudly. "Chef O'Toole would like to give you his compliments."

Everyone in the room stops what they're doing and turns their focus to the door. Paul walks toward the entryway, and I follow closely behind him.

"Hi, everyone," James greets us with a cocky smile. "Lord knows if anyone understands how busy you are, it's me. I don't want to take up much of your time, but I had to tell you all how much I enjoyed my meal. Chef Weston, you put together quite an impressive team."

"Thank you, Chef," Paul says, extending his hand.

James accepts the handshake. "That pot pie was genius. I'm assuming you made that one yourself?"

"Yes, I did, I'm glad you enjoyed it," Paul replies.

James nods. "There was only one dish I enjoyed more, the sushi sampler. It was fresh, inventive, and delicious. It was everything a plate of food should be. I'm assuming that one was yours as well?"

"Unfortunately, I can't take credit for that one." Paul blushes, and I'm too worried about his bruised ego to enjoy James's compliment. "The sushi dish was the work of this fine chef." Paul gestures to me. "Chef James O'Toole, may I introduce Chef Kiara Sands."

I extend my hand and try not to tremble as James takes it into his. "It's a pleasure to meet you, Chef O'Toole."

"Likewise... please, call me James." He smiles at me, and I am oddly drawn to him. I know Paul is right… on the show, James acts like a pompous, perverted egomaniac. But in person, he's devastatingly attractive.

"Thank you, James... I'm glad you enjoyed the dish," I stammer. Paul shoots me a look and I know he knows I'm about to lose my cool.

"You can't be more than twenty-one. How long have you been cooking?"

"I've been cooking for as long as I can remember, but I'm only in my second year of culinary school," I explain. "And I'm nineteen."

"A natural talent which is even better. What do you think about New York City?" he asks quickly.

"New York City? I'm not sure I understand..."

"My restaurant is there," James explains with another cocky smile. "I'm always looking for the best new talent. Whatever Weston is paying you, I'll double it. I'll also pay your moving expenses... all you have to do is say yes."

"Thank you very much, Chef, but I can't possibly accept," I say slowly. "I'm not even a real chef, I'm an apprentice... I don't get paid, I get class credit."

"Even better!" James laughs. "I'll give you a paid apprenticeship and set you up at the Culinary Institute in New York, if you want. But I have to tell you, you'll learn more working with me than you'll ever learn in school."

"Thank you, again, but I have to pass," I insist.

"Are you sure..." James begins.

"The lady said no, O'Toole," Paul growls. "I've done my part. I served you a meal. I let you parade yourself through my kitchen... I've given you every courtesy, and you're trying to steal one of my best chefs. We're done here. Charlotte will see you to the door."

"No hard feelings, man," James says with a shrug and a laid-back smile. "You can't blame a guy for asking for what he wants. It's been a pleasure, I can see myself out. Is it all right if I enjoy a drink at the bar before I leave?"

"If you'd like to pay for a drink, be my guest," Paul says roughly.

"Thank you," James says with mocking gratitude as he turns back toward the doorway. "Though if I'm paying, we can't really call me your guest." The door swings shut behind him.

I turn to Paul and squeal, "I can't believe that just happened!"

"I don't know what you're so excited about," he snaps. "He's an ass... he offered you a job because you're hot. I can't believe the nerve of that man!"

"People said *you* offered me the job because I'm hot, and you insisted that it was all about my food. Were you lying?" I snap back.

"Of course not, Kiara, that's different."

"What's different about it? Nothing at all, except James probably doesn't have a knocked-up one-night stand hanging around and ruining everyone's fun!" I exclaim.

Paul's face turns red with fury. "If you ever talk about my child like that again, so help me, Kiara..."

"I'm sorry," I say quickly. "I crossed the line, I know that. We're both riled up, and I, for one, am exhausted. I'm going to take a quick break. I'll be outside."

I walk away without giving him a chance to respond. I make it to the back door quickly and slip out into the alley. The backside of Fission is dark and full of dumpsters, so I walk to the side of the building and sit on one of the benches reserved for waiting customers. I take several deep breaths and try to process all of the conflicting emotions I'm feeling.

On one hand, I know Paul is probably right about James. He does show favoritism to the more attractive female competitors on the show. It wouldn't shock me if his job offer wasn't based on my cooking abilities. But he had no idea who made the starter when he first raved about it, so his compliments on the sushi had to be genuine.

Paul's reaction was completely unacceptable. He should be happy for me... he should be proud of me. His snippy attitude makes me wonder if he's jealous of the attention I got from the celebrity chef. Something tells me that regardless of how much Paul protests, O'Toole's opinion of his food really meant something to him.

With a sigh, I stand and walk toward the front entrance of Fission. There's not a handle on the exterior of the back door, and I don't want to stand there knocking until someone in the kitchen hears me. As I round the corner of the building, I walk straight into James O'Toole.

"Lovely bumping into you again," he tells me with a sly grin.

"Sorry..." I stammer. "I was just heading back inside."

James reaches into his pocket and retrieves a business card. "Consider my offer a standing one, and give me a call when you decide you want to work for a real chef."

I take the card from his hands. As I search for a cleaver response, he leans down and brushes a soft kiss across my cheek.

Until next time," he says softly before he walks away.

I stand stunned for a few moments, my cheek still burning from the touch of his lips.

"Excuse me, ma'am... are you all right?"

I look to my right and see a tall, muscular, athletic man.

"Yes, yes, I'm fine," I assure him quickly. "I just got lost in thought for a second, that's all."

"Well, you look like a woman with many important thoughts," the man says kindly. His Southern accent is thick and charming which reveals that he's not a native Texan.

"They're not important, just distracting," I explain. "I'm Kiara Sands, I work in the kitchen. May I ask where your accent is from?"

"Hello, Kiara Sands, my name is Chase Abbott and I am from South Carolina." He smiles with a twinkle in his eyes.

"It's a pleasure to meet you, Chase. I have to get back to the kitchen, but I hope you enjoy your meal," I tell him as we walk inside Fission.

He reaches for my hand, lifts it to his lips, and kisses it softly. "It was a pleasure to meet you too, Kiara... I don't mean to sound forward, but would you consider having a drink with me after your shift?"

"I'm sorry," I blush, "but I'm involved with someone."

"All right," Chase agrees easily. "But you haven't seen the last of me, Kiara Sands."

I smile sheepishly, extract my hand from his, and make my way back to the kitchen. I can sense Chase's eyes on me until I'm safely behind the door.

"Having a good time?" Paul snarls.

I turn and see him standing in front of the service window. My heart sinks when I realize he must have seen Chase kiss my hand.

"I was just talking to the customers," I explain dryly. "Nothing happened, he just kissed my hand. What was I supposed to do, slap a paying customer in the face for being nice to me?"

"The two of you looked pretty friendly," Paul says with a tone of accusation.

"He kissed my hand," I repeat hostilely. "He didn't get me pregnant. I'd appreciate it if you don't start with me right now."

"Fine, whatever you want," Paul grumbles. "Robbs and Patrick are going to clean up tonight. Let's go home."

"Only if you snap out of this mood," I tell him. "Otherwise, I'll go to my place."

"Come home with me, Kiara." Paul gives me a heart-melting smile once more, and I reluctantly agree.

Chapter Three

Jenny and Robbs walk around the Austin Food Truck Food Court, eating and plotting their next step in taking down Kiara Sands.

"I'm telling you, Jenny, I've got her wrapped around my little finger," Robbs insists. "She's starting to trust me, I can tell. She'll be confiding in me in no time, and then I'll be able to work her like a puppet."

Jenny holds her expanding belly and sighs. "I hope so, Robbs. This baby will be here in no time, and I want her out of our lives before then. There's no way I'll be able to pull everything off if nosey, perfect Kiara is still around."

"You could be honest," Robbs reminds her. "I mean, I don't want this baby to be mine any more than you do, but if it is, the truth will come out eventually. It may be better for you if you lay all of your cards out on the table now."

Jenny shakes her head adamantly. "No, this baby is Paul's, and that's the end of it. He's so excited, Robbs, you should have seen him at the doctor's office. He's going to spoil the baby rotten, and take care of me, too. Kiara could ruin everything though... she's already been bitching about the amount of time Paul and I are spending together. I can just see her counting every dime he gives me and the baby. She's a control freak, and we have to get her out of the way.

"Your wish is my command," Robbs answers sarcastically. "Remember, it's going to cost you."

"You know I'll take care of you," Jenny coos. "You just make sure that Paul is in the position to take care of me. You still haven't explained how you're going to get rid of her... what is your diabolical plan?"

"It's simple." Robbs shrugs. "I'm going to become Kiara's new best friend. It doesn't take much to get her and Paul at each other's throats these days. And I admit, if I didn't hate the bitch so much, I'd be on her side. Paul totally left her hanging yesterday with that delivery problem. Luckily, yours truly was there to save the day. As she lets her guard down, I'll start planting little ideas in her head... how Paul takes advantage of her, how she deserves better. I'll make her see the light and dump him before the baby gets here."

"I hope so," Jenny says, her voice full of doubt. "Otherwise, I'll only be getting standard child support, and the three of us can't live off of that."

With a sigh, I pull my Honda into a parking spot at the Austin Food Truck Food Court. It's Friday afternoon, and I had yet another fight with Paul. I woke up this morning to an empty apartment, and I'd assumed Paul had left early to pick up the rest of the food order from Lansing's. Imagine my surprise when I arrived at the kitchen and found him asleep at his desk. After I woke him, Paul explained that he'd left the apartment early so he could meet with the realtor again. He'd seen three more apartments, then decided to take a quick nap at Fission.

"If you're not going to pick up the order, you may as well put up the closed sign and go sleep at home," I'd insisted bitterly.

"You know how stressed and exhausted I am," Paul had argued. "Can't you and Robbs make another run to the farm? It's not like you won't be paid for your time."

I reminded him that Robbs was off today, and he'd promised to stop putting me in these types of positions. He suggested I take his Land Rover to Lansing's.

"Are you sure you want me to do that?" I'd snapped. "Men work at the farm, one of them might talk to me. And after the attitude you gave me last night, I know you hate it when other men talk to me."

The argument devolved from there, and it became obvious that Paul and I needed a break from each other. I stormed into the kitchen, asked Patrick to cover for me for the day, and fled the building.

I love food, and when I'm upset it's the only thing that comforts me. The Austin Food Truck Food Court has over thirty vendors… it's the perfect place to drown my sorrows. I slip some cash into my pocket, stow my purse under the passenger seat of my car, and set off for the trucks.

I walk around the food court and survey my options. I'm tempted to try something exotic, but my desire for familiar comfort food wins out and I stop at Mama's Café for fried chicken and waffles.

The food court is busy, and as I wait for my order I observe the other diners around me. The blend of people is as eclectic as the variety of cuisine, and I lose myself in my people watching. I marvel at the ability of food to bring people together. My attention is drawn back to the present when the vendor calls my name. I retrieve my order and settle at a small, shaded picnic table set apart from the crowds.

The food is amazing… the waffle is soft and sweet, while the chicken is spicy and cooked to perfection. As I eat, I reflect on my relationship with Paul. In the beginning, we'd seemed like such a perfect match. I'd let myself believe he would be different from everyone else, that he understood me and that the relationship would be easy. Now here I am, in love with a man who is expecting a child with another woman… and who bites my head off when another man so much as looks at me. He's being such a hypocrite, and I have no idea how to deal with him.

My seat away from the crowd allows me to continue people watching, and I'm shocked when two familiar faces appear in the distance. Jenny and Robbs are walking through the food court, hand in hand.

What the hell are they doing together? I keep a careful eye on them, ensuring they don't see me. From what Jenny told Paul and me, she hasn't seen Robbs since the apprenticeship competition ended. She's assured me several times that she's seen Robbs for who he really is and wants nothing to do with him. And in the two months Robbs and I worked side by side in the kitchen, he's made no mention of Jenny at all. In fact, he's one of the few people at Fission who hasn't tried to grill me about the situation with Jenny, Paul, and the baby.

He's been hiding this... they both have. I *knew* I couldn't trust them. I have to know what they're doing together. I toss my trash into a nearby receptacle, circle the crowd, and approach Jenny and Robbs from behind. They stop in front of a taco truck, and I quickly position myself off to the side of the line and turn my back to the couple. I'm in the perfect position to overhear them without being seen, and what I overhear is shocking.

"I'm so glad you were able to take the day off," Jenny tells Robbs. "I missed you this past week. It's getting hard for me to sleep by myself."

"Don't worry, babe," Robbs assures her. "We'll be together for good before you know it. We just have to wait for our plan to fall into place."

Rage fills me as I listen to them speak. I can't believe the two of them are together, and I wonder what else they've been lying about over the past few months. When did they start hooking up? And why have they been hiding it? If Robbs is going to be with Jenny, and be in the baby's life, Paul has a right to know about it.

"Once the baby is here, you'll hold all of the power," Robbs continues. "Paul will have to play by our rules if he wants to see the kid."

"It will be perfect, won't it?" Jenny laughs. "We'll have Paul's money, *and* we'll be able to use him as a free babysitter."

Their order is up… they collect their food and make their way to a table. I've heard enough, and I know the longer I eavesdrop, the more likely they'll see me. I hide myself in the crowd once more and make my way back to the parking lot.

Once I'm safely in my car, I consider what I should do with the information I learned. On one hand, what Jenny does in her free time isn't any of my business, or Paul's. If she wants to be with Robbs, we have no right to stop her. After all, we wouldn't want her interfering with our relationship. But on the other hand, there is a baby involved. Jenny knows that Paul and I are involved and that I will be part of the baby's life… Paul deserves the same courtesy. And if Jenny and Robbs are planning on using the baby to wield some kind of control over Paul, he definitely needs to be warned. I fetch my purse from the passenger floorboard, retrieve my cell phone, and send Paul a quick text.

I learned something you need to know about. Can we call a truce and meet at the café in twenty minutes?

Less than a minute passes before I receive his response.

On my way back from Lansing's, have to unload order. Meet you in an hour?

I text back and tell him an hour will be fine. I'm relieved he didn't ask me to meet him at Fission. My news won't go over well, and I don't want to give our coworkers any more reasons to gossip than they already have. I drive aimlessly for forty-five minutes, practicing my speech in my head. I decide that a 'rip the Band-Aid' approach will be best, and I prepare myself for Paul's reaction.

I pull up to the café located down the block from Fission. I step inside and see Paul is already waiting. I join him at the table.

"Hey, baby," he says softly as I approach. "I know I'm starting to sound like a broken record, but I'm so sorry I snapped at you earlier."

"I appreciate that, Paul, but that's not what I need to talk to you about." I place a comforting hand on his forearm and repeat everything I overheard at the food court. The color drains from Paul's face as I speak.

"So the two of them... you think they're together?" he asks incredulously. "That doesn't make any sense. Jenny's been adamant about her dislike for Robbs. And as hard as she's tried to hide it, we both know she still has feelings for me. Are you sure you overheard correctly? That they're involved and not just friends?"

"It was pretty obvious to me they are," I answer softly. "But that's not what has me worried... they seem to be planning something... they're going to use the baby as a way to use you... I'm worried for you *and* the baby."

"What the hell is Jenny thinking?" Paul demands. "Why would she be with such a douche bag? She could do so much better than that asshole! I've got to talk some sense into her."

I'm panicked and taken aback by his reaction, especially his insistence that Jenny wouldn't date Robbs because she still has feelings for him. I'd expected Paul to be furious, but not jealous.

"Like I said..." I begin slowly, "I'm worried about you and the baby. Jenny doesn't seem to be thinking like a mother. In fact, she's acting like a selfish opportunist. You can't confront her about this or she'll know I was spying on her. I think our best approach is to keep what we know to ourselves and start looking in to the legal actions we can take once the baby is born."

Paul shakes his head rapidly. "We're not going to bring the courts into this. Jenny is a great girl, and she'll be a good mom. I have no intention of separating my child from its mother. You know how persuasive Robbs can be... he's got to be the one behind all of this."

I nod in agreement. I know better than Paul just how persuasive Robbs can be. In a way, it's his fault that there's a baby on the way in the first place. He came up with the plan for Jenny to sleep with Paul as a way to force me out of the apprenticeship competition. Paul has no idea he was behind it. When Jenny had confessed and apologized to me, I'd agreed to keep Robbs involvement to myself.

"It may have been Robbs' idea, but Jenny's going along with it," I remind Paul. "We can't stop them from being together, but we can protect ourselves, and the baby, from the inevitable fall out."

"Like hell we can't stop them from being together," Paul snaps. "She's the mother of my child. I get a say about who she spends time with," he says. "You have no idea how much I hate this, Kiara. Life would be so much easier if..." He looks at me and stops himself.

"Go ahead, finish," I snap. "Life would be so much easier if you and Jenny were together. The two of you and the baby could be a happy little family, and you wouldn't have to worry about another man being in the picture. Just say it, Paul!"

"Kiara, that's not what I meant," Paul insists. "Yes, given the current circumstances, life would be easier if I loved Jenny, or if I was having a baby with you. But neither of those are the case, and we have to make the best of things as they are."

"You go on and on about how much you hate this, but I assure you, I hate it even more," I tell him. "I overheard all of this information, and my first instinct was to protect you and your child. Then I tell you what I learned, and your big issue is the fact that Jenny is seeing someone else. You can deny it all you want, but you're jealous."

"Kiara, you're wrong," Paul tells me. "There's not even a small part of me that wants to be with Jenny."

"But you don't want her to be with anyone else either, do you?" I demand. "Just like you have no time to spend with me but you fly off the handle if I have a conversation with another man. You're being such a hypocrite, Paul. I should have just kept my mouth shut and let you go on thinking that Jenny's sitting at home every night pining away for you." I abruptly push my chair away from the table and stand.

"Kiara, wait," Paul insists.

"No," I retort. "I'm going home... to *my* home. Maybe Jenny and Robbs have the right idea. Maybe you deserve whatever they have planned for you. Don't come crying to me when it all falls down around your head."

With that, I gather my things and storm out of the café.

Chapter Four

"Okay, if we do the prime rib special tomorrow night, we can do Yorkshire pudding or beef wellington for Wednesday's lunch," Paul suggests. It's Monday morning, and the two of us are working on Fission's weekly specials menu. Lansing's delivery truck is back up and running, and we need to get our order placed before noon.

"I love beef wellington," I tell him. "And it's hearty enough to serve as a dinner special. We could do the prime rib tomorrow, the duck on Wednesday, and then the wellingtons on Thursday... space out the protein selection a bit."

Paul quickly agrees with me, and the menu for the week is complete. He calls in the order while I return to the kitchen to start prepping for the lunch rush.

We've been getting along a little better over the last few days. After I stormed out of the café, Paul gave me a few hours to calm down and then showed up at my apartment. He took the night off from the restaurant and cooked dinner for the two of us. We haven't talked through our issues so much as ignored them, but I'm thankful for the peace in whatever form it comes. Paul did agree not to confront Jenny about her relationship with Robbs. Our plan for now is to keep our eyes open and wait for them to make a mistake... we'll confront them after.

While Paul continues to insist that he's not romantically interested in Jenny, I'm finding it harder and harder to believe him. Part of me is convinced that he's only telling me what I want to hear so I won't leave him. I think he wants Jenny and I to both stay devoted to him, and to dote on him at every turn. I want to be able to trust him, but deep down I know the only person I can trust is myself.

"Good morning, Chef." Robbs greets me with a friendly smile as he enters the kitchen.

Speaking of untrustworthy snakes...

"Good morning, Robbs," I reply with a smile. "Did you have a good weekend? Any hot dates you want to talk about?" I say teasingly, knowing there's no way he'll tell me about his relationship with Jenny.

Robbs laughs. "No hot dates, but thanks for asking... you know this is the first time you've treated me like a real friend? It's good to know you care."

"Don't read too much into it, Robbs, I was just making conversation."

"I know." He nods. "But five months ago, you'd have ignored me. I call that progress."

"I guess it is, in a way," I agree.

"You know, Kiara, I'd like for us to be friends," he tells me seriously. "I know you know about my involvement in Jenny and Paul's one-night stand. I know, in a way, I'm responsible for the awkward situation the three of you are in now. I want you to know it was never my intention to complicate your life so drastically. It was a shady, cowardly way to try and get what I wanted and if I could go back and change things, I would.”

“Thank you for admitting that,” I tell him with false sincerity. “It was a cowardly, underhanded thing to do... and pointless, I might add.”

“Yeah,” he agrees with a grin, “because you stomped my ass and won the apprenticeship anyway. I hope we can put the past behind us and move forward. I know things are tough for you right now. If you ever need someone to vent to, I'd be happy to listen.”

I bet you would be. “Thanks, Robbs. I'd just like to stay focused on my work. And speaking of work, your prep list is ready.” I gesture to the list I'd left on his station.

“Yes, Chef, I'll get right on it,” Robbs replies.

As he makes his way to his station, Paul emerges from the office. “Good morning, Robbs,” he says tensely. Robbs returns his greeting and Paul turns to me. “I put the order in with Lansing's. They'll deliver tomorrow. I have a meeting scheduled with a new seafood supplier. Do you mind handling things while I'm gone? It shouldn't be more than an hour or so.”

“No problem,” I reply. “Cole and Michael will be here soon. We can make it through the lunch rush without you.”

“Great.” He leans down and plants a kiss on the top of my head. “Call me if anything comes up.” He nods a goodbye at Robbs and disappears through the kitchen doors. I throw a glance at Robbs' station and see he has his ear buds in, so there's no pressure for me to carry on a conversation with him. I collect what I need from the walk-in cooler and the pantry and start my prep work for the day. Michael and Cole arrive on time, and the lunch rush goes smoothly until an unexpected visitor arrives in the kitchen.

"There you are!" Chase exclaims as he steps through the swinging door. "You're a hard woman to track down, you know that?"

"What are you doing here?" I ask in shock.

"I wanted to see you," he answers simply. "I came in on Friday, but the hostess out front said you'd left unexpectedly. I had practice over the weekend, and had to cram for a test yesterday. I passed it with flying colors, and I thought my luck would continue and I'd find you here. And I was right!" He beamed.

I'm so surprised I have no idea where to begin. "Practice...?"

"Off-season football," Chase explains with a grin. "I'm an offensive lineman for Texas State."

"Ah, I see... and you wanted to find me because...?" I look around the kitchen and see all eyes are on me and Chase.

"Because you're beautiful, and our first meeting was entirely too short. I was hoping you'd agree to have dinner with me sometime."

"I'm sorry but I have a boyfriend," I tell him quickly. "I think I mentioned that the first time we met."

"You did." Chase pauses. "And I can accept that. I didn't come here to ask you out on a date, I came to ask you to be my mentor."

"Your what?" I ask in disbelief. "I don't know anything about football..."

Chase laughs. "That may be, but you obviously know your way around a kitchen, and my true dream is to be a chef. I was hoping you could give me some pointers, tell me about different culinary schools and explain how someone as young you are landed a job in one of the best restaurants in Austin. The dinner would be strictly business, I promise."

I know he's flattering me, and it's working. "I'm not actually a chef here," I explain modestly, "I'm an apprentice."

"Tomato, tomotto." Chase smiles. "You're obviously living the dream. I'd like to pick your brain about the industry... unless, of course, your boyfriend is one of those broody jealous types who doesn't let you talk to other guys."

"Who I talk to is no one's business but my own," I reply defensively. I glance at the wall clock and realize Paul will be back from his meeting any minute. I turn back to Chase. "It's getting busy in here, let me walk you out."

Chase and I walk out of the kitchen and through the crowded dining area. We don't speak again until we're outside and safe from the prying eyes and ears of my coworkers.

"I'd be happy to give you some pointers about culinary school, if that's what you're here for," I tell him.

"Honestly, I'd love to take you out on a real date, but I'll settle for anything I can get," he answers with a sweet smile.

"All right..." I hesitate. "Do you know Ivy?"

"The French place by the outlet mall?" Chase asks.

I nod. "I can meet you there tonight around eight, if you're free."

A satisfied grin spreads across his face. "Tonight at eight sounds fantastic. I'll see you then."

As we speak, my eyes dart up and down the street on the lookout for Paul's Land Rover. The last thing I need is for him to pull into the parking lot while I'm talking to Chase. Chase can tell I am distracted and he gracefully gives me an out.

"I know you've got work to do, so I'll get going," he says politely. "I'll see you tonight... dinner's on me since you're being kind enough to give me advice."

We say our goodbyes, and I quickly return to the kitchen. I get several inquiring looks from my coworkers but I ignore them all. Five minutes after my return to the kitchen, Paul arrives.

"How did the meeting go?" I ask him.

"Great, their prices are much better than our current seafood supplier. And the rep gave me some fresh sea bass to sample... I've already dropped it off at the apartment. What do you say we grill it tonight? We could throw together a quick salad and try out the new product."

I blush against my will. "Actually... I kind of have plans tonight. It's nothing important, I can cancel if I need to. I was going to meet with Katrina, remember her?"

"Your friend from culinary school?" he asks.

I nod. "She's about to try out for an apprenticeship at a restaurant in Dallas. She wants some advice on how to handle the pressure."

"No problem," Paul assures me. "I'm glad you're going out with your friend. You need to have time like that for yourself. The sea bass will keep until tomorrow."

"Are you sure?" I ask hesitantly. I feel guilty for lying to him, more so because he believes me so easily.

"Positive. I want you to enjoy yourself. And lord knows if there's anyone who can help Katrina land an apprenticeship, it's you."

"Thanks, baby." I smile.

"Of course," he assures me again. "This will give Jenny and I a chance to sit down and talk. There are still a lot of decisions we need to make about the baby... unless you have a problem with that? If you want, we can wait and talk to her together..."

His mention of Jenny erased all of the guilt I felt at lying to him about Chase. "You two go ahead and talk," I insist. "You're right… there are a lot of things you still need to decide. I trust you'll keep my feelings in mind when you make your decisions."

"Kiara, I appreciate the way you've been handling all of this. To know that you love me enough to accept all of this baggage... it means the world to me. I promise I will make all of this worth it. I will spend my life making this up to you."

I hear his words, but I can't make myself believe them.

Chapter Five

I arrive at Ivy promptly at eight o'clock. I'd left work early so I'd have time to get ready. As I shift my car into park, I lower the rearview mirror to ensure that my hair and makeup were still perfect. I'm happy with what I see. My chestnut hair falls in curls around my shoulders, and my dark eyes sparkle behind bronze eyeliner. I step out of my car and smooth my cornflower blue sweater over my charcoal pants.

I step into the restaurant and see that Chase is already at a table. Our eyes meet, and he crosses through the dining room to greet me.

"You look fantastic," he says.

"Thank you," I say graciously. "I may have gone a bit overboard. I work all of the time, so I hardly ever go out. It was nice to have an excuse to get a little dressed up."

"So, no time to go out... is this my first lesson in being a professional chef?" he asks with a smile.

"Absolutely... if you're not willing to work at least a hundred hours a week, you need to rethink your career choice," I tell him.

"Well, I'm glad you were able to get away tonight." He pulls out my chair. I take my seat and he gently pushes me forward before taking the chair opposite me. I promised myself I would keep this professional, but as Chase sits before me, I feel oddly drawn to him. He's broad and muscular, not the type I normally go for at all. But his kind brown eyes and Southern gentleman charm is a welcome change after dealing with Paul's moodiness and drama.

"I'm sorry, but I'm dying to know," I say with a playful grin. "You play college football *and* you want to be a professional chef? How does that work, exactly? Don't most college players want to become professional players?"

"Most do, yes," Chase agrees. "And unlike most, I probably could go pro. I just don't want to." He shrugs.

"So you're playing for a scholarship or something?" I ask.

"In a matter of speaking," he sighs. "It's my dad's dream for me to play in the NFL. He played college ball but he never went pro… it's one of the biggest disappointments in his life. He's been training me for the NFL since I was old enough to hold a football. My scholarship covers tuition, but he pays all of my expenses and gives me an allowance so I can concentrate on two things… playing football and keeping my grades up so I'm allowed to play football."

"So... you're not interested in becoming a chef at all? You just saw that as your 'in' with me?"

"No, no, it's not like that at all. I do want to be a chef. I'm good at football, and I like it okay, but to be honest I'm tired of getting slammed into all of the time.

I'm eligible for the draft in six months, so I have to decide what I'm going to do soon. I was hoping you could tell me about culinary school, what it's like to work in a real kitchen... the pros and cons, if you will. I want to make sure it's really what I want and decide if it's worth ruining my relationship with my dad."

"Chase, I'm so sorry. That sounds awful. How does your mom feel about it?"

"My mom died having me," he answers softly. "It's just me and Dad. I love him, and he did the best he could on his own. But he's... intense."

I soften even more toward Chase as he tells me about his parents. I feel remarkably at ease with him, and soon I find myself telling him about my past.

"When I was sixteen, I came home from school one day to find that my parents moved away without me. I've been on my own ever since," I tell him. I go further into details about how they sold drugs to support their habit. They were the only family I had and now I don't even know whether they are still alive.

"So you understand," he says softly when I finish. "No offense, but I feel better about my family after learning about yours."

"No offense taken," I assure him. "It's been rough. But I've fought my way to the top. As you said earlier today, I'm living my dream. And if I can do it..."

"Then I certainly can, I know." He blushes. "If I like what you tell me about being a chef, I'll find a way to become one. So, let's get started... I have a ton of questions for you, if you don't mind."

"That's what we're here for," I tell him, more to remind myself than to reassure him.

"You said you never have time to go out, but you mentioned several times you have a boyfriend. Were you with him before you got the job? Does the job put a strain on your relationship?"

"My relationship is... complicated," I say slowly. I search for the words to continue but my cell phone chimes and rescues me. "Excuse me for a second. Lesson number two on being a chef, you're always on call." I don't recognize the number on my screen. I answer with a nervous "Hello...?"

"Kiara, this is James O'Toole. I can't stop thinking about your food. I tracked your number down through the Culinary Institute. I have to ask you again to reconsider my job offer. I believe if you come to work with me, I can help you become a world renowned chef."

"Thank you, Mr. O'Toole," I stammer. "But I can't accept the job. My life is here."

"You're not listening to me, Kiara," he replies insistently. "I know I have a reputation, but I assure you that is not what's behind this offer. As I'm sure you know, I critique other people's food for a living. We do All Star *Kitchen Wars* episodes, and I've tasted dishes from some of the best chefs in the world. Your dish blew them all out of the water. I insist you come to work for me and let me help you develop your talent. I have all of the right connections to help you succeed."

He's describing everything I've wanted since I was nine years old, and I'm tempted to accept the offer on the spot. I have a sudden moment of clarity and, remembering the speech I'd given Paul about considering my feelings in *his* decisions, I resist the urge to say yes right away.

"Mr. O'Toole, your offer is incredibly tempting. Can I have some more time to consider it? I'll call you at this number once I've made up my mind."

"That's fine. And Kiara? When you call me back to accept, feel free to call me James." I could almost hear a smile on his face as he disconnected the call.

"Was that what it sounded like?" Chase asks in disbelief. "Did James O'Toole just call and offer you a job?"

"Yes," I admit.

"That's a fantastic opportunity, Kiara. Wow, James O'Toole... I'm impressed." He smiles. "I'm assuming that you need to talk to your boyfriend about this?"

"I hate to cut this short, but I do. I promise I'll make it up to you. We'll get to your questions next time."

"I'll hold you to that." He stands, pulls my chair out, and helps me to my feet. "You go on... I'll wait and take care of the check."

"Thank you," I tell him with a hug.

"Kiara... for what it's worth, if your relationship is complicated, maybe this offer from O'Toole is a sign... this isn't an opportunity you turn down."

"I'll keep that in mind," I tell him before I turn and walk away.

<<◇>>

I call Paul as I drive toward his apartment.

"Hey, babe," he answers somberly.

"Are you all right?"

"Fine, just frustrated." He sighs. "Turns out Jenny and I have different opinions on important things. What's up with you? I didn't expect to hear from you until later."

"Something's come up," I explain quickly. "I'm on my way over. Do you need anything?"

"Just to see you," he says softly. "I'm glad you're coming home."

I promise to see him soon and disconnect the call. I know his argument with Jenny will make my news even harder to hear, but I know I have to tell him about it. Chase was right… no one in their right mind would turn down the chance to work with James O'Toole. I love Paul, but if he truly loves me, won't he want what's best for me?

I pull into his apartment complex, park my car, and gather my resolve. I climb the stairs and use my key to let myself in to the apartment. I'm greeted by the aromas of lemons and thyme as I step through the doorway.

"Hi, babe," Paul calls from the kitchen. "I'm starving so I went ahead and cooked the fish. It's ready, if you're hungry."

"Thank you, but I'm not... so what did you and Jenny fight about?"

"A better question is what *didn't* we fight about." He sighs. "She doesn't want to find out the sex of the baby, I do. I want her to breast-feed... she hates the idea and insists that formula is just as good. The only thing we did agree on was sharing custody."

"Well, that's the most important decision," I say positively. "And it would be hard for her to nurse if you're going to share custody."

"I don't need you to play devil's advocate." He groans.

"I'm sorry... and I think I'm about to make things worse. Paul, I got a phone call a few minutes ago. James O'Toole doesn't want to take no for an answer. And I admit, his offer sounds amazing. He has all of the right connections. If I go work with him for a while, there's no telling how far my career could go."

"Connections?" Paul asks with a sneer. "It's supposed to be about the food, Kiara, remember? Not some sell-out, corporate-run money-machine."

"You're not being fair, Paul," I insist. "It's not like you're giving your food away for free. And if someone's willing to pay me generously to do what I'm passionate about, why in the world should I turn that down?"

"After everything we've been through... after everything we've shared, you're going to leave me? We're supposed to be a team... it's supposed to be you and me against the world, remember?"

"It still can be," I tell him hotly. "If you could put your jealousy aside and be happy for me. I've put all kinds of issues aside for you."

"And there you go bringing up the baby again," Paul snarls in frustration. "Are you ever going to stop acting like a martyr? I made a mistake. We weren't even together yet. What do you expect me to do, abandon my child? Maybe you're more like your parents than you'd like to think."

"You know how I feel about people who abandon their children." I can't believe he's hitting below the belt. "I can't *believe* you'd accuse me of that. I'd never want you to abandon your child, but you expect me to abandon my dream. Everything always has to be about what *you* need, what *you* want. I have a clear picture of what I want, and accepting O'Toole's offer is the fastest way to get there."

"Admit it, you're attracted to him," Paul sneers. "And you love the idea of being in the spotlight. Do you think he'll let you on *Kitchen Wars* if you give him a blow-job?"

"You're one to talk about sleeping with the help," I retort.

"That's me, always the bad guy. I sleep with inappropriate people, I'm a selfish arrogant ass and you deserve better. Celebrity chef James O'Toole better, am

I right?" He leans over me and for the first time I smell the whiskey on his breath.

"That's it," I say firmly. "I'm leaving. Call me when you sober up and you're capable of having an adult conversation about this. And find someone to cover my shifts until then."

"Kiara, wait," he calls after me.

I leave the apartment without looking back.

Chapter Six

I check the time on my dashboard clock as I pull into the parking lot of Shirley's Diner. Jenny called this morning and asked me to meet her for lunch. I went for a run and lost track of time, so now I'm fifteen minutes late. I park my car and rush into the restaurant.

"I'm sorry," I say quickly as I slide into the booth. Jenny is bigger since I last saw her and she looks miserable. "I went jogging and forgot my phone. I hope you didn't wait on me to order."

"Are you kidding me? Now that the morning sickness has passed, I have to eat all of the time. I ordered before I even sat down." As she speaks, a waitress arrives with a platter of pancakes, bacon, hash-browns, and eggs.

She sets the food in front of Jenny and turns to me. "Can I take your order, or do you need a few more minutes to decide?"

"I'll have exactly what she's having," I say as Jenny covers her entire plate in maple syrup. "Well, maybe not exactly." I laugh.

"Don't knock it till you've tried it," Jenny says with a sigh. "Food is the only vice I have left these days... I choose to enjoy it."

"Jenny, I know things have been tough, and I know I haven't been there for you. I felt like you and I had become real friends before this happened, and there's no reason that has to change. I promise to be a better friend from this point forward."

As I talk, I notice Jenny's mood change. She tenses and shifts awkwardly in her seat.

"Oh yeah, you want to be my best friend? Are you going to send me post cards from New York?" she hisses.

My face turns hot with fury as I realize what her words mean. "You talked to Paul?" I ask angrily.

"Of course I talked to Paul. He's devastated. And since we're now connected for life, I'm obligated to be his shoulder to cry on."

"Does he know you're here?" I ask suspiciously.

"No, he doesn't, and we're going to keep it that way. I wanted to talk to you alone. What exactly do you want from him, Kiara?"

"This is none of your business," I tell her, remembering the day I saw her with Robbs.

"That may be," she admits, "but I'm asking anyway. Explain to me what you want to happen... pretend I'm your friend."

"I want to take the job with O'Toole," I confess. "And I want Paul to support my decision. People have long-distance relationships all of the time. I'll be making enough money to fly in a few times a month, and Paul can come visit me in the city. It will be tough, but it would only be for a year or two. I'll gain experience with O'Toole and then move on. We could make it work, and in the end, everyone is happy."

"How naïve can you be?" Jenny asks in disbelief. "The only person who's happy in that situation is you. You think Paul will be flying across the country to see you? Have you forgotten he's about to be a father? Paul doesn't want a glamorous life, he wants to settle down and build a life for this baby. And he wants you to be a part of that life. But if you're not up for it, Kiara, you need to accept that job and never look back."

I'm astounded she has the nerve to talk to me like this. "That would clear the way perfectly for you, wouldn't it?" I snort. "You, Paul, and the baby could be a happy little family. Or you'll lead him to believe that while you and Robbs milk him for everything he's got... that's the plan, isn't it?"

"I don't know what you're talking about," Jenny insists.

"I saw the two of you together... at the food trucks... you had tacos." I stare coldly into her eyes.

"I don't care what you think you saw, or what you think you know," Jenny snaps. "I'm trying to protect my family... you did have one thing right. Paul, the baby, and I could be a happy family... if you'd just get out of the way."

I stand and throw a twenty dollar bill on the table. "Be careful what you wish for, Jenny," I warn before walking away. "You just might get it."

I flee the restaurant and collect myself on the sidewalk. I am dazed after the encounter, and a confusing blend of emotions fills me as I try to process what happened. I decide to take a walk and clear my head before I get behind the wheel.

Shirley's Diner is located in one of Austin's trendy boutique districts and the area is pedestrian friendly. I browse the shop windows as I think about my life. I don't know if my relationship with Paul is even worth fighting for. So many things seem stacked against us and the more complicated things become the more miserable we are. And a part of me knows Jenny is right. If I wasn't in the picture, the three of them could have a chance at being a real family.

Except that she's scheming with Robbs. But I've warned Paul that the two of them are plotting together, so if something does happen, it's not my fault. I don't know why he can't see Jenny for who she is. *Because she's having his baby. He needs to see the best in her, not the worst.* As I walk, I realize that if Paul was forced to choose between Jenny and me, she would win. Not because he loves her more, but because she's the mother of his child.

Can I be happy in a relationship where I'll always come third? And what's the alternative? Picking up my entire life and moving clear across the country? Am I ready for that?'

Paul isn't the only factor in my hesitation to leave Austin… the city has always been my home. My few happy childhood memories took place here, as well as all of my struggles. I grew up here, I survived here, and the thought of leaving my history behind me is bittersweet.

I can always come home.

My thoughts are interrupted by the ring of my cell phone. My heart races and I can't help but hope Paul is on the other end of the line. When I left his apartment last night, I hadn't expected so much time to pass before I heard from him.

I look at the screen and my heart sinks. "Hi, Chase."

"Hello, rock star," he greets me. "I wanted to check in and see if you've made a decision yet. I'd like to start bragging that I'm friends with James O'Toole's apprentice."

"I'm still thinking about it," I say.

"Well, I think best on a full stomach. And I still owe you dinner. Are you free tonight? I'll feed you, and I'm a great listener if you need to talk... I assume that if the decision is this hard for you to make, you're not getting much support."

"You assume correctly," I tell him. "To be honest, dinner is what I need right now. It will be a change to talk things over with someone who doesn't have an agenda."

"I never claimed I don't have an agenda." Chase laughs. "But it's not a dishonest, selfish one."

"I'll settle for that." I laugh in return. "How about seven o'clock at Thai Palace? It's pretty close to my apartment."

"I love a good buffet," Chase agrees. "I'll see you tonight."

<<<>>>

I spend the rest of the day pacing my apartment, waiting for Paul to call. I steal a glance at my wall clock and see that it's already five thirty. I decide that a long, hot shower is what I need to snap out of my anxious mood. I walk into my bedroom and study the clothes hanging in my closet. I don't want to overdress again, so I grab a pair of boyfriend jeans and a fitted flannel button up. I stop at my dresser for socks and panties, and make my way to my bathroom.

I turn on the water, light aromatherapy candles, and dim the lights. The room is already filled with steam as I step underneath the spray. As the water dances over my tense muscles, I try to remember if I've ever felt so overwhelmed with emotion. When my parents left, I didn't have time to feel anything. I had to focus on physical survival, keeping a roof over my head and food in the refrigerator. I'd been so determined then, so sure of what I wanted out of life. And now, I have a chance to live that dream in New York City.

But on the other hand, I also have a chance for something I never thought I wanted. Things are so complicated with Paul, but I love him so much. The idea of spending my life with him, the two of us working and living side by side, is heartwarming. I can even get excited about the baby, as long as Jenny keeps a respectful distance.

And there's Chase... sweet, bright-eyed Chase who's determined to win me over. I am playing with fire, meeting him for dinner, but I can't help myself. He's so charming, and there's something about him I find irresistible. It's also nice to spend time with someone my own age. Chase doesn't have the life experiences that Paul does, but he doesn't have all of the baggage either.

I rinse the conditioner out of my hair and turn off the water. I step out of the shower feeling more confused than when I'd stepped in. I wrap myself in a towel, dry off, and pull on my clothes. I blast my hair with a blow-dryer and weave it into a loose braid. I decide to go easy on my make-up. I dust my face with powder, swipe on mascara and lip gloss, and check myself in the mirror. I look good, casual but put together.

I'd chosen Thai Palace not because I love buffets but because it's within walking distance and I'm in the mood to drink. I step into the living room and check the time. I have twenty minutes before I need to leave the apartment so I grab a beer from the refrigerator and pop the top. That's one bonus of having an older boyfriend. My fridge is always stocked with beer. I sip it slowly and feel warmth spread through my body. At 7:40, I toss the empty can into the trash, slide into my denim jacket, and grab my purse.

I step out into the cool, crisp air and head south. Thai Palace is on a corner lot, six blocks from my apartment. It's been my go-to takeout place since I moved into the area… everyone there knows me, and I don't get carded when I order alcohol. I arrive at the restaurant ten minutes early… Chase is stepping out of his car.

"When you said this place was close to your apartment, I didn't realize you meant within walking distance." He greets me with a smile. I walk across the lot to meet him and he wraps me in a friendly hug.

"I felt like having a few drinks, and I like to walk," I explain as we walk arm and arm into the restaurant.

Cho, one of the owners, greets us with a smile from behind the hostess counter. "Hello Kiara, it's good to see you. It's been such a long time."

"You know how the restaurant business is," I reply.

"Time consuming." She nods. "You're favorite table is open. Take a seat… I'll be there shortly with your water and tea. Are you having the buffet, or would you like menus? Everything's pretty fresh..."

"The buffet is fine with me," I tell her. Chase nods in agreement.

"Sake?" Cho asks.

"Please," I say graciously.

Chase and I fill our plates before sitting down at our table. Our drinks are already waiting for us, along with a relish tray of homemade sauces, chutneys, and pickled vegetables.

"The aroma is amazing." Chase grins as he twirls a forkful of Pad Thai.

We spend a few minutes eating in comfortable silence. Chase cleans his plate in record time. "Do you mind?" He lifts the sake bottle.

"Of course not," I insist. He pours himself a glass and refills mine. I single to Cho for another and push away my mostly empty bowl of beef pho. I am full and satisfied, and the warm wine loosens my tongue.

"You know, this is the first meal I've had today...," I say.

"Things are that bad, huh?" he asks sympathetically.

I nod. "I'm being pulled in so many different directions. I don't know what I'm supposed to do."

"What do you want to do?"

"I want to go to New York," I confess. "I've never been more scared of something, but I've also never been more excited. I want to follow my dream, and I know this could be my shot. But I'm not sure I can leave if it means losing the person I love..." I sigh. "I'm sorry... I know that's probably the last thing you want to hear about."

"It's fine, Kiara," Chase assures me. "I was expecting the topic to come up. You can talk to me about anything. Though I must say I'm surprised your boyfriend isn't more supportive. Why can't he move to New York with you?"

Cho arrives with our second stone decanter of sake. "Would you like some dessert? I finished a pot of the coconut tapioca that you like so much."

"That sounds fantastic," I agree quickly.

"Make it two," Chase adds. Cho disappears back to the kitchen and Chase turns to me. "So, why can't your boyfriend move with you?"

I pour myself another glass of sake, drink it in one gulp, and tell Chase about my relationship with Paul.

"So he can't go with you because he's about to have a baby with a former employee he had a one-night stand with?" Chase asks in disbelief. "And you're tempted to stick around because...?"

"Because I love him… at least, I did love him. I fell hard, and then a baby unexpectedly arrived in the picture. Things are so complicated between us now… I don't know how I feel."

"I think you feel stifled and trapped," Chase suggests softly. "Kiara, I don't mean to be bold, but do you have any idea how amazing you are?" He pours yet another glass of wine. "You're beautiful, you're amazingly talented... It's no wonder Paul doesn't want you to accept that job. He doesn't want you to get out there and realize all of the other options available. You could do so much better... you deserve someone whose entire focus will be on you."

I'm not sure if it's the sake or Chase's words, but I am emboldened. I lean across the table and plant a soft kiss on his lips.

"You want to get out of here?" I ask as I pull away.

"I can't drive..." he answers, gesturing to the empty sake decanters.

"You don't have to, remember?" I say. "I'll ask Cho to pack our desserts to go. I, for one, intend to work up an appetite."

Chapter Seven

"Robbs, I'm telling you, the bitch saw us at the food trucks," Jenny says in a panic. "I don't know how much she overheard, or if she told Paul, but she definitely doesn't trust us."

"Relax, babe," Robbs says reassuringly. "There's no way she said anything to Paul. I work with him almost every day, there's no way I'd still have the job if he thought I was plotting against him."

"I don't know..." Jenny says hesitantly. "I'm afraid Kiara's going to cause us a lot of trouble."

Jenny and Robbs drive through town on their way to Thai Palace. Jenny has a craving for their mango chili chicken, and Robbs hopes the food will calm her mood.

"Let me handle Kiara," Robbs tells her. "I think she's warming up to me. She wasn't at work today. Paul was in a horrible mood and everyone's talking about how there's trouble in paradise. We'll grab a quick bite, I'll take you home, and then I'll stop by Kiara's apartment. I'll tell her I'm worried about her since she wasn't in the kitchen today. It'll give her an opening to vent, and then I'll encourage her to leave Paul's sorry ass."

"I'm not sure the plan is going to go quite so smoothly," Jenny replies. "I told you, she's already suspicious of us. If you show up at her apartment, she'll see right through you."

Robbs pulls into the parking lot of Thai Palace and finds a spot in front of the large picture window. "Will you look at that...?" He whistles.

"What?" Jenny asks. He gestures toward the inside of the restaurant. Kiara is sitting at a table with a strange man.

"I guess the three of us have the same taste in food... we keep ending up at the same places at least," Robbs says with a laugh. "But who is that guy?"

"I don't know, but they seem awfully cozy, don't they?" Jenny says as she studies the scene in front of her.

"Indeed..." Robbs nods.

Jenny gasps as Kiara leans across the table and kiss the stranger. "Oh my god, babe, do you know what this means?"

"It means that Kiara is going to ruin everything for herself, not for us." Robbs smiles. "I think you have a phone call to make. It's your duty, after all, as the mother of Paul's child to make sure he doesn't get screwed over."

"That's what I'm going to say, at least." Jenny retrieves her cell phone. She dials Paul's number and he answers on the second ring.

"Hey, is everything all right?" he answers.

"Yes, I'm fine, the baby's fine," Jenny assures him quickly. "But there's something you need to know. There's no easy way for me to say this, Paul, but I just saw Kiara. She's with another man... I don't know who he is, but they seem awfully enamored with each other."

"I'm sure he's one of her friends from school," Paul answers quickly. "She's been spending time with some of her old friends lately..."

"Paul, have you spoken to her since the last time we talked?" Jenny asks softly.

"No," he admits. "I'm so ashamed of the way I acted last night, I was afraid to call her."

"Paul, I know you don't want to believe she would cheat, but..."

"Jenny, I don't want to hear it," he interrupts harshly. "I appreciate you listening to me vent last night, but I don't need you calling me to tattle on my girlfriend. Kiara would never cheat on me. We'll work things out, and I need you to stay out of it."

"All right," Jenny snaps. "But don't come crying to me when she breaks your heart." Jenny hits the 'end' button on her cell phone screen. She wishes she could slam the phone down for dramatic effect.

"I take it didn't go well," Robbs says inquisitively. "Let me guess, Paul insisted that Kiara can't possibly be doing anything wrong?"

Jenny shakes her head. "I wanted to tell him about that kiss, but he cut me off. He probably wouldn't have believed me anyway. He's blind when it comes to her."

"Lucky for us, he's blind to most things." Robbs grins. "Don't let him upset you. Whether Paul wants to believe it or not, his girl is screwing around on him. It's only a matter of time before their relationship falls apart. At this point, we can just sit back and watch."

<<◇>>

I'm more intoxicated than I realized, and I have to hold on to Chase for support as we walk back to my apartment. He's carrying our tapioca in a small bag and seems to be in disbelief at what's happening.

"Kiara, are you sure...?" he asks as we get closer to my building. "I mean, you've had a lot to drink... we both have... and..."

"I'm positive," I interrupt him. "For the last few months I've been living a boring, grown-up life. I'm nineteen years old, for god's sake, and I've been shopping for diaper genies for my boyfriend's bastard kid. I want to act my age, even if it's just for tonight."

"So... you want to use me?" Chase asks as we climb the staircase.

"That's not what I meant," I tell him. "But if that's how you feel, nothing has to happen. We'll go inside, I'll make a pot of coffee, and when you're sober, you can go home. I'm attracted to you, Chase. I'm attracted to you. I don't know what that means. I don't know what I'll want tomorrow. But tonight, I want to be with you." I lean against my door and look him in the eyes as I speak.

A smile spreads across his face. "That's all I needed to hear." He leans into me, pressing me into the door. His lips find mine and we kiss hungrily, like animals who've just been uncaged. After a few minutes, I push him away and unlock the door. We stumble into the living room, our hands groping for each other's clothes. I walk backwards until I feel the couch bump against my calves, then I fall and pull Chase down on top of me. His muscular, athletic body is heavy and the weight pushes me into the cushions.

"Let's switch things up before I accidentally crush you." He laughs, sits up and pulls me onto his lap. I wrap my arms around him and run my fingers through his soft, shaggy hair. He slowly unbuttons my shirt, kissing my flesh as it's exposed. His lips send shivers through my body and I get wet with desire. I pull his T-shirt over his head, and I can't help but stare at his well-defined arms.

Chase buries his face in my cleavage as he wraps his arms around me and unhooks my bra from behind. He licks and nibbles at my erect nipples, and I can feel his hard cock push against me through our jeans. I reach down and undo his belt buckle… he wiggles out of his pants and lays me on my back once more.

Chase runs his tongue from my earlobe to my waistband. He outlines the top of my jeans with soft, sweet kisses, tugs off my pants, and tosses them to the floor. Things have been so complicated lately, Paul and I haven't made love for weeks, and my body is burning with desire.

"Take me," I beg Chase. "Take me now."

"Shh... be patient." His head disappears between my legs, and I cry out in pleasure as his tongue lashes against me. He traces clockwise circles around my clit before plunging it into my aching hole.

"You taste so good, Kiara," he says as he comes up for air. He dives into me again, this time rubbing my clit firmly with two fingers while thrusting his tongue into me.

"I want you," I cry out. "I want to feel you inside me."

"Not until you come," he tells me in a teasing, sing-song voice. "Relax. Don't think about anything but what's happening right now, in this moment."

His head disappears again and I let my legs fall open wide. He switches things up this time and slides his fingers inside me while his tongue teases my clit. I lay back and close my eyes, giving myself over to the sensations. He finds my G-spot and strokes it firmly… I feel my climax build and lose all control of my body. My hips buck toward his face as I explode in pleasure. Chase laps my juices hungrily, pulls away, and retrieves a condom from his discarded jeans.

"Let me," I coo. I take the package from him, open it, and slide the rubber down his long, throbbing shaft. Holding Chase's cock in my hand, I get wet all over again. He's long and thick, and I can't wait to hold him inside me.

"Take me," I urge once more. I lie back on the couch and wrap my legs around his waist. He hovers over me… I reach down and guide his cock to my warm tunnel. "I want it all."

Chase pushes all of the way into me. The tip of his cock hit the back of my pussy wall, and I clench my muscles around him.

"Oh god... don't stop. Please don't stop." I settle into a rhythm of clenching and releasing, while Chase remains motionless above me. I look up and I'm surprised to see him staring into my eyes.

"You're amazing." He pulls out an inch and pushes back in. "I could stay inside you forever."

I clench him tighter in response, and he continues to rock in and out of me, increasing his speed with each thrust. Abruptly, he pulls away.

"I don't want to come yet," he explains through heavy breaths. "Let's change things up." He turns me over onto my stomach. I crawl to the edge of the couch, balance my elbows on the arm, and shake my ass at him.

"Does this work for you?" I ask in a teasing voice.

"Absolutely," he agrees quickly. He moves behind me, takes my hips in his hands, and pushes his cock back in to my now dripping pussy. "You're so wet." He moans as he slides in and out. I push back against his thrusts. He releases his grip on one of my hips, reaches around, and strokes my clit softly.

"Two can play that game," I moan playfully. I reach between my legs and cup his balls in one hand. I roll them around in my hand, careful not to grip them too tightly.

"Kiara, I'm going to come," he warms.

"Give it to me, Chase," I demand. He pounds into me forcefully, and the raw, animalistic passion is overwhelming. My body ignites in a second orgasm. The waves of pleasure course through my body and it's not until they pass that I realize Chase has reached his own release. He slides out of me and we collapse on the couch, wrapped in each other's arms.

As I lay with Chase's arms around me, I can't help but think about Paul. I wonder what he's doing right now, and who he might be with. There's no way he avoided the restaurant today, but he should be home by now. Why hasn't he tried to call me?

"A penny for your thoughts?" Chase says, bringing my focus back to the present. "I hope you're not having regrets..."

"Of course not," I assure him. "I was thinking I'm too tired to move to the bed."

"Tell you what." He smiles. "I'll carry you to bed and tuck you in before I head home."

"You're not spending the night?" I ask, trying to hide the relief in my voice.

"I can't tonight," he explains. "I have an early practice in the morning... in fact, I should get going."

"All right," I say as I sit up. He stands, dresses, and takes me into his arms as promised.

"I love this room." He carries me through the doorway, reaches down with one hand, pulls back my covers, and deposits me on the bed. I slide between the sheets and he pulls the blankets over me and sits down.

"And the bed is comfortable... I'll have to remember that for next time."

I reach up, pull his face to mine, and kiss him softly. "Thank you for a wonderful night."

"Trust me," he replies. "The pleasure was all mine."

Chapter Eight

I wake to a pounding on my front door. I roll over, and my brain throbs against my skull. Too much sake, I think as I roll out of bed. I don't know what time it is, where I left my cell phone, or who could possibly be making such a racket behind my door. I pull on my long, well-worn bathrobe and stumble into the living room. I peek through the peep hole and am filled with both relief and guilt when I see Paul's face staring back at me. I reach for the doorknob but stop myself and glance toward the couch. My outfit from last night is still lying haphazardly discarded on the floor. I cross the room quickly, gather the clothes, and toss them into my bathroom hamper. I return to the door and open it calmly.

"Hi," I greet Paul casually.

"Kiara, I've been so worried about you. I've been trying to call all morning. I know I should have called sooner, and I know that you're pissed at me. I deserve it. Can I come in and talk?" he asks nervously.

As he speaks, my mind is filled with images of my night with Chase. I don't know how I feel about my infidelity, but I can't process that with Paul standing in front of me. I study him for a moment and open the door wider.

"I guess we do need to talk," I agree. "I'm sorry I missed your calls. I promise I wasn't ignoring you. I did a little drinking last night, and I forgot to put my phone on the charger before I went to bed," I tell him as he follows me into the apartment and shuts the door behind him.

It's all right. If you were ignoring me, I deserved it," he insists. "Kiara, I was wasted when you came over the other night. I had a horrible fight with Jenny and I took all of my anger out on you."

"You've been doing that a lot lately," I tell him honestly. "And I'm getting tired of it. I get the brunt of your bad moods because you don't want to upset Jenny. I know she's pregnant and hormonal, Paul, and I know you're afraid to piss her off. But that doesn't mean you get to keep punishing me for her actions."

"I know, Kiara, and I promise I'll do better." He sighs. "I realize this is no one's idea of the perfect relationship. This isn't how life is supposed to happen, and I had a hard time accepting the consequences of my actions. And I hate that you have to deal with those consequences alongside of me."

"I hate it, too," I tell him. "Not the baby, of course," I add quickly. "None of this is the baby's fault, and I know I will love it once it gets here. But I'd be lying if I said I don't resent Jenny's presence in our lives."

Paul nods. "You were right about her, Kiara. I think she is plotting something. She called me last night and tried to tell me that she'd caught you cheating. Said she'd pulled up at Thai Palace and you were there with another man."

I feel the color drain from my face and panic fills my heart. "I was there..." I confess. "I met a friend for dinner..."

"I know that whatever she saw, it was innocent," Paul interrupts me. "I told her that if you were out, you had to be with a friend from school. It was Marcus, I'm assuming?"

I had a sauce class with Marcus, and Paul and I ran into him and his boyfriend at the farmer's market a few weeks ago. We're friendly, but I've never spent time with him socially. "Yes, it was Marcus," I lie. "What exactly did Jenny accuse me of doing? What did she claim to see?"

"I didn't give her a chance to accuse you of anything," Paul answers quickly. "I cut her off, told her I trust you implicitly, and that the last thing I need is for her to try and cause trouble."

"Thank you for standing up for me," I tell him with a sigh.

"You don't have to thank me," he insists. "I love you, Kiara, and I will always stand up for you. I promise I will never let Jenny come between us."

"I appreciate that..." I reply slowly, "but you know that Jenny isn't our only problem."

"You're talking about O'Toole's offer." Tears well up in Paul's eyes. "Kiara, I can't stand the thought of being away from you. I know this could be a fantastic opportunity for you, but it could also be a disaster. You're the only thing that's kept me sane these last few months, and I can't imagine going through everything with the baby without you by my side. I want my child to know you, and to love you the way I do. And please keep in mind that James O'Toole isn't your only path to success... if you stay here, we can conquer the culinary world together." He sighs, crosses the room, and takes me into his arms.

"Please, tell me I haven't lost you," he says quietly. "Please tell me you'll stay here, where you belong."

I sink into his embrace. "Oh, Paul... I love you so much. I'm so sorry," I tell him with tears in my eyes.

"Baby, you have nothing to be sorry for," he tells me affectionately. "I'm the one who's sorry... I'm sorry I ever let Jenny into Fission."

I wipe my eyes as I pull away from him. "You'll feel differently about that once the baby's here. We both will."

"Does that mean you forgive me, and that you're going to stay in Austin?" he asks hopefully.

I stare into his eyes… this man has his problems, but he loves me. And I spent last night rolling around naked with a stranger. The guilt I feel is overwhelming and I say a quick, silent prayer that Paul never finds out about my tryst with Chase.

I smile softly and wrap my arms around Paul once more. "The only place I'm going is to work with you."

<<◇>>

I stand in front of my prep station, slicing beef for tonight's kabobs. I'm trying to concentrate on the work in front of me, but I'm distracted by guilt and confusion. I told Paul that I'd turn down O'Toole's offer, but in my heart I can't let go of the idea. I'd also told Paul that the dinner Jenny had caught me at was innocent, but it couldn't be further from the truth.

I know I have to stop seeing Chase, but I can't accept it either. He represents my youth and my freedom, and part of me can't help but wonder if he's the man I'm supposed to be with. Things would be easy with Chase... not perfect, but less complicated than my relationship with Paul.

"Chef Kiara?" Megan's voice interrupts my thoughts. I turn and see her standing in the kitchen doorway… she looks incredibly nervous.

"What is it, Megan?" I ask her impatiently.

"There's someone here to see you," she says. Chase's face immediately pops into my head. "It's James O'Toole," she continues quickly. "I don't think Paul wants him here, but he says he won't leave until he speaks to you."

I take a deep breath in frustration. Is it too much to ask for a few moments of peace? "You're right… Paul is with his realtor but he'll blow a gasket if he shows up and sees him. Tell Mr. O'Toole that I'll meet him at the café down the street in ten minutes."

Robbs throws me a curious glance, but I ignore him.

"Yes, Chef," Megan replies with a nod. She disappears back into the dining room.

Every eye in the kitchen is on me as I stow my beef in the walk-in and slip out the back door. I walk to the café quickly. James is waiting at a booth when I arrived.

"I took the liberty of ordering you an espresso," he says as I approach the table.

"I hope you ordered it to go," I tell him sharply. "I can't stay long… I'm prepping for the dinner rush."

"I understand you're busy," he replies harshly. "I'm a busy man myself. In fact, I'm catching a flight back to New York tonight. That's why I had to see you. Do you have an answer to my offer?"

I squirm uncomfortably in my seat. "Actually..."

"That's what I was afraid of." He takes a deep breath. "You're going to turn me down. I have to tell you, Kiara, I'm not used to hearing the word 'no'. Do you know how many people beg for the chance just to cook for me? Do you know what they would give for the chance I've offered you?"

"This is a bad time...," I say defensively.

"That's bullshit," he argues. "I think you're scared. You're young, and you're afraid to leave your comfort zone. I had a feeling you were going to turn me down, so I came here prepared to sweeten the deal. Not only will I pay you generously during the apprenticeship, after a three-year period I will help you launch your own restaurant. If you're interested in television, I can also put you in contact with all of the right people."

"All of this because of a plate of sushi?" I laugh nervously.

"It was a damn fine plate of sushi." He shrugs. "Kiara, I don't know what's holding you here, but I suspect it may be an infatuation with Paul Weston. I'm not usually one to gossip, but if you're looking for a good man, you need to look somewhere else."

"What in the hell are you talking about?" I snap.

"Defensive," he sighs. "You are hung up on him."

"I think it's a little hypocritical of you to talk about another man's reputation," I retort.

"That may be true. Lord knows, I've earned my reputation, but at least I admit it. I don't run around acting like I'm something I'm not," he replies calmly.

I sigh and stare at him, trying to find a hint of dishonesty in his face… it isn't there. "All right," I say, giving in. "What have you heard about Paul?"

"My pastry chef at The Madden Crowd went to culinary school with him. She says he's a talented chef, but a bit of a flake when it comes to relationships. She was smart enough to stay away from him, but in their four years of school, she noticed a pattern. Paul would get serious with women incredibly quickly. And then he'd leave them just as quickly."

"That doesn't sound like him at all." As I defend Paul, I remember a day from my first week at Fission. I'd been in the women's restroom, and I'd overheard two waitresses gossiping about Paul's player reputation. Maybe I don't really know him.

James shrugs. "Perhaps he has changed. But even if that's the case, he's not worth passing up this kind of opportunity." He glances at his watch. "You need to get back to work, and I have a plane to catch. Tell you what, Kiara, consider this an open offer. You have my card… if you ever want to come to New York, give me a call."

We stand… I extend my hand and James accepts it. But instead of shaking it, he pulls me close, leans over, and plants a firm kiss square on my lips.

"You need to be reminded that Paul Weston isn't the only man on Earth." He winks at me, and turns to walk out of the café.

I'm flushed with surprise and panicked by what just happened. I toss a ten down on the table and rush out of the café like I'm fleeing the scene of a crime.

I have to stop this, I tell myself as I walk back to Fission. No more meeting men who aren't Paul. I'm not a cheater... I've never been a cheater. But I am a cheater. In the last twenty-four hours, I've kissed two other men and had sex with one. I don't know what's gotten into me, but I do know I have to get control of it.

I groan internally as I step through the front door of the restaurant. Chase is sitting at the bar waiting for me. What is with today? Why can't they leave me alone at *work*?

I cross the room over to Chase. He can tell that I am not happy to see him. "What are you doing here?" I hiss. "Now that you know about Paul, I thought you'd be smart enough to stay away."

"I'm sorry," he whispers. "I know I shouldn't have come. But I made an important decision, and I want to tell you about it."

I check my cell phone for the time. Paul shouldn't be back for another twenty minutes or so. "I have ten minutes. I'm sorry for being snappy, Chase, but I have a lot of work to do."

"It's all right... can you sit down?" He gestures to the seat opposite him. I sit and signal Megan for a cup of coffee.

"So what is this decision you made?" I ask after she delivers my steaming cup.

"I decided not to go out for the draft. I'm going to tell my dad that I don't want to be a football player... I want to be a chef. I'm going to finish out next semester at Texas State, and transfer to the Culinary Institute in the fall... if I can get in, that is."

"Oh, Chase, that's so exciting!" I tell him. "But I'm surprised to hear it. What made you decide to go for it? I never even got around to answering your questions..."

Chase smiles. "To be honest, your inability to make your decision helped me make mine. You're a fool if you turn down that job, Kiara. I was thinking last night that if I was given the offer you were, I'd jump all over it. And then it dawned on me that I'll never get that kind of chance if I don't go to culinary school. When I realized that, I knew what I had to do."

"When are you going to talk to your dad?"

He takes a deep breath and exhales slowly. "Tonight... I'm making him dinner at my place."

I laugh. "Going to show off a little? Impress him with your talent before you shock him with your news?"

"Something like that." He nods.

I open my mouth to speak, but I'm startled by the sound of a throat clearing behind me. A look of panic spreads across Chase's face.

"Kiara, are the kabobs threading themselves this evening?" Paul asks harshly.

"Sorry, Chef," I say weakly. "Paul, this is Chase. He's starting at the Culinary Institute in the fall, and he asked me for some advice about his class schedule." I say, struggling for an explanation.

"How nice of you to take such a personal interest in the customers," Paul says softly. I can hear the sarcasm in his voice, but I don't think Chase notices it. "It's a pleasure to meet you, Chase. If you don't mind, Chef Sands is needed in the kitchen. Best of luck to you at the Culinary Institute." He glares at me with a look that tells me it's time to leave.

"Yes, Chase." I awkwardly rise from my seat. "Good luck at school."

He nods at me, thanks us both, and Paul leads me by the arm back to the kitchen.

"How was your meeting with the realtor?" I ask innocently. "Did you find anything worth showing me?"

"She showed me a three bedroom I am thinking about putting an offer on. How was your meeting with O'Toole? I trust you told him what he could do with his offer?"

My first instinct is to ask him how he knows that I saw O'Toole. My eyes fall on Robbs and I answer my own question. "I turned down his offer," I tell Paul. "And he's flying back to New York tonight, so we don't have to worry about him showing up anymore."

"That's a relief." He sighs and follows me to the walk-in and helps me carry the kabob ingredients back to my station. "The meat should have been put in marinade an hour ago," he says critically.

"I'm slicing it razor thin, Paul, the flavor will be fine."

"Kiara... that guy, Chase. He's the one I saw you with last week... in the dining room." Paul says slowly. "Is he...? I mean... have you...?"

I know where the conversation is going, so I cut in. "I've only ever seen him here, Paul," I assure him. "He's interested in cooking, and he enjoys our food. I was wearing my jacket when I met him, and he asked if I had time to give him some pointers. I joked that he'd have to catch me in a slow time here, and today he did just that."

Paul lets out a sigh of relief. "So he's not the one Jenny saw you with? It really was Marcus?"

I set my knife down on the butcher block and stare into his eyes. "Paul, do you really expect me to answer that question?" I ask him. The anger in my tone is meant more to hide my guilt for lying than it is to challenge his questions of suspicion.

His face softens. "Of course not," he says. "Just do me a favor, all right? Don't sit down in the dining room with that guy again. The gossip around here is bad enough without us adding to the ammunition. Can you handle that?"

"Sure baby," I quickly agree. "He's just a customer... it's no big deal."

Chapter Nine

"Do you want some hot chocolate?" I call to Paul from his kitchen. I toss a K-cup into his Keurig and pull the handle… rich, creamy hot chocolate fills my cup and lifts my mood. Three days passed since Chase showed up at Fission. I tried to call him a few times, but he hasn't returned my messages. He is probably pissed at the way I treated him after Paul showed up that day.

It is for the best if Chase and I don't see each other again. Or rather, my brain understands that. My heart, on the other hand, is a different story. I find myself longing for his muscular arms to be wrapped around me. A few times, Paul caught me daydreaming and asked what was on my mind. I had to cover fast, and I think he is starting to expect that something's up.

"I'd love some, baby, thank you," Paul calls back at me from the living room. He's lounging on the couch, waiting for *Iron Chef* to start. I fill another cup with hot chocolate and carry the drinks into the living room. As I take my seat, the opening scenes introduce the *Iron Chef's* opponent. This week, it's Chef Carly Simms, the pastry chef from The Madden Crowd.

"Oh my god, I know her!" Paul exclaims. "We went to culinary school together. I can't believe she's working for O'Toole. That's all the more reason you didn't need to go to New York."

"You know her?" I ask with convincing surprise.

"I know her." Paul blows on his hot chocolate. "And she's a nut case. She came on to me on our first day of school. I passed on it and I dodged a bullet. A couple of other guys in our class dated her, and she went full blown stalker on them."

"Interesting..." I reply. Maybe James's source on Paul isn't as reliable as he thinks she is. "If she's crazy, I'm surprised she's in such a prestigious position..."

"Don't get me wrong, she's talented... she's not as good as Claire, but no one is. And maybe she's grown up a little. I know I'm not the same person I was back then," Paul says.

"What kind of person were you back then?" I tease.

"One that wouldn't be worthy of you," he answers seriously, looking deeply into my eyes. He sits his mug on the coffee table and takes me into his arms. "Kiara, do you have any idea how much I love you? And how happy it makes me that you're staying here?"

"I love you, too, baby." I smile. "And I'm happy to stay here. We're going to have a fantastic life together."

Paul grabs me by the face and envelopes my mouth with his. He kisses me urgently, and I feel his erection poke against my leg. I reach down and stroke him through his pajama pants.

"Oh, Kiara..." he groans. "It's been so long... why have we gone so long...?"

"I don't know, baby," I say softly. "But do you want to change that?"

He bucks against my hand. "You know I do," he whispers into my ear. I stand and walk toward his bedroom, leaving a trail of my clothes behind me. Naked, I spread out on the bed. Paul enters the room a few moments after me. He's naked as well, and he climbs on top of me on all fours. He kisses me softly as he hovers above me.

"I want you now." He moans.

"Then take me now," I reply. I open my legs and angle my hips up toward him.

"No... roll over," he begs. "Please..."

I do as he asks and in one quick motion Paul buries himself inside me. He thrusts hard and fast, but I am not warmed up yet. "Slow down, baby." I grimace.

"Sorry...," he says as he slows his movements. He bends over my back and plants a soft, single kiss on the nape of my neck. He keeps his pelvis still as he wraps an arm around me and teases my nipples with his fingers. Finally, I am wet.

"Better...?" he coos as my juices pour over him. He begins thrusting again without waiting for my reply. I try to keep my mind in the moment, but memories of my night with Chase keep popping into my head. The sex with him was so tender, so different from what's happening now. As I remember the feeling of Chase's tongue lashing my clit, Paul explodes inside me. I feel him go soft, and I lower my hips, releasing his spent cock from my unsatisfied pussy.

"Oh, baby, that was amazing." Paul sighs. "Did you come?"

"Hell yeah, I did," I lie with a smile. We both know I am not being honest, but Paul seems happy to go along with my story. He settles under the blankets and pulls me into his arms. I rest my head on his shoulder and try to hide my frustration.

"Kiara, I meant what I said earlier," he tells me. "We're going to have a fantastic life together... you, me, and the baby. I was thinking about what you said before... about researching what legal action we can take with Jenny. Under any other circumstances, I'd hate the idea of separating my child from its mother. But if she's plotting against us, and planning on using the baby to get to me, I don't think we have any other choice. I think we need to sue her for full custody."

"Full custody...?" I ask in disbelief. "I was talking about child support, and visitation, Paul! I think you need to get the courts involved in everything... to protect your assets. How will you manage things if you have full custody?"

"Well... I thought I'd have your support," he answers moodily. "We'll have to hire outside help, but we could work alternate shifts at the restaurant. We could come up with a schedule that gives us both plenty of time home with the baby."

"Paul, I'm your apprentice!" I remind him. "How am I supposed to learn anything from you if we work separate shifts?"

"I can teach you at home," he answers angrily. "I thought you'd be on board with this idea, Kiara. I know you hate the idea of having Jenny in our lives. If we raise the baby together, we can eliminate most of that. We could be a real family..."

I can't believe what I am hearing, and my lack of excitement is hurting Paul's feelings. "I'm sorry, I wasn't expecting this," I explain quickly. "You have to understand, while it's a noble idea, it's incredibly overwhelming. I'm nineteen years old, Paul, I don't know if I'm ready to be someone's mother..."

"I know I sprung this on you, but I'd appreciate it if you'd consider the idea. This is my child, Kiara. It's my job to protect him or her from anyone who wants to use them for their own agenda... even if it is their own mother."

"I understand..." I agree softly. "And if this is what you want, we'll find a way to make it work."

If this is what you want, we'll find a way to make it work. My words to Paul echo over and over in my head as I shower. It's seven in the morning, and Paul has gone to the farmer's market to get fresh ingredients for our breakfast.

I was awake in bed all night thinking about Paul's idea, and how quickly I'd gone along with it. There is no doubt in my mind that I'm not at all ready to be a mom… if I were, I'd have gotten pregnant myself. I take much care to ensure I don't end up with a child before I'm ready, but here I am, ready or not.

The longer I contemplate the situation, the angrier I am with Paul. Not because he's asking me for support, but because he refused to support me in return. The words I spoke last night were what I'd wanted Paul to say when O'Toole made his offer. *If this is what you want, we'll find a way to make it work.*

As the shower sprays over me, I reach another realization. If I stay here, I have to accept that Paul's wants and needs will always come first. I love Paul, and I'll love the baby once it's here, but I'm not sure the love will be enough to keep me from resenting both of them. I am not naïve... if I go along with Paul's plan, I'll be the one doing most of the child care. His career will come before mine, and my life will become a revolving schedule of diaper changes, nap times, and play dates. In a few years, my cooking time will probably be limited to family meals. I'll be the best bake sale mom, but the idea is bittersweet.

I contemplate the road my life is about to take as I think about Chase. I wonder if he's talked to his dad yet and, if so, how it went. I wonder if he's been thinking about me the way I think about him.

I step out of the shower, wrap my hair in a towel, and pull on Paul's bathrobe. I walk to the living room, retrieve my cell phone from my purse, and dial Chase's number. I'm relieved and surprised when he answers.

"Hello?" he says harshly.

"Hey, it's Kiara. I haven't heard from you for a few days. How did things go with your dad?"

"Worse than I'd ever expected," he replies bitterly. "My father accused me of shaming our family. He said that cooking is for women and queers, and that no son of his was going to some fairy cooking school. When I tried to defend my idea, he snapped. He's cut off my credit cards and made it clear that I now pay my own rent. If I agree to go out for the draft, he'll start bankrolling me again."

"Oh, Chase, I'm so sorry." I sigh. "I know your dad is upset right now, but I'm sure he'll come around."

"I love how you're so sure about my life and what I should do, and yet you can't make one damn decision for yourself," he snaps.

"What are you talking about?" I ask… my feelings are hurt by his tone.

"You encouraged me to follow my dream, but you won't follow yours. You went on and on about how I should stand up for what I want. I listened to you, and now I lost everything. I should have followed your example and not your advice."

"Chase, you're upset, and you're taking it out on me… it would be best if I give you some space and some time to calm down."

"Maybe you should just stay out of my life for good," he says sharply. "After all, I'm just your boy toy, right? Someone to play around with when your boyfriend pisses you off?"

"Chase, that's not how I think of you…" I argue.

"Do me a favor, Kiara, and don't think of me at all. Forget you ever met me." The line goes dead. I stare at the screen for a minute before returning my phone to my purse.

Chase's attitude hurts me more than I expected it to. Maybe I care about him more than I realized. But it doesn't matter now… staying away from him is for the best. My heart hurts, and I return to the bed and lay down.

Chase hates me, Paul wants me to settle down and raise his child, and James wants to turn me into a world-renowned chef. As much as it pains me, I know the choice that I have to make. I retrieve my phone again, pull up the last call from James, and dial the number. The call goes to voicemail, so I leave a quick message. I end the call and dial Paul.

"Hey, baby, I'm almost home," he tells me.

"I'm so sorry, but I need to head out," I tell him. "My super just called. The plumber will be at my place soon to fix my clogged shower drain."

"I didn't realize you had a clogged drain," he replies.

That's because I don't. "Did I not mention it to you? I guess I was busy. It's no big deal, but I need to get over there and let him in."

"Do you want me to go with you?" he offers. "I can make breakfast at your place."

"No, don't worry about it. You go on to the restaurant. I'll be in as soon as the plumber finishes up."

"Take the day off if you want," Paul suggests. "I don't think we'll be busy, most of the traffic will be on the other side of town near the music festival."

I forgot we were expecting a slow weekend. "All right... if you're sure. See you tonight, at your place?"

"I'll try and get home early. Love you, Kiara."

"I love you, too. I'll see you tonight." I disconnect the call and rush out of the apartment before he gets home.

Chapter Ten

"Hello?" An irritated voice greets me on the other end of the line. I've been calling James all day and at nine o'clock at night he's finally answered.

"Hi, James, this is Kiara Sands. I did a lot of thinking, and I decided to accept your offer."

"Isn't that interesting?" he replies. "I have to tell you, Ms. Sands, I heard quite a bit about you since we last spoke. I'm no longer certain you'll be a good fit at The Madden Crowd."

"May I ask what you heard...?" I reply nervously.

"I spoke with one of the chefs in your kitchen, a Mr. Martin. According to him, you have a habit of juggling more than one man at a time. Mr. Martin also said you let your personal life distract you from your work. After speaking with him, I have to wonder if I just happened to catch you on a good day. I am no longer confident that you'll be able to turn out quality food on a consistent basis."

"Mr. O'Toole, please..."

"Mr. Martin also informed me of how you received the apprenticeship position in the first place," James continues. "And I must say that while I love a girl who's willing to put out to get what she wants, I have no use for one who screws around on her boyfriend. Especially when that boyfriend is a colleague of mine..."

"So now you care about Paul?" I snap. "Last week you were telling me that he's not worth my time."

"Yes, and now I realize you're the one who's not worth it. Now, if you'll excuse me, I have a kitchen to run. Consider my offer off the table and don't bother me again."

He ends the call. I stare at my phone again in disbelief as a single tear rolls down my cheek.

"Baby, will you toss me the nutmeg?" Paul calls from across the kitchen. Every chef on staff is packed into the kitchen, and we're running full speed to keep up with our Sunday brunch crowd.

"Here you go," I call out as I toss the spice container.

A little over a week has passed since James O'Toole rescinded his job offer. Instead of dwelling on my disappointment, I throw myself into my new life with Paul. He signed the contract on the three-bedroom apartment yesterday, and we'll both be moving in next week. I gave my notice to my landlord and most of my things are already in boxes.

Paul and I agreed that after the baby is born, he'll continue running Fission, and I will return to culinary school. It is the schedule that will work best for us, and I'm all right sacrificing the apprenticeship as long as I can still get my degree. I have a feeling that raising a baby and working together would put a strain on our relationship, and I'm actually looking forward to having a normal schedule again.

We haven't spoken with an attorney yet, but we booked an appointment with one on Wednesday. I am nervous about the meeting, and it has nothing to do with confronting Jenny. I watched enough television to know what the lawyer is going to say first... Paul will have a better chance of getting full custody of his child if he and I are married. We may not be able to prove that Jenny is unfit, so we'll have to show that Paul and I are a better fit to raise the baby. And while there are plenty of places in the country that allow unmarried couples to adopt, this is Texas. The court system is old fashioned here, and a judge will be most likely to side with the married, stable parent.

I found a way to be happy about the changes in my life, but the idea of legally binding myself to Paul sends panic through my body. I'd feel differently if the marriage was motivated by romance, but in this case it's just legal red tape that takes away my last bit of freedom. If the meeting with the attorney goes as expected, I'll go along with the plan and say my 'I do's'. I just can't find a way to be happy about it.

I flip the bread pudding French toast in front of me and throw a glance in Paul's direction. He's bent intently over a saucepan, ensuring the eggs in the water are poached to perfection. I watch him pull the eggs from the water and gently assemble an order of crab Benedict, and I'm reminded of why I fell in love with him in the first place. Paul sets one egg of to the side and I return my attention to the task in front of me. The French toast is browned to perfection… I plate it with a dollop of fresh whipped cream and a ramekin of maple syrup and carry it to the service window.

I return to my station to find a hot *croque madame* waiting for me.

"I thought you might be hungry," Paul calls out. I look up and see him back at his own station.

"Thank you, baby," I tell him. I eat the sandwich in four bites. It is delicious and it reminds me of the first night we spent together in the kitchen. Maybe marriage isn't such a scary thing... I wash down the sandwich with long gulps of Diet Coke.

Paul assembles another plate of food, carries it to the window, and walks to my station. "I was thinking that takeout would be the perfect way to end this busy day. Want to order Indian and curl up with a movie after work?"

I smile at him, a plot forming in my mind. "That sounds good, but I'll need to go by my place first. I need to pick up a few things."

"What could possibly be left there?" he teases. I accumulated quite a collection of things at his place.

"Just a few personal items," I answer casually, "nothing you need to worry about."

"All right... I can get you out of here early. I'd rather miss you in the kitchen than at home." He gives me a heart-melting smile and I know, if it comes to it, I won't hesitate to walk down the aisle if that is what he needs me to do.

As promised, Paul gets me out of the kitchen by eight o'clock. "I'm going to try and get out of here early, too. I should be no later than nine-thirty," he says as he walks me to my car.

"Alright, baby. I'll see you then." I climb into my car and rush to my apartment. I run up the stairs, unlock my door, and head straight for my bedroom. I find what I'm looking for at the bottom of my sock drawer.

The lingerie is silky and black, with a garter belt and stockings that match the nearly see-through bodice. I bought the outfit months ago, right before we found out about the baby. I'd stuck it in the drawer and forgotten all about it until this afternoon. I carry the lingerie to the bathroom, undress, and step into the shower. I take care shaving my body smooth… Paul likes my pussy soft and bare. Once I'm satisfied with my grooming, I turn the water off and step out of the tub. I'd kept my head out of the shower spray, so my hair is damp but not wet. I am pleased with what I see in the mirror… I have a tousled, sexy appearance and decide to leave my hair as it is. I apply bold make up and then put on the lingerie.

I walk back to the bedroom and slip on my tallest high heels. I add a black trench coat, and I'm ready to head to Paul's. It's always been a fantasy of mine to do the 'naughty trench coat' surprise, and I hope Paul is as excited about it as I am. I drive to his apartment, careful to obey all traffic laws… the last thing I need is to get pulled over by a cop in my current attire.

I pull into the parking lot of Paul's building, and I'm pleasantly surprised to see that his truck is already in its usual spot. I step out of the car, belt my coat tightly, and make my way to his door. I let myself in with my key and am greeted with a horrific shock. Paul and Jenny are both in the living room, wrapped in each other's arms.

I stand silently and watch the scene in front of me. A few long moments pass before Paul pulls away and sees me in the doorway.

"Kiara... this isn't..." he stammers.

"It isn't what, Paul?" I demand. Tears fall from my eyes as I watch him scramble for an explanation.

"This isn't what it looks like." He sighs. "We were talking about the baby... we decided to find out the gender, and Jenny has agreed that if it's a girl, we can name her after my mother." He smiles hopefully.

"That's great," I tell him. "But I don't understand what it has to do with what I walked in on."

"Kiara, Paul is telling the truth," Jenny pipes in halfheartedly. "You're overreacting. The three of us are going to be raising this baby together. It would be best if you and I could get along. But you can't fly off the handle every time you see Paul and I together."

"You know what, Jenny?" I snap. "I'll do you one better. I'll pack my shit right now and get out of your way. You and Paul can raise the baby, and I'll get on with my life."

"Jenny, I think you need to leave," Paul says firmly. He walks her to the door and she leaves in silence.

"Kiara..." Paul begins.

I glare at him fiercely, turn, and set off for the bedroom. I grab my luggage out of his closet and start tossing my things inside. Paul walks in as I'm dumping my designated drawer into the bag.

"We were just talking, I swear," he says softly.

"Yes, you were making plans about the baby together. What about our plans, Paul? Remember those? The ones we made together?" I cry loudly. Satisfied that all of my things are gathered from the bedroom, I drag the luggage to the bathroom and start packing my toiletries.

"Kiara, I haven't forgotten. I am just having second thoughts... if Jenny can be agreeable and we can all get along, wouldn't it be best for the baby if we're all involved in its life?"

I collapse onto the floor. "I can't take this anymore, Paul. It's like living a nightmare over and over again. I can't keep dealing with all of the drama, all of the back and forth. I know deep down you want to be with her, that you want a family. Just let me leave... I'm doing us all a favor."

"That's not true," he argues quietly. "If you leave now, you'll destroy me."

I think of everything I gave up, all of the sacrifices I made to make him happy. "Well, you already destroyed me, so I guess we're even." I say, rising to my feet. I zip my luggage shut and roll it toward the door.

Paul stands in the doorway, refusing to let me pass. "Kiara, don't do this. I don't know what I'd do without you... I'll fall apart."

"You'll figure it out," I insist. "I'm done putting your needs ahead of mine. I want you to be happy, Paul, I do. But I want me to be happy more. And your life... it's too much for me," I tell him sadly. "You can also consider this my resignation... I'll have someone drop my jacket off at the restaurant."

He steps out of the doorway and lets me pass. I roll the luggage down the hallway and leave the apartment without another word.

After a long night's sleep, I wake rested and ready to start my day. When I got home from Paul's last night, I caught my reflection in my stainless steel refrigerator and remembered that I was dressed in a trench coat and lingerie. The sight of myself and the memory of how happy I'd been just a few hours before broke my heart, and I'd collapsed onto the kitchen floor and cried until there were no tears left in my body. From there, I'd moved to my bed and assumed the fetal position.

I gave myself a few hours to mourn the death of the life I thought I would have, and then I'd forced myself to snap out of it and look toward the future. I managed to fall asleep easily, but now I realize I haven't eaten anything since early yesterday afternoon. I roll out of bed, slip my feet into my soft fleece slippers, and set off for my kitchen.

I examine the contents of my fridge and pantry… my selections are limited. I didn't stock up on groceries in anticipation of my move. I have no plans for the day, and decide to eat out for breakfast, then spend the rest of the morning at the farmer's market.

I walk back to my bedroom, throw on some loose jeans and a baggy sweatshirt, pull my hair into a messy bun, and slip my feet into my Converse. I look young and sloppy, but it is comfortable. It's about time I acted my age. I grab my purse and walk out the door.

I drive a few blocks to a small, locally owned coffee shop. The shop isn't crowded, and I tuck myself in to a small corner booth. The waitress arrives and I order a pot of regular coffee and a slice of vegetable quiche. She brings me the coffee, mug, and cream pitcher quickly. I pour myself a cup and pull out my spiral notebook.

I have a lot of decisions to make and details to take care of, and I find it's always best to stay organized. I write 'To Do' on the top of the page and start my list. First, I will call my landlord and ask if I can stay on in my apartment. I only gave notice a few days ago, so I doubt he has already found a new renter. Still, as having a home is more important than anything, my first call will be to him.

Next on my list is school. I've been receiving college credit for the hours I work at Fission. There's only three weeks left in the semester, and I hope the work I've already completed will be enough for a passing grade. I dread calling Chef Lee to tell her I am leaving for personal reasons again. She will be disappointed in me, but I will deal with it. I can start back to normal classes over the summer semester... that was the plan even if I stayed with Paul.

If only I'd accepted James O'Toole's offer when I had the chance... I'd be well on my way to a brand new life instead of picking up the pieces of my old one. I can't change the past so I have to make the best of things as they are now.

I thought about Chase a lot since I decided to go back to the Culinary Institute. He'll be in the beginner classes, but we'll run into each other on campus, if he sticks to his guns and follows his dream.

The waitress delivers my breakfast and I continue thinking about Chase as I eat. He was another opportunity I let pass me by, but maybe, just maybe, it's not too late for us. I finish my quiche, push my plate away, and dial his number. I am surprised when he answers.

"Kiara?" he asks. "I'm surprised to hear from you."

"Hi, Chase..." I take a deep breath. "You can hang up on me if you want... I deserve it. I've been thinking about you a lot lately, and am wondering how you've been."

"Actually, I've been thinking about calling you," he says in a friendly tone. "Can we meet in person? I'm free for lunch... I could meet you somewhere near Fission if you can get away."

"I'm off today," I quickly reply. "In fact, I'm off indefinitely."

"You have a lot to catch me up on, too. So you can meet me? I get out of class at noon... we can go anywhere you'd like."

"How about twelve-thirty at The Rib Shack?" I suggest.

"A good southern boy never turns down barbecue." He laughs. "I'll see you then."

Chapter Eleven

I arrive at the restaurant ten minutes early. And as usual, Chase is already waiting. He was friendly on the phone but I am not sure what to expect when I see him. I step into the dining area and my fears subside. Chase greets me with a wide smile, stands, and crosses the room to greet me.

"Kiara, it's so good to see you." He wraps one arm around my shoulders and plants a soft kiss on my cheek.

"It's good to see you, too." I let him guide me to the table. "How have you been?"

"I've been keeping well," he says. "You were right... I needed time to calm down. Once I did, I realized that telling my dad was the right thing to do. I expected him to disapprove, but when it actually happened it hurt more than I thought it would. I took that hurt out on you, which wasn't fair. I'm sorry."

"It's all right... how are things with your dad now?"

"Getting better... he's speaking to me again, at least. He said that the way I stood my ground told him that I am serious about being a chef. He didn't realize there were so many ultra-masculine chefs these days until he started watching the Food Network. He still wants me to go out for the draft, and my credit cards are still shut off, but I think he'll come around, eventually."

"I'm so happy to hear that," I tell him. The waitress arrives and we order a rack of ribs with fries and onion rings to share.

"This calls for a celebration... it's just too bad we're not old enough to celebrate properly." I laugh.

"I can think of another way for us to celebrate." He replies with a devilish smile. "But first, I need to hear what's been going on with you. You're not working at Fission anymore... does that mean what I think it means?"

I nod. "Paul and I aren't together anymore," I confess with a casual shrug. "Things have been over for a long time... neither of us wanted to admit it. I just reached a point where I couldn't pretend anymore."

"That's understandable." He agrees. "So when did you break up?"

"Last night," I tell him… he chokes on his ice tea. "Are you alright?" I ask.

He nods and clears his throat. He takes another drink and stares at me. He is upset but I have no idea why.

"You broke up with your boyfriend last night, and you called me first thing this morning? No offense, Kiara, but I have no intention of being your rebound guy... and it seems like that's what you're looking for..."

I understand his concern, but I shake my head. "That's not what I'm looking for at all, Chase," I assure him. "Yes, I'm attracted to you. But I just got out of a serious relationship and I have no desire to jump straight into another one. I want to be young, act my age... honestly, I just want to be your friend."

"Like friend friends or friends with benefits friends?" he asks cautiously.

"Like pig out on a rack of ribs, grill on the weekends, go to the farmers market together friends," I explain. "I want to spend time with you... I want to get to know you. If something romantic develops from it, bonus. If not, no problem. Do you think you can handle that?"

He eyes me with a smile. "Will you help me with culinary school? Like, tutor me and teach me all of your pro tricks?"

"Of course I will," I assure him. "That's what friends do. A few weeks with me, and you'll be the star of your class."

"That would sound kind of cocky, if I didn't know that you were handpicked by one of the best chefs in the country," he teases. "And by the way, as your friend, I have to tell you that turning down O'Toole's offer was a dumb-ass move. I won't be letting you get away with that kind of shit in the future."

"Please, don't ever mention O'Toole to me again," I ask. "I'd like to pretend that the whole mess was just a bad dream."

The waitress delivers our enormous platter of food. The ribs are charred perfectly and falling off the bone… the fries and onion rings are crisp and salty. We eat in silence until we're both stuffed, and we each order a cup of coffee.

"So what are your plans from here?" Chase asks. "Want to hang out... you know, as friends?"

"I have to unpack," I tell him. He looks confused so I explain how close I'd come to moving in with Paul.

"I think you dodged a bullet here, Kiara. Tell you what, I'll come over and help you unpack," he says.

"Really? I would appreciate it...," I reply hesitantly. "If you don't mind..."

"It's not like I'm helping you move... I'm helping you stay put." He smiles. "Now, is there anything we need to do before we go to your place?"

"I have no groceries," I confess. "I was going to go to the market after breakfast, but I had a bunch of phone calls to make and didn't have time to stop before I came here."

"Well then, the market it is. Which one do you go to?"

"There's one in my neighborhood. Why don't you follow me back to my place and we can walk from there?"

"Sounds good."

Chase pays the check, we leave the restaurant, and make the short drive back to my apartment. I grab my grocery bags from the trunk of my car, and we set off down the sidewalk.

It's about eight blocks away. I usually drive, but I'm so stuffed, I want to walk off that meal," I explain.

"I walk everywhere on campus. I like taking things slow," he says... the double meaning in his words is crystal clear.

"That's good to hear," I tell him with a grin. The moment is interrupted by my ringing cell phone. I retrieve it from my purse, and I am shocked by the number on the screen. "Oh my god, Chase, it's James O'Toole!" I squeal. *Maybe he's changed his mind.*

"Answer it!" Chase encourages me. I swipe my screen and lift the phone to my face.

"Hello?" I ask with obvious confusion in my voice.

"Kiara, this is James," he says quickly. "I'm so relieved I was able to get a hold of you. I'm afraid I overreacted the last time we spoke... I apologize for that."

"Apology accepted," I reply, perhaps a bit too quickly. "May I ask what made you change your mind?" I can't believe he took the time to call, much less that he apologized to me... I am surprised that he thought of me at all.

"I received an interesting phone call from Paul this morning... I take it you never told him that I rescinded my offer? He seemed to think that you'd turned me down to stay with him."

"I never bothered to tell him the truth," I confess. Chase and I step into the farmer's market… he grabs a basket and browses the aisles as I continue my conversation with James. "Paul and I stopped bothering with a lot of things... that's why we broke up."

"Yes, he mentioned that. Anyway, Paul called me to apologize for steering you away from the job at The Madden Group. He encouraged me to extend the offer again, and assured me that you'd accept it this time. I told him that I'd spoken to Mr. Martin, and that I wasn't interested in working with you anymore."

"I see..." I sigh.

"I'm not finished," James assures me. "Paul filled me in on your back story with Martin, and explained that he's not someone who can be trusted. When I got off the phone with Paul, I made some more calls and heard the same stories from a lot of people. According to my contact at Escoffier, Robbs has been on disciplinary probation twice since he started attending the college. They were all happy to get rid of him when he won the chance for the apprenticeship at Fission."

"Disciplinary probation?" I ask. "Somehow, that doesn't surprise me."

"Kiara, I'm sorry I believed him. I see now that he's just jealous and trying to make trouble for you. If you're still interested in the job in New York, it's yours."

Adrenaline rushes through my body and for a moment I am convinced I imagined his words.

"Kiara?" he asks. "Are you still there?"

"I'm here," I assure him. "You caught me off guard, that's all."

"I understand. Do you need to take some time to consider the offer again?"

"No," I reply quickly. "I accept your offer, James. I'd love to come work with you in New York."

"That's what I wanted to hear." I can almost hear the smile on his face. "Text me your email address, and I'll send you all of your information. As soon as you know when you can leave Austin, I'll book your ticket. You'll be put up at a hotel until you're able to find a place in the city, and your moving expenses will be paid, of course."

"Thank you so much," I stammer. "You're being so generous."

"I'm being selfish, Kiara." He laughs. "You're going to be one of the biggest chefs of your time, and I want to be known as the one who discovered you."

"I'm going to do a fantastic job for you, I promise."

"I know you will. Text me your email, and I'll talk to you soon."

He ends the call. I stow my phone in my purse and search for Chase in the crowd. I find him at a table of fresh root vegetables.

"I didn't know what you need, so I grabbed what I like," he explains sheepishly, lifting the basket. "How did it go with O'Toole?"

"You aren't going to believe this, Chase!" I exclaim. "He offered me the job again... this time I accepted!" I expect to see excitement on his face but instead there's only disappointment.

"That's great," he says halfheartedly. "I guess that means I don't need to help you unpack."

I decide, for the moment, to ignore his attitude. I survey the items he's gathered. "I'll grab a fresh chicken, and we can roast everything together for dinner. I'll give you your first cooking lesson," I joke.

He gives me a stiff smile. I grab the bird and pay for the groceries. As we walk back to my place, I confront Chase about his mood.

"Are you mad at me?" I ask.

"No," he tells me, "I'm just surprised that you told O'Toole yes on the spot like that... I thought you'd want to talk something like that over first..."

"Talk it over... with you."

He shrugs. "It's stupid, I know. It's not like you have to ask for my approval..."

"At lunch, you said you'd never let me make a mistake like that again," I remind him. "I thought I had a clear understanding on where you stood on the subject."

"You're right," he says as we arrive at my building. "I'm going to miss you, that's all. I was looking forward to being your friend... and seeing where that leads."

"We can still be friends, Chase," I assure him. "I care about you a lot... More than I expected, too. We can Skype... I don't know anyone in New York. I'll need someone to talk to..."

I pull a roasting pan out of my cabinet. Chase pulls a knife from the block on the counter and starts chopping the vegetables for our meal.

"If my dad reinstates my credit cards, I can fly out and visit once a month," he suggests as he peels a parsnip.

"I can show you around the city." I smile. "And I can come visit you... though probably not as often."

"You're going to be a busy, hot shot chef. I'll take on most of the traveling... There are good culinary schools in New York, aren't there?" he asks softly.

"Yes..." I agree slowly. I like Chase, and I'll miss him when I leave, but I'm not ready for him to move to New York with me.

He notices my hesitation and smiles. "I don't mean now," he laughs. "But maybe later... after we see where this goes..."

"You seem like you're in a better mood," I say as I pat the chicken dry with a roll of paper towels.

"I am," he agrees. "Kiara, I have a confession. That day at Fission, when you pretended you barely knew me? I know it was because of Paul, but it broke my heart. I felt like I'd lost you... and then you call this morning, and I think that I have a real shot. Then this afternoon..."

"James O'Toole called and now I'm moving halfway across the country," I finish. He nods. "I know it's overwhelming," I tell him. "But I have a confession, too... I haven't been able to stop thinking about you since the first night we met. There's something about you that makes me feel comfortable... at home, almost. I can't turn down this opportunity for a second time, but I don't want to lose you either. I hope you feel the same way, and that you'll be patient with me."

Chase sits the knife down on the counter, crosses the room, and puts his arms around me. "If you want to try and have a long distance... friendship, then consider me in."

Chapter Twelve

I take one last walk through my apartment before leaving it forever. My things are packed in boxes, which are stacked around piles of furniture on the living room floor. My essentials are going straight to New York… everything else is going to an Austin storage unit, and I'll have it shipped once I find a rental in the city.

Leaving the bulk of my things in Texas was Chase's idea. He pointed out that storage units, along with everything else, are four times more expensive in New York. Chase has been incredibly helpful and supportive over the past week. We spent every day together, and I'm not looking forward to saying goodbye. But I do know I have to.

Ever since that fateful day that Patrick chose me for the apprenticeship competition, I've lost control of my life. I let someone through my walls and then when things went wrong, I was too proud to admit I'd made a mistake. I kept giving and compromising, until I'd turned into someone I didn't recognize. By accepting James's offer, I am taking back my life. I won't sacrifice that for anyone, even sweet Chase.

The honk of a taxi brings my attention back to the moment. I sold my car to one of Chase's teammates… he is picking me up and taking me to the airport, but there's something I need to take care of before he gets here. I grab my Fission jacket from my closet and meet the taxi at the curb. It's nine a.m., so I give the driver Paul's home address and then work up my resolve as he drives through town.

I haven't spoken to Paul since the night I found him with Jenny. I appreciate that he called James O'Toole, but I don't trust the motives behind it. To me, his actions seem less like an attempt to right a wrong, and more like a desperate attempt to win me back. But whatever the motives, I know I have to see him face to face before I leave. I need closure so I can move on. I know there is a good chance that I'm about to find Jenny and Paul together, but if that's the case, so be it. In fact, it might make moving on a lot easier.

The driver pulls into the parking lot of Paul's building. I ask him to leave the meter running and wait, and I'm relieved when he agrees. I am not planning on staying here long, and I want to be able to make a quick escape. I climb out of the cab, take a deep breath, and make my way to Paul's door. I knock firmly and remind myself to stay strong.

Paul opens the door and greets me with a look of shock. He's wearing a T-shirt and pajama pants, and his hair is disheveled. "Kiara...! Come in... what are you doing here?"

He opens the door wider and I step inside. The house is a mess and has an odd, ripe smell. "I came to say goodbye." I peek into the kitchen and see a pile of empty beer bottles on the counter.

"I thought we already said goodbye." He snorts. "Remember? Last week when you flung your shit into a bag and walked out on me?"

"You're drunk," I say as a statement, not a question. "It's nine-fifteen in the morning, Paul."

"Yeah, pretend you give a damn." He takes a seat on the couch.

"Why don't I make you a cup of coffee?" I suggest impatiently.

"Do what you want." He waves me away. I disappear into the kitchen and slip an espresso cup into the Keurig. I leave the coffee black and return to the living room. Paul is still on the couch, his eyes red from holding back his tears.

"Drink this," I tell him, extending the cup. He accepts it and drinks it in one long gulp.

"I'm sorry, Kiara." He sighs. "And not just for right now... but for everything. I don't know where it all went wrong."

I don't want to get in to this with him, so I change the subject. "Paul, I came over to say goodbye because I'm leaving for New York this afternoon. I accepted the job at The Madden Crowd... I wanted to return this." I pull my Fission jacket from my purse. "And I wanted to thank you for the opportunity to work with you. The personal issues aside, I do appreciate everything you taught me."

Paul shakes his head. "How can you do that, Kiara? Put everything personal aside? I am dying without you... please don't do this... please stay."

"You know I can't do that," I tell him. "But you can't keep throwing your life away. Who's been running the kitchen while you're drowning your sorrows in booze? You have to get it together or you're going to lose everything... the restaurant, the baby..."

"Ah, yes." He snorts. "The baby, that's the best part! I haven't told you!" He laughs... it is obvious the coffee hasn't sobered him up one bit. "Yes, Jenny and the baby. The wrench that busted up our relationship... guess what?" he asks with a disturbing grin.

"What...?" I reply nervously.

"The baby isn't even mine! How do you like that?" He laughs.

"What do you mean the baby isn't yours?" I gasp. "When did you find out...? How did you find out?"

"A week ago," he tells me, "after I found out that Robbs sabotaged your offer from O'Toole. I went to his apartment to confront him and fire him, and guess who I found in his bed?"

"Jenny," I say softly.

"Yep... and even then, I still thought the the baby was mine. I ranted and raved at the two of them, and I told Jenny that I was going to take her to court for full custody... that no child of mine would be raised by a lying whore. I reminded her that I have money, success, and influence, and she's unemployed. That's when she lost it. She told me that I'd never get custody of a child that isn't mine. Robbs put his hand over her belly, and the picture became pretty clear," he says.

"Oh god, Paul, I'm so sorry," I say sincerely. "To find out like that... it must have been awful. I take it that's when all of this drinking started?"

He nods. "And to answer one of your previous questions, Patrick is running the kitchen. He's done it before when I've gone on vacations... I haven't been throwing my life away."

"That's a relief to hear. So... was a paternity test done, or are you taking Jenny's word for it that the baby isn't yours?" I ask nervously.

"I don't need a paternity test," he tells me harshly. "Honestly, a part of me was suspicious from the beginning. I mean, I used a condom... correctly... it didn't make any sense that the baby was mine, but she assured me that there were no other candidates."

I am surprised that he is taking Jenny at her word, but it is not my place to argue with him anymore. The real truth of the baby's paternity will come out eventually, but I don't care what it is and I am glad I won't be here to deal with the fallout.

"Paul, I have a taxi waiting... I need to be going. I'm sorry about the baby. I know you were looking forward to being a father." I lay my chef's jacket over the arm of his sofa and make my way to the door.

"Kiara," he calls after me. "Wait!" I turn and meet his eyes. "I was looking forward to being a dad, but I was looking forward to raising the baby with you. The whole situation was too much for you to deal with, and I understand that. But our circumstances have changed! There's nothing to keep us apart anymore, don't you see that?"

"Paul, please don't do this," I tell him with tears in my eye. "It wouldn't work... too much has happened. We both need to start over, rebuild our lives."

He shakes his head. "No, we need to rebuild our life together. I refuse to accept that it's over. I'm going to win you back, Kiara. I don't care how long it takes, or what I have to do, but I'm going to remind you why you fell in love with me... and I'm going to make you do it again."

My tears are flowing faster now and I struggle to find the right words. "I won't be here to fall in love with you again. I'm leaving Austin today, and I have no reason to ever come back. Please, for your own sake, let me go."

Paul takes my chef's jacket off the arm of his couch. "You know, you returned this to me once before... and then you realized you made a mistake. I have faith that history will repeat itself... you'll see that we're meant to be together. I'm going to keep this in the office for you until you come home. And for the record, I know how to get to New York. There's nowhere you can go that I won't follow. I'll do whatever it takes to show you how much I love you."

He stands from the couch and walks toward me. He has a heart-melting smile on his face and I know that if I don't move, I'm going to find myself in his arms. As tempting as it is to hold him one last time, I back away and open the door.

"Good bye, Paul," I tell him as I step into the hallway.

"Until we meet again," he replies with determination.

I retreat to the taxi... I racked up a fifty-dollar fare and I still have to get home. As the driver pulls onto the street, I'm saddened as I realize the implications of Paul's news. If only we'd known from the beginning that Jenny's baby was Robbs', not Paul's, our lives would be completely different. We'd be happy... drama free. *That is if Jenny is telling the truth about Paul not being the father.* At this point, there's not much that Jenny and Robbs could do to surprise me... except act like decent people.

As heart-wrenching as it is to think that my relationship with Paul was destroyed because of a lie, I know, baby or no baby, I'm better off without him. After spending so much time with Chase, I can see now that Paul is selfish and demanding. I see it because Chase is the opposite, and I'm enjoying the difference. I hope Paul doesn't follow through with his plans to try and win me back. I still love him, but after everything that's happened between us, I know I'll never be able to trust him again.

I don't know if Chase and I will continue our relationship after I move, but I want to try. I let him kiss me twice over the past few days. Both were light and sweet, more romantic of a kiss than you'd give your mother but not so passionate that they led to anything else. *I meant what I said that day in the barbecue place... I want us to really get to know each other before we get serious.* Chase says that in the South, the relationship I want is called 'courting'. We personalized the term to 'long-distance courting' to fit our situation.

I check the time on my phone as the taxi pulls up to the stoop of my building. My heart races... Chase should be here anytime, and in just two hours I'll be on a plane on my way to my new life. I don't know what I'll find in New York City, but I am confident that, aside from Chase, it will be better than everything I'm leaving behind.

-To be continued in Book 3-

Book Three

Chapter One

I STEP into my steam shower, seal the door behind me, and turn on the spray. As the hot water falls over my aching muscles, the enclosed walls trap the relaxing steam in the stall. I reach for one of my fancy new aromatherapy body washes and marvel at the way my life has changed in the last month.

I'd arrived in New York City four and a half weeks ago, shell shocked and numbed by Jenny's revelation: Robbs was the father of her unborn child, not Paul. I tried to tell myself that the news didn't change anything, but deep down I knew the truth. If Jenny had been honest from the beginning, Paul and I would still be together. I've been thinking about that a lot since I arrived in the city, and I still can't decide if that would have been a good thing or a bad thing.

The flight landed at JFK Airport at ten p.m. on a cold March night. Having had to take care of myself since the age of sixteen, I'd never had the money to visit Dallas, much less somewhere as far away as New York City. James O'Toole, my new boss, had arranged for a car to pick me up from the airport and take me to The Plaza, where I'd be staying until I found an apartment. I'd told James that I'd be happy to stay somewhere more affordable, but he'd laughed off the suggestion and insisted that I have the best. That was my first sign that life in New York would be unlike anything I'd ever experienced.

As the Town Car carried me through the city, I became so absorbed in my new hometown that I completely forgot about Paul, Jenny, and all of the drama I'd just left behind. New York had an amazing energy, and I was ready to be a part of it. As we crossed the bridge into Manhattan, I pulled out my cell phone and blocked Paul and Jenny's numbers. I wanted to cut all ties with my old life so I could fully experience my new one. All ties that is, except for Chase.

When I arrived at the hotel that first night, a package was waiting for me at the front desk. I waited until I was alone in my elegant room before opening it. The box contained a subway pass, individual maps of each borough, an electronic planner, and an envelope. I broke the seal and found a letter and a Platinum card. The letter was from James, telling me that he'd be out of town for the next month filming the overseas finale of *Kitchen Wars*.

You've got a lot of work to get done before I get back. I've listed forty of the greatest restaurants in the city in the enclosed planner. I expect you to visit all of them and have critiques ready when I return home. I've also made several appointments for you. They are listed in the planner as well. The real estate agent will show you apartments within the budget I authorized. Use the credit card for your meals and to pay everyone else.

I'd immediately scanned through the planner; not only would I be meeting with the real estate agent, I also had meetings scheduled with a hairstylist, a personal shopper, and my new faculty advisor at The Culinary Institute of New York.

My first week in the city was an absolute nightmare. Between making it to all of my appointments and fitting in one of my assigned restaurants, I barely had time to take a breath. But on my third day, I met with the amazing Myra Owens, who showed me my dream home. It was the third apartment I looked at, and I immediately knew that I had to have it. I now live in a spacious studio; it's modern and elegant, with hardwood floors and quartz countertops. It's only a one bedroom, but it's more than enough space for me. I still haven't recovered from the shock of learning just how much James O'Toole was willing to spend to keep me happy in the city.

I lather the citrusy soap over my body and reach for the shampoo that was custom blended for my hair. Frankie, the stylist James had sent me to, was a genius blend of chemist and artist. He'd given me highlights and lowlights and then whipped up several products for me to take home. When I'd pulled out my Platinum card, he'd shaken his head.

"Mr. O'Toole has already taken care of it," he'd told me.

Each of the personal shoppers I'd met with had said the same thing. When I'd called James and insisted that I couldn't accept any more gifts or favors from him, he'd simply laughed.

"I'm in the limelight," he'd explained. "Photographers follow me everywhere I go. As my apprentice, you'll now be photographed just as much as

I am. I insist that you look your best at all times. Anything less would be contradictory to my brand."

From that point on, I hadn't felt bad about spending his money. I ordered everything I wanted from the restaurants I visited, to the point that I often took half of it home for later. I didn't worry about the price of the clothes I bought on Fifth Avenue, and I added enormous tips to every receipt I signed. After all, generosity had to be good for 'the brand'.

But my four weeks of play time have run out; James flew in last night, and I have to report for my first day on the job in an hour. I turn off the water and step out onto the heated stone floor. I wrap myself in a fluffy towel and head into my closet to decide what to wear. I assume that I'll be spending most of my day in the kitchen, covered in a chef's coat, so I select a pair of lightweight black slacks and a designer white silk T-shirt. I put on a light layer of makeup before sliding into the clothes and blast my hair with a blow dryer. I stop with my hair still a bit damp, gather it in the middle of my head, and weave it into an intricate braid. I twist the braid into a bun, secure it with bobby pins, and pronounce myself ready for the day.

One of the best things about my new apartment is its location. I'm within walking distance of both Central Park and The Madden Crowd, the five-star Michelin restaurant that is now my place of employment. After a quick stop in my kitchen to fill my travel mug with coffee, I grab my keys and leave the apartment. I ride the elevator down six floors, walk through the marble entryway, and step out onto the busy sidewalk.

I've walked my route several times in the past few weeks, trying to gauge how long it will take to get to work. My best time has been eleven minutes, the worst twenty-seven. I've learned that the time of day plays a big role in how fast you can move about the city. Today, the trip takes me just under fifteen minutes; I'm fifteen minutes early for work.

The Madden Crowd may be the only fine dining restaurant in New York that I haven't sampled yet. James had been adamant that I not step into the place until he returned; it didn't really make sense to me, but I'd felt it pointless to argue. An apprentice's job is to do as they're told, and I didn't want to start off on the wrong foot.

I take a deep breath and pull open the birch door. A thin, blonde woman in a fitted black dress greets me with a look of confusion. I glance around at the customers in the dining room and realize that I'm horribly underdressed.

"Hello," I greet her sheepishly. "My name is Kiara Sands. I'm supposed to start working with Chef O'Toole today… I'm sure there's a back entrance or something that I'm supposed to use…" I trail off.

"Just a second…" She pushes her long hair to the side and reaches for an earpiece. I realize that she's wearing a discrete intercom system, and I'm impressed with how up-to-speed the place is technology-wise. As I wait for the woman to turn back to me, I take a closer look at the dining room. The restaurant has clean white walls adorned with delicate, intricate birch carvings. The scenes depict all sorts of nature elements, and the sleek stone floors draw the look together perfectly. It's one of the most beautiful restaurants I've ever stepped foot in.

The blonde turns back to me with a stiff smile. "Chef Sands? Chef O'Toole will be up shortly."

"Thank you," I tell her warmly. "I'm sorry I didn't get your name?"

"I'm Vanessa," she tells me with an air of boredom.

"It's very nice to meet you, Vanessa."

"Do I hear that charming Texas drawl?" James calls out playfully as he approaches. He greets me with a hug. "Kiara, I'm so happy you're here. Forgive Vanessa's greeting; the staff usually enters through the kitchen. You didn't know, and that's my fault. I was so tired when I landed last night that I forgot to send you an email."

"It's no problem," I assure him. "I've just been admiring the dining room. Did you design the restaurant yourself?"

"Oh, please." James laughs with a dismissive wave. "Of course not. I hired a designer… a team of them actually. And that was after I hired the market researchers and the branding specialists… I'm glad that you like the place, though. Follow me, and I'll show you where the real genius happens."

He leads me across the dining room and through a set of swinging birch doors. My jaw drops as I lay eyes on the kitchen. I'd thought that Fission was luxurious. In The Madden Crowd kitchen, each chef had their own work area twice the size of the kitchen in my Austin apartment. The appliances are state of the art and plentiful; six ice cream machines churn on the back wall while pheasant, venison, and elk spin in a massive rotisserie. A staff of sixteen works on the food without shooting a single glance in our direction.

James sees the look of awe on my face and smiles. "The money I've spent on you so far kind of makes sense now, doesn't it? What's a five-hundred dollar haircut to a man with a three-million dollar kitchen?"

I'm too impressed by the kitchen to be put off by his arrogance. "This is amazing… I can't believe that I get to work here."

"Not just yet," James tells me with a smile. "First, I thought we'd go to my office, and I'll explain the apprenticeship position."

I think the position is pretty straightforward, but again, he's the boss. "Lead the way," I tell him with a smile. The right wall of the kitchen has two doors. The second obviously leads to the walk-in cooler; I follow James through the first.

The room is small but clean, with just enough space to hold a desk, a filing cabinet, and two chairs. James sits behind his computer, and I settle in across from him.

"I take it that you've completed your homework and have tried the restaurants I listed in your planner?" he asks as he shuffles through his top drawer.

I nod.

"Fantastic. Consider that an ongoing assignment. Food trends are constantly revolving. It's imperative for an executive chef to always be aware of what his… or her… competitors are serving. Did you bring your critiques?"

"Yes." I hold up a thick spiral notebook.

"Jesus, don't you have an iPad?" he asks in disbelief.

"Until last month, I was a struggling culinary student." I laugh. "If I'd known that an iPad is required, I would have charged one."

"They're not required, but I'll order you one anyway. They're fucking useful… okay," he says, turning back to my notebook. "We'll go over your thoughts on everyone else's food after we've made some of our own. But before we start cooking, I want to explain what your normal day will be like. I run things a lot differently than Weston. You're *my* apprentice, which means that you work with no one else. I'm in the kitchen Thursday, Friday, and Saturday nights and all day Sundays… when I'm not traveling or shooting the show, of course. On Tuesdays and Wednesdays, I come in and work the end of the lunch rush through the beginning of dinner hours. My sous chefs can handle things on their own, but I like to be here at least a couple of hours a day. My schedule will be your schedule. Any questions?"

"Is there a set day that you usually do menu planning?" I ask.

"Carter handles all of the menu planning," he tells me. "That's my lead sous chef. I let him know when there's something specific I want to make, but otherwise I let him take the reins."

I nod. "I assume he does the inventory and ordering as well?"

"Of course not," James laughs. "Raven, my kitchen manager, handles all of that."

"You have a really large staff," I observe.

"That's the secret of running a successful business without having to live in it," he explains with a shrug. "The most important aspects of being an executive chef aren't taught in culinary school. You have to know how to spot talent in others and how to delegate to those people. Otherwise, you lose your mind and then your business. Like your old boss Weston," he adds with a cocky grin.

"What do you mean, like Paul?" I ask. "Fission is doing incredibly well… at least it was just a month ago."

"You haven't talked to him then? That's good." James gives me an approving nod. "Paul Weston doesn't deserve you, in his kitchen or anywhere else. I'm glad you've cut off contact with him."

"There's only one person from Austin that I'm still in contact with, and it's not Paul," I tell him. "But what were you talking about before? Is Fission in trouble?"

James shrugs. "I'm sure he's still filling seats, but word in the industry is that he's burning out fast. His menu's been static, the kitchen is sending out sloppy plates… he's stopped paying attention to the small, important details. If he doesn't snap out of it soon, he'll be closing the doors within the year."

"Well, I hate to hear that, but Paul Weston is no longer any of my concern. Back to the topic of my schedule… I'm used to spending twice that amount of time in the kitchen… what else will I be doing? And what will I do when you're shooting the show or on vacation?"

"You'll be doing whatever I'm doing," he explains. "If I'm shooting *Kitchen Wars*, you'll come to the set. If I'm doing an interview, you'll tag along to that as well. As far as my vacations, you're always welcome to join me, or you can relax and have free time to yourself. Your salary will remain the same, regardless of the amount of time we spend cooking."

I'm completely confused. The whole point of serving as an apprentice to a talented chef is to learn how to improve your food. James sees the confusion on my face and smiles again.

"Look, Kiara, I know that most chefs spend a hundred hours a week in the kitchen, showing their apprentice all of the tricks of the trade. I don't have time for that, which is why I hardly ever take on apprentices. But you've already got the talent; there's not much that I could teach you about food that you don't already know, or won't learn from the culinary institute. I don't intend on grooming you for a life in the kitchen. I want to groom you for a life in the spotlight, a life like mine. How does that sound to you?"

I take a moment and think about how elegant and expensive my life has become over the last four weeks. And if James does what he's promising, this is only the beginning. I could have a life of glamour and adventure… travel the world and taste all kinds of exotic cuisine.

I look at James and smile. "A life in the spotlight sounds just fine to me."

Chapter Two

James and I return to the kitchen for our four-hour shift. He doesn't bother to introduce me to any of the other chefs, so I nod politely and vow to make my own introductions when I have a chance.

He does give me a tour of the kitchen. His walk-in cooler is almost as large as the dining room; beef ages on large hooks in a far corner and fresh seafood chills on ice. Between the walk-in and the pantry, there's probably almost half a million dollars' worth of food in the kitchen.

I spot a case of black beluga caviar and realize that I'm completely unfamiliar with the restaurant's menu. I don't want to admit my ignorance, so I act unfazed as I survey the expensive ingredients. Luckily, I don't have to act for long. He leads me to his cooking area, which is three times the size of the rest. He pulls a menu out of a drawer and tosses it on the butcher-block table.

"Look through this. Pick one dish, and I'll teach you how to make it from start to finish," he instructs.

"We aren't supporting the kitchen staff?" I ask with confusion.

"Have you already forgotten our entire conversation?" James laughs. "My kitchen doesn't need any support. I can oversee and teach at the same time. I'm great at multi-tasking."

"Okay," I agree quickly. *This is NOTHING like Fission. Is this really happening? Do I get to skip all of the hard stuff?* Most chefs have to start as prep or line cooks and work their way up. I'm still in culinary school, and I don't even have to cook for the guests.

"Kiara… the menu." James pushes the small binder my way and brings my attention back to the present.

"Right," I answer quickly as I flip open the cover. The menu is extensive. The appetizers take up two pages, the entrees four. A single page of desserts completes the binder. The overall theme of the cuisine seems to be game meats and seafood cooked with modern techniques; I can't wait to get started.

"Is this what we'll be doing every time we're in the kitchen? Just practicing dishes one on one?" I ask him.

James nods. "Unless we have a big VIP party or half the staff gets sick."

"Then let's just start with the first appetizer and work our way through the whole thing," I suggest.

"All right, he laughs. "Though I reserve the right to switch things up from time to time."

"Deal."

"Okay, most of the apps are pretty simple, so we'll do three of them today. We'll do the squab breast pot-stickers, venison kabobs, and the roasted shrimp cocktail," he suggests.

"Sounds good to me," I agree quickly. I can't wait to taste the food, and I eagerly follow him to the pantry. We gather what we need and move on to the walk-in. James sets the pantry basket on the floor and turns to me as I study the protein shelves.

"I'm glad you're here, Kiara." He leans in close; quickly wraps me in an embrace and puts his lips to mine. He kisses me lightly and then pulls away. I don't realize what's happening until it's too late.

"Let me say something, before you slap me." His arms are still around me, and I don't try to pull away.

"I'm listening…" I tell him.

"First… what just happened? That's not why I hired you. And if you never want it to happen again, that's fine. But we're two attractive adults, who have a lot in common. We're going to be spending a lot of time together… so if you ever need to… scratch an itch, as they say… the offer is on the table."

He stares at me longingly as he waits for my response. His turquoise eyes are piercing and smolder with an intensity that I can't resist. This man is responsible for the last four weeks, the most amazing month of my life. He's also drop-dead gorgeous, famous, and incredibly wealthy. The man has his own 'brand' for god's sake; a girl could do a lot worse.

I take him by the back of the head and pull him in. Our lips meet again; we tease each other with light kisses and then amp up the passion. He pushes me against the food rack, and I wrap my legs around his waist. James reaches up my T-shirt, and I have a flash of sanity.

"We can't do this," I tell him. "Not here. I refuse to earn that kind of reputation. What happens in the privacy of our own homes is one thing, but I'm not going to jeopardize my career."

James laughs, backs away, and sets me on my feet. "You're smart, Kiara… and driven. I like that. I'm smart and driven, too. And you're absolutely right; this isn't the place for this to happen… just remember that it's always an option."

"I'll do that," I tell him. "Now can we please go cook some appetizers?"

Robbs Martin sits in a small diner in an upscale area of Manhattan. He is disguised in a convincing black wig and thick, black plastic glasses. He has become a regular at the place, much to the dismay of the restaurant staff. When he isn't bitching about the price of his food, he is offering unsolicited advice about how it could be improved. Most of the time, he just drinks coffee and stares out the window.

Robbs' life has gone to hell in a hand-basket, and he knows exactly who to blame: Kiara Sands. The quiet little bitch had somehow woven her way into his life and destroyed everything he had. She'd stolen the apprenticeship out from under him by sleeping with the boss. Sure, Paul pretended to hand the decision over to a couple of the other chefs, but everyone knew that was just a way to cover his own ass. Patrick and the rest of the chefs knew damn well who they had to award the position to if they wanted to keep their own jobs once the competition was over.

And as if stealing the apprenticeship wasn't enough, Kiara had come in like a wrecking ball and demolished his plan B. If he'd gotten his way, Robbs would still be quietly working alongside Paul, thinking of ways to help Jenny spend the child support money the executive chef would be doling out for a kid that wasn't even his. But instead, Kiara had put the idea of full custody in Paul's head. When Paul threatened Jenny with the idea, she panicked and admitted that the baby was really Robbs'. Paul had promptly fired him and taken out a restraining order against the couple.

But he's not the one who should be worried, Robbs thinks smugly as he watches Kiara's building. He'd been relieved when Kiara moved into a building without a doorman. It had been hard to keep an eye on her while she was staying at The Plaza. There was no way for him to get to her there.

That's not a problem anymore, he reminds himself with evil satisfaction. *She is right out in the open. I can get to her whenever I want.*

Robbs turns back to the waitress and signals for a refill of his coffee. He looks back to Kiara's building and smiles in amusement at what he sees. *I guess I'm not the only one who can find you, Kiara.* He smiles.

The waitress arrives with the coffee pot and notices the grin on his face. "In a good mood tonight, Tom?" she asks; Robbs had been smart enough not to give anyone his real name.

"Yes, Wanda," he grins, "there's nothing more heartwarming than a reunion of old friends."

<<◇>>

The rest of my day with James is uneventful compared to our three hot minutes in the cooler. A part of me, a big part, knows that I have no business getting involved with my new celebrity boss, even if it is only casual. But he's done so much for me, and he's so good looking…

Chase, I remind myself, *Chase is a GOOD guy, and if all goes well he'll be moving here soon… I can't get involved with my boss.*

James seems to sense that I'm rethinking our encounter but he doesn't push it. We spend the next three and a half hours preparing the appetizers. James' technique is flawless, and I know that I've done the right thing by moving to New York. Paul had always insisted that James was a fraud, but I see now that was his jealousy talking.

We finish cooking and carry our plates to James' office. He pushes his personal intercom and orders a bottle of wine from the bar.

"Now comes the part where we enjoy our meal, and I read over your critiques of the restaurants I had you visit," he explains.

"So… you're going to read it quietly, and I'm just going to sit here?" I ask. "We aren't going to… discuss them?" I feel awkward at the idea of sitting silently as James critiques my critiques.

"I'll read fast and then we'll discuss them. Eat, while the food is hot."

Another woman in a fitted black dress enters with a bottle of wine, a bottle of chilled sparkling water, and two glasses. James doesn't bother to introduce me to her either; she deposits the drinks on the desk and turns back to the door without saying a word.

"Thanks, Monica," James calls after her as she leaves.

"Are you ever going to actually introduce me to my coworkers?" I tease.

"I'll get around to it eventually, I guess," he answers dismissively as he opens my notebook. He skims the pages while I nibble at a pot-sticker and drink more wine than I should. He finally finishes and studies me silently for a while before speaking.

"You have an excellent palate and impeccable taste in food. The same taste as mine," he adds with a devilish smile.

"Thank you." I throw a glance at the clock; it's getting late, and I have class in the morning.

James sees that I'm getting antsy and offers me an out. "I know that you have class tomorrow, if you need to get home and prep for it, I completely understand. I'll see you Wednesday." He stands and walks me to the door.

I thank him and make my way to the kitchen exit; the back door leads to an alley, but fortunately it's also close to the street. The sky is dreary; I walk three blocks from the restaurant and the clouds open up with rain. I pull my umbrella from my bag and speed walk toward my apartment; I stop short, half a block away. Sitting on my doorstep, getting drenched in the rain, is Jenny Foster.

<<<>>>

I see her, but she doesn't see me. I sigh and resume my walk home. I don't know how Jenny found me or what she wants, but I do know that I can't avoid her. It's best to just get it over with, I tell myself as I approach her. She sees me and smiles sheepishly.

"Hi, Kiara."

"Jenny… what are you doing here?" I ask coldly.

Tears well in her eyes. "I didn't have anywhere else to go… could I come up? Just for a minute… I didn't realize how cold it is up here, and then it started raining."

I finally notice that Jenny is wearing a lightweight cotton dress and ballet flats; spring must already be in full force back in Texas. Jenny's shivering and, while I don't care about her comfort, I do care about the well-being of her innocent baby.

"Follow me," I tell her. "You can put on my bathrobe, and I'll dry your clothes."

I unlock the front door; Jenny follows me through the entryway, and we ride silently up the elevator.

"This is a really nice building. You must be doing well here," Jenny observes as I fumble with my keys. I finally find the right one and slide it into the lock.

"I'm doing great," I tell her as I push open the door. "Leaving Austin behind was the best decision I ever made."

I watch her face as she observes my apartment, and I know that she's impressed. "The bathroom is down that hall," I tell her, "first door on the left. I'll make some hot tea while you change."

Jenny nods and disappears down the hallway. I step in to my kitchen and set a kettle to boil. I fill two balls with loose tea and toss them into mugs. Jenny reappears just as the kettle starts to whistle.

"This is an amazing apartment… I can't believe this kitchen," she says in awe.

"James insisted that I have the best appliances possible," I explain. "He says that a chef is only as good as his tools."

I take her wet dress to the nearby laundry room and toss it into the dryer. "It'll be dry and warm in about half an hour," I tell Jenny as I return to the kitchen. "Which should be just enough time for you to explain what you're doing here."

Jenny looks down and blows on her steaming mug; she seems to get lost in thought for a moment before responding. "Back in the beginning… before Robbs and Paul… I thought that you and I were really becoming friends. I know that I fucked up royally, I know that I lied to you and that I ruined what you had with Paul… but I'm desperate, Kiara. I don't know where to turn. The baby will be here in just a few months, and I have no one to help me."

Instead of feeling pity for her, I feel rage. "Let me get this straight." I begin calmly. "Paul wants nothing to do with you because the baby isn't his… and I'm assuming that the second Paul's money was no longer a possibility, Robbs kicked you out on your ass, too… and now you're coming to ME for help? You think that since I'm making good money now, I'll forgive you and let you freeload off of me? Seriously, Jenny?"

"For god's sake, Kiara, I'm pregnant and alone," Jenny sobs. "Don't you have any compassion?"

"Both of those things are entirely your fault," I remind her. "Along with a laundry list of other things."

"I'm sorry, Kiara," she says again. "But I didn't know what else to do. I sold my car and all of my furniture before I left Austin. I thought maybe… if I can't stay here… I could find my own place… and maybe we can hang out… I could have a chance to make things up to you."

"First of all, there's no way you're staying here," I tell her firmly. "Second of all, I don't believe you. You're not looking for redemption, Jenny, you're looking for another free ride. You won't find it here, so if that's all, I'll go get your dress."

I walk back to the laundry room, thankful that Jenny isn't trying to argue with me. I'm in no mood for anymore of her pleas and insincere apologies. I return to the kitchen, toss the dress to her, and stomp into the living room. Five minutes later, she appears in the doorway, once again wearing her lightweight dress. I sigh and stomp over to my coat closet. I grab one of the oversized hoodies that I usually jog in.

"You should be able to get into this," I tell her as I toss her the sweatshirt. "I may lack compassion, but I won't have you catching your death of cold walking around in the rain. Don't bother returning it, I can afford more." I coldly open the front door.

Jenny steps out in the hallway and turns back to me. "Thank you for the sweatshirt, Kiara. I'm going to make everything up to you, I promise. You may hate me now, but I'll find a way."

I slam the door in her face without responding.

Chapter Three

As I cram the last of a club sandwich into my mouth, my cell phone starts to ring. I look at the screen and roll my eyes. James knows my class schedule… why in the hell is he bothering me today?

In order to fit in enough credit hours to maintain my scholarship and still have plenty of time for work, I'd scheduled all of my classes on Tuesdays and Thursdays. Tuesdays are my heaviest days, and I'd had just enough time between Saucier and Pastry to run home for a quick lunch.

I glance at my oven clock and see that I have an hour before I have to be in class; it will take me half that to get back to campus. I look at my crumb-filled plate and wonder if saving money will always be my first instinct. Here I am living in an expensive Manhattan apartment, rushing around like a chicken with my head cut off to save a few bucks on food.

I'm having trouble accepting my new life and my new spending budget because I just don't trust that it will last. Being in the city and working for James has given me the same kind of rush I had at the beginning of my relationship with Paul. I've learned the hard way that those types of feelings never last. I'm happy here in New York, but my new life hangs in the mercy of James O'Toole. Once again, I've found myself in a situation where my life's happiness depends on a man I don't trust.

With a tired sigh, I sling my bag over my shoulder and set off for the subway. As I maneuver the busy streets, I have the overwhelming feeling that someone is watching me. I look over my shoulder several times but I don't spot anything odd, just a hoard of people, all trying to get somewhere fast.

Assuring myself I'm just being paranoid, I arrive at the subway station and rush onto a train. I find a seat in the back, where I can see everyone else in the car. I don't recognize anyone and nobody pays much attention to me, so I feel even more confident that I was overreacting on the street. The train pulls into the station, and I have an uneventful walk to campus. I arrive at my classroom with only two minutes to spare.

Next week, I'm eating lunch nearby, I promise myself as I slide into a seat. My classmates are already settled around me; Chef Ballard, a tall, stern man with no patience for foolishness, enters the room and class begins.

"Good afternoon, Chefs," he greets us. "We've covered all of the fundamentals, so today we're actually going to do some cooking. We're going to start with a simple pastry choux. That should be basic knowledge at this point in your education, but I need to see where everyone is at, technique wise. Everything you need has already been placed at your stations. You have one hour."

My classmates and I all stand at once and make our way to the station. I'm by no means a five-star pastry chef, but I spent enough time with Claire in the Fission kitchen to feel confident about the task at hand. As I cut my butter into the pastry flour, the sensation that I'm being watched returns.

Maybe someone's trying to copy my technique. Do NOT turn around. I repeat the reassurances over and over in my head, but I only feel more anxious. The sensation gets more intense, and I give in to the urge to look behind me; no one is there who shouldn't be.

I tell myself I'm just not used to the city yet, but the anxiety doesn't subside. I feel like I'm in a horror move, in that brief moment when the heroine realizes that she's in trouble but trouble hasn't actually appeared yet.

"Kiara Sands!" a familiar, unwelcome voice calls out happily behind me.

I jump and cringe at the same time. I take a deep breath, turn, and meet him with a cold stare.

"What are you doing here, Robbs?" I ask angrily but as quietly as possible.

"I was in the city, so I thought I'd come visit. I wasn't sure where you live, so this was the only place I could think of to track you down."

"There are thousands of student on this campus," I tell him as fear fills my body. "There's no way you just happened to walk into the right classroom."

Chef Ballard is approaching, and he looks pissed.

"So maybe I hung out outside for a while and waited until I saw you," Robbs says with a shrug.

"Chef *Sands*!" Chef Ballard hisses as he approaches. "I don't know how that school in Texas runs things, but here at The Culinary Institute of New York, we act like professionals. Guests are not allowed in the classroom."

"I apologize, Chef Ballard," I tell him quickly. "Robbs didn't know any better. He was just leaving, weren't you, Robbs?" I take his arm and try to lead him to the door.

Robbs doesn't budge. Instead, he turns to Chef Ballard and I brace myself for the disaster I'm sure is about to happen.

"Actually, Chef, I did know better but I came here anyway. You see, I'm something of a chef myself, and I've been trying to get in to the New York program. I guess there's been some sort of miscommunication or technical error, because my admission has been stalled. Forgive me, but I know that you sit on the admissions board… I was hoping that I could cook for you, dazzle you with my skill, and then you could get the ball rolling for me in time to enroll for summer classes."

Chef Ballard regards Robbs with silent distain for several long moments before turning to me. "Get this… person out of my classroom."

I nod at him, take Robbs by the arm once more, and glance around the classroom. No one is working on their pastry choux. Instead, all eyes are on me and the nightmare I thought I'd left behind.

"Robbs, please," I beg him. "Just go."

"Kiara, if I didn't know better, I'd think that you aren't happy to see me," he says loudly, still grounded to his spot. "I bet you'd be happy to see Paul… or anyone else you could sleep with to get ahead. That's why we never got along, isn't it? You like people who can give you something… money, prestige… and you know just how to get it, don't you?"

I have never felt so mortified in all of my life. I wish that I could just sink in to the floor and never have to see Chef Ballard or any of my classmates ever again. I open my mouth to insist that Robbs leave, but he cuts me off. He turns to Chef Ballard.

"Tell me, big guy, are you screwing her yet? If not, you totally can. Offer her an A, and I'll bet she'll do anything you ask." Robbs sneers.

"That's it," Chef Ballard exclaims. "Young man, I don't know who you are, but I'll be sure to get your name from Chef Sands. After this little stunt, I will ensure that you're never accepted into this fine institution. You have thirty seconds to leave, or I am alerting security."

"I'll go, I'll go," Robbs insists, holding up his hands in defeat. "I just thought that you might like to know who you're working with. Kiara, I'll be seeing you."

He walks through the room and out the door with his head held high and a cocky grin spread. I don't feel any relief; forty-six pairs of eyes are trained on me, trying to figure out what just happened.

"I'm so sorry," I tell Chef Ballard. "I knew him in Austin… we weren't friends. And nothing he said about me is true."

"True or not, what just went on here is completely unacceptable," he replies harshly. "In all of my years as an instructor, I've never witnessed anything so… so unsavory. Chef Sands, please gather your things. You've proven to be quite the distraction tonight, and the rest of the class still has dough to finish."

"But…"

"But nothing, Chef Sands. You are dismissed for the night. You may return to class next Tuesday, if you've managed to rid yourself of unwelcomed guests by then."

He nods and turns away from me, and I know that the conversation is over. I roll up my knives, toss them into my bag, and leave the room feeling defeated.

<<◇>>

Robbs is waiting for me just outside of the building. My rage returns full force when I lay eyes on him.

"What the *fuck* are you doing here?" I insist angrily. "And what the *fuck* was that?"

"Out of class so soon, Kiara?" he asks mockingly. "I thought I'd be waiting another hour, at least."

"I got kicked out. Congratulations, are you happy? You did what you came here to do. You can leave now." I try to turn away, but he grabs me by the arm.

"But, Kiara, I *haven't* done what I came here to do. All that up there with your teacher and your classmates? That was just a bit of fun… call it the icing on my cake," he says with an evil look in his eyes.

"Take your fucking hand off of me," I growl and pull free from him. "Tell me, Robbs, what did you come here to do?"

"To make you apologize, of course." He grins. "You ruined my life, Kiara Sands. You're going to acknowledge that, and you're going to make it up to me."

"I will do no such thing," I tell him with a laugh. "Everything you're dealing with, you've brought on yourself. And I pray every day for Jenny's baby… having the misfortune of having you as a sperm donor."

Robbs remains unfazed by my words. Instead of reacting, he looks at me with hell-bent determination and smiles. "You're going to apologize to me one day, Kiara. And you're going to pay for what you've taken from me."

Robbs looks at something behind me and takes a few steps back; I turn and see a campus security guard approaching us.

"Excuse me," the guard calls out from ten feet away. "Ma'am, are you Kiara Sands?"

"Yes," I answer with relief.

"Ms. Sands, Mr. Ballard called the office about ten minutes ago and asked us to make sure that you made it off campus okay… he said you'd had an unwanted visitor, and he was concerned about your safety." The guard looked directly at Robbs while speaking to me.

"Thank you, Officer Parker," I say, reading his badge. "Yes, Mr. Martin doesn't seem to understand that I don't want to speak with him. I'd appreciate an escort off campus."

Officer Parker nods and leans in toward Robbs. "Look, man, I don't know what's going on here, but I'm sure that you don't want any trouble. If the lady doesn't want to talk to you, that means you walk away. Ms. Sands, I'm ready when you are."

I nod at him and turn to Robbs. I feel emboldened by Officer Parker's presence and say more than I should. "Look you sad, pathetic excuse for a man. I'm sorry that Paul fired you for trying to pass your own kid off as his. I don't know what kind of delusional world you've slipped into, but none of your problems are my fault. Stay the fuck away from me, or I'll make you sorry you ever stepped foot in the city."

I turned away from him and Officer Parker and I started walking down the sidewalk. "You don't own New York, Kiara," Robbs calls after me. "You can't make me stay away."

Chapter Four

The walk to the edge of campus takes five minutes, and I'm sad to part ways with my protector. Officer Parker offers to call the NYPD and help me file a harassment report, but I don't have the energy to wait around for a unit to drive out. I assure him that I'll be just fine and set off for the subway station.

Three blocks away from campus, I realize that I'm still in trouble. I don't know where he is, but I know that he's still close by, watching me. A sick feeling spreads from my stomach through the rest of my body as I realize that Robbs probably knows where I live. I pick up my pace, tossing quick glances over my shoulder as I rush toward the subway station. While looking for Robbs behind me, I run smack dab into a thick, solid body.

"Kiara? What's wrong?" another familiar voice asks.

I look up in disbelief. *What the fuck is going ON? Why are they ALL suddenly HERE?*

"Nothing's wrong, Paul," I answer with a resigned sigh. "Everything's perfect… what are you doing here?"

"I came to find you," he explains simply. "Please, Kiara, I came all this way. Will you sit down and have a cup of coffee with me?"

As he looks at me hopefully, I scan the crowds around us for any sign of Robbs. He's nowhere to be found, and I breathe a little easier.

"Kiara, are you sure that you're all right?" Paul asks again.

"I'm fine," I quickly reply. "And you're right. You've come all of this way, the least I can do is sit down and drink a cup of coffee with you. I actually know a great place nearby. Follow me."

I turn and walk back toward the college. Paul follows me, and I have to admit that it's exhilarating, knowing that he's come all of this way to see me. The walk to Maude's takes ten minutes; we travel them in silence.

"This is a quaint little place," Paul observes as we step into the coffee shop. Maude's is decorated in the same Roaring Twenties décor it's had since it opened its doors in 1923. The equipment is modern, and the baristas make a fantastic cup of coffee.

"The coffee is good, and it's inexpensive," I tell him. "I stop in between my classes for caffeine boosts."

We place our orders at the counter; the barista tells us to take a seat and promises to deliver our coffees to the table. Paul and I slide into opposite sides of a booth; sitting here face to face, we're forced to actually speak to each other.

"You were right about their prices being low… though I'm surprised you even worry about that anymore. From what I hear, you're living the good life these days," Paul tells me.

"And who are you hearing from?" I ask. "Jenny?"

He nods. "She called me the other night, after she left your place. She said that Fission could damn near fit in your apartment."

"So what if it would?" I ask defensively. "Since when is it a crime to be successful?"

"Kiara, I'm sorry. I didn't mean it that way… I think that we got off on the wrong foot, can we just start over?"

"We've already started over… so many times," I sigh.

"I know." He blushes. "That's not what I meant."

"So we'll start over, like I just bumped in to you. What are you doing here, Paul? You said that you needed to see me, but you haven't said why."

"Isn't it obvious?" he asks me with a sad smile. "I needed to see you because this last month has been hell. I owe you an apology for the way I treated you that last time you came to my apartment."

"You owe me apologies for a hell of a lot more than that," I remind him.

The barista arrives with our coffees, and we sit quietly until he leaves.

"I know that, Kiara," Paul continues. "And if you give me a chance, I will make all of it up to you. I just need you to come home, I can't function without you."

"I'm happy here, Paul," I tell him quietly.

"I know that you are," he sighs. "Why wouldn't you be? I know that I can't compete with O'Toole. I don't have millions of dollars, and I can't put you up in a fancy apartment. But I love you, Kiara. My life is empty without you. Please say that you'll consider giving me another chance. We can put all of the bullshit with Jenny and Robbs behind us. We can have the life we were supposed to have all along."

"It's not that easy." I study his face and remember that there was a time I'd have done anything to hear those words. I've imagined this moment over and over again, but the reality is nothing like I'd expected. I don't feel a rush of love, or relief, or anything really, except pity. Paul stands and slides into the booth next to me.

"I know that it won't be easy," Paul agrees. "But nothing worth having is… I love you, Kiara. You're good for me. And I don't know how much longer I can go on without you."

He puts one arm around my shoulder and flashes that heart-melting smile. It's as powerful as ever, and I'm helpless to resist him. I lean in to his embrace and our lips meet.

Paul's touch is familiar, but it's no longer exciting. I kiss him eagerly, trying to find a hint of our old spark; nothing's there. I pull away and study his face silently for a while.

"Look, Paul," I finally sigh. "I appreciate the apologies, and I forgive you. But I think that it's just too late for us…"

"I understand," he replies stoically. "Can we at least be friends? I'd love to hear about your time in the city… if you have the time."

I signal the barista for two more coffees. "What do you want to hear about?" I ask him.

"Everything," he replies.

I don't want to rub my new life in his face, so I stick to the subject of food. I tell him about my classes and all of the restaurants I've visited since my arrival. I mention that I'm enjoying my new job at The Madden Crowd, but I don't offer any details on the fabulous kitchen or the luxurious menu. I leave James out of the conversation completely.

"It sounds like you're really making a life for yourself here," he tells me. "I'm happy for you… and I'm proud of you, Kiara." I can tell that the sentiment is genuine.

"Thank you. I feel bad. I've been doing all of the talking. How are things back at Fission?" I ask, remembering what James had said about Paul's downhill slide.

He takes a deep breath, exhales slowly, and replies, "Better now. I let things go for a little while, but I went back to work two weeks ago and the kitchen is back on track. It's understaffed at the moment. I haven't had a chance to interview new prep cooks… and I doubt that I'll ever take on another apprentice."

"Don't say that," I insist. "You're a talented chef, Paul, and you're an excellent teacher. I wouldn't be here today without everything I learned from you."

"Thanks, but I think you're giving me too much credit. You're standing on your own talent, Kiara. I was just the first to spot it… and I guess that's not even true. If anyone gets credit for discovering you, it has to be Patrick." He sighs and looks at his watch. "It's getting late. I'm sure you have a full day ahead of you tomorrow. Can I walk you home?"

"I'm headed to the subway. I can make it on my own," I assure him.

Paul nods and reluctantly rises to his feet. "Can I walk you to the station then?"

I consider the offer and, remembering that Robbs may be lurking somewhere close by, I accept. We walk to the subway in a comfortable silence. Paul reaches for my hand several times out of instinct, but catches himself and pulls away. We arrive at the station, and I offer him a hug. He pulls me into a tight embrace and for a moment I wonder if he'll ever let me go. Finally, he releases me and steps back.

"Have a safe trip home," I tell him awkwardly.

"You, too," he says with a hesitant smile. "Kiara, you can insist that you're fine all you want, but I know you. Back at the coffee shop, you kept glancing out the window. You've been on edge and overly alert since we left. Something is bothering you… are you scared of something?"

"No, of course not," I answer quickly. I know Paul as well as he knows me, and I can tell that he doesn't believe me.

"All right," he sighs. "Keep it to yourself if you insist. Just promise me something, Kiara. If there's ever someone or something that makes you afraid, you will tell me. I may not be your boyfriend anymore, but I still love you. If you're ever in danger, or in need, I want to know about it."

"If I ever get into a situation that I can't get myself out of, I'll give you a call," I tell him.

Paul shakes his head with a smile. "I guess that's as good as I'm going to get… I swear, Kiara, you and your stubborn, independent ways, You're a force to be reckoned with, you know that?"

I laugh and look down at my phone. "The next train leaves in a few minutes… I need to get going. Goodbye, Paul."

"Until next time, Kiara."

Chapter Five

James and I sit in his office, looking over next week's food order. After my run in with Robbs and my late cup of coffee with Paul, I had a horrible, restless night. I try hard not to fall asleep while James explains how he figures menu prices.

"Kiara!" he cries out. "Are you with me?"

I jump in my seat. "I'm sorry… I had a really long night last night. I'm fine to work my shift, I promise. I just need a cup of coffee."

"Late night, huh?" he asks with a sly grin. "Is it all right if I admit I'm jealous of the guy?"

"Not really," I tell him with a teasing grin, "but there's nothing to be jealous of. It wasn't that kind of night."

"Well, I hope that you're not too tired for the field trip I have planned for this afternoon."

"Field trip?"

"It's a surprise. Go out front and have Marcus make you an espresso. I'll be out in a few minutes and we'll get going," James instructs me.

"All right…" I leave the office, wondering what in the world I'm getting myself in to. Surely this is work related. Although this would be a great way to trap me into a date…

I stop at the bar and ask Marcus for a double shot of espresso. So far, the combination bartender/barista is the only employee James has introduced me to. He's around my age, with rich mocha skin and a sparkling personality that keeps the bar area packed full. He brews my double shot and slides it across the bar just as James appears.

"Make me one of those," James demands. I'm shocked by his harsh tone but Marcus just nods and brews the coffee. "Ready to go?" he asks after Marcus passes him his drink.

"Lead the way," I tell him.

Instead of walking through the dining room and exiting through the kitchen door, we leave through the front. A black convertible Roadster is parked right in front of the building.

James opens the passenger door with a wide grin. "You're chariot awaits."

"You have a car in the city?" I ask. "Isn't that kind of unnecessary?"

"Sometimes I like to leave the city," he explains with a shrug. "I have a place upstate, and I hate being chauffeured."

"So… are we going upstate?" I ask.

"Yes," he tells me, "we're going on a food adventure."

"Oh yeah?" I ask with a smile. "That sounds like my kind of adventure… care to explain further?"

"There is a cooler in my incredibly undersized trunk," James tells me with a smile. "Along with everything we need to start a campfire. Spring is blooming in New York, and you and I are about to gather the freshest food available. Local farms have roadside stands set up. We're going to stop at each one, and at the end of the line, we're going to a beautiful little park to cook over an open fire."

If this is a date, it's a damn good one. "I love this idea," I tell James.

He nods. "I haven't completely jumped on the farm-to-table bandwagon, but I do like to eat the freshest, best foods available."

His mention of the farm-to-table movement brings Robbs back to the forefront of my mind, and I shudder involuntarily.

"What's the matter?" James asks.

I sigh and decide that it's best to tell James what's going on. Robbs has already shown up at my school; there's nothing to stop him from walking into The Madden Crowd. "Do you remember Robbs Martin?"

"The asshole who called and told me all of those lies about you?" James asks. "Of course I remember him… is he the reason you had a late night?"

"Yes," I tell him. I decide that it's in everyone's best interest to keep Paul's visit to myself. "Robbs showed up at my pastry class last night. He embarrassed the shit out of me, told my instructor that I'd sleep with him for a good grade."

"That's disgusting," James says. "What the hell is he even doing in town?"

"I don't know… I got the impression that he's here to make my life a nightmare. He seems to blame me for everything that's happened to him lately… Chef Ballard kicked him out, and then he dismissed me from class for the rest of the night…"

"Do you want me to call the school?" he asks quickly. "I can tell your instructor about Robbs' history of mental instability… I heard an earful about it when I called Escoffier asking about him."

"I'm a grown woman, James," I remind him. "I can take care of myself. I've been doing it for a long time…"

I feel comfortable with James, and if he asks what I mean by a long time, I know that I'll tell him the truth about my past. But my statement doesn't peak his curiosity, and he continues on about Robbs.

"I almost hope that little punk has the nerve to try and pull something like that at the restaurant. I'll hand him his ass on a silver platter," James tells me. "You don't think he'd actually try to hurt you, do you? I *knew* that I should have told the real estate agency to put you in a building with a doorman."

"Robbs is too much of a coward to actually hurt anyone," I assure him. "He's all bark and no bite. Besides, he's probably already back in Austin… I don't want to think about him anymore."

"Fine by me, just let me know if he continues to be an issue."

"I will," I promise. The buildings around us grow farther and farther apart, and I know that we're leaving the city. Spring is more evident in the suburban area; the only green plants I've seen in Manhattan are the ones in Central Park.

"It's beautiful out here," I tell James as we pass a small field of wildflowers.

"Wait until you see it in the fall… all of the leaves start changing and the air feels crisp. We'll have to make this a once-a-season adventure," He suggests.

"You won't hear me argue with that," I tell him. "How far until our first stop?"

"About fifteen minutes." James flips on the radio as we turn onto the old country highway. Our first stop yields a bundle of ramps and a container of foraged mushrooms. I want to buy everything the stand has to offer, but James reminds me that we have several stops to go.

At our second stand, we add a bundle of arugula and a homemade herb vinaigrette. We continue down the highway, adding spring carrots, an assortment of peppers, and a bottle of local wine to our collection. Our last stop is at an organic, free-range farm where we buy a freshly plucked chicken and a single, giant ribeye.

"Are you hungry yet?" James asks as we slide back in to the Porsche.

"Famished," I answer quickly. "How far away is the park?"

"It's right around the corner."

He's not exaggerating. James exits the farm and takes the first left off of the highway. Fifty yards later, he pulls down another driveway that leads to a small but beautiful park. There's plenty of play equipment, a sand pit, and six picnic tables; each table area has its own cast-iron grill.

"Here's hoping that at least one kind soul cleaned up after themselves," James says as he inspects the grill.

The first three are loaded with ashes, trash, and remnants of charcoal briquettes; the fourth is relatively clean. James fetches our supplies from the trunk and deposits them on the table. He turns to me and smiles.

"All right, let's see what you've got," he tells me.

"You mean I have to do everything… by myself?" I'm starving and the last thing I feel like doing is slaving away over a hot grill.

"All by yourself," James tells me. "It's easy to be a good chef when you have access to a fully stocked cooler and pantry. I want to see what you can do with limited, simple ingredients. You have salt, pepper, and everything we've bought today."

"This feels like something you'd do on your television show," I observe. "Are you also going to give me a time limit?"

"No." He smiles. "If you're hungry enough, you'll get it done quick… do you need me to start the fire?"

"I'm from Texas, remember. I know how to start a fire." I arrange a pyramid of charcoal in the iron box and douse it with lighter fluid. I toss in a lit match and flames engulf the briquettes. I let the lighter fluid burn off while I crust the steak in kosher salt and fresh ground pepper. I slide the chicken into a Ziploc bag, drown it in the vinaigrette, and leave it to marinate while I attend to the fire. I spread out the hot coals and gingerly place the proteins onto the grate. While the meat cooks, I prep the vegetables. The carrots and the poblano peppers are prepped for the grill while everything else gets chopped for a salad. James pours us each a glass of wine while I work.

The chardonnay has bright, apple overtones; I quickly finish my first glass.

"So," James says as he pours me a refill. "I think this would be a good chance for us to get to know each other a little better."

It IS a date. AND he's making me cook. "What would you like to know?"

"I don't know… the basics, I guess."

My urge to be honest about my past has subsided, so I decide to go with my standard lie. I told James that I'd had a happy childhood and wonderful parents. I forced out a single tear as I explained that my mother and father had passed away in a car accident when I was a teenager. James tried to act sympathetic, but I didn't want to linger on the topic. After explaining what happened to my parents, I launched into all of the details of my education.

"And you know the rest from there," I tell him. "I won a spot in the competition, I won the apprenticeship, and two months later you walked into the kitchen and changed everything." I laugh as I pull the meat off the grill.

"Changed for the better, I hope?" James asks with a smile.

"Of course," I tell him as I toss the vegetables onto the grill. I slice the meat while James starts telling me about himself. I finish plating the food, and he pauses his story long enough to devour his entire plate.

"That was phenomenal," he tells me as he wipes his mouth with a napkin.

"Thanks," I tell him, pouring another glass of wine. The more I drink, the more my mind wanders back to those stolen moments in The Madden Crowd's walk-in; I resist the urge to reach across the picnic table and run my hands through James' silky blond hair. With so much wine in my system and my stomach contently full, my restless night starts to catch up with me. I yawn, and James gets the hint.

"You must be exhausted; let's get going. I'll pack up if you want to go get settled in the car," he offers.

"Are you sure that you're all right to drive?"

"I've been sipping the same glass of wine since we got here, I'm fine," he assures me.

I stand and stretch for a minute before walking to the Porsche. I drift off to sleep before James makes it to the car.

<<◇>>

"Kiara...?" James gently nudges me awake. I stretch as much as I can in the cramped passenger seat of the tiny car, yawn, and look out the window. We're right outside the apartment building.

"I slept the whole way home?" I ask in embarrassed disbelief. It's dark outside. I pull my phone from my purse and see that it's nine p.m.

"Yes," James chuckles, "but don't worry. You didn't drool or snore or anything... in fact, you're pretty damn cute when you're asleep."

"Thanks." I blush. "And thank you for today. I really did have a lot of fun. I can't wait for our summer road trip."

We sit in awkward silence for a moment; James places a hand on my thigh. "So... do you have any plans for this evening?"

I know what he's hinting at and, after our magical day, I'm game for a little more fun. "I don't have any plans... and I'm caught up on everything for my classes tomorrow. Would you like to come upstairs?"

"I thought that you'd never ask." He shuts off the engine, and we climb out of the car. We walk through the lobby; once we're alone in the elevator, James wraps his arms around my waist, sticks his hands in my back pockets, and gives me a passionate kiss while he squeezes my ass. Normally, this kind of move would turn me off; somehow, with James it feels incredibly erotic.

The elevator doors open, and he releases me. I fumble for my keys as we walk to my door; James pulls my hair to one side and kisses the back of my neck as I struggle with the lock. The key finally turns in the cylinder; I turn the knob and push the door open, ready to drag James into my bedroom and have my way with him. Instead, I stand motionless and stare into my apartment in disbelief.

Everything has been completely destroyed. The cushions of my new leather living room furniture have been torn open, the stuffing strewn across the floor. My flat screen television is shattered, and my DVD collection lies in shards near a far window.

"What the *fuck*?" James exclaims.

I stand speechless. Robbs *does* know where I live, I realize with a sinking heart. He has to be behind this, I just hope that I'll be able to prove it. I take a deep breath and turn to James. "I told you that Robbs is crazy. I guess we should survey the rest of the damage and call the police."

James is suddenly standoffish and silent. He nods and walks toward my kitchen; I follow and find that all of my plates and glasses have been busted against my marble floor. The appliances look unharmed, but the contents of my fridge have been smeared across every surface of the room.

James pulls out his phone and studies the screen for a moment. "Oh shit, Kiara, I completely forgot that I have to be somewhere… I'll hire a cleaning company to come in and deal with this mess and arrange for new furniture to be delivered. The renters insurance will cover it."

"Okay…" I agree softly. Five minutes ago, all he had to do tonight was me… I guess James is the type of guy who doesn't stick around for the tuff stuff.

"Text me and let me know what the cops say," he continues. "I'll see you tomorrow night at the restaurant… unless you want to take the day off?"

I shake my head. "I'll be there."

Unless the bastard comes back and kills me after you leave.

James walks back through my demolished living room and opens the door. "Text if you need anything," he tells me before disappearing.

I sigh again, pull out my phone, and dial 911. The dispatcher listens impatiently to my story and gives me a short lecture on dialing 911 for a nonemergency before connecting me with the local precinct. The dispatcher there takes down my address and phone number and promises that an officer will be out as soon as one's available.

"Please don't touch anything before the officers arrive," the dispatcher advises me before hanging up.

I stow my phone in my back pocket and decide that I have to check the rest of the apartment. I walk down the hallway and push open the bathroom door. The vanity mirror is shattered, just like my television; the intruder also made a fragrant but expensive mess with my custom-blended beauty products.

With all of the damage I've already seen, I dread looking in my bedroom. But I know that it has to be done, so I leave the bathroom and continue down the hall. I push open the door and feel relief for the first time since I arrived home. Everything is still in place; the intruder spared the room during his rampage.

I collapse on the bed and think about calling Paul; I *had* promised to let him know if I felt like I was in trouble. Instead, I pull my phone from my pocket and call Chase. I get his voicemail and leave a short, generic message and ask him to call me when he can. I end the call and stare blankly at my phone.

James didn't seem too concerned about the break-in, and I don't want to talk to Paul about it. I know that he'll come running back to New York to rescue me and that's the last thing I need. Jenny's probably still in the city, but I don't know how to contact her and I'm not sure I want to. So I just sit on my bed, realizing that I have no one to turn to. My doorbell rings and shocks me out of my self-pity.

I rush to the front door and glance out the peephole. Two uniformed officers are waiting in the hallway.

"I'm sorry, but could you please hold up your badges?" I call out through the door.

"Of course," the older officer replies. He and his younger partner pull their badges from their hips and hold them a few feet from the peephole. Satisfied that they're not imposters, I unlock the door and let them in.

"Kiara Sands?" the older officer asks as they step inside.

"Yes, thank you for coming so quickly."

The younger officer whistles. "Damn, someone really did a number on this place."

The older officer nods. "Ms. Sands, I'm Officer Delco and this is Officer Mantooth. We'll inspect the damage and take pictures, and then we'll have some questions for you."

"Of course." I nod. "I'll just stay right here… all of my seating has been destroyed." I gesture to my ransacked living room.

"That will be fine, Ms. Sands," Officer Delco agrees as he pulls a digital camera from his pocket.

I stay rooted in place while the officers inspect my apartment. They return about twenty minutes later.

"Ms. Sands, can you walk me through your day? What time did you leave the apartment… what time did you get back? Did you notice anything unusual in the building or outside?"

I explain that I'd left for work around ten a.m. and arrived home just a few minutes before calling the station. I didn't notice anything strange this morning, but I haven't really been in the neighborhood long enough to know what belongs and what doesn't.

The officers nod as I speak. "So you're new to the city then?" Officer Mantooth asks.

"Yes."

"Do you know many people in New York? Someone who may hold a grudge against you?" Officer Delco asks.

"The only person I really know in the city is my boss, James O'Toole. And I was with him when this happened."

"James O'Toole… the celebrity chef?" Officer Mantooth asks. I can tell that he's impressed.

"Yes," I tell him. "And like I said, I know he didn't do it. There is someone else that I think may be behind this…" I take a deep breath and tell them about Robbs. I spare the more personal details, but I give them enough information to explain why I think he's the one who destroyed my home.

"I see," Officer Delco says when I finish. "And were you and this Mr. Martin ever… involved?"

"Absolutely not," I answer in disgust. "We just worked together… and like I said, he blames me for the problems he's been having with his career. He thinks I stole a job from him, and he hates me for succeeding where he's failed."

"Okay," Officer Delco replies. "One last question and then we'll get out of your hair. Did you have a chance to really check out the apartment and see if anything's missing?"

"I haven't noticed anything missing," I tell them. "But I don't really own any jewelry or anything like that. Everything I own of any value was broken, not stolen."

Officer Delco nods again. "That's in line with a harassment break-in… which this definitely is. It was definitely personal; you need to watch out for yourself. There's no sign of forced entry, which means that we're dealing with someone who has a copy of your key or has experience picking locks."

"No one has a copy of my key," I assure him. "And I have no idea if Robbs knows how to pick a lock or not."

"We'll run a background on him when we get back to the station," Officer Delco assures me. "And we'll call the airports and find out when he arrived in the city and if he's left yet. We'll catch whoever was behind this, Ms. Sands. In the meantime, I want you to change your locks and think about investing in an alarm system. Mix up your routes for work and school; it will make it harder for a stalker to find you. Don't let yourself sink into any routines until we've wrapped up the case."

I assure him that I won't and escort them to the door. Both officers hand me their card and tell me to call any time before disappearing into the elevator.

I lock myself in the apartment and lean against the door. James promised to send a cleaning crew tomorrow, but I can't look at this mess for another second. With a determined sigh, I gather cleaning supplies from my ruined kitchen and set in for a long night of work.

Chapter Six

Robbs sits in a small, rundown motel room staring at the screen of his cell phone. He watched happily as Kiara arrived home with James and discovered her ransacked apartment. He was smugly satisfied when O'Toole ran out of the apartment just a few minutes later.

He just wants to fuck you, Kiara. He doesn't want to deal with all of your bullshit.

When the police arrive, Robbs is glad that he sprang for the camera system that included audio. It had been difficult to pick Kiara's lock, but once he was inside the apartment, his work had been easy. He'd cussed Kiara as he shattered all of her new things. She didn't deserve the upscale apartment or any of the fancy things inside it. The apprenticeship at Fission should have been Robbs'. O'Toole should have offered *him* a job at The Madden Crowd. In Robbs' mind, Kiara had stolen everything Robbs had coming to him, and he wasn't going to let her get away with it.

He watches as the cops inspect each room of Kiara's apartment. He's relieved when they don't find any of his hidden cameras; he can't afford to buy new ones if the cops find and confiscate the first set. The cops reappear in the living room, and Robbs listens as Kiara accuses him of the crime.

"You can talk all you want, bitch, but good luck proving your theory," Robbs shouts at the screen. He'd been careful in the apartment. He'd slid on gloves before picking the lock and slipped on surgical shoe covers just inside the door. A stocking cap had ensured that no stray hairs would be left behind, though he doubted that the police would bother looking for DNA evidence at a break-in where nothing was taken.

The cops hand Kiara their cards, and Robbs watches her escort them to the door. Robbs expects her to break down now that she's alone, but instead she heads to the kitchen for a broom and dustpan.

"Clean all you want, Kiara," Robbs whispers. "I'll be back."

<<◇>>

I sit at my kitchen island and finish my last cup of coffee. It's Saturday, three days after the break-in. I'd spent most of Wednesday night cleaning the apartment; James' cleaning crew arrived early Thursday morning and finished the job. As promised, James had also replaced all of my ruined furniture, kitchen supplies, and beauty products. A locksmith had installed the strongest locks available along with an alarm system equipped with a small video camera. If the intruder, who I know was Robbs, tries to come back, I'll have the proof I need to put him behind bars.

I've followed all of Officer Delco's advice and, so far, life has been uneventful since Wednesday. I haven't had that feeling of being watched, and I certainly haven't spotted Robbs lurking in any corners. But it's only been three days, and I'm not ready to let my guard down.

The police checked in yesterday to let me know that they were unable to find any flight records for Robbs Martin. He either drove across country or he flew in under an assumed name. Officer Delco thinks that the former is more likely; airport security has been incredibly tight since 9/11, especially for passengers flying in to The Big Apple. The NYPD issued a BOLO for Robbs' SUV and promised to keep me updated on their progress.

James arranged for the apartment to be cleaned and my things to be replaced, but he hasn't actually mentioned the break-in to me. I've taken my cues from him and haven't brought up the subject either. Chase called me back later Wednesday night, but I'd been cleaning and hadn't felt like taking a break. I spoke with him yesterday, but I didn't mention the break-in. Chase is a good guy, a real Southern gentleman, and if he thought for one moment that I was in danger, he'd drop everything and rush to my rescue. He has his own studies and career to think about, and I don't want him sacrificing anything to help me.

I glance at the oven clock and see that I still have an hour until I need to leave for work. I debate taking a long walk, but decide against it. Instead, I take my coffee to the living room and flip on my new television. As I search for something to watch, my cell phone chirps; I look down and see Paul's number on the screen. I know that I can't avoid him forever, so I swipe the screen to answer.

"Hi, Paul," I say causally.

"Hey, Kiara. I just wanted to check in and see how things are going in the city."

"You mean since you were here four days ago?" I laugh.

"Yeah, I guess that's what I mean… so? How are you."

I think for a moment before answering. I don't want Paul rushing back to the city, but it would be nice if he could check out Robbs' apartment and hangouts to find out if he's returned to Austin. I take a deep breath and tell him everything.

"He was there on *Tuesday*?" Paul exclaims angrily. "And you didn't *tell* me! That's why you were so upset, why you seemed distracted. For the love of god, Kiara, why didn't you say something?"

"I didn't want to be rescued," I tell him. "I still don't. But if you could ask around Austin, find out if he's back in town or when he was last seen in the area, it would help. I'm sure that the police are making calls, but you could do a much more thorough job."

"Kiara, I'll do whatever you want but you *have* to come home. I can't bear the thought of you alone and vulnerable in the apartment."

"I'm not vulnerable," I insist. "And if you remember, I'm alone by choice."

"Kiara, I made a mistake. Haven't you punished me enough? Don't put yourself in danger just to spite me."

"Nothing I've done has been to punish you, Paul," I insist impatiently. "I'm here for ME Paul, for MY career. I'm moving on, and you should do the same."

"Are you moving on with O'Toole?" he snarls.

"That's none of your business," I tell him firmly. "Look, I'm sorry that I asked you to look into things… I'm sorry that I told you anything about this at all. Don't worry about checking up on Robbs, and don't worry about me."

"Kiara…" he begins to argue.

I hang up the phone before he has a chance to continue.

Chapter Seven

"Kiara, how long until the mousse is ready?" James calls from across the kitchen. I've been at work for six hours, and I haven't had one free moment. On top of the restaurant being slammed, James and I are prepping for the monthly, members-only wine night we're hosting after the dining room closes.

The Madden Crowd's wine night is one of the most popular attractions in Manhattan. Members of the official Madden Crowd pay a hefty fee to enjoy this and other perks, and prepping for it is incredibly stressful.

"It'll be ready in about ten minutes, and then I'll move on to the duck," I assure him.

"Speed it up!" he demands. "You don't just have to get the food prepped before service, you have to get cleaned up, too!"

Not only am I cooking for the wine night, I will also be enjoying the wine and appetizers with our guests. James continues to amaze me with his business savvy. He uses the monthly event to test new recipes; he explained that it's important for us to sit with the customers and gauge their reaction to the food. I arrived at work with a pair of black slacks and a silk top to wear to the event; James examined my clothes, then took me to his office and presented me with a tiny emerald dress.

"You have to stand out, Kiara," he told me. "Not blend in with the middle-aged customers at the table. You can get ready at my place once we're done in the kitchen."

James lives just one block away from the restaurant; I don't even want to know what his apartment is worth, but I'm excited to see it for myself.

"I can help with the duck, Chef," Monica calls out from her station. Monica is The Madden Crowd's roasting chef, the perfect person to help me get out of the weeds.

"That would be great, Monica," James replies. "Kiara started marinating them hours ago, they should be ready for the oven."

Monica sets off for the walk-in and James crosses the room to my station. "I don't want you to be nervous about tonight," he tells me softly, "but I hope that you're ready to talk to *a lot* of stuffy rich people. They're all going to love you after being stuck with my boring ass for so long."

"I can handle it," I tell him. "Though I'd be more comfortable in my own clothes… I'm not sure that dress will even fit… and it doesn't go with my shoes."

"Nonsense," he tells me. "The dress will fit you perfectly, and the color will go great with your hair and skin tone. I have a great eye, I know that it's your size. And black flats match everything, though I'd prefer you in some sexy kitten heels," he finishes with a sly smile.

"All right," I relent. "The mousse is finished, so if you don't need anything else, I'll go ahead and go to your place to get ready."

"I've called the doorman; he'll let you in to the apartment," James tells me. "I'll be there shortly, I just want to check with Marcus and make sure that all of the wines that need to breathe have been opened already."

"Okay, I'll see you there or back here." I exit from the kitchen door and take the short walk to James' apartment. As promised, his doorman is expecting me and escorts me to the elevator. There are forty buttons to choose from; the doorman slides a key into a small hole and hits the button marked "P".

Of course he lives in the fucking penthouse. The doorman and I ride to the top of the building in an awkward silence. I wonder what he's thinking and how many other women he's taken on this same ride. The bell chimes, and the doors open directly into James' home.

The apartment has an open floor plan, with tall ceilings and stone floors. The far wall is solid glass, offering a breathtaking view of Manhattan. I stand motionless, still in the elevator car, and take in the view.

"Have a good evening, Chef Sands," the doorman tells me. The statement reminds me of his presence and I step out of the car.

"I'm sorry, I guess I was a little taken aback by this place," I explain. "It's amazing."

He nods. "Mr. O'Toole has excellent taste in everything. Again, have a good night."

The elevator doors close and he disappears. I glance around James' home; I'm tempted to snoop through his things and learn more about him, but it seems a little too voyeuristic. Instead, I set off down the hallway in search of the bathroom. I find it behind the second door I open; it's even more extravagant than I'd imagined. The shower is made of hand-painted tile; the Jacuzzi tub is deep and big enough for four people. I lay my garment bag across the countertop and pull off my work clothes. I consider hopping in the shower for a second to rinse off the smell of the kitchen, but I remember that James isn't far behind me. I don't want him to show up, find me naked in his home, and consider it an invitation.

I probably shouldn't be here at all when he gets here. I know that the wine night is important to James, but with all of the sexual tension between us, I'm not sure we'd be able to control ourselves alone in his house. I pull the emerald dress over my head and check my reflection in the mirror.

James was right; the dress fits me perfectly, hitting just above my knee and hugging me in all of the right places. I pull my powder and lip gloss from my purse and freshen up my makeup before leaving the room. I race to the elevator and push the call button; I'm relieved when the car arrives empty. I ride to the lobby, say goodbye to the doorman, and I'm back at The Madden Crowd in a matter of minutes. I walk in through the kitchen; James' jaw drops when he lays eyes on me.

"You look amazing," he tells me with a wide smile. "I can't believe you got dressed so fast. I was just about to head back to the apartment."

"Is there anything you need me to do while you're gone?" I ask.

"No, I don't want you to lift a finger. You look like a piece of artwork. I don't want you to ruin that dress before the guests get here. You can hang out in the office or up at the bar; I'll be back in thirty minutes, at the most."

"Okay," I tell him. "I'll probably go have a drink… calm the nerves."

"Just one though," James warns. "Don't get sloppy drunk on the clock."

"I know how to behave myself," I argue with a smile.

James leans close to me. "I bet you're pretty good at misbehaving, when the situation calls for it," he whispers with a suggestive smile.

"I guess you'll just have to wait and see," I tease.

He smiles and steps away. "I've got to get out of here before you get me all worked up. The wait-staff has the seating arrangements for tonight under control. If any questions come up before I get back, you can reach me on my cell."

I assure him that the restaurant will be fine without him for twenty minutes, and he finally leaves. I walk through the kitchen doors and find an empty stool at the bar.

"You look lovely, Kiara," Marcus tells me.

"Thanks… could you pour me a shot of whiskey?"

"Nervous?" he asks. "I understand. I was a wreck before my first wine night. I'd just finished my sommelier training, and I was certain that I'd make a mistake. But you'll be fine, I promise. The event is much more relaxed than you'd expect." He slides my shot across the bar.

I shoot it quickly and debate whether or not to have another. Marcus seems to be reading my mind.

"I know what you're thinking, but I can't pour you another one," Marcus tells me. "We're only allowed one drink before the event starts. Just be patient, you'll be drowning in wine soon enough."

"Kiara?" a voice calls from behind me.

Not again. I spin my stool around. "What are you doing here, Paul?" I stare him coldly in the eye and wait for his explanation.

"What am I doing here?" he asks incredulously. "What the hell do you mean, what am I doing here? There's a psycho stalking you and breaking into your apartment. I drove by Robbs' apartment building and talked to the manager. He's been gone for six weeks, he didn't give notice, he just disappeared. The last time anyone saw him was the day after you moved here. I spoke with some of his neighbors, since I was already at the building. Robbs is unbalanced, Kiara, even more than we'd realized. You have to come home with me!"

I don't reply. Instead, I keep my eyes on James, who entered the dining room just a few moments after Paul and positioned himself directly behind my ex.

"Kiara has a home, Weston," James snaps.

Paul jumps in surprise at the sound of James' voice. He turns and sneers at him for a moment before speaking. "This is between Kiara and me, O'Toole. She's in danger and from what I can tell, no one here is doing anything to protect her. Austin is her home. That's where she belongs, and I'm taking her back with me right now."

"Over my dead body," James replies. "She doesn't want to go back with you, man. She doesn't want anything to do with you. Why can't you just get that through your head and go back to where you came from? You can't give her what I can… she deserves better than you."

I'm tense in my seat; I feel a light poke on my shoulder and spin back around to face Marcus.

"It looks like you could use this, and James isn't paying attention. Shoot it fast." He slides me another shot of whiskey. I down it quickly and turn back to the dueling men.

"You don't know her," Paul insists. "And don't pretend that you give a damn about her career. I know what kind of slime you are, O'Toole, and I'll be damned if you get your hands on my girl."

I've had enough. I jump up from the stool and move in between them. "James, thank you for trying to deal with this, but I'm a grown woman and I can speak for myself." I turn to Paul. "What do I have to do to get it through your head that I'm done? I've said it over and over again, I've ignored your calls, hell, I moved across the country. What more will it take to make you realize that you *have* to move on?”

“Kiara, please…” Paul begs.

“*Stop it!*” I tell him. “Listen, I’ve done this as nicely as possible, Paul. This is my place of employment and what you’re doing right now is harassment. You claim that you’re here to protect me from Robbs, but you’re almost as bad as he is. Get out of here or I’m calling the police.”

“You know, Kiara has a point,” James says smugly. “She’s convinced that Robbs was the one who broke into her place, but with the way you’re acting right now, I’m not so sure… where were you on Wednesday, Weston?”

“How *dare* you!” Paul snarls.

“Chef O’Toole?” Marcus interrupts. James turns to him and Marcus nods at the front door; the first Madden Crowd members have arrived and are waiting to be seated.

“Thank you, Marcus.” James smiles and turns back to Paul. “As Chef Sands just said, this is our place of business and you aren’t welcome. So get your sorry ass out of here and don’t come back.”

I loop my arm through James’ and walk with him to greet our first guests without a single glance back at Paul.

"Kiara, I'm really impressed with the way you handled everything last night," James tells me as a waitress appears with our mimosas. I'd made it through my first wine night with flying colors; I charmed the guests and they all seemed to love the recipes I'd created.

"Thanks," I tell him. "I'm actually looking forward to the next members' meeting. Everyone was really nice."

"I'm glad you enjoyed yourself, but that wasn't what I was talking about," James tells me.

"Oh… yeah." I sigh and take a long sip of my drink.

We're sitting at a small, private table at The Plaza, enjoying Sunday brunch. The meal had been James' idea. He was horrified to learn that while I was staying at the hotel, I hadn't attended their famous Sunday event.

"Everyone in New York brunches," he'd told me. "We'll go tomorrow."

"I hope that Weston finally got the hint and went straight to the airport from the restaurant last night," James continues. "I swear, he has some kind of nerve to show up and demand that you go back with him."

"Yeah," I agree. "He's like that about everything… it's always all about him. He's good at playing it off and making you believe that he has your best interests at heart, but really he's just taking care of himself."

James nods. "He's a manipulative bastard. To be honest, Kiara, no one in the industry takes him seriously… no one important, that is. That was one of the reasons I was so determined to get you away from him. You have more raw talent than he ever will, and he'd have never let you rise to the top. You would have drowned at Fission."

"I know," I tell him. "I'd really rather not talk about Paul anymore, if it's all the same to you."

"I'll never speak his name again, if it makes you happy. Are you happy here in the city, Kiara?" James asks with genuine concern.

"It's been like living in a fairytale," I tell him.

"Complete with an evil villain." He laughs. "You haven't had any more trouble at the apartment, have you?"

"No, unless you count last night when I tripped the silent alarm by accident." I laugh. "I completely forgot about it; the cops showed up about ten minutes after I got home. I was about to take a shower and I answered the door in my ratty old bathrobe."

"Ratty or not, I'm sure that you in a robe was a tantalizing sight. One I'd like to see sometime…" His eyes sparkle with the comment and despite my best efforts otherwise, I melt in my seat.

I stare at him daringly. "That can probably be arranged. If you play your cards right."

"Oh yeah? How's this for a start?" He pulls a small turquoise box from the pocket of his navy blazer. I recognize the iconic color immediately, and I can't believe that this is happening.

"I don't know what's in that, but I'm positive that I can't accept it," I tell him as he slides the box across the table to me.

"Consider it an early birthday present," James suggests. "I spotted it the other day and knew that you had to have it."

"My birthday isn't until summer," I tell him.

"I know that," he replies. "And when it rolls around, feel free to remind me that I've already given you your present. Please, Kiara, just open it… it makes me happy to make you happy."

I lift the cover from the box; a giant ruby ring sits inside. I stare at it, speechless.

"See, it's your birthstone. That's why you had to have it… try it on," he prompts me.

I gingerly lift the ring from its box and slide it on to my middle finger; it's a perfect fit.

He smiles. "I told you, I have a great eye for sizes. It looks amazing on you, Kiara… though I wouldn't wear it with your emerald dress unless you want to look like a sexy Christmas tree."

"That's perfect," I joke. "I already have my outfit for The Madden Crowd's holiday party." I lift my hand and admire the ring on my finger. The wide, white gold band is intricately cut and the stone looks beautiful against my skin.

The waitress delivers our meals, and we eat silently for a while. The food is amazing, and I inwardly scold myself for not trying it sooner. When the waitress returns with our check, James slides her a hundred-dollar bill and tells her to keep the change.

"Are you this generous all of the time, or are you just showing off for me?" I tease.

"I started my restaurant career bussing tables at a burger joint," James explains. "I practically lived off my tip shares. When I eat out, I like to take care of the people who are taking care of me."

"I see… you know, you're a bit of a surprise, James O'Toole," I tell him.

"How's that?"

"I guess I just expected you to be more—"

"Of an ass?" he interrupts with a laugh. "That's what most people expect from me. I'm glad you see me differently now."

"I'm glad, too… but you have to stop buying me stuff. You're already paying me a more than generous salary and I don't even want to know what my apartment is costing you. I'm here to work, not to be taken care of."

"But I like spoiling you," he argues. "Like I said, it makes me happy… there's something else that would make me even happier."

"What's that?"

James reaches into his blazer pocket again and pulls out a Plaza key card. "I have a room… if you want to join me."

Everything in me says to turn down the offer; James is my boss, my success in the city depends on him, and I'm not at all ready to jump in to another relationship. But James is so damn hot, and I just can't help myself.

"I'd love to join you. Lead the way."

Robbs paces the sidewalk across from The Plaza, waiting for Kiara to emerge. After waiting for almost two hours, he knows that the two chefs are doing more in the hotel than enjoying overpriced Eggs Benedict.

I knew she was fucking him. That's how the little bitch gets everything. I need to find a female executive chef who will let me sleep my way to the top. If being a good lay is enough to get an apprenticeship, I'd have my pick of offers.

Robbs has been growing more and more agitated since he'd broken in to Kiara's house. He'd been hoping to catch something good on the surveillance cameras, but so far all he'd seen was Kiara doing boring shit all by herself. He'd thought he'd at least get a few good nude shots, but the stupid little bitch gets dressed in her walk-in closet, and he hadn't thought to put a camera there, and the bathroom camera was set at a bad angle. Robbs had watched the locksmith install Kiara's new security system, and he hadn't yet figured out a way to bypass it.

Paul Weston's arrival in the city also had Robbs stressed out. He'd seen his former boss on the streets that night while he was following Kiara. Robbs had also been across the street from The Madden Crowd when Paul crashed that pretentious wine party. He'd watched Paul exit the place in a hurry and assumed that he was heading back to Austin. After all, Paul had his own fancy restaurant to run. Imagine Robbs' surprise when he'd arrived at the diner across from Kiara's building and spotted Paul sitting in a far booth. Robbs had been lucky and realized that Paul was there before he entered the restaurant. The diner was the only place to sit and watch the building, so Robbs had been forced to retreat back to his hotel. When he'd arrived at the café that morning, he'd been relieved to find the place completely empty.

He continues pacing and throwing looks toward The Plaza doors. How long does it take to fuck? As Robbs walks back and forth on the block, he notices that a couple of shopkeepers are paying attention to him. He knows that he's been on the sidewalk for far too long, and that it's only a matter of time before one of the workers calls the cops and reports his suspicious behavior. Robbs knows that at least a couple of New York cops are looking for him after the break-in, and he can't afford to take any chances. With a sigh, he moves north and keeps walking.

I'm going to make you pay for making this so difficult for me, Kiara, he vows silently. As he makes his way back to the diner, he fantasizes about all of the evil things he's going to do to Kiara once he finally has her to himself.

Chapter Eight

James leads me to the elevator bank on the far wall of The Plaza lobby. He passes the regular cars and heads to the single elevator that requires a key card to enter.

Of course he rented the penthouse, I think happily. My regular room here had been elegant and beautiful; I can't wait to see what the high-priced suite looks like. The doors slide open, and we step inside. The doors shut again; James wraps me in his arms, and we kiss passionately as the elevator climbs to the top of the building.

"I've wanted you for so long, Kiara," he tells me with a groan. I can feel his throbbing erection against my hip, and I can't wait to free it from the confines of his designer jeans. I grind against him, longing to feel him inside me. The doors open directly into the suite; James and I stumble into the living area, still entwined in each other. James pulls my dress over my head and tosses it to the floor; I stand before him in my matching black lace panties and bra.

"You're so beautiful," he tells me as he strips out of his own clothes. His chest is smooth and muscular, and I can't wait to feel his skin against mine.

"You're not so bad yourself," I tell him with a sly grin.

James lifts me into his arms, and I wrap my legs around his waist. His enormous, stiff cock rubs against my clit as he carries me into the bedroom. He tosses me onto the king-sized bed and crawls on top of me. In one swift motion, he buries the entire length of his cock within me.

I'm a little caught off guard; I'd been expecting at least a little foreplay, but I guess James likes to just get down to business. He thrusts into me, stretching my pussy to accommodate his large love muscle.

"You like that, don't you?" He breathes heavily.

"Yes," I tell him, mimicking his passion. I try to clear my mind and concentrate on the moment. James may not be the most attentive lover, but it's been a long time since I've had sex and I'm aching for release.

"Give it to me, James," I encourage him. He replies by increasing his pace. I angle my hips until I feel the tip of his cock bump up against that magic button deep inside me. Waves of pleasure course through my body; I reach down and finger my clit as James jackhammers away.

"Oh god…" he moans. "Oh *God*…"

As I start climbing to release, James pulls out abruptly and comes on my stomach. I'm startled and disappointed that he finished before me, but I assume that he'll make sure I come, too; I soon realize that that is just wishful thinking. James rolls off of me, climbs out of the bed, and sets off for the living room.

"Are you thirsty?" he calls out to me.

"Yes," I reply. I wait in bed for a few minutes and realize that he's not coming back. I roll out of bed and pull on a plush Plaza bathrobe before returning to the living area. James is lying on the couch, drinking a bottle of sparkling water and watching television.

"Hey," he greets me. "The mini fridge is stocked, help yourself."

I grab a bottle of my own and take a seat near him on the couch. He's watching Iron Chef, yelling at the screen the way most people cheer on their favorite sports team.

"I beat Bobby Flay, you know," James tells me as the show cuts to commercial. "I was on the show a couple of years ago. He's my mother's favorite chef… she was almost disappointed that I won."

"Do your parents live in the city?" I ask.

He shakes his head. "Florida… I bought them a place there a few years ago. What about your parents, are they back in Austin?"

I'm shocked by his question; I'd given James my standard cover story to explain my parent's absence during our trip through the countryside.

He wasn't even paying attention. He doesn't care at all. I sigh and decide to tell him the truth. "I don't know where my parents are. I haven't since I was sixteen years old. They were drug addicts; I came home from school one day, and they'd moved without me."

James stares at the television without responding. The show is back on, and Michael Simon is working on a complicated recipe that's stolen James' attention.

"James?" I ask. "Are you listening?"

"Yeah, yeah," he replies, his eyes fixed on the television. "You came home from school and they were gone. It sounds like you're better off without them. Did you see what Simon just did with that *foie gras*?"

"No… I guess I missed it." I sigh. *You selfish bastard. You talk a good game, but you're even worse than Paul. All you care about is yourself.*

"Simon is amazing," James continues. "I wish he'd have been an option when I was on the show… I have my agent working on getting me a second appearance. If she lands it, you can serve as my sous chef."

"Great." James remains mesmerized with the show, and I'm filled with the overwhelming urge to escape. I wait until the next commercial break to announce my plans.

"I've got a bunch of work to do before class on Tuesday… I should probably head home," I say softly.

"All right," James answers. "Do you need cab fare?"

I can't imagine taking his money and leaving the room without feeling like a complete prostitute.

"My boss pays me well," I remind him as I get dressed. "I can pay for my own taxi."

"All right… well, I'll see you tomorrow then," he tells me casually. As the elevator doors open, the show comes back from break. I step into the car; James doesn't glance back at me. The doors close and the elevator carries me back to the ground floor. I step out, quickly cross through the lobby, and escape to the street. As I wait for a taxi, I wonder just how bad of a mistake I've made.

<<◇>>

My alarm clock jars me awake at nine-thirty a.m. I roll over and groan as I slap the snooze button. I have a horrible hangover; my head is throbbing and my stomach is churning angrily. I know that I don't have time to make it to the bathroom; I roll over and get sick in my bedside trash can.

Oh my god… I wonder if James would be pissed if I call in sick. I know that he would be, so I don't bother making the phone call. I pull on my bathrobe and pad into the kitchen. I start a pot of coffee, retrieve a bottle of water from the refrigerator, and down it in one big gulp. I look through the cabinets for something that won't upset my stomach and settle on a small bag of ginger snaps. I pour a mug of black coffee and after a quick detour to the bathroom for ibuprofen and Pepto, I retreat back to my bed. I have three hours before I have to be at The Madden Crowd; I hope it's enough time to pull myself together.

I settle back under my blankets and see that the notification light is blinking on my phone. I swipe the screen and see that I've missed a call from Jenny. She's called once a day since she showed up on my doorstep and I've yet to answer a single call. She leaves a message each time, always casual and friendly as if all of the lying and deceit never happened. I don't know why she thinks that we'll ever be friends and, like Paul, I hope she gets the point sooner rather than later.

James hasn't called or texted since I left the hotel last night; I can't decide if I'm happy about that or not. After his reaction to my coming clean about my past, I know that the two of us will never be a real couple. James is a big talker, and an even bigger spender, but when push comes to shove, he's no better than Paul. All he cares about is his life; he just wants me to be an accessory in it. I've had one night stands that I regret, but none as much as I regret sleeping with James.

Maybe Robbs is right. I mean, I *do* keep sleeping with my bosses… and now, if I want to keep my job, I'm stuck in a relationship that I don't want and I'm not ready for. I sigh, roll over, and crawl out of bed. I set off for the shower and stand under the hot spray until the water runs cold. I turn off the tap and stay in the steam for a bit, trying to sweat out the alcohol that's lingering in my system. After awhile, I start feeling lightheaded and open the glass door. The fresh air gives me a head rush, but I don't get sick again so I know that I'm on the mend. I wrap myself in my bathrobe and set off for my closet.

My walk-in is almost as big as my old Austin apartment, and I've developed a habit of using it as a dressing room. It makes me feel like Carrie from *Sex in the City*, only she had an even bigger closet and a much more impressive wardrobe. I pull on a pair of my black work slacks and a lightweight purple blouse. I walk back to the kitchen for another mug of coffee, and watch last night's news before taking off for The Madden Crowd.

As I walk the busy streets, that eerie feeling of being watched fills me once more. My eyes dart back and forth down the street, and I pick up my pace. I arrive in The Madden Crowd kitchen, sweaty and out of breath.

"All right, Chef?" Monica asks as I lean against the cooler door.

"I'm not sure," I tell her. "Is Chef O'Toole here yet?"

"No, he called earlier and said he was running late. He also said that you can take the day off, if you want to. I was about to call and tell you when one of the fryers went out. It's back up and running now."

"I can stay," I tell her. "Unless James doesn't come in at all… I'll wait awhile and see. I'll be at the bar drinking our espresso supply."

"Yes, Chef," she replies with a smile.

I make my way to the bar and deposit myself on a stool. Marcus is off for the day and the relief bartender isn't as chatty. I sit and drink my coffee quietly until once again, my peace is interrupted by an unwelcomed Texan.

"Kiara," Paul says softly as he takes the stool beside me. "Please, can I just talk to you?"

The dining room is full of lunch guests, and I don't want to make another scene. "Why are you here, Paul? What in the world could you possibly have to say now?

I've explained that I'm finished. I'm not coming back. Not to Fission, not to Austin, and certainly not to you."

"Kiara, I have one favor to ask you and afterward I'll leave. I promise, I'll get on a plane, go back to Texas, and you can forget that I exist, if that's what you want. Just do one thing for me first."

"What is it?" I ask with a frustrated sigh.

"Close your eyes…" he directs me. "Close them and let your mind wander back to that very first night we spent together… remember how happy we were then? How simple everything was? A tornado tore into our lives, Kiara. I admit that I could have handled things better, but I was completely out of control of the situation. Jenny and Robbs were lying and manipulating both of us… try to clear all of that from your mind… just focus on that first night… think about the way my lips felt against your body… the way we moved together in perfect harmony."

I want to hate Paul, but his words are hypnotizing. I *do* remember the way his lips felt against my bare skin, and I think about our first night together more often than I'd like to admit. Paul puts a hand on my shoulder, and I lean into his touch.

"Don't you miss me, Kiara?" he whispers. "Don't you miss us?"

I do, and I'm about to tell him so.

"What the *hell* is going on here?" James' voice booms from across the room. I open my eyes and see him standing in the kitchen doorway; his hands are on his hips and his face is full of rage. He crosses the restaurant in three strides and grabs Paul by the collar of his shirt.

"Didn't I tell you to stay the hell away from my place?" James demands. "You really don't understand shit, do you, Weston?"

Paul doesn't flinch; he stares coldly into James' eyes. "Get your fucking hands off of me, O'Toole."

"Keep your fucking hands off of my woman!" James counters. A heartbroken look spreads across Paul's face; I feel nothing but anger. James and I had a one-night stand; we're not a couple. He has no right to tell anyone that they can't touch me.

Paul recovers from his initial shock, pulls an arm back, and punches James squarely on the jaw.

James hits the floor and a dozen diners rush to his aid. One of them grabs Paul from behind and drags him out the front door. I chase after them and make sure that Paul isn't seriously hurt.

"Kiara, please," he says again after the burly customer returns to the dining room.

"Just leave, Paul," I insist. "I heard what you said, and I promise to think about it. I'll call you soon, but you have to get out of here right now, unless you want to end up in jail for assault. Someone's probably calling the cops as we speak."

"But you'll call me?" he asks hopefully.

"I'll call you," I agree, "if you leave right now."

Paul wraps me in a soft hug, kisses the top of my head, and sets off down the street. I turn to go back into the restaurant, and James steps out the front door.

"Is he gone?" James bellows; he's holding an ice pack to his jaw but it's swelling anyway.

"He's gone," I assure him. "Why the fuck did you provoke him like that? I'm not your woman."

"That's not what you said last night," he reminds me with a sly grin. The fact that he's trying to flirt in this situation infuriates me, and I can't be around him a moment longer.

"Look," I tell him, "Monica mentioned that you said I can have the day off… I'm going to take you up on that offer. I'm exhausted, hung-over, and all I want to do is go back to bed."

"You're going to leave me like this?" James exclaims. "Your crazy ex-boyfriend just tried to break my jaw, and you're going to go home and take a nap?"

"I think that you can take care of yourself, James. Besides, you put your hands on him first, remember?"

"Kiara, if you leave…" he begins.

"Don't give me an ultimatum right now, James. I promise, you won't like my answer."

"Fine," he snaps. "Go take a nap. But be back here for the dinner rush."

"But it's Monday," I remind him. "We don't work the dinner shift on Mondays."

"I don't, but you do tonight," he tells me. "Be back at six-thirty; you'll report to Monica."

"Fine," I tell him with a dismissive wave. "I'll see you later."

I make it home almost as quickly as I'd made it to work. I let myself in to the apartment, remembering to disable the alarm after I lock the door. I go to the kitchen, grab myself a beer, and return to the living room. I collapse on the couch and consider my options while I enjoy some hair of the dog.

I know that if I decide not to continue a relationship with James, I'll lose my job at The Madden Crowd. Which means that I'll lose my apartment; James has paid for almost everything since I arrived in New York, so most of my salary is stowed away in my savings account. And although James has been incredibly generous and started my salary the moment I arrived in the city, I still can't afford to stay in New York if I quit my job.

Going back to Austin doesn't seem like an option either, mostly because I don't have much to go back to. Even Chase will be gone soon; he's accepted a scholarship to a culinary school in South Carolina, where he grew up. I sold my car before I left town, and I know for a fact that my apartment has already been leased.

The most discouraging part of returning to Austin is the idea of having to call Chef Lee and explain to her that I've once again left a prestigious job for personal reasons. She'd criticized me harshly for what went on during the Fission apprenticeship competition; I'm not sure that she'd even consider letting me back in to the Austin program at this point.

So I'm on my own… that's nothing new. And I've survived much worse than this, I remind myself, thinking of my parents. I wonder where they are right now and if they're thinking about me, too.

Stop it, I scold myself. Wherever they are, they aren't wasting any thoughts on me. I need to make a decision.

I finish my first beer and fetch a second. I'm not sure what the long-term future holds, but I'm certain that I won't be going in for the dinner shift. As I sip the frothy liquid, my cell phone rings. It's the restaurant's number; there's a chance that it's not James, so I answer.

"Kiara, we're getting slammed. A new show is opening on Broadway tonight, and the early rush is kicking our asses. I need you to come back in now," James tells me quickly.

"I can't do that," I say softly.

"Damn it, Kiara, I'm sorry for calling you my woman, but you need to get over that. You have a job to do," he says angrily.

"I'm sorry, James, but I'm not coming back in tonight. If it's busy now, it will be dead by the time I get there. I'm staying home… I need some time to think," I explain.

"Kiara, get your ass back to this kitchen right now, or you're finished here," he says with an impatient sigh. His attitude makes my decision incredibly easy.

"I guess I'm finished then," I tell him without any emotion. "I'll pack my things and be out of the apartment before the end of the month. I can either leave the ruby here or I can have it messengered over. You can text me if you think of anything else."

"You're overreacting," James insists. "Is this about Paul?"

"No, it's not," I tell him honestly.

"Well, if you don't want to be with him, what's the problem? Please, Kiara, just come back. My jaw hurts… I need you." His tone is sweet, but I hear the manipulation in his words.

"I'm not coming back," I tell him. "I'd been thinking about leaving before Paul showed up. Now I know that it's the right decision."

"Kiara, you need to think long and hard about what you're doing here," James warns. "You're going to regret this, and by then it will be too late."

"The only thing I regret is coming here in the first place. I wish I'd made a boring fucking salad that night you showed up at Fission; then, I'd have never had the misfortune of meeting you," I tell him sharply.

"Kiara…"

"I have to go now. I have packing to do." I end the call before James has a chance to reply.

Chapter Nine

Across town, Jenny Foster is leaving her small studio apartment. Jenny's neighborhood may as well be in a different world than Kiara's; it's rundown, infested with New York's famous giant cockroaches, and hookers openly peddle their wares on the street. But the tiny, rundown apartment is all Jenny can afford. She normally doesn't leave the apartment at night, but the baby is craving Thai food, and Jenny can't afford to pay the delivery fee. She gathers her things and opens the front door; she's shocked to find Robbs in her hallway.

"Hey, Jen," Robbs greets her with an evil grin. "Did you really think that you could hide from me?"

"I didn't realize you were looking for me," she answers dismissively as she walks toward the staircase. The building doesn't have an elevator, but Jenny's unit is on the third floor so the staircase isn't much of an inconvenience.

"Did you really think that you could just run off with my child and I wouldn't care?" Robbs asks.

"Oh, so now it's your child?" Jenny snaps. "When I told you I was pregnant, you told me to get rid of it. That's why I lied to Paul in the first place; I want this baby but I didn't think that I could do it on my own."

"You can't hold my initial reaction against me, Jenny. You weren't jumping for joy at the thought of motherhood. I came around, just like you did," he argues.

"Yeah, you came around all right," Jenny snorts. "As soon as Paul started footing all of my bills, I couldn't get rid of you. But when that ended… when I told the truth and asked you to claim YOUR child, you started talking about abortions again… I was four months pregnant then, Robbs. Do you know what a monster that makes you?"

"Well, you'll be happy to know that I've changed my mind again. This baby is mine, Jenny, and I won't let you keep me from it."

"Ha," she laughs sarcastically. "You keep calling the baby 'it'. Some father you are; you don't even know your kid's gender."

"Do you know?" Robbs asked.

"Of course I do, but I'm not telling you because you are never going to lay eyes on this baby. I love my child, and I will do whatever it takes to make sure that it's safe, happy, and healthy. And that means that I have to make it impossible for you to find him or her. Now, if you'll excuse me, MY baby wants Thai food. I trust that you can find your way back to where you came from."

Jenny tries to move past Robbs; he grabs her by the arm and flings her into a wall. "You're not going anywhere, you baby-stealing bitch." Jenny lies on the floor, her arms guarding her swollen belly, and Robbs continues. "You're no better than that bitch Kiara. You both get off on stealing what's mine. But you know something, Jenny? Kiara's going to get what's coming to her. I'm going to hurt her so badly, she'll wish that she'd never won the spot in the apprenticeship competition. When I'm finished with her, she'll never land another job because no one will ever want to fuck her again."

He pulls a switchblade from his pocket and flips it open. "I can't wait to cut a map into that pretty little face of hers… maybe I should practice on you first."

The pure evil in Robbs' eyes sends adrenaline coursing through Jenny's body. Robbs is between her and the door of her apartment; she knows that she has no chance of making it back inside and locking Robbs out. She jumps from the floor and races for the stairs.

Jenny moves as fast as she can but her weight and awkwardness make it hard for her to move quickly. Robbs waits until she's halfway down the staircase before running after her. He catches up to her on the second floor landing and grabs Jenny by the hair. She stops abruptly and falls backwards.

"Please, Robbs," she sobs uncontrollably. "Please… the baby."

"The baby?" Robbs laughs. "The baby that I'm not allowed to see? I've got news for you, Jenny, if I can't have it, neither can you." He grabs her by the hair again and pulls her to her feet. Jenny prays that someone will hear their struggle and come to her rescue, but no help arrives.

"I'll see you in hell," Robbs sneers. "You go first."

Robbs slams his knee into the small of Jenny's back and sends her soaring down the staircase. She hits halfway down and tumbles to the first floor landing. Robbs calmly climbs down the staircase behind her. When he reaches Jenny's body, he bends down and searches for a pulse. He finds a faint one, but with the amount of blood pouring out onto the floor, Robbs knows that Jenny doesn't have long. He pulls on a stocking cap and steps out onto the street.

Sorry it had to end like that, Jenny. But don't worry... you'll have company in hell soon.

With more satisfaction than he has felt in months, Robbs sets out for Kiara's apartment.

Chapter Ten

After hanging up on James, I spend three hours packing my things. It's an easy task, since I still have the boxes I used to move in. This is by far the nicest place I've ever lived, but the price of staying is just too high. I refuse to stay in a situation where a man has control of my life. I've been on my own for far too long to change now. I will miss this apartment though.

I'm leaving behind everything James paid for, including the furniture, televisions, and practically everything in the kitchen. I haven't decided where I'm going yet; Austin would be the logical choice, which is why I've decided that I can't go back there. Between Paul and Robbs, I'd never have another moment of peace if I returned to Texas.

Maybe California would be nice. I've always wanted to see wine country… or I could go somewhere in the Midwest… no one would ever think to look for me there. All I want to do is disappear, to wipe the slate clean and start fresh. I've made a mess of everything; I need to be somewhere that no one knows me, where I can reinvent myself as the woman I want to be.

I flip open my laptop and log on to a discount airline ticket site. I compare ticket prices to several destinations; the cheapest tickets are to California, so I take it as a sign that that's where I'm supposed to go.

As I start the checkout process for a flight leaving in two days, my cell phone rings.

I glance down at the screen; it's a New York area code but I don't recognize the phone number.

"Hello?" I ask, hoping that the call is from the police and that they've finally found Robbs.

"Hello," a kind, female voice replies. "My name is Bridget. I work at Grace Memorial Hospital. I'm trying to reach Ms. Kiara Sands."

"This is Kiara," I reply, wondering why in the world I'm getting a call from the hospital.

"Hello, Ms. Sands. I'm sorry to call with bad news, but a friend of yours, a Ms. Foster, was just brought in to the emergency room. She's in pretty bad shape and hasn't regained consciousness, but we found her identification in her purse. Your name and number were behind her driver's license, with instructions to contact you in case of an emergency."

"Oh my god!" I gasp. "Jenny's been admitted? What happened? Is the baby all right?"

"Ms. Sands, all I can tell you right now is that she's here, and that she was brought in by ambulance. The doctors are with her now, but since she's unconscious it would be helpful if you came in and helped us with some details. The more we know about Ms. Foster's medical history, the more effectively we can treat her," Bridget explains.

"Yes, of course," I reply quickly. "I'll be there as soon as possible."

I hang up the phone, grab my purse, and rush out the door without setting the alarm. I hail a taxi at the curb and ask the driver to get me to Grace Memorial as quickly as possible. I'm grateful to see that the streets aren't busy. As we barrel through the city, guilt consumes me.

I should have answered her calls… I should have been there for her. What if she doesn't make it? And what in the world happened in the first place?

The driver pulls up to the emergency room entrance; I toss a twenty at him and jump out of the car. The emergency doors swing open, and I rush to the nurses' station.

"Hello, my name is Kiara Sands," I tell a small blonde behind the desk. "I'm here for Jenny Foster… I got a phone call, but no one could tell me what was going on."

"Yes, Ms. Sands, I'm Bridget," the blonde replies. "Ms. Foster has been taken up to surgery. If you'll follow me, I'll take you to the I.C.U. waiting area."

"I.C.U.?" I ask in a panic. "Is it that bad? What the hell is going on?" I ask as I follow Bridget to the elevator.

"Ms. Foster never regained consciousness before surgery, so we're not sure exactly what happened. A neighbor found her at the bottom of a staircase. We're assuming that she lost her balance and took a bad fall… it's sad, but these things happen more often than you'd think."

"So… the baby?" I'm afraid that I already know the answer, but I need to hear the words out loud.

"The doctors are doing everything they can… since we weren't able to question Ms. Foster, it's hard to predict the outcome. Do you know how far along she is? Or the gender of the baby?" Bridget asks. "The more developed the fetus is, the better chance it has… and if they have to deliver early, a little girl would have a better chance of survival than a little boy… that's how it is with preemies."

"She's about six months along," I tell Bridget; I'm ashamed of myself for not being able to provide more information. "I'm not sure if she's having a boy or girl… I'm not sure that Jenny even knows," I confess. The elevator doors open, and we step out onto the third floor of the hospital.

Bridget leads me to the waiting room and puts a comforting hand on my shoulder. "A doctor should be in soon, and there's a coffee machine just down the hall. Is there anything else I can get you before I get back to my station?"

"No," I tell her. "Thank you for everything."

Bridget nods. "Ms. Sands? If things go badly during surgery, Jenny is going to need a lot of support. Do you know how to contact any of her family?"

"No," I tell her. "Her parents are incredibly conservative… they cut ties with her when she told them she was pregnant."

And I cut ties with her, too, I think with tears in my eyes. I left her all alone, and now she could be dying.

Bridget sees my tears and offers to send the hospital chaplain to wait with me. I insist that that isn't necessary, and Bridget reluctantly leaves me alone in the waiting room. I sit there for what seems like hours; finally, a tall man in surgical scrubs enters the room. I'm the only one waiting, and he approaches me.

"Are you here for Ms. Foster?" he asks. I nod and introduce myself. "Hello, Ms. Sands, I'm Doctor Porter. Jenny pulled through surgery well; she's in a regular recovery room, I.C.U. won't be necessary. She should recover just fine, physically, but I'm afraid…"

"The baby didn't make it," I finish.

He nods. "There was just too much damage. Jenny's placenta detached, and the baby's oxygen supply was cut off too long. She also had some internal bleeding of her own; I got her out, but it was too late for us to save her."

"It was a girl?" I ask sadly. "Does Jenny know yet?"

"A nurse will tell her when she wakes up, unless you'd prefer to give her the news yourself."

"I would, please," I tell him. "I don't want her to hear it from a stranger."

"All right then, I'll take you to recovery now so you can be there when she wakes up."

I stand, gather my resolve, and follow him to the recovery area. Jenny is still out; her left arm is in a sling, and she has bruises on the right side of her face. I take a seat next to her, hold her hand, and try to figure out how to break the bad news.

<<◇>>

An hour and a half later, Jenny stirs in her hospital bed and slowly opens her eyes. She struggles to speak, and I realize that her mouth is dry. I quickly pour her a glass of ice water from the pitcher on the bedside table.

"Drink this," I tell her softly. "It will help." I hold the cup up to her lips and tip the water in to her mouth. Jenny sips slowly and leans back against her pillow.

"You're here," she says quietly, holding her stomach. Tears fill her eyes; I don't have to break the news to her, she already knows. "She didn't make it, did she? It was too soon…" Jenny breaks down in sobs and I climb into the bed next to her. I wrap my arms around her and let her cry on my shoulder until she has no tears left.

"I'm so sorry, Jenny," I tell her through my own tears. "I should have been there. I should have let you stay with me. This never would have happened."

"It's okay," she tells me. "He would have found me no matter where I was."

"He…?" I ask. "Jenny, what happened? The nurse said that you were unconscious when the ambulance brought you in. One of your neighbors found you at the bottom of the staircase. Everyone just assumed that you lost your balance and fell… but that's not what happened, is it?"

She shakes her head and tears fill her eyes again.

"Robbs?" I ask, even though I already know the answer.

She nods. "I was going out to pick up some Thai food. Maggie… that's what I named the baby… she loved when I ate spicy foods… she'd roll around for hours after I ate anything hot." She sighs and takes a moment to compose herself before continuing. "Anyway, I opened my front door and he was in the hallway. He had an evil look in his eyes, like nothing I've ever seen. He yelled and accused me of taking off with his child. He didn't even want her, Kiara! He told me so all of the time. He said he changed his mind, and I provoked him. I told him I didn't want him in the baby's life, and I threatened to disappear… to make sure he never met her… this is all my fault, Kiara!" She breaks down in sobs again and collapses on my shoulder.

I rub her back and try to offer her comfort. "This isn't your fault, Jenny. The only person responsible for this is Robbs. We have to call the police. What happened tonight was murder."

Jenny nods. "If we don't stop him, he'll kill both of us, Kiara. He threw me down the stairs and left me for dead. And he's coming for you too, he told me so. He said that he was going to hurt you so bad you'd wish you'd never met him."

"I already wish that I'd never met him," I tell her as I climb out of the bed. "I'm going to find a nurse and let them know that you're awake. I'm also going to have them call the police." I rummage through my purse until I find Officer Delco's card. I carry it to the nurses' station, and after I tell them that Jenny is awake, I explain that I need to call the police. I ask if I should call from the hospital phone or if I can use my cell.

"Just use our line." The nurse hands me the bulky receiver. I dial Officer Delco's number; he answers on the first ring.

"Delco."

"Officer Delco, this is Kiara Sands. You were at my apartment last week; it' had been ransacked and I told you that I suspected Robbs Martin was behind it?"

"Yes, Ms. Sands, I remember you. I'm sorry I haven't checked in lately, but we haven't been able to track down Mr. Martin. He hasn't bothered you again, I hope?"

"Not me," I tell him, "but there's been an incident with a friend of mine. Robbs showed up at her apartment tonight and threw her down a flight of stairs. She was six months pregnant, and the fall killed her baby. I understand that the crime didn't happen in your precinct, but I wanted to speak to someone who's already familiar with Robbs."

"Which hospital are you at?" he asks quickly.

"Grace Memorial."

"I'll be right there," he promises. "Precinct issues won't be a problem since I'm already running an open investigation on Martin. I'll contact the local P.D. and see if they want to send out their own officer to meet me."

"Thank you, Officer Delco."

"I'm sorry about your friend," he replies. "If I were better at my job, Robbs would have been in jail tonight."

"I think we're all blaming ourselves," I told him. "But that won't bring the baby back. We have to find him, Officer Delco."

"We will," he assures me. "He's a criminal, and all criminals eventually make mistakes. I'll be there in twenty minutes… I'll speak with you then."

I thank him again, hang up the phone, and return to Jenny's room.

"The police are on their way," I tell her. "The officer who's coming is already familiar with Robbs. He's been looking for him since last week, when someone broke into my apartment."

"What!" Jenny exclaims. "So he's already come after you?"

I shake my head. "I don't think he was coming after me, per se. I think he just wanted to rattle me that night. It worked too… I had a state of the art security system installed. You'll stay with me when they release you. We'll be safe there."

I don't tell Jenny that I've lost my job and will have to be out of the apartment in two weeks. I don't mention that I have no idea where I'm going after or what my next step is. There will be time for that, but she's been through too much tonight, and I don't want to put any added stress on her.

"Thank you, Kiara. I don't deserve your friendship, I know that. I lied and I used people, and now I'm paying the price. I've lost my little girl because I'm a horrible person and I never deserved her."

"Jenny, that's not true," I insist. "You made mistakes, but you're a good person. And no one deserves this."

She continues to sob and a nurse comes through the curtain with a syringe in her hand.

"There, there, Ms. Foster," the nurse says kindly. "I know that this is hard. The doctor left orders that you can have a sedative, if you want."

Jenny shakes her head. "No, the police are on their way, and I need to be awake to talk to them."

"Jenny, that can wait," I assure her. "If you need to rest, the cops can come back later, when you feel more up to this."

"*No!*" she insists again, this time more forcefully. "My baby is gone; I'm her mother and it was my job to protect her. I failed her in the worst way possible. *I am going to help find her murderer!*"

The nurse looks confused, and I realize that no one at the hospital knows the true story of what happened.

I turn to Jenny. "That's fine, Jenny, you don't have to take anything you don't want to take." I turn to the nurse. "Can I speak with you outside for a moment?"

"Of course," she replies. We step to the other side of the curtain and I quietly fill her in on the story.

"That poor girl, no wonder she's so distraught. I'm a mother myself… if someone had done this to me… I just can't imagine. It's standard procedure for the doctor to order a psych consult after a miscarriage. I'll call down and see if we can speed things up on that, and I'll make sure everyone knows what's going on. The last thing she needs is someone putting their foot in their mouth and making her feel worse."

"Thank you," I tell her. "I've already called the police. Once they leave, I'll talk her into taking the sedative. When will she be moved to a regular room?"

"Anytime, now that the anesthesia has worn off. I'll see if I can get that sped up, too."

"Thank you. That would be great. Could you arrange for a cot for me? I don't want to leave her here alone."

"Absolutely. Jenny is lucky to have you for a friend… she's going to need you for awhile. On top of the emotional trauma, her hormones are going to be completely out of whack for the next month or so." She returns to the nurse's station to make the arrangements; I remain rooted to the floor, full of guilt after listening to her words.

I've been a horrible friend. But there's nothing that I can do about that now. All I can do is be better from now on.

With a sigh, I step back through the curtain and return to Jenny's side.

Chapter Eleven

"I'm so sorry, ladies, but we haven't been able to find Martin yet," Officer Delco tells Jenny and me. It's been three days since Robbs attacked Jenny; it seems that he's vanished off of the face of the earth.

"No flight records or anything?" I ask with frustration.

"Nothing," he sighs. "We've put out an A.P.B; every security checkpoint at every airport in New York has his picture. If he tries to leave the state by plane, we'll get him. From what we've been able to gather, he hasn't shown back up in Austin. We have officers there looking for him as well. We've put a trace on his credit cards and cell phone, but there hasn't been any activity on anything."

"So he's using cash and a burner phone," I say.

Officer Delco nods. "And that will make it harder to find him, but I promise you that we won't give up. Warrants have already been issued for him. As soon as he turns up, he'll be charged with the attempted murder of Jenny, the first-degree murder of little Maggie, and a laundry list of other charges like stalking and harassment… I know that that doesn't make anything better, but I promise that Robbs Martin will be stopped."

Jenny nods with tears in her eyes. She's been crying a lot these past few days; I completely understand, but it makes me feel helpless. There's nothing that I can do but sit here with her, hold her hand, and let her know that she's not alone. I haven't made any promises about everything being all right because I'm not sure that it will be. I see her pain, but I can't empathize; I can't imagine the grief she's feeling.

"Have you tracked down his parents yet?" I ask.

"I've found his dad, but he swears that he hasn't seen Robbs in months," Officer Delco tells us. "According to him, Robbs has always been a bit unstable. He was a difficult child and an even more difficult teenager. He was arrested twice for assault and battery while he was still a minor, but his records were sealed when he turned eighteen. His dad says that he tried to treat Robbs with a firm hand, tried to force him into therapy, but his mother was the complete opposite. She coddled him and made excuse for his actions. The parents are divorced; I haven't been able to reach his mother."

"Can't you send an officer to her house?" Jenny demands. "Surely there's good cause to search her home."

"I can do that, as soon as I find an address on her," Officer Delco explains. "She's been as hard to track down as her son. I assure you, I have an entire team of officers working on this case. We are taking every lead seriously, we just have to be patient and wait for Robbs to slip up. In the meantime, I wish you'd reconsider letting me post a guard at your door."

Jenny shakes her head. "I don't want the attention, and it's not necessary. I know Robbs Martin, Officer Delco. He's a coward… he'd never come after us here. If he comes for us, he'll wait until we're alone. He's not going to walk into a crowded hospital."

"If you insist." Officer Delco sighs. "I need to get back to the precinct. I'll be back after my shift. Is there anything else I can bring either of you?"

We both thank him and tell him we're fine. Since we've been at Grace Memorial, Officer Delco has gone above and beyond to be as helpful as possible. I haven't wanted to leave Jenny, so he went to each of our apartments and gathered clothes, toothbrushes, and our cell phone chargers. He visits several times a day, each time with a small gift to help us pass the time in the hospital room. Books, magazines, and playing cards are scattered across the bedside table.

"All right then, I'll see you in a few hours. Call me if you need anything, or if you think of something that may help us find Robbs."

He exits the room, leaving Jenny and I alone. We sit quietly for a long time, our eyes fixed on the television. A commercial for *Kitchen Wars* comes on and I cringe, knowing what's about to happen.

"Look, there's James," Jenny says, pointing at the screen. "Oh my god, Kiara, I completely forgot about your job! Is he all right with you missing so much work? I'd be fine if you need to leave for awhile… I really can't believe that you've been here so long."

"I'm here because I want to be," I insist. "And James isn't missing me at The Madden Crowd. I quit about an hour before the E.R. called and told me about… that I needed to come here.”

“You quit your job?” Jenny gasps. “Why in the world would you do that, Kiara? That was a once in a lifetime opportunity.”

“I just wasn’t a good fit with the rest of the staff,” I lie. “And I’m not happy in New York. I don’t belong here. I was actually trying to decide where to go next, before everything happened.”

“You don’t want to go back to Austin?” she asks.

“I didn’t think that I had anything to go back to,” I explain. My eyes start tearing up. “I feel so alone, Jenny… ever since my parents.”

“I’m sure you have, Kiara,” she interrupts. “I know that losing them in that accident was terrible for you.”

I remember that Jenny doesn’t know the truth about my parents. This is basically the only friend I have in the world, and she doesn’t even know me. I wipe my tears and tell her the truth.

“I’m sorry I lied before,” I tell her after giving her the full story. “It sounds stupid now, but I felt like I couldn’t trust anyone… and I didn’t want to be pitied. I’m so sorry…”

This time, Jenny is the one to wrap a comforting arm around me. “It’s okay, Kiara, I understand.”

“You do?” I ask.

"Of course I do. The two people in this world that you were supposed to be able to trust and rely on betrayed you. You were forced to grow up and take care of yourself long before you were supposed to. I don't know how you survived it, but it makes total sense that you'd have trust issues after that… thank you for trusting me with the truth now."

"That's it?" I ask. "You're really not mad at me? I've been raking you over the coals for months for not being truthful, and you're going to forgive me just like that?" I can't believe the kindness and understanding she's showing me.

"I forgive you, just like that," she tells me. "My lie was worse than yours… and you've forgiven me, right?"

"Yes," I tell her. "I should have forgiven you immediately. I should have been there…"

"Kiara, we can't keep going back and forth like this." Jenny sighs. "I don't blame you for anything. Can we just start over? Leave the past in the past and move on from here?"

"Absolutely," I agree. "We just have to figure out where we're moving on to… do you want to stay in New York City?"

Jenny shakes her head vehemently. "God no, I don't care if I ever set foot in this city again."

"Do you want to go back to Austin?"

She considers the question for a moment before answering. "I do. I understand why you might not want to, but for me Austin is home. My parents are close… if they ever speak to me again.”

“Then we’ll go home,” I tell her. “Texas is my home, too, even if it wasn’t always a happy one… did you let go of your apartment before you came here?”

She nods. “I broke my lease, I sold my car… and I’ve burned through almost all of my savings.”

“I sold my car, too, but I have a little money in the bank,” I tell her. “We’ll figure something out. We’ll get a one-bedroom if we have to, until we both get back on our feet. We’ll find a way to make it work.”

“I don’t know, Kiara.” Jenny hesitates. “I don’t feel right, letting you foot the bill for everything.”

“Don’t worry about it,” I assure her. “I’m sure the time will come for you to return the favor. That’s what friends do, right?” I smile.

“Right.” She smiles back. Jenny yawns and a nurse comes in with her afternoon pain medicine. Her surgical incisions are healing nicely, but her left rotator cuff is torn. She’ll need surgery to repair it, but her doctors think that it’s best to wait until all of her other injuries have healed. The nurse hands her the small cup of pills; Jenny tosses them in her mouth and chases them with water. The nurse leaves; Jenny rolls over and looks at me.

“I’m exhausted… I’ll probably be out for awhile. You can leave if you want to. Go home and take a nap in a real bed, I’ll be fine,” she insists.

I shake my head. "I'm fine here. I'm not going anywhere without you."

<<◇>>

Robbs steps out of Kiara's steam shower and wraps himself in her bathrobe. After leaving Jenny's apartment a few nights ago, he'd headed straight to Kiara's. He'd been amped up and ready to get rid of her, but when he was a block away from her building, he'd spotted her jumping into a taxi. That's when he'd pulled his phone out and turned on his spy cam app. He rewound the footage and watched her receive the call from Grace Memorial.

Damn it, that bitch is still alive, he'd thought when he realized that the call was about Jenny. His mood improved when he watched Kiara run out of the apartment without setting her alarm. Equipped with his lock pick kit, he'd let himself into her home. He'd spent hours going through her clothes and keepsakes, careful to put everything back exactly how he'd found it.

Robbs had accidentally fallen asleep in Kiara's bed that first night. He woke up the next morning in a panic, and then realized that there was no reason to worry. Kiara must have stayed at the hospital. He lounged in the bed for awhile and a new plan formed in his head. He climbed out of the bed, dressed quickly, and retrieved the hidden camera from Kiara's kitchen. He rode the elevator down to the lobby and reset the camera so that it pointed directly at the building's entrance.

Now I'll know when she gets back… I'll hide somewhere in the apartment and catch her off guard.

He returned to the apartment and eagerly awaited Kiara's return. Several hours passed and he grew bored watching the small screen on his phone. He flipped on the television and was shocked to see his own face looking back at him. He turned up the volume and listed to the local news report.

"Mr. Martin is wanted in connection to an attempted murder last night," the news anchor announced. "He's also suspected to be behind several stalking and harassment incidents. The police believe that he is armed and dangerous. Anyone with information on the whereabouts of Robbs Martin is asked to contact the Manhattan precinct of the NYPD."

Damn it! I can't risk going out for awhile… I have to wait until a new story hits and this blows over… Once I finish off Kiara, I'll stick her in the pantry and stay here for a few days… I'll take care of Jenny once the heat dies down. She'll go back to Texas… it will be easier to get to her there.

But things didn't go as Robbs had planned. A few hours after watching the news program, a uniformed officer stepped into the lobby. He wasn't positive that the cop was headed to Kiara's, but he knew that he couldn't take any chances. He hid in the pantry; a few moments later, he'd heard Kiara's door open.

Robbs kept his breathing steady and his eyes focused on the screen of his cell phone. He watched as the officer collected a toothbrush, toothpaste, deodorant, and a razor from Kiara's bathroom. From there, the cop moved on to Kiara's bedroom and disappeared into the closet. He emerged a few moments later, the bag in his hands much bulkier than it had been when he entered.

What the fuck is going on? Robbs wondered. His question was answered a few moments later when the cop's phone rang.

"Delco. Yes, I'll get right on it… No, I haven't made it to the hospital yet. Ms. Sands refuses to leave Ms. Foster's bedside, so I offered to pick up some essentials from each of their apartments… Friday, at the earliest. The doctors said that she can't leave until she's no longer vulnerable to infection… No, I haven't heard back from the Austin P.D. yet… All right, keep me posted."

Officer Delco left the apartment; Robbs left the pantry and returned to the couch. He'd spent the next three days making himself at home in Kiara's apartment. He ate her food, he used her shampoo, and he tried on every single article of her clothing.

Wrapped in Kiara's bathrobe, Robbs makes his way to the living room. He collapses on the couch and checks the clock. The evening news is about to start, so he flips on the television. The network has been keeping the public updated on the search for him, as well as Jenny's condition. The opening credits flash across the screen and Robbs turns up the volume.

"Good evening," the male anchor begins. "At the top of the program, we have an update on the search for suspected murderer Robbs Martin. The police have received hundreds of leads but so far, the criminal remains at large. One of his victims, who is still unnamed, is improving at a local hospital. Anonymous sources tell us that the victim will be released tomorrow and moved to an undisclosed location. The NYPD asks again for anyone with information about Mr. Martin to call the Manhattan precinct. They also asked us to remind the public that Mr. Martin should be considered armed and dangerous. Now, in other news…"

Robbs flips off the television. *She is being released tomorrow. Kiara's been there this whole time. I bet they'll both come back here. This is the last place anyone would ever expect to find me… they'll think it's safe here… this is perfect.*

Robbs is excited and aroused by the idea that in twenty-four hours, both of the women who ruined his life will be dead; he doesn't spare a single thought for his daughter. He sets off for Kiara's kitchen, takes a beer from her refrigerator, and celebrates the end of his troubles.

Chapter Twelve

"All right, Ms. Foster, you're cleared for discharge," Doctor Parks announces with a smile. The nurses drew several vials of blood from Jenny this morning for lab work. Doctor Parks has just given her a thorough exam and seems satisfied with her recovery.

"Thank you for everything," Jenny tells him.

"You're more than welcome," he replies. "I wish there had been more I could do. I've taken the liberty of having your prescriptions filled at the hospital pharmacy," he tells her, pulling three pill bottles from the pocket of his white exam coat. "That will save you an errand and help you get out of town as quickly as possible. I've also made an appointment for you with one of the best orthopedic surgeons in Austin. You'll see him next week, and he'll schedule your surgery. He already has your records."

"Thank you so much," I tell him. "You've been so helpful… everyone has."

"It's the least we could do, Ms. Sands," he says. "Jenny is in your hands now. Please, both of you, get out of the city as quickly as possible. Find someplace where no one would think to look for you and stay there until the police apprehend that monster."

"We will," I assure him. "Jenny's booked on a flight out this evening. I'm going to stay the night at my place and tie up a few loose ends. I'll join her in Austin tomorrow."

Doctor Parks nods his approval. "Good luck, girls. Take care of each other." He leaves the room and I turn to Jenny.

"Are you ready to go?"

"I've been ready to leave since the moment I got here." Jenny is more depressed today than she's been since the attack; I know it's because she'd spent months imagining the day she'd leave the hospital with her baby. Instead, she's leaving with a broken heart and a target on her back. "Do you really think we'll be able to get out of the city without him finding us?" she asks softly.

"I don't know," I admit. "But we have to try." We leave the hospital room and ride the elevator down to the lobby. We climb into a waiting taxi, and Jenny gives the driver her address.

"Are you sure that you feel like going back there?" I ask. "I can pack your things on my own… we could go sit in a café or something until it's time for your flight."

"No, I have to go back. I know it will be painful, but I need the closure. Delco promised to have a guard at the door, so we'll be safe," she reminds me.

A half hour later, we arrive at her building. I'm shocked to see the horrible condition of the neighborhood, and I regret even more that I hadn't taken Jenny in when she'd arrived in the city. But I'd promised not to apologize anymore, so I don't say anything.

Jenny blushes as we step through into the entryway of her building. "This isn't nearly as nice as your place…"

"Don't worry about that," I insist. "You should have seen some of the places I lived with my parents after they started all of their shit. A couple of the apartments make this place look like the Taj Mahal."

We climb the three flights of stairs to Jenny's floor. It's a slow trip, as Jenny's still incredibly sore from the attack and stiff from spending a week in a hospital bed. As promised, a uniformed officer is standing guard at her door. He greets us as we approach.

"Good afternoon Ms. Foster, Ms. Sands. Everything's been calm here. You ladies go on in and get packed; I'll make sure nothing happens to you. Ms. Sands, when we're done here I'll head over to your apartment."

"Thank you, Officer Michaels," I say, reading his badge.

Officer Michaels opens the door for us, and we step inside. Jenny has only been in New York for a few weeks, and she'd arrived with a single suitcase. The apartment had come furnished, so it only takes us a few minutes to pack her things. I can tell that Jenny is exhausted, so I suggest that we relax on her couch until it's time to head to the airport.

"No," she insists. "I needed to see this place one last time, but now I want to leave. Let's go to a café, like you suggested, and we'll run through our plan again."

"Whatever you want," I reply with a smile. "We'll find somewhere near J.F.K. Let me carry that," I add, taking the suitcase from her hand. I extend the handle and roll the suitcase into the hall. Jenny follows and gives the door a final slam behind her.

Accompanied by Officer Michaels, we walk back down the staircase and out onto the sidewalk. He waits with us until we find a cab and promises to see me at my apartment.

"I'll make sure that the place is clear for you before you get there," he promises.

I thank him and shut the taxi door.

"Where to?" the driver asks impatiently as he pulls away from the curb.

"Our final destination is J.F.K.," I tell him. "But we don't have to be there for a few more hours. Do you know of a place near there that we could sit and drink coffee for awhile?"

"Sure thing," the driver replies.

Jenny looks out the rear window of the taxi until her building disappears. With tears in her eyes once more, she faces forward, takes my hand, and says, "Thank you, Kiara."

I squeeze her hand in reply, and we ride the rest of the way to the café in silence.

Robbs paces the floors of Kiara's apartment, impatiently awaiting her arrival. He checks his watch and cusses the fact that he can't leave the apartment without the risk of being arrested. He knows that the police will probably catch up with him eventually, but he's determined to get rid of Kiara and Jenny first.

He'd been tempted to venture out and find a safe spot to stakeout the hospital. As much as he longed to know what was going on and when Kiara and Jenny would be out in the open again, he knew that going to Grace Memorial would be the equivalent of walking into the police station and turning himself in. The cops are assholes, but they're not stupid. They were sure to have lookouts posted outside of the hospital, waiting for him to show up. They'd probably send someone home with the girls to check the place out, but Robbs isn't concerned about that. If a cop walks through the door with the women, he'll meet the same end they do.

Robbs has had a lot of time to think and plan since he arrived at Kiara's apartment. That cop, Delco, had taken her laptop to the hospital, but her desktop had been a godsend. He'd lifted some credit cards the day before he attacked Jenny, in anticipation of having to make a quick get-away after taking care of Kiara. He used the cards to buy a bus ticket to Virginia and a plane ticket from there to Mexico City. He had his black wig and glasses on hand to disguise himself during his flight from the city.

Robbs had also used the desktop to try and determine how far the search for him had traveled. He browsed local and national news sites and was confident that he'd be safe once he left the northeast. Texas was the only exception; the news outlets there were running more stories about his case than the ones in New York. It seemed like everyone Robbs had ever met had come forward to tell their Robbs Martin stories. Every single one of them insisted that the current accusations against him weren't at all surprising.

Robbs stops cold in his tracks as he watches a new uniformed officer enter the lobby of Kiara's building. He waits hopefully, expecting Kiara and Jenny to appear any moment. Instead, the cop walks alone to the elevator, steps inside, and reaches for the buttons as the door closes and cuts off Robbs' view.

Shit! What's going on now? He rushes to the pantry and shuts the door behind him. He stays there for almost ten minutes but doesn't hear the front door open. He quietly opens the pantry and creeps to the front door. He looks out the peephole and sees the cop standing guard in the hallway.

They're not with him, but they must be on their way, he realizes happily. He sets off for Kiara's kitchen to get ready for the big event.

<<<>>>

"All right," I say to Jenny as I roll her suitcase into the airport. "Do you have your ticket?"

"It's in my purse," she answers nervously. "Kiara, are you sure that we should do this? Maybe I should stay with you tonight and we can fly home together tomorrow. Or you could leave with me now, and we could send someone to pack up your things… I hate the idea of splitting up… Until they find Robbs, I feel like we're safer together."

I shake my head. "You have to leave tonight. All signs point to Robbs still being in the city, which means this is the last place you should be. I have to be out of my apartment by the end of next week, which is finals week for Chase, so I can't ask him to come out here and get my things. I'll be fine, Jenny. Officer Michaels will be here to check things out, and I have the alarm system. I'll be in Austin by lunchtime tomorrow."

"You could ask Paul to come pack for you," she suggests stubbornly. "When he called, he said that if we need anything, all we have to do is ask."

"I don't want any favors from Paul Weston," I insist. "I'm done with that type of guy, Jenny. All I want is to get back home, find a place to live, and focus on putting my life back together. If I ask Paul for anything, I'll be opening the door to let him back in my life."

"All right," Jenny sighs. We approach the security checkpoint where we'll be forced to part ways. Jenny turns to me, and I wrap her in a gentle hug.

"Chase will be at the airport to pick you up," I remind her. "He's taking you back to his place. He's going to stay with a friend in his building and give us his apartment until we find our own."

"He seems like such a nice guy… but I'm afraid it will be awkward, getting picked up by a stranger," Jenny says nervously.

"The moment you meet him, you'll feel like you've known him forever," I assure her. "Now get going, I don't want you to miss your flight."

"I love you, Kiara," Jenny says as she hugs me again.

"I love you too, Jenny. I'll see you tomorrow," I promise.

Jenny walks up to the security desk, hands the clerk her ticket and driver's license, and is quickly issued a boarding pass and shuffled into the line for the metal detectors. I make my way back to the sidewalk, where my taxi is still waiting. I give the driver my address and my cell phone chimes. I fetch it from my purse and see Officer Delco's number on the screen.

"Hello?"

"Kiara, did you get Jenny to the airport safely?"

"Yes, I just left her. I stayed until she went through security."

"Great," he says with a relieved sight. "Look, Kiara, I had to pull Michaels from your place. There's been a homicide in the district, and it's all hands on deck. I hate to ask this, but can you stay away from the apartment for a few more hours? I'll call and let you know when I can meet you there. I really don't want you going in to the place before an officer has a chance to check it out."

"That's fine," I tell him. "I'll talk to you soon."

I hang up the phone and sit silently for a moment. I really just want to get my stuff packed and get it over with, and I'm confident that the alarm system will have kept out any intruders. I decide to go on home as planned; Delco may get irritated when he learns that I went in to the apartment on my own, but by the time he finds out it won't matter anymore.

The taxi pulls up at my building; I pay the driver and add a generous tip. As I step out onto the sidewalk, I realize that this is the last time that I'll be 'coming home' to this apartment. The thought doesn't sadden me at all. I step into the lobby, hit the elevator call button, and wait patiently for the car to arrive. I scan the lobby while I wait; something seems off but I can't place what it is. The elevator doors open, and I step inside. I rush of anxiety hits me as the elevator climbs to my floor; I try to shake it off, assuring myself that anyone would be rattled after everything that's happened these last few weeks.

The elevator arrives at my floor; I step into the hallway and everything seems normal. I unlock my apartment, push open the door, and reach for my alarm keypad. That's when I remembered that I'd run out of the apartment without activating the alarm.

Shit, I think as I realize that the alarm is disabled. Did I forget to turn it off when I left? I must have, I ran out of here so fast. I make my way to the bedroom and deposit my bags on the floor. I don't bother unpacking the clothes Officer Delco had brought to the hospital, but I do need to check some stuff on my laptop. I pull the computer from my bag and carry it in to my kitchen.

As I make my way around the house, I realize that nothing is where I left it. The ottoman is in front of the couch instead of the chair, a single chair is pulled out from the dining room table, and one of my silk nightgowns is lying across the kitchen island. I rush back to the bedroom to retrieve my phone. I fumble through my purse until I find it; Officer Delco answers on the first ring.

"Kiara… is everything all right? I'm at the crime scene now, it's worse than I'd expected. We may have to wait until tomorrow morning to get your apartment packed up. Do you…"

"Officer Delco, I'm in the apartment now," I admit quickly. I don't give him a chance to lecture me. "There are a lot of things out of place. I thought maybe you'd done it when you came and picked up my stuff, but then I saw a piece of my lingerie in the kitchen… I'm assuming that that wasn't you?"

"Kiara, get out of the apartment right now," he demands. "I'm getting in my car, but it will take me at least twenty minutes to get there. Don't stop to take anything, just get out. Go to that diner across from the building, I'll meet you there. Have you received any calls from the alarm company?"

"I forgot to set it," I confess. "I'm so sorry, Officer Delco, I should have listened to you. I'm sure this is nothing, I'm probably just on edge after everything that's happened."

"It's not nothing," he insists. "I'm turning on my siren, I'll be there in ten. I've got to make some calls and explain why I've just left a crime scene. Get *out* of that apartment, Kiara," he demands again before ending the call.

I stick my phone in my back pocket, grab my keys from my purse, and rush down the hallway. As I near the front door, a voice calls out from behind me.

"Hello, Kiara."

I turn and stare into the evil eyes of Robbs Martin.

-To be continued in Book 4-

Book Four

Chapter One

I SEARCH Robbs' eyes for any sign of humanity, but all I see is wild rage. I know there's not a chance that I'll be able to talk my way out of this, but I try anyway.

"Robbs," I say calmly. "What are you doing here?"

"I've been waiting for you, Kiara. I've been waiting for a really long time. You don't think you're leaving, do you?" He gestures to the keys in my hand. "You just got here."

He takes a couple of steps toward me, and I instinctively back away. "You haven't answered my question, Robbs. What are you doing here?"

He pulls one of my chef's knives from his back pocket and points the blade at me. "I'm here to give you what you deserve. You know as well as I do that you've slept your way to the top. This should have been *my* apartment. You stole it from me, just like you stole the apprenticeship back in Austin. I could outcook you all day long, but I just can't satisfy the executive chefs quite the same way you can. It's not fair."

Just stall him. Delco is on his way. Just keep him talking until the cops get here.

"Robbs, you're clearly upset. But so far, you haven't done anything that you can't come back from.

I'm sure that any decent attorney could keep you out of jail. Please don't do anything to make things worse for yourself." I try to keep my voice even. I don't want Robbs to have the satisfaction of seeing my fear.

He lets out an evil laugh. "Nice try, Kiara, acting like you're worried about *me*. It's completely unnecessary, I have a foolproof plan all worked out." He takes another step toward me.

I remain rooted in place. I don't want to put any more distance between myself and the front door.

"As soon as I'm done with you," he continues, "I'm going to go finish what I started with your slutty little friend. I thought I'd done the job right the first time, but the bitch just wouldn't die, would she? I wasn't counting on a neighbor finding her. But I learned from that mistake. You'll be cold before anyone finds you. And once Jenny is taken care of, I'll disappear. I'm a master at reinventing myself. I'm thinking a life near the beach is in order. The sun and fresh air will be good for me, after all of the hell you've put me through."

"You'll never get away with it," I tell him defiantly. "The cops will grab you the moment you try to go near Jenny. You'll never hurt her again, and you'll rot in prison if you hurt me."

"They'll have to find me first," he snarls. "And even if they do, any punishment they give me will be well worth it. Knowing that you're in the ground will be the warm blanket that keeps me warm in prison."

He lunges at me and knocks me in to the hallway wall. The back of my head hits the hard sheetrock, and I slide to the floor. I feel dizzy, and it takes me several moments to focus my eyes. When I finally do, I see Robbs moving toward me with the knife.

Where the hell is Delco?

Robbs bends down and grabs me by the front of my shirt. I lean into the wall as he pulls me to my feet. I've never been a particularly religious person. I've kind of always thought that if God did exist, he'd forgotten about me a long time ago. But in this moment, with Robbs holding me against the wall and pressing the cold blade to my neck, all I can do is pray.

Please help me. Please send someone. I'm not ready to die.

I hear the crack of the front door being kicked open, and a rush of relief fills me.

Thank you. I can't believe that worked. Thank you.

"Kiara?" Paul cries out. "Kiara, are you here?"

Robbs is caught off guard by Paul's sudden appearance, and I'm able to wiggle out of his grip.

"I'm here, Paul," I call out through my tears. I race down the hallway, followed closely by Robbs. "So is Robbs! He was here when I got home!"

Paul rounds the corner into the hallway and quickly gets between me and Robbs. "Get out of here, Kiara! Go to the diner across the street and wait for me. I'll take care of this trash."

"NO, NO, NO!" Robbs screams. "Get the fuck back here, you bitch."

"Paul, he has a knife!" I warn as Robbs lunges for him.

Paul hits the wall but isn't knocked out.

"*Go*, Kiara," Paul demands again. He grabs a hold of Robbs' wrist and keeps the knife at bay. I'm torn between wanting to stay and help him and wanting to get the hell away as fast as possible.

Paul can handle him. And if he can't, I don't want to be here for Robbs to slice into next. I'll call the cops from the diner.

I race toward the door and find it splintered, barely hanging from its hinges. I step through the wreckage and race for the elevator. I listen for sounds from my apartment but I can't hear anything. My ears are still ringing from hitting my head on the wall. The elevator doors open, and I jump inside. My heart pounds as I descend to the ground floor and escape to the sidewalk. I cross the street and step into the diner, but I still feel an overwhelming urge to flee.

What the FUCK happened to Delco?

A tired, middle-aged brunette approaches my table. "What can I get you?" she asks halfheartedly.

"Coffee and water, please," I quickly reply. She leaves, and I pull my phone from my back pocket. Delco had promised to be here in ten minutes, but that was twenty minutes ago. I dial his number.

"Kiara, I hit traffic. I'm still about ten minutes out. Was it Martin? Is he still there?"

"It was him. He tried to kill me. He would have killed me, but my ex-boyfriend showed up and kicked the door in. I'm safe now, in the diner across the street. Paul told me to wait for him here, but so far neither of them has left the building. Robbs had one of my professional butcher knives. I… I don't know if Paul was armed. "

"Kiara, you don't sound like you feel safe," Officer Delco quickly replies. "And I'm not sure that you are. If Robbs is the one who walks out of that apartment, he'll come straight for you. What time is your flight scheduled?"

"Ten o'clock tomorrow morning."

"Were you able to get anything out of the apartment? Do you have cash?"

"I have my purse and my keys. There's about a hundred dollars in cash in my wallet."

"Okay, great. I want you to calmly step outside and hail a taxi. Take it to Airport Suites. My brother-in-law is a manager there. I'll call ahead and let him know that you're coming. He'll put you in the closest room to the front desk and arrange for someone to escort you to airport security in the morning. Bruce will cut you a deal, and let you pay for the room in cash. I'll call you there as soon as I know what's happened at your apartment."

I pull a five-dollar bill out of my wallet and toss it on the table to cover my check. I try to remain as calm as possible as I step back outside, but I can't keep my eyes off of my building. I know that Robbs could walk out at any moment. At this point, I wouldn't put it past him to attack me on the street. To my relief, an empty taxi is waiting just down the curb. I jump inside and give the driver the name of the hotel. As my building disappears in the rearview mirror, my anxiety finally begins to subside.

I guess that prayer thing really worked. Thanks for sending Paul. If you're still listening, I'd appreciate it if you could get him out of there safely.

I pace the worn carpet of my hotel room, waiting for my phone to ring. It's been two hours since I arrived at Airport Suites, and I still haven't heard from Delco. As promised, Bruce had put me in the room directly across from the front desk. I feel safe here, but I'm dying to know what happened back at my apartment.

I'm startled by a knock at my door and cautiously peek through the peep hole. Delco is waiting on the other side of the door; I fling it open.

"Did you get Robbs? Is Paul okay?" I ask urgently.

Delco steps into the room, rolling my largest suitcase behind him. "Robbs was already gone when I got there," he tells me with a sigh. "Mr. Weston was knocked out. He's fine now. Paramedics checked him out on scene. He'll have a hell of a headache for the next few days, but no lasting harm was done."

"So he got the knife away from Robbs?" I ask with relief. I'm upset that Robbs is still on the loose, but relieved that Paul wasn't hurt.

"Yes, according to Paul's statement, Robbs was on top of him with the knife but he was able to wrestle it away. That didn't slow Robbs down much though. Paul took a few punches to the head. Apparently Robbs didn't want to kill him, or he'd have grabbed the knife again once Paul was out."

"Where is Paul now?"

"He's on his way to the airport. He wanted to come to you, but I convinced him to give you some space. You mentioned he was your ex-boyfriend, I wasn't sure if you'd want to see him or not. I promised that you'd call him when you're ready."

"Thank you, Detective Delco. You've really gone above and beyond for Jenny and me."

"My sister went through something similar to this," he explains. "She lives in Los Angeles. A LAPD officer saved her life and put her stalker behind bars. I take cases like this pretty personally. I figured the last thing you'd want to do is go back to your apartment, so I took the liberty of bringing this." He gestures to the suitcase. "I had a female officer pack some of your things, I hope that you don't mind."

"Of course not, thank you. And you're right, I never want to see the inside of that apartment again. The rent is paid up through the end of the month, so I'll see if I can get a friend to fly out and pack up the rest of my personal things. I don't know what to do with all the furniture… I've still got a storage unit full of stuff in Austin."

"I have a suggestion. My niece just rented a new apartment in the city. She could pack up your personal things and ship them to you and in exchange, you could sell her the furniture at a discount."

"That would be perfect. In fact, if she'll clean the apartment after she packs up, she can just have the furniture."

"I'm sure she'll be delighted. Is there anything else you need before you fly out tomorrow?"

I shake my head. "No, I just want to take a long, hot bath and then sleep until it's time to leave this city."

"After what you've been through, I don't blame you. Did Jenny land in Austin safely?"

"Yes, she sent me a text about an hour ago. I didn't tell her what happened tonight. I figured she has enough to worry about. What's being done to find Robbs?"

"We've put out an APB. The airports, bus terminals, and train stations all have his picture. I've got people processing your apartment now, looking for signs of how he got in and how long he may have been there. One of our tech guys is going through the history on your desktop to see if he researched any destinations or bought any tickets."

"He said that he was going after Jenny again when he was done with me," I tell him.

"I've alerted the Austin PD that he could be on his way. I wish that there was more we could do."

"I wish there was, too." I sigh. "I know I'll be looking over my shoulder until Robbs is behind bars."

"Can you and Jenny stay with your friend Chase until he's caught? I hate the idea of you two girls on your own."

"Once Chase finds out about tonight, he'll probably organize a rotating guard of his football buddies. Robbs will have a hard time getting to us if we're surrounded by college linebackers," I joke.

"I like the sound of that. I hate to leave you, but I really need to be getting back to work. Have a safe flight tomorrow. You have my number. If you need anything at all, just give me a call. I'll let you know if the crime scene techs find anything in your apartment."

I walk the detective to the door. "Thank you again for everything, Detective Delco."

"You're welcome, Kiara. I'm sorry that you didn't have a better time in The Big Apple."

"It wasn't the city. I was trying to escape my past, but it just followed me here. Tomorrow, I'll fly home and face it. For now, I just want to sleep."

Chapter Two

I spend most of the night trying to get to sleep, but I'm haunted by the memory of Robbs' evil glare. At four-thirty, I give up on the idea of rest and call the airline. They have a seat available on a six-forty flight to Austin, so I change my reservation. By five-fifteen, I'm on the hotel shuttle to the airport.

We pull up to the departure gate, and the shuttle driver helps me unload my suitcase. I can't help but be on edge. As I move through the airport, I keep my eyes peeled for any sign of Robbs. Delco assured me that Robbs would never be able to get past airport security, but he's evaded the police so far. I don't feel safe until I'm finally on the plane. The flight is nonstop to Austin, so once we're safely in the air, I recline my seat and drift off to sleep.

"This is your captain speaking. We're now approaching Austin for landing. Please secure your tray tables and carry ons, buckle your seatbelts, and return your seats to the upright position. Local time is eleven-thirty a.m."

The pilot's booming voice wakes me up, and I move my seat up as directed. I gaze out the window as we begin our descent. When the wheels touch down on the runway, I feel at home.

I stay seated and let the other passengers rush off the plane. I'm groggy from my nap and don't feel like fighting through the mad dash. I pull my cell phone from my purse and turn it on. It chimes immediately, and I see that I have six new voicemails. I dial in to my messages as I exit the plane.

"Hey, Kiara, it's Chase. It's nine o'clock, I just wanted to make sure that your flight is still scheduled for ten. A couple of guys from the team are going to come stay with Jenny so I can pick you up at the airport. Give me a call back if you get a chance before you board."

There's no point calling him now. I'll just grab a taxi to the apartment.

I delete Chase's message and move on to the next.

"Kiara, it's Paul. Look, I promised that detective that I'd give you some space, but I'd really like to know that you're okay. I gave my statement last night and then hopped a red eye back to Austin. I'll be at the restaurant all day, but I'll keep my phone on me. Check in if you don't mind, just a text is fine."

He did save my life, the least I could do is call him. I'll do it after I get home.

I delete the message and stick my phone back in my purse without listening to the rest of the voicemails. I'm sure that they're all from Chase, Jenny, or Paul, and I'll be talking to all of them soon enough. I make my way to the baggage terminal just as the conveyor belt starts moving and luggage starts falling from the shoot. I retrieve my suitcase and roll it out onto the sidewalk. A line of taxis are waiting at the curb. I hop into one just as my cell starts ringing. I look at the screen and recognize the Culinary Institute's phone number. I give the driver Chase's address and answer the call.

"Hello?"

"Hello, may I please speak with Ms. Kiara Sands?"

"This is Kiara Sands."

"Ms. Sands, this is Ruby Miller from *Le Cordon Bleu*. I regret to inform you, but you're scholarship for the current semester has been revoked."

"What?" I ask in shock.

"If you'd like to continue your current classes, tuition will be due by the tenth of next month. If you cannot pay the tuition in full, you will be dropped from the class rosters. Any questions can be directed to the Board of Admissions and Student Services. Have a nice day."

It takes me a few moments to realize that she's ended the call.

"I'm sorry," I say to the driver, "but I need to make a detour. I'd like to go to the *Le Cordon Bleu* campus."

"No problem," he assures me.

We travel through my hometown, but I'm too distracted to take in the familiar sights.

What the hell has happened now? I haven't even called to transfer back to the Austin campus yet. Why did they call me, instead of New York? And what reason could they possibly have for revoking my scholarship?

Sure, I missed some classes while Jenny was in the hospital but surely they understand the special circumstances.

"Am I dropping you here, or waiting?" the driver asks, snapping my attention back to the present.

"If you can leave the meter running, I'd appreciate it," I reply. "I may be awhile, but I don't want to lug my suitcase around campus."

"It's your money. It makes no difference to me whether I'm moving or not."

"Thanks, I'll try to be fast."

I slide out of the taxi and rush through the main entrance of the administration building.

"Can I help you?" the receptionist behind the counter asks in a perky voice.

"I hope so. My name is Kiara Sands. I just got a phone call from Ruby Miller regarding the status of my financial aid. Is there any way I could speak with her?"

"I'm sorry, but Ms. Miller only sees students by appointment. Would you like me to put you on her schedule?"

"Yes, please, as soon as possible."

"No problem, I'll just need your student I.D. card."

I retrieve the card from my wallet and pass it to her.

"All right, Kiara Sands," she says to herself as she types my information into her computer. She hits "enter" and frowns.

"Is there a problem?"

"I'm sorry, Ms. Sands, but your I.D. number has been flagged. If you'd like to inquire about your financial aid package, you'll have to submit a hearing request to the Admin Board."

"How do I do that?"

"I can do it for you now," she replies, her fingers racing over the keyboard. "It may take a couple of weeks before you hear back from them. And I should warn you, they only approve a fraction of these requests. Once they make a decision, they usually stick with it."

"Ms. Miller said that my tuition for this semester will be due on the tenth. What happens if I don't get a meeting with the board before then?"

"You'll have to pay the tuition or drop your classes. If you formally drop them, it won't affect your grade point. If you wait for the teachers to drop you, you'll end up with incompletes."

I sigh. "Okay, can I also get a copy of my bill? I've always been a scholarship student. I'm ashamed to admit this, but I don't even know what my classes cost."

"Of course," she replies, hitting even more keys. Her printer spits out a single sheet and she passes it to me. "Good luck, Ms. Sands."

"Thank you."

I glance down at the figures and feel like I've been hit in the stomach. I still have most of my New York salary in the bank, but it won't be enough to cover living expenses *and* the tuition. I fold the bill in half and stick it in my purse as I walk back to the taxi.

"Thanks for waiting. The original address now, please," I tell the driver.

"No problem." He smiles.

Robbs has to be behind this. I don't know who he called or what he said, but this has to be his fault.

We get closer to Chase's apartment building, and I put on a brave face to greet my friends.

"Kiara, what are you doing here?" Chase steps out of the doorway, and I walk into the apartment. "We weren't expecting you for hours. I was about to run some errands before I picked you up from the airport."

"I had a change of plans. Where's Jenny?"

"She's sleeping. That's pretty much all she's done since she got here yesterday. The poor girl, I can't imagine how she must be feeling. I've taken some pretty bad hits on the field, but I've never been as banged up as she is."

"She's got an uphill battle, that's for sure. How's her mood?"

"Better than I expected. She's sad, that's obvious, but she's also got a sense of peace about her. I think that she's just relieved to be back in Austin."

"That makes two of us."

"So what happened? Why did you change your flight? Not that I'm not thrilled to see you."

"I had a rough night. I don't want to tell the story more than once. Let me go wake Jenny."

A cloud of concern covers Chase's handsome face. "Okay… I took the couch last night. She's in my bedroom. It's the second door on the left."

I make my way down the carpeted hallway and gently knock on the door. "Jenny?" I call out softly as I push it open. Thick black curtains are drawn over the windows, and the room is dark.

Jenny stirs in the far corner. "Kiara?" she replies through a yawn. "I didn't mean to sleep all day. How long have you been here?"

"Relax, I caught an earlier flight. It's just a little after noon. Do you mind if I turn on the light?"

"No, I need to get up anyway. Did Chase tell you the news?"

"No… Jenny something happened last night that I need to tell you about. Can you come out in the living room with us?"

"Oh my God, what is it now?"

"Exactly what you think it is," I reply gravely.

Jenny and I make our way back to the living room, where Chase is pacing impatiently.

"So what did he do this time?" he demands. "I'm assuming whatever happened last night, Robbs was involved."

I nod and take a seat on the couch. Jenny perches next to me. Her long blonde hair is tangled around her head, but her eyes are clear and focused.

"Just tell us, Kiara," she insists. "I can take it."

"Robbs was waiting for me when I got back to the apartment yesterday. When the ER called to tell me you'd been brought in, I rushed out without setting the alarm. I have no idea how long he'd been there. He confronted me with one of my chef's knives and threw me against a wall. He'd have killed me, but Paul busted the door down and I got away."

The color drained simultaneously from Jenny and Chase's faces. "He was in the apartment?" Jenny asked.

"What was Paul doing in the city?" Chase piped up.

"I don't know why Paul was there, but I'm glad he was. I got away and called Detective Delco. When he got there, Robbs was gone and Paul was unconscious."

"Oh my *God*," Jenny gasps. "Is Paul okay?"

"He's fine," Chase replies.

"How do you know?" I ask, completely confused.

Chase blushes. "I took your old apprenticeship at Fission," he admits. "Paul approached me about it weeks ago. You'd just left for New York, and he'd just fired Robbs. He needed help, and I need the experience. I hope that's not awkward for you."

"If you can handle it, so can I," I quickly reply. "It doesn't matter much anyway. I'll be eternally grateful to Paul for saving me last night, but I don't want him in my life. You working at the restaurant isn't awkward for me."

"I'm glad." Chase smiles. "Anyway, I talked to Paul this morning. He knows that Jenny is here, and he gave me a couple of days off. But he never mentioned anything about being in New York or rescuing you from Robbs last night."

"He probably knew I'd want to tell you myself."

"Why didn't you tell us sooner?" Jenny asks. "You should have called last night as soon as you were safe. Or at least called this morning when you changed your flight."

"I wanted to tell you in person, so you could see for yourselves that I'm fine. I knew if I told you over the phone, you'd just worry until my plane landed."

"Did Delco have any leads on where Robbs is headed next?" Chase asks.

"There are techs going through the apartment for clues. But I think it's pretty safe to assume that he'll come here. I know I said we'd be out of your hair in a few days, Chase. But we may need to stay a little longer."

"So he didn't tell you the news," Jenny says with a smile.

"No, what's going on?"

"I called my super yesterday," Chase tells me. "The unit across the hall is open. It's a two bedroom, so you'd have plenty of room. I explained your situation, and he agreed to let you do a month-to-month lease. I know you might not want to live across the hall from me indefinitely, but it would be a great arrangement until Robbs is behind bars."

"That couldn't be more perfect," I agree quickly. "When can we sign the lease?"

"You don't even want to look at it first?" Chase laughs.

"I don't need to. the location is all that matters. And the money, of course, but I'm sure that I have enough in savings to cover the deposit and first and last month's rent."

"I thought you'd feel that way." Jenny beams. "Chase called the super again this morning. He'll be here at five with the paperwork and keys."

"And I talked to some of the guys on the team. They're going to empty out your storage unit tomorrow and move everything in for you," Chase adds.

I let out a sigh of relief. "That's a few less things to worry about at least."

"You don't have *anything* to worry about, Kiara. Neither of you do, not anymore. I'm not going to let anything else happen to you," Chase promises.

"I'm afraid that will be harder than you think," I warn him. I tell Chase and Jenny about my scholarship.

"But they didn't say *why* they revoked it?" Jenny asks.

"No, Ms. Miller hung up the phone before I could ask and the receptionist wouldn't tell me anything. All she said was that my I.D. number had been flagged."

"They can't just revoke your scholarship based on the word of a crazy person," Chase insists. "I'm sure there's something we can do. We'll find a way to come up with the tuition money."

"Kiara, maybe we shouldn't sign the lease," Jenny suggests. "You need to pay for school, and you shouldn't have to take care of me."

"No, Jenny, we have to have a place to live. And I've already told you, I *want* to take care of you. Chase is right. We'll figure something out."

"Kiara, my sister Madison moved to town a few weeks ago. She has a degree in Academic Administration, and she's working at the college. I was pissed when she first showed up. I'm convinced that my dad talked her into coming here so he could keep tabs on me. I could give her a call and see if she can pull some strings with the Board. At the very least, she can probably make sure you get the hearing."

"That would be fantastic, Chase," I reply with a yawn.

"After the night you had, you must be exhausted. I was going to go to the market before I picked you up. I don't really have much food in the house right now. You go take a nap. I'll call Madison on my way to get groceries."

"I am really tired," I confess.

"You can have the bed. I'm going to take a shower," Jenny announces. "I haven't done anything but sleep since I got here yesterday. I still have the stench of the city on me."

"You girls make yourselves at home and call me if you need anything. My neighbor Sherman works from home. I'm going to stop by on my way out and have him keep his eyes and ears open while I'm gone."

"I'll never be able to thank you enough for all of this, Chase," I tell him.

"Your safety is all the thanks I need."

Chapter Three

"Kiara, wait a second!"

I turn impatiently and see Paul running across the parking lot. I pull my phone from my purse and check the time. It's one-fifteen, and my meeting with the Administration Board is set for two o'clock.

"Hi, Paul. Look this isn't really a good time."

"Kiara, I don't mean to crowd you. I know that you needed space, but I had to see with my own eyes that you're okay. Every time I close my eyes, I see that maniac standing over you with that knife. I had to get that image out of my head."

"I'm fine," I assure him. "Thanks to you, all I had was a headache and a sore shoulder. I really appreciate you showing up, and I don't mean to be rude, but I really do have to leave. There's a problem with my financial aid, and I have a meeting with the Administration Board in less than an hour. If I miss it, I'll lose my scholarship. I've worked too hard to get where I am, you know that. I'm more than halfway through school. I have to finish. And to do that, I need them to reinstate my aid."

"What if you didn't have to depend on the aid?"

"That would be great, but that's not going to happen. I promised Jenny that I'd help her get back on her feet. I signed a lease on our apartment three days ago. I'm going to have to work full time along with going to school or we'll be out on the street in a matter of months."

"You could come work for me," Paul suggests slowly. "Patrick put his notice in a few weeks ago. He's opening his own restaurant, but he agreed to stay on until I find his replacement. You could take the job, I'll pay you what I've been paying him. I won't be out any extra money, and you can pay your tuition."

"I can't very well be your full-time sous chef and get through school."

"Yes, you can. I'll flex around your class schedule. I need to spend more time in the kitchen anyway."

I hesitated and looked at my phone again. There's no way I can make it to the meeting on time. I should have left the apartment earlier, but Jenny's still healing and needs so much attention right now. "I don't know, Paul. With our history, I don't think it's a good idea for us to work together. And with Chase working as your apprentice… things could get unnecessarily *complicated*."

"Look, I know we're over. And I know that's my fault. But I feel responsible for bringing Robbs into your life. If I hadn't chosen him for that damn competition, none of this would have ever happened. I should have looked in to his background before letting him in to my kitchen. Let me make it right by helping you out. I promise I won't try anything inappropriate.

And if you and Chase want to be friends, I'll stay out of your way."

This is a horrible idea. There's no way this will end well. But what choice do I have? I have to keep a roof over our heads. And if I'm working at Fission, we can live comfortably instead of struggling week to week.

I eye Paul carefully. "You never told me what you were doing in New York that night. How did you end up at my apartment at exactly the right time?"

"Chase was at work when you called to tell him about Jenny. I overheard his side of the conversation, and I asked him to keep me updated. When he told me that Jenny was flying home a day before you, I got nervous. I didn't like the idea of you being alone and vulnerable in the city. So I got on a plane and flew out to check on you. I got to your apartment and heard you and Robbs fighting on the other side of the door. So I kicked it in."

"If I come back to work for you, you have to promise not to hover over me. I appreciate you saving me that night, but it doesn't give you a free pass to show up unannounced whenever you'd like."

"Understood, I'll treat you like any other employee. I'll always care about you, and I'll always want you to be safe. But I know that I can't watch over you twenty-four seven."

"All right," I sigh. "When should I start?"

"Come in at nine in the morning. Bring your class schedule, and we'll figure out your work schedule around it. And bring me your tuition bill. I'll take care of it up front and deduct a little from your check each week."

"Thank you, Paul."

"Like I said, it's the least I can do. If I could go back in time and erase Robbs Martin from our lives, believe me I would. Do the cops have any leads on him yet?"

I shake my head. "No, but that reminds me that I need to call Delco back. He left a message this morning. He said that they didn't have any new leads on Robbs, but that there was something else he wanted to talk to me about."

"I hope everything's all right. I'll get out of your way, see you tomorrow?"

"I'll be at Fission at nine. Thanks again. The job really will help me out."

"You're welcome. I know you've got people in your corner, but I want you to know that I'm here for you if you need anything."

I give Paul an awkward hug goodbye and walk back into the apartment building. The elevator carries me to the third floor, and my phone chimes as the doors swing open. I look down and read the text.

Kiara, it is vital that I speak with you ASAP. I'm not at the precinct so call me on my cell.

I know I need to call Detective Delco back, but I just can't bring myself to dial the number. Since Jenny and I have been back in Austin, we haven't talked much about what happened in New York. I've enjoyed living in our bubble of denial, and I'm not quite ready to pop it. I decide that what I need is a hot bath and a long nap. I'll wake up in a better, braver mood, and I'll return Delco's call then.

<<◇>>

"Okay, so if everything goes as planned, you'll have classes on Tuesdays and Thursdays. I can cover lunch and dinner shifts on those days. When will you know if the school's accepting your transfer?" Paul asks. It's nine-thirty, and I've been back at Fission for almost an hour.

"I don't know. With everything that's going on with my scholarship, I forgot to put in the transfer request until yesterday. I called after I missed my meeting with the Admin Board. They rescheduled me for next week. The receptionist said we'd discuss my transfer then, so for now my schedule is completely open."

"I'm sure that the meeting is just a formality. You've had a rocky year, Kiara. They probably just want to check in and make sure that you're getting your life in order. At the most, they'll put you on academic probation. You'll show them that you're stable, and they'll reinstate your aid."

"I hope you're right. I know I've been a pain in their asses. First I bounced back and forth between campus and the apprenticeship. Then there was that god awful scene Robbs caused in New York. I really won't blame them if they toss me out."

397

"Speaking of Robbs, have you heard anything from the cops?"

"I still haven't returned Delco's call," I confess. "After my nap yesterday, Jenny and I cooked dinner together and watched a movie. She was in a good mood, and I didn't want to bring her down by mentioning New York."

"Kiara, you have to know what's going on! Robbs could be on his way here right now! I insist that you call him back right now."

"Paul, you're overstepping. We've talked about this. If I'm going to work here—"

"I'm not overstepping. I'm being reasonable. Call Delco back, and I'll go start prepping for the lunch rush." He stands and makes his way to the door. "I have his card, Kiara. If you don't call him, I will."

I pull out my cell as he leaves the office. Delco answers on the first ring.

"Kiara, is everything okay?"

"Yes, Jenny and I are fine," I quickly assure him.

"I've left you several messages. When you didn't return my call, I got worried."

"I'm sorry, Detective Delco. We've been so busy getting settled in…"

"It's fine, Kiara. I know that you want to forget everything that happened here, but until Robbs is behind bars, I need you to keep in touch with me."

"I'll do better," I promise.

"Listen, I called because the tech team finished processing your apartment. I'm afraid that they found something quite… concerning."

"What is it?" I ask, bracing myself for more bad news.

"There were several small surveillance cameras hidden in the apartment. Robbs must have planted them there when he broke in the first time. They were cheaply made, low-range spy cams. He probably picked them up at Shaper Image or somewhere like that."

"You're saying that Robbs was watching me for weeks?" I ask in disbelief.

"It seems so. We also found a camera in the lobby of your building. It was pointed right at the elevators. The bastard could have been in your apartment when I stopped by to get your things."

"Did you find anything that would suggest where he's going next? Is there any chance he's finally gotten discouraged and decided to disappear for good?"

"There's always that chance, but it's miniscule. People like Robbs see obstacles as challenges, not detours. The harder we make this on him, the more he'll want to prove himself. We didn't find anything to suggest where he's going next, but we have to assume that he's on his way to Austin, if he isn't there already."

"Jenny and I took an apartment across the hall from my friend Chase. Another neighbor works from home, so I think we'll be safe there. Someone will always be watching."

"Since you've been back in Austin, have you noticed anything suspicious?"

I take a deep breath and let it out slowly. "I haven't seen anything, but I'm pretty sure that Robbs has interfered with my financial aid." I tell Delco what's happening at the college.

"So they didn't give you any indication of *why* your aid was revoked?"

"No, they said that we'd discuss it at the meeting, but I wasn't able to make it. They rescheduled me for next week. I'm not positive that Robbs was involved, I haven't been the most dependable student lately. But I've kept my grade point up, and I did well on all of my exams."

"If your gut's telling you that Robbs is behind it, you're probably right," he assures me. "I wish that there was something that I could do about your scholarship, but I'm afraid my hands are tied there."

"You've already done more than enough. If Robbs was behind it, he'll be discredited as soon as he's arrested. I'm at work right now. It's my first day back, and I need to get off the phone, but I promise that I'll keep in touch from now on."

"All right, Kiara. Call me if you need anything."

I end the call and stow my phone in my purse.

The bastard was watching me. He saw me sleeping, changing clothes. God I hope there wasn't a camera in the closet.

Knowing that Robbs had an unfiltered view into my life is almost more than I can bear. I've never felt so violated, so exposed. I break into a cold sweat as I picture him hovering over a computer, watching my every move. I jump when I hear a knock on the door. It opens slowly and Paul peers into the office.

"Is everything okay?" he asks, his voice full of concern.

I quickly gather my composure. "Yes, everything's fine. Delco just wanted to make sure that Jenny and I were getting settled. He doesn't have any new leads on Robbs."

"He'll slip up eventually and the police will find him," Paul assures me. "And until then, we'll keep you safe. Are you ready to get to work?"

"Yes," I reply honestly. With everything that's going on in my head, work is exactly what I need to distract me.

"Then I guess all that's left to do is give this to you again," Paul says with a smile. He opens the closet door and pulls out my chef's jacket.

"How many times have we passed this back and forth?"

"I don't like to think about that. Let's just get to the kitchen and do what we do best."

Jenny sits at the kitchen table in her new apartment, studying job ads on the Internet. She's felt helpless and depressed since she lost baby Maggie, but she knows that it's time to start putting her life back together. Kiara has been great about paying rent and all of their deposits, but Jenny feels like a burden and is determined to help out.

Jenny has had a lot of time to think about the mistakes she's made and what she wants for her future. All she's certain of is that she doesn't want to be a chef anymore. Winning her spot in the apprenticeship competition was the worst thing that had ever happened to her. Jenny takes that as a sign that she is meant to do something else.

Jenny's first passion had always been theater, but her conservative parents hadn't seen acting as a suitable career choice for their daughter. Culinary school had been a compromise. Cooking gave Jenny the artistic outlet she craved, and her parents thought it would be a great way for her to find a husband. They were certain that as soon as their daughter found the right man, she'd settle down and be a proper housewife.

But when Jenny got pregnant out of wedlock, her parents had disowned her. There was nothing to stop her from following her dreams, but she had a long way to go before she'd be ready to break into the industry. She needed to take some refresher acting classes and put together a portfolio, not to mention the fact that Austin wasn't the place to land any starring roles. Jenny would need to move to California or back to New York. And all of that would take money. As she considers the job ads in front of her, she's startled by a noise at the window.

Jenny jumps up from her seat and instinctively backs away from the window. She remembers that she's on the third floor and cautiously approaches the glass and parts the curtains. The parking lot below her is dark, and she can't find the course of the noise. She pushes her face to the glass to get a better look and jumps away when a rock bounces off the window.

Jenny can't see Robbs, but she knows that he's there. She turns off all of the lights in the apartment and peeks out the living room window. Finally, she spots him. He's standing close to the building, directly under the kitchen. Jenny grabs her cell phone, rushes out of the apartment, and knocks on Sherman's door.

"Jenny, are you okay?" he asks when he opens the door. His gray eyebrows furrow in concern on his mocha forehead.

"I'm sorry, Sherman. Can I come in? Robbs is outside, or he was at least. He threw rocks at the window."

"He's outside! Get in here, I'll go take care of this."

"No! Please don't leave me. I came here because I'm afraid to be alone. I'm calling 911, please just stay. He could get past you, or he could hurt you, and I'd be all alone. He'll kill me, Sherman, please."

"Okay, okay, child," Sherman answers soothingly. He steps back into his apartment and Jenny follows him. "I'm not going anywhere, and no one's going to hurt you. Let's call the police and then I'll call Chase and Kiara."

"Thank you," Jenny sobs. She collapses on Sherman's couch and dials 911.

Chapter Four

"That wasn't so bad, was it?" Chase asks. We've just worked our first full day together in the Fission kitchen and it went better than I'd ever expected.

"It was a blast. You're really becoming a fantastic chef, Chase. I like working with you."

"I have to say, Paul was more pleasant than I expected him to be. Does he know that you and I…?"

"He knows that we're friends and that I care about you. And he knows that he and I are over. He doesn't know that we slept together while I he and I were still dating."

"Yeah, I figured he was in the dark about that one or otherwise I wouldn't have a job."

"I hope Paul doesn't become a problem. I really need the sous chef salary right now, and I'd never be able to make this much anywhere else. I'm going to start looking for a car next week, so you don't have to keep chauffeuring me around."

"I don't mind at all. It's easy since we work together. But I know you want your freedom back." Chase pulls into the parking lot of our building. We round the corner and immediately spot blue lights bouncing off the windows.

"Shit, what's happened now!" I gasp. A single cop cruiser is parked in front of the entrance. Chase pulls up next to it, and I jump out of the car.

"I'm Kiara Sands," I tell the uniformed officer who's standing next to the cruiser. "Has something happened to my roommate? Her name is Jenny Foster. We just moved in to the building. Is she the one who called you?"

"Yes, Ms. Sands. My name is Officer Jones, and my partner Officer Marquez is upstairs with Ms. Foster. Robbs Martin paid her a visit this evening. He didn't get into the building. He just bounced rocks off of the window. We see this type of thing a lot. I'm sure it's just a harmless case of harassment, but we'll keep an eye on the building tonight."

"A harmless case of harassment?" Chase demands. I turn to see that he's parked the car and is moving to join us. "I thought that Detective Delco from the NYPD alerted you all about Robbs. He's tried to kill both of the girls, Officer. There's nothing harmless about him."

"I'm sorry, Mr…?"

"Chase Abbott," Chase replies, extending his hand.

Officer Jones accepts it and gives him a firm shake. "I'm sorry, Mr. Abbott, I'm unaware of the history of the case. We responded to the 911 call because we were in the area. My partner went upstairs to take statements. Since Mr. Martin had caused trouble in the parking lot, we decided I'd stay here and keep a lookout in case he comes back."

"You think that he'll come near the place if he sees those lights flashing?" Chase asks impatiently.

"No, I don't, Mr. Abbott. That's why the lights are flashing, to keep him away. Once Marquez finishes up with the statements, we'll go back to the precinct and file the official report. We'll review the information from the NYPD and get back with you as soon as we have a plan on approaching the case. Your restraining orders against Mr. Martin did pop up on the cruiser's laptop, so we'll charge him with violations."

"Thank you, Officer Jones. If it's all right, I'd like to go check on Jenny now."

"Of course, Ms. Sands, here's my card. It has Officer Marquez's number listed as well. We patrol this neighborhood regularly, so if Mr. Martin makes another appearance, give us a call."

"Thank you," Chase tells him. He opens the door for me, and I race into the apartment building. I don't have the patience to wait for the elevator so I bound up the staircase with Chase trailing behind. I reach the third floor landing and find Jenny in the hallway with Officer Marquez.

"Jenny, are you all right?" I ask as I throw my arms around her. "We saw the patrol lights as soon as we pulled in and I thought that he'd hurt you again."

"I'm fine," she assures me meekly. "Just shaken a little, that's all."

"I presume you're Ms. Sands and Mr. Abbott," Officer Marquez chimes in.

"Yes, and you're Officer Marquez. We met your partner in the parking lot. He didn't seem to be very informed about the case," Chase tells him.

"I'm sorry about that, Dave and I agreed it would be best if one of us kept watch downstairs. Ms. Foster was kind enough to call Detective Delco in New York, and he brought me up to speed on the specifics of the case. We're going to increase patrols in the neighborhood and make sure that Martin's picture gets in every patrol car in Austin. I apologize that that hasn't been done already, but with transfer cases things sometimes fall through the cracks."

"But you'll keep a closer eye out from now on?" Chase asks.

"Absolutely. I've also given Ms. Foster my contact information. If you need anything at all, just give me a call. To be on the safe side, you might want to install stronger locks on your door. Martin didn't get into the building this time, but from what Detective Delco said, I think it's safe to assume that he'll be back."

"I'll install new deadbolts first thing in the morning," Chase says quickly.

"If you're finished with me, Officer Marquez, I'd really like to go lie down now," Jenny says softly.

"Of course, Ms. Foster. We'll stay close by tonight, and I'll speak with you tomorrow."

Jenny, Chase, and I take turns shaking the officer's hand and escape to our apartment.

"Are you sure that you're all right?" I ask Jenny once we're safely inside.

"I'm fine, I just don't understand why Robbs is doing this. We don't deserve it, Kiara," she says with tears in her eyes. "Why won't he just stop?"

"Jenny, it's impossible to understand the motives of a crazy person," Chase tells her softly. "You'll go crazy yourself trying to figure it out. The best thing to do is remember that you're safe now and try not to let him get to you."

"That's easier said than done," she replies with a weak smile.

"I don't like the idea of you girls being alone tonight, even with me right across the hall. What if I crash on the couch tonight? I'm a light sleeper. If anyone tries to get in, I'll stop them before they get to either of you."

I hesitate at the idea but Jenny brightens at the suggestion. "I would sleep better if you were here," she admits. They turn to me.

"If you really don't mind, that would be great," I relent. "I've got a box of extra blankets and pillows. I'll make up the couch for you."

"I can take care of it," Chase insists. "Is the box in the closet?"

I nod, and he retrieves the bedding. I turn back to Jenny. "Do you need anything? If you're hungry, I can make a quick dinner."

She shakes her head. "You've been cooking all day, and I don't have an appetite anyway. I just want to go to bed."

"Do you want me to stay with you until you go to sleep?" I offer.

"No," she says with a sad smile. "I need to be alone for a while. I'll see you in the morning."

"Okay, if you're sure. Goodnight."

"Sleep well," Chase adds. "I'll be right here if you need anything."

"Thanks, guys." Jenny disappears to her bedroom, and Chase and I share an awkward look.

I decide to address the elephant in the room. "Chase, I know that there was a time I'd have let you sleep with me instead of on the couch. But—"

He quickly interrupts me. "You've got a lot to deal with right now, Kiara. I admit that I want to pick up where we left off before you moved to New York, but I can be patient. Right now, you need a friend, not a new relationship. So that's what I'm going to be."

"Thanks, Chase. You have no idea how relieved I am to hear you say that. For the record, I'd like to pick things up where we left off, too. But I need to feel like myself again first."

"I understand completely. And like I said, there's no rush. I'm not going anywhere. But I think you need to go to bed. You look exhausted."

"I am," I confess. "Do you need to get anything from your place?"

"I'll pop over and grab my toothbrush and some pajamas. Don't worry about me, just get some rest."

I give Chase a long, hard hug and make my way to my bedroom. I don't know if I'll be able to sleep, but I know I have to try.

Chapter Five

"No!" I scream. "Get off of me!" One moment Robbs is standing over me, wielding the butcher knife. The next, I'm upright in my bed, shaking and sweating.

It was just a dream. You're safe, Robbs didn't hurt you. You got away. It was just a dream.

My eyes adjust to the darkness, and I glance at my bedside clock. It's three in the morning, but I feel wide awake.

Chase is asleep in the living room, but maybe I can heat up some milk without waking him.

I have a long day of work ahead of me and I need as much sleep as I can get. My mother used to make me warm milk when I was restless or upset. It's one of the few comforting memories I have of my otherwise disastrous childhood, and I crave the familiar warmth.

I slowly crawl out of bed, pull on my bathrobe, and slide my feet into my slippers. I open my bedroom door, careful to stay silent. I pad down the hallway and into the living room. Chase is sitting on the sofa, watching television with the volume turned low.

"Are you all right?" he asks as I step into the room.

"I'm fine, I just had a bad dream, that's all. I was going to heat some milk. Do you want some?"

"No thanks, that's never really worked for me. And besides, I need to stay alert."

"You're working the same hours I am tomorrow, you need your sleep," I argue.

"I can handle one sleepless night," he assures me. "I doubt that I'd be able to sleep tonight if I tried."

"Has Jenny gotten up at all?"

He shakes his head. "How do you think she's doing, really? I know that she's putting on a brave face, but this has to be torture for her."

"I think she's really struggling. She blames herself for what happened to the baby. She thinks that taking Maggie was God's way of punishing her for lying about Paul being the father."

"That doesn't make any sense. God's not like that," Chase insists.

"That's not what Jenny was raised to believe." I tell Chase about Jenny's super-conservative, super-religious family.

"So they think that God would condone them abandoning their child when she needed them the most? That's the most ridiculous thing I've ever heard. My dad can be difficult, but he'd never do anything like that."

I shrug. "I know it's sad, but those are the parents she was stuck with. We all can't be as lucky as you," I tease.

"Is that why you were able to forgive her so easily, because you relate to her family problems?"

"That's part of it, I guess. I also realized that I'd been acting like a complete bitch. Holding a grudge against her didn't do either of us any good. And if I'd forgiven her in the first place, everything might have turned out a lot differently."

"It sounds like Jenny's not the only one blaming herself for what Robbs has done," Chase observes. "You couldn't have known how much danger she was in. How much danger you were both in."

"I know that in my head, but I can't get my heart to agree," I confess. "If I'd been there, if I'd let her stay with me, Maggie might still be alive. We'd be ordering a crib instead of a memorial stone."

"I think that you should both talk to a professional. There are support groups for women who've been in your situation."

"I've done some research, and I think I found a great place for Jenny to go."

"You *both* need to go," he says again. "You've been through almost as much as she has. Robbs tried to kill you, too. You may not have the physical scars like Jenny does, but if you don't talk to someone, the emotional scars may be just as bad."

"I thought I could talk to you."

"You can always talk to me, but I'm not a professional. And I can't imagine what it feels like to be in your shoes. I'd like for you to talk to someone who does, even just once."

"Okay," I quickly agree.

"That was easier than I expected."

"You've done so much for me, and you've asked for nothing in return. If you want me to talk to a professional, it's the least I could do."

"Thank you, Kia…"

"Shh… did you hear that?" I ask, raising my hand to silence him.

Chase shakes his head and quietly rises to his feet.

"There it was again," I whisper. There's a soft scratching noise coming from the other side of the front door.

Chase looks through the peep hole and backs away from the door. "Kiara," he whispers in an even tone. "I want you to go to Jenny's room and lock the door. Call the police and tell them that Robbs is trying to break into the apartment."

"What are you going to do?" I ask in panic.

"I'm going to stop the bastard, but I'm not opening this door until you're locked in Jenny's bedroom. Grab your knives on your way, in case he gets through me," Chase directs firmly.

I'm filled with anxiety but I do as he says.

"Jenny, wake up," I whisper harshly as I gently shake Jenny's shoulder.

She rolls over and opens her eyes. "Kiara, what's going on?"

"Robbs is in the hallway," I tell her urgently. "We've got to call the cops. Where's your cell phone?"

"It's on the dresser, I plugged it in before I went to bed. He's out there?" she asks anxiously.

Before I can answer, we hear a loud crash in the living room.

"Yes, he's out there. He may be in the apartment now. Grab one of my butcher knives from the pouch," I tell her as I grab her phone. I don't have time to look for Officer Marquez's card, so I dial 911.

"Emergency services, how may I assist you?" a calm, female voice answers.

"My name is Kiara Sands. I live at 129 Melrose Street, apartment 317. There's a dangerous man trying to break in to my apartment. His name is Robbs Martin. We filed a report about him earlier this evening."

"Okay, Kiara, I'm dispatching officers to your location now. I'm going to stay on the line with you until they get there. Where are you in the apartment?"

"My roommate and I are locked in her bedroom. A friend was staying on the couch, and I think he's gone after Robbs on his own. We heard a loud crash a few minutes ago, but it's been quiet ever since."

"I need you to stay exactly where you are until the officers arrive. My name is Brenda, just try to stay calm, and let me know if you hear any more noises."

"Thank you, Brenda."

"Can I have your roommate's name?"

"Jenny Foster. And Chase Abbott is the man who went after Robbs."

"Thank you… is it still quiet?"

"Yes."

"Officers Jones and Marquez are pulling into your parking lot now, and two more units are on their way. Does anyone at the scene need medical attention?"

"Jenny and I are fine, but I don't know about Chase."

"Okay, Kiara, I'm going to dispatch an ambulance, just in case."

The doorbell rings, and Brenda hears it on her side of the line.

"The officers are right outside, Kiara. I'm going to disconnect now."

"All right, thank you, Brenda."

I toss Jenny's phone on the bed. "I'll go make sure that's the cops. You stay here, and I'll come get you once I'm sure it's safe."

"No." She shakes her head. "I'll come with you."

Jenny crawls out of bed and loops her arm through mine. We make our way to the living room and find the coffee table overturned.

"That must have been the crash," Jenny observes quietly. "I wonder where Chase is."

"Wherever he is, we owe him. He managed to get Robbs out of the apartment."

The front door stands ajar; I open it all the way and let Officers Jones and Marquez into the apartment.

"Did you catch him?" I ask hopefully. I know the answer by the grave look on their faces.

"No," Officer Jones replies. "Robbs had already fled the scene when we got here. Your friend managed to get in a few good licks, but Robbs was too fast for him. Chase was able to get a partial tag off of the getaway car, as well as the make and model. We'll run the numbers through the DMV database. There's a chance Robbs is using a stolen tag, but even a small lead is better than no lead at all."

"Where is Chase now? Is he all right?" I ask urgently. I can't stand the thought of Chase getting hurt while trying to protect me.

"He's fine. He's probably going to have a black eye, but Robbs didn't fight back much. He had to know that he's no match for Chase. That boy is built like a linebacker."

"He was a linebacker."

"That's not surprising. Anyway, he's downstairs with the paramedics. They want him to stay there until his adrenaline wears off. Sometimes people don't realize how badly they're hurt in the heat of the moment. I imagine they'll let him come back up in another half hour or so."

"I'm so glad he's okay." I breathe a sigh of relief.

"You've got a good friend there, ladies. You're lucky he was on your couch. Would it be possible for him to stay with you until this matter is resolved?"

"I'm sure that we can work something out."

"Great. I know the two of you have had a long night, so if you can give us quick statements, we'll get out of your hair."

"Of course," I agree. I tell the officers that Chase and I were talking on the couch when we heard the noises, and I locked myself in Jenny's bedroom while he went after Robbs. "There's really not much else to tell. We heard the crash and then it was quiet until you got here."

"Do you have anything to add, Ms. Foster?" Officer Jones asks softly.

"No, I was asleep when Kiara came in. She told me what was going on and we stayed put until you got here."

The front door opens, and Chase walks in to the living room. A large red welt covers his left cheekbone but otherwise he seems unharmed.

"The bastard got away from me. I'm so sorry, he was just too fast."

"That's okay," I tell him with a hug. "I'm just happy that you're all right. I heard the crash and thought that he'd attacked you."

Chase shakes his head. "No, that was me. When I looked through the peephole, I saw Robbs trying to pick the lock. I flung the door open really fast and caught him off guard. He was still bent over so I grabbed him by the torso and tossed him into the table. He jumped up and hit me. He was probably halfway down the stairs by the time I got back on my feet. I made it to the parking lot just as he was jumping into his car. It was a black or dark blue Camry, I got part of the tag number. It'll be easier to find him now, right?" he asks the officers hopefully.

"Yes, I just explained to the ladies that we're going to run the partial against the dark Camries in the DMV database. If we get a hit, we'll put a BOLO out on the car. If the partial matches a stolen tag, we'll at least have another avenue to investigate. I know that this is torture, but we'll find Robbs eventually. Guys like this always get sloppy. It's only a matter of time before he's behind bars."

"That's what everyone keeps saying," Chase says impatiently. "I just hope it happens before he hurts anyone else."

"Detective Delco in New York seems to think that nothing will detour Robbs. In your opinion, will he still try to get to us here now that he knows Chase is protecting us?" I ask the officers cautiously.

"In cases like this, it's best to hope for the best but plan for the worst," Officer Marquez advises. "Get these locks changed out ASAP and if you can afford it, have a security system installed. If either of you are familiar with firearms, it may be a good idea to get one."

"I refuse to live with a gun," I insist. "But some pepper spray is probably a good idea."

"We've got plenty at the station, I'll bring some over tomorrow and show you how to use it," Officer Jones offers.

"If you don't need anything else tonight, we should be getting back to the precinct," Officer Marquez chimes in. "There's another unit outside, Officers Vicker and Charles. They're going to stay put for the night. You all try to get some sleep, and we'll check in as soon as we learn something."

"Thanks again, Officers," Chase says as he walks them to the door.

"I can't believe this keeps happening," Jenny sobs as soon as the officers are gone.

"I know, Jenny, but it will all be over soon," I promise. "We've proven twice tonight that he can't get to us here. From what Delco said, the harder we make it, the more determined he'll be to hurt us. That means that he'll keep trying, but the cops are watching the apartment now. The next time he makes a move, they'll be waiting for him."

"Do you really think so?"

"I know so," I assure her. "Why don't you take one of the sleeping pills they gave you at the hospital? I know that you hate feeling groggy, but you really need to get some rest. Your body is still healing. Go get back in bed, and I'll bring you a bottle of water."

"Okay, thanks, Kiara. And thank you, too, Chase. I hate to think about what could have happened to us if you weren't here."

"You're more than welcome, Jenny. I'm happy to keep you safe. Get some rest, and I'll see you in the morning," Chase tells her with a kind smile.

"I'll be there in a minute," I call after her as she disappears into her room.

"Be honest," Chase says in a lowered tone. "Do you really believe that the police are about to find Robbs? Or were you just saying that to make Jenny feel better."

"I was just saying it to make her feel better," I reply honestly. "But I really hope it's true."

"All right, ladies, two pancake platters with bacon, eggs, and hashbrowns. It's refreshing to see young girls who aren't afraid to eat. Can I get you any refills?" Marsha, our perky waitress, sets our breakfast plates down on the table.

"Another pot of coffee would be great," Jenny replies. A week has passed since the night Robbs tried to break in to our apartment. He hasn't made a move since, and this morning I was finally able to talk Jenny into getting out.

"You were right. I needed this," she tells me between bites of bacon.

"I thought some fresh scenery would make you feel better. I know that you're on edge but staying cooped up in the apartment isn't going to help anything."

When we left New York, I'd hoped that being back home would help Jenny heal. And in the first few days, that seemed to be the case. But after Robbs showed up at the apartment, she became even more reserved than before. I want to help her but I'm not sure how.

"I haven't felt like facing the world," Jenny admits. "I reach for my belly sometimes when I first wake up. I forget that she's gone until I feel my empty stomach. I guess I've been trying to figure out how I'm supposed to go on without her."

"I can't imagine how hard that is. Chase mentioned something last week. He thinks that we should talk to a professional, or at least someone who can empathize with what we're going through. I've done some research, and there's a domestic violence survivors' group that meets at the Methodist church down the block from the apartment. They have meetings on Mondays, Wednesdays, and Saturdays. One of the ministers' wives is a therapist, and she leads everything. Does that sound like something you'd be willing to do?"

"At this point, I'm open to anything that might help. But I think that what I really need is a job. I feel like a burden on you, and I want to start pulling my own weight."

"Jenny, don't ever feel like you're a burden. I'm making plenty of money right now, almost as much as O'Toole was paying me at The Madden Crowd. I don't want you to jump into anything you're not ready for because you're worried about a paycheck."

"It's not just the money," Jenny explains. "I need to find a purpose. A few months ago, Maggie was my entire reason for existence. I need to find something to fill my time so I can ignore the void."

"I can understand that," I tell her. "I'm not thrilled about working for Paul again, but when I'm in the kitchen, everything else just disappears. All that matters is that the best food possible gets put on the plate. And I'm better at doing that than handling everything else that's going on."

"That's exactly it," Jenny agrees. "I need to feel like I'm good at something again. Honestly, I don't remember the last time I felt that way. It must have been during the apprenticeship competition, before I fucked everything up."

I'm suddenly struck with an idea. "Why don't you come back to the restaurant? Paul has been surprisingly great about everything, I'm sure he'd give you a job."

"I don't want to be a chef anymore," she tells me. "I'm not sure of much, but I'm sure of that. Besides, I doubt Paul wants me anywhere near his restaurant. It would be too awkward being around him all day."

"So you could wait tables. I know he's hiring servers right now. Five of them followed Patrick to his new place. Think about it. You'd make great tips, you wouldn't have to be in the kitchen with Paul, and Chase and I will be close by in case anything happens. I've hated leaving you alone while I'm at work. This would solve all of our problems. Consider doing it until Robbs is captured, at least."

"The waitresses there do make really good tips," Jenny agrees. "And I do have serving experience. I guess I'm in, if it's all right with Paul."

"I'm sure it will be fine," I assure her. "I'll talk to him about it tonight. How's your shoulder been feeling? Do you think you'll be able to carry a tray?"

The doctors in New York City had scheduled an appointment for Jenny with a local orthopedic surgeon, but she'd missed the appointment. She doesn't have health insurance, and I know she was too proud to ask for my help with her medical bills. Instead, she's been doing rehabilitation exercises she found on YouTube.

"My shoulder's getting stronger, I think I'll be able to manage," she answers. "If not, I can always carry the trays with my other arm."

"It's settled then. Once you're on Paul's payroll, you'll qualify for the health insurance again. And I'm not going to take a dime of money from you for bills until you get checked out by the orthopedic surgeon."

"You don't have to do that," she insists.

"I know that. But I'm going to do it anyway."

Chapter Six

I knock anxiously on Paul's office door. Our seafood vendor missed today's delivery, and dinner service was an absolute nightmare. I know that Paul's in a horrible mood, but I promised Jenny that I'd come home with an answer about the waitressing job.

"Come in."

I crack open the door and stick my head inside. "Are you busy? Or do you have a minute to talk?"

"I have a minute, but not much more," he says impatiently.

I step into the room and close the door behind me. Paul is bent over a pile of paperwork and nursing a pint of beer. "I know you've been slammed today, but there's something I want to talk to you about."

"Slammed is an understatement. If I'd known that Patrick was going to steal half of my staff on his way out, I'd have started interviews a month ago. The overtime I'm having to pay everyone else is about to break me."

"That's actually what I wanted to talk to you about. I was hoping that you'd let Jenny take one of the serving positions."

Paul's mouth drops, and he takes a moment to recover from his reaction. "I'm sorry, but that's a horrible idea. I know that you've forgiven Jenny, but I don't trust her. And I can't have someone I don't trust in my restaurant, handling my money."

"Paul, please just consider it. I know that what Jenny did was awful. She knows it, too. She thinks that losing her baby was punishment for lying to you about being the father. She's really changed, and she needs this. And I would feel better if she's here instead of home alone. Until Robbs is captured, she's a sitting target."

"That's not my problem, Kiara. To be honest, I don't know how or why you're friends with her again, let alone living with her. I hate that she lost the baby and no innocent child deserves to have their life ended before it even begins. But Jenny's already proven who she is."

"She made a mistake, Paul," I remind him softly. "And if I'm recalling correctly, we were all guilty of that. You knew better and you slept with her anyway and I told almost as many lies as she did. We're no better than she is, and Robbs manipulated us all. It's time for us all to be better people. You said that you gave me the sous chef position to make up for bringing Robbs into my life. If that's true, you owe the same to Jenny."

Paul is quiet for a minute, and I know I've made a point he can't argue with.

"All right," he finally agrees. "I'll give Jenny one of the serving positions. I'll pay her the standard starting wage and the first hint I get that she's being shady, she's out of here."

"That's not going to happen," I assure him. "You'll see. Thank you for giving her another chance."

"I'm not doing this for Jenny, I'm doing it as a favor to you," he replies. "And I'm going to expect a favor in return."

"Paul, I'm not going to sleep with you," I say sternly.

"That's not the kind of favor I was talking about, but it's nice to know where your head is," he replies. "The next time I'm in a jam, I expect you to bail me out. I've got two holes in tomorrow's schedule. Do you think Jenny's up to working a double?"

"I'm sure she'd be thrilled to. Chase and I will give her a ride when we come in in the morning."

"Is there anyone else in your building who needs a job, or can I get back to work now?" Paul asks sarcastically.

"No, that's all. Thank you again. You're not going to regret this."

"I hope not, because if I do, I'm holding you responsible."

"Are you sure you're ready for this?" I ask Jenny as Chase drives us to Fission. "It's not too late for me to call Paul and tell him you'd rather start tomorrow."

Jenny shakes her head. "I'm grateful that he's giving me a chance, and I'm happy to have somewhere to be. I can't call in on my first day. I have to prove to him that I've changed. I just hope that Robbs stays clear of Fission. I know that you guys will be in the kitchen, but even that will seem like a long way away if he shows up and tries anything."

"Everyone at the restaurant knows what's going on with Robbs," Chase tells her. "They're all going to keep an eye on you and make sure you're safe. And if he does try to attack you again, there will be plenty of people to grab him and hold him until the cops come. I really think you'll be okay."

"I think you're right. I'm anxious right now, but I know I'll feel better once I'm actually working."

"It will be nice, all of us working together," I comment. "Maybe we can run to the café and relax for a while between the lunch and dinner rushes."

"Is it strange, Kiara? Being back at Fission, I mean. We both left thinking we'd never see the place again. I'm kind of afraid that going back will feel like defeat," Jenny confesses.

"I had the same worry, but when I walked in, I felt like I'd never left. This will be good for you. Being back at the restaurant has made it easier for me to pretend that New York never happened."

"I'll never be able to pretend that," she says sadly. "But I'm looking forward to the distraction."

"Well, ready or not, here we are," Chase announces as he pulls into the Fission parking lot.

"Talking to Paul will be harder than anything, and I'll be with you for that," I assure Jenny as we exit the car. I put a comforting arm around her as we walk toward the kitchen entrance, but she brushes it away.

"I love you, Kiara, but I don't want them to think I'm fragile," she says in a low voice.

"Of course, I'm sorry," I reply.

Chase holds the door open for us, and we step into the kitchen. Raoul, Robbs' replacement, is already hard at work at his prep station. The rest of the kitchen is empty.

"Good morning, guys," Raoul greets us. "This must be Jenny. I'm Raoul, it's nice to meet you."

"It's nice to meet you, too," Jenny replies. I watch the tension disappear from her shoulders, and I'm thankful to Raoul for his friendly greeting.

"Jenny needs an apron and a ticket pad," I explain to Raoul. "Is Paul here yet?"

"No, he called about ten minutes ago and said that he won't be in until the dinner rush. Rachel has you stuff in the dining room, Jenny. She's ready to start your training whenever you are."

"Has anyone made coffee?" I ask.

"There's a fresh pot at the bar," he answers without looking up from the scallions he's chopping. "Would you mind bringing me a refill?"

"Of course not."

"Good luck, Jenny," Chase says as he pulls on his chef's jacket. "I'm going to start on my prep list, but Kiara and I will be right here if you need us."

"Thanks," she replies anxiously. She lowers her voice so that only I can hear her. "Will you find a way to warn me when Paul gets here?"

"Sure," I tell her as we step into the dining room. "But if he comes in through the main entrance, just smile, say thank you, and go on about your business."

"You must be Jenny," Rachel says as she approaches us from the hostess station. "I'm Rachel, I'll be training you. Paul tells me that you already know your way around this place, so the next couple of days are more of a formality than anything else. Are you ready to get started?"

"Absolutely," Jenny replies eagerly. "I'll see you after lunch, Kiara."

"Good luck." I smile and squeeze her hand. Rachel leads Jenny to a booth and starts going over the table sections while I pour three steaming mugs of coffee. I return to the kitchen and see that Claire has arrived in my absence.

"Good morning, Kiara, is Jenny here yet?" Claire asks.

"Yes, Rachel's training her now. I guess Paul let everyone know that she's back?"

Claire nods. "He sent out an email last night. I'm surprised you talked him into giving her a job again, but I'm glad that you did. I've always liked you and Jenny. You both caught a raw deal having to work with Robbs and I'm glad that Paul's doing something to make it right. I've told him a million times that he needs to run background checks before he hires people."

"It's not Paul's fault," I tell her. "No one could have predicted how crazy Robbs would get."

"That's bullshit, I spotted the little weasel for what he was the moment I laid eyes on him," Claire argues. "I know that he had Jenny convinced for a while, but how Paul didn't see through his act is beyond me. If I'm correct, you've shared my opinion of him since the beginning."

"You're right, he always gave me a creepy feeling."

"Is everything still quiet at your place?"

I nod as I pull on my chef's jacket and retrieve the prep list Paul left at my station. "Yes, he hasn't been back since last week. Not that we know of, at least."

"He's not going to come near them as long as I'm around," Chase calls out from his corner station.

"You're lucky to have such a great friend," Claire tells me with a laugh. She follows me to the walk in and helps me load chafing dishes with today's ingredients. "So what's going on between you and Chase? It's just us girls in here, so answer honestly."

"Chase has been amazing," I gush. "I don't know how I'd have gotten through the last few weeks without him."

"You realize that he's in love with you, right?"

"We started dating a little before I moved to New York," I admit. "We were taking things slowly and then O'Toole called and offered me the job again. Now I wish to God that I'd turned him down, but at the time it seemed like the perfect escape. I know that Chase wants to pick up where we left off now that I'm back. I want that, too, but I'm just not ready for it yet."

"Does Paul know that the two of you dated before?"

"No, and I'd appreciate it if you don't mention it. Chase deserves this apprenticeship. I don't want him to lose it because of Paul's jealously.

"I understand completely. For what it's worth, I really like you and Chase together. He's a real gentleman, unlike Paul the Neanderthal."

"I didn't realize that you have a problem with Paul."

"I don't, but I'm just his employee. If I were you, I'd have a huge problem with him. I like that you're back here. With you and Chase in the kitchen, Paul keeps his distance. I cook better when I don't have to deal with his attitude."

The door of the cooler swings open, and Chase appears in the doorway. "What's the holdup, ladies? This food isn't going to prep itself."

"Thanks for that earth-shattering revelation," Claire teases with a smile. "We were just having a little girl talk, nothing to concern yourself with."

Claire and I step out of the cooler and deposit the food on my station. "I'm going to set my dough to knead and then go get some coffee. Does anyone need anything from the dining room?"

We all assure her that we're fine, and I focus my attention on the food in front of me. Today's lunch special is a seared Ahi tuna with a wasabi crust and fennel lime dipping sauce. I start slicing the whole fish into steaks and, just as I'd described to Jenny, all thoughts of what's happening outside of the restaurant are pushed from my mind. The other scheduled chefs file into the kitchen but I hardly notice them. All that matters is that I do justice to the amazing ingredients in front of me. Before I realize it, the lunch rush is over and the kitchen staff dwindles down to me, Chase, and Raoul.

"Oh my God, is it already two o'clock?" I ask, finally looking up from my station.

"Yep," Raoul replies. "There are a few late customers in the dining room, but the real crowd has cleared out. Your tuna looked delicious. Is there any left?"

"There are a couple of crusted steaks I haven't seared off yet. Do you want me to make one for you?"

"I can do it, I'm sure that you want to check on Jenny," Raoul replies.

Jenny! I forgot she was here! Surely everything's fine or someone would have come and gotten me.

I wash my hands at the sink, pull off my chef's jacket, and walk toward the dining room. I'm anxious to hear about Jenny's first shift but I try to appear calm and nonchalant as I approach Rachel.

"Is Jenny still here?"

"Yes, she just ran to the bathroom. She did really good considering how long it's been since she's waited tables. There was one weird moment when she spaced out on me for a second, but she recovered well and I don't think that the customers noticed."

"She zoned out at a table?" I ask. "Who were you waiting on? What type of customers?"

"It was a young couple and their baby."

Oh no! Seeing the baby must have brought back all kinds of emotions.

"Like I said," Rachel continues. "Jenny recovered pretty quickly and the customers didn't notice anything."

"How long ago was this?"

"A couple of hours maybe. To be honest, I lose track of time when I'm on the floor. She's been fine ever since though. I'm happy she's here. As soon as she's trained, I'm taking a day off."

"I know you need one. I'm going to go find Jenny. Thanks for everything, Rachel."

"No problem," she calls after me as I make my way to the ladies room.

"Jenny?" I say softly as I push open the door. I find her standing in front of the mirror applying lipstick.

"Hey, Kiara, that was a crazy shift! I'd forgotten how busy it gets around here," she greets me happily.

"So everything went well?"

"It was perfect." She grins. "Rachel said I can probably start taking tables on my own tomorrow. Which means money in my pocket sooner rather than later. I know I didn't love the idea of working here again, but I'm so glad you talked me in to it. I think being around people is just what I need."

I study her for a moment, looking for any sign that she's trying to hide her real feelings. She seems genuinely content, so I don't bring up the family Rachel told me about.

"I'm glad that you're enjoying yourself. Are you ready to run to the café for lunch?"

"Would you mind terribly if we just eat here?" she asks. "There are a couple of new things on the menu that I'm dying to try. Have you had the Kailua pork? It looks delicious."

"It is delicious, and there's plenty in the walk in. You go grab us a table, and I'll heat some up."

We leave the bathroom, and I rush to the kitchen to get our food. Paul could show up at any minute, and I don't want Jenny to have to deal with him on her own.

"What's going on? I was about to leave to meet you at the café," Chase says as I step into the kitchen.

"Jenny spotted the Kailua pork and won't be satisfied until she tries it," I tell him with a smile. "We're just going to eat in the dining room."

"You go join her. I'll make us all a plate and join you in a few minutes," he insists. "I know you want to be with her when she sees Paul for the first time."

"It bodes well for you that you can read my mind like that," I reply with a suggestive grin.

"Whatever gets me ahead." He laughs. "I'll see you soon."

I walk back to the dining room as Chase sets off for the walk-in. I push through the swinging doors just as Paul walks through the front entrance. Jenny's facing me, and I make my way to the table quickly.

"Where's our food?"

"Chase is getting it. Jenny, Paul just walked in," I warn her.

Jenny takes a deep breath and sits up straight in the booth.

"You'll be fine. You'll feel much better once we get this over with," I assure her.

Paul spots us on his way through the dining room and heads for our table. "Jenny," he greets her with a curt nod. "I take it your first shift went well?"

"It did, Paul, thank you," she replies with confidence. "I owe you an apology. I owe you a lot more than that, really, because saying I'm sorry doesn't begin to make up for what I've done. But I want you to know that I truly regret everything I did before. I appreciate you giving me another chance, and I'm going to prove to you that I deserve it."

That was pretty good. Her voice didn't break once. I wonder how long she's been practicing.

"You're right, Jenny, an apology doesn't even begin to make up for anything. I understand that you're in danger right now, a danger that you brought upon yourself. But Kiara is determined to protect you, and I really am shorthanded. I trust that once Robbs is behind bars, you'll want to move on to a job with fewer complications," Paul replies harshly. "While you are here, there will be no need for you to step in to my kitchen." He turns on the spot and continues on to the kitchen.

"I'm so sorry, Jenny. He was completely out of line," I say quickly.

"No, it's fine," she assures me. "I didn't expect him to roll out a welcome mat. I'm lucky he's giving me a chance at all. He has no reason to trust me. Ah, there's Chase with our food."

I turn and see Chase approaching with a huge tray. "I'm going to go grab a salad," I tell them as Chase distributes our plates. "I'll be right back."

"You're going to go confront Paul about his attitude," Jenny corrects me. "It's not necessary, but I know better than to try and stop you. Just take it easy on him, he really is doing us both a favor."

"What's going on?" Chase asks.

"I'll explain," Jenny insists. "You go get your 'salad'."

I cross the dining room and throw open the kitchen doors. Paul is sitting at the butcher block island, studying a newspaper.

"What the hell was that?" I demand.

He looks up at me and scowls. "In my office, Chef Sands."

I follow him into the office, and he quietly shuts the door behind me. "Don't you *ever* speak to me like that in my kitchen again. *You are my employee*, that is *all*. You've made that abundantly clear on several occasions. And if any of my other employees dared to address me the way you just did, I'd toss them out on their ass."

"I'm sorry, *Chef Weston*," I reply mockingly. "But if you don't mind, could you please explain to me why you had to be so rude to Jenny? Did you let her come back because you're willing to give her another chance? Or did you just do it so you can torture her?"

"I let her come back as a favor to you, which I believe I've already explained. I never promised to be nice to her. That wasn't part of the deal."

"I'm sorry, I didn't realize that I'd have to ask you to act like a decent human being. Call me crazy, but I thought you'd do that all on your own. She just lost her *child*. Don't you think that she's been punished enough?"

"I think that it's time you went back to your table. You've only got twenty minutes until I need you back in the kitchen and the same goes for your little boyfriend. And by the way, since the regular employee rules now apply to you, those pork plates will be coming out of your check. At the employee discounted price, of course."

"Of course," I reply angrily. "I'll be back in the kitchen directly, *Chef Weston*." I back out of the office and slam the door behind me.

I was right. Coming back here was a terrible mistake. Now how in the world am I going to get out of it?

Chapter Seven

I wake to my blaring alarm, roll over, and slap the snooze button. It's nine a.m., two weeks since Jenny's first day back at Fission and our first full day off together. Jenny's scheduled to meet with her orthopedic surgeon in an hour, and Chase and I are meeting for breakfast. I roll out of bed and stumble into the bathroom.

Before I strip down to take my shower, I search every nook and cranny of the room to make sure that there are no hidden cameras. This has become my normal routine when I'm alone in the apartment. We haven't seen any signs that Robbs has been in the house, but I don't want to take any chances. I still haven't told anyone that he'd watched me in New York. I think that in some ways keeping the information to myself makes it less real, and I don't want to give Jenny and Chase anything else to worry about.

I'm satisfied that the bathroom is camera free, so I strip out of my pajamas and step under the steaming water. I shower quickly and return to my bedroom to survey my wardrobe. I'm still not completely ready to take things to the next level with Chase, but I want to look nice for him. I decide on a pair of skinny jeans, brown boots, and a white, gauzy peasant top that sets off my dark hair. I highlight my green eyes with gold liner, glide on some lip gloss, and head for the living room. Jenny's already dressed and ready for her appointment.

"Good morning," I greet her. "Are you ready to go?"

"Yes, are you sure that you don't mind me taking the car?"

"Not at all, I'm riding with Chase to the diner. He can bring me home before he goes in to work."

"I hate that we couldn't all have a day off together."

"It works out pretty well for me." I smile. "I can have quality time with him over breakfast, and we can have girl time tonight."

"You look fantastic. Can I take that as a sign that you're finally going to give that poor boy a chance?"

"I'm close," I tell her. "I know that Chase would never hurt me. And he's been fantastic through all of this. I'm just not sure that I trust my own judgment. I remember how happy I was when Paul and I first got together and now, when I think about how wrong I was…"

"You wonder what else you were wrong about," Jenny finishes. "I feel the same way, in some respects. But you have to move forward. You can't punish Chase for Paul's mistakes. And you need to forgive yourself for yours."

"You've been paying attention at the meetings," I say with a grin. Jenny and I have gone to two of the domestic abuse survivors meetings together, and she's gone to three more on her own. I've been amazed at how much progress she's made in such a short amount of time. It was the meeting leader who finally convinced her to see the doctor again, and I'm thankful that someone was able to make her see reason.

"I'm so glad that you convinced me to go. You'd be surprised how many of the women there have been in my exact situation. We like to think that all of our babies are up there playing together in heaven."

It's the first time I've heard Jenny mention her lost daughter with any sense of peace and I wrap her in a hug.

"I'm sure they are. And I'm sure that Maggie will be the first one in line to greet you when your time finally comes."

Jenny wipes a single tear from her eye. "Enough of all this emotional nonsense, I have an appointment to get to, and you've got a hot man waiting across the hall. See you back here in a few hours?"

"Sure," I agree as we walk into the hallway. Jenny steps into the elevator, and I knock on Chase's door.

"Hey," he greets me with a wide smile. "You look beautiful. I'd almost forgotten what you look like out of your Fission uniform."

"You clean up pretty good yourself." Chase's broad, well-defined chest is covered by a fitted blue button up and khaki shorts reveal his toned calves. The shirt sets off his clear blue eyes perfectly and a rush of attraction courses through my body.

"Thank you," he replies. "I'll have to change before I go to work, but I thought it would be nice to put on real clothes for a change. So where would you like to have breakfast? Claire told me about a great new Jewish deli that opened on Central. Want to check it out?"

"That sounds fantastic, unless their bagels suck. That's the one thing I really miss about New York."

"We'll try them out and if they don't measure up, we'll make a batch at home. Sound good?"

"Sounds perfect," I agree.

Chase locks his door, and we step into the elevator. He reaches for my hand as we step out into the lobby, and I don't pull away. We walked to his car, and he opens my door for me.

He really is a true Southern gentleman.

We ride to Central Avenue in a comfortable silence, and I'm amazed by how at ease I feel when I'm around Chase. The feelings I have for him are unlike anything I've ever experienced, which is why I'm so hesitant to rush things. The last thing I want to do is mess this up.

Chase pulls in to a parking spot right in front of the deli and takes me by the hand again as we step inside. We take seats at a small two top and a plump, elderly woman approaches the table.

"Good morning, can I get you a pot of coffee or some hot tea?"

"I'd love some tea, thank you," I reply. "Do you make your bagels in house?"

"Of course we do."

"Great, I'd also like an everything bagel with lox and cream cheese."

"The same for me please, but I'd like coffee," Chase adds.

"Perfect, I'll have it right out." She smiles.

"So, Jenny's at her appointment now?" Chase asks once we're alone.

"Yes, finally. I thought she was never going to see reason but she came around. I hope that he tells her good news. She really did try hard to rehab that shoulder on her own."

"I'm sure she'll be fine. Have you heard from the cops lately?"

I shake my head. "No, Delco still checks in every couple of days, but no one has any news. I don't want to get my hopes up but I'm starting to think that Robbs finally got tired of the game and disappeared."

"From your mouth to God's ears," Chase replies as the waitress delivers our drinks.

"Your food will be right up; we're just toasting those bagels," she tells us before leaving again.

"So no news on the Robbs front. Have you heard anything back from the college?"

I blush and lower my eyes.

"Kiara, what is it?" Chase asks, his voice full of concern.

"Ruby left another message on my phone yesterday. She said that I've missed too many meetings and that the Board won't reschedule again. I haven't been to a class since the week Jenny was attacked back in New York. Even if they did reinstate my scholarship and approve my transfer, there's no way I could catch up now."

"There has to be a way," Chase insists. "I'll call Madison again and see if she can do something. She knows what you've been dealing with. I'm sure that she can explain it to the Board."

"You don't have to do that, Chase. I know that Madison is new to her job. I don't want her to alienate herself from her coworkers by going to bat for me. They've made it pretty obvious that they don't want me at the school, and I know how to take a hint."

"You can't just give up. You've worked too hard. And you won't want to work at Fission for the rest of your life."

"That's the truth."

"It's much easier for a chef to get a business loan if they have a culinary degree."

"I'm aware of that, but there's nothing more I can do about it right now. This semester is a lost cause, no matter what happens. I'll reapply in the fall and hope for the best."

"Okay," he relents. "But if you change your mind about calling Madison, all you have to do is ask."

"Thank you."

The waitress reappears with our food, and we spend the next few minutes eating in silence. The bagel is chewy on the outside and soft in the middle, just like it's supposed to be, and I know I've found a new favorite place to eat.

"Well, there won't be any need for us to make them ourselves," Chase says after he swallows his last bite. "That was delicious."

"Good thing, too," I agree. "It's not like we have loads of free time for leisure cooking. I can't remember the last time I made a meal at home."

"I know, that's the one part of this career that surprises me. I love cooking, but when I get home I just don't have the energy for it."

"Speaking of school, how long of a waiver did they give you to do the apprenticeship?"

"A year. I'll go back to regular classes next summer."

"That's perfect. Now that Jenny's earning a paycheck, too, I'll be able to put some money back. I should have plenty saved by the time you finish the apprenticeship."

"What will you need money for?"

"To quit my job, if I don't find something else before then. I can barely stand to be around Paul now, I can't imagine staying there after you leave."

"Aww… that's kind of sweet. But I thought that Paul was going easy on you? He's certainly been more than fair about your salary."

"He's going easy on me, but he's still being awful to Jenny and I can't stand it. I don't know how Jenny's managed to keep her cool. If he talked to me the way he talks to her, I'd slap him in the face."

"If another few weeks go by without Robbs showing up, it might be safe for her to find a new job. Though it'll be hard for her to make the same money she's making now."

"That's the problem we're both having. We need the money, so we're stuck there for the time being."

"You're both talented women. I'm sure that other opportunities will pop up before you know it. Though I have to admit, I'd love to see you slap the shit out of Paul. I wish that I could help out with your bills… sometimes I think that I should have taken my dad's advice. I could be making a small fortune right now if I'd gone out for the draft, and you and Jenny wouldn't have to worry about money."

"Chase, that's the last thing I'd want you to do. You hated the idea of going out for the NFL. And with my luck, you'd have been drafted by some godforsaken East Coast team and I'd never get to see you. I'd much rather put up with Paul and have you here with me than be a kept woman who's always alone."

Chase smiles slyly. "Be careful. The way you're talking it sounds like you think of me as more than a friend."

I blush for the second time that morning. "Of course I think of you as more than a friend, Chase. You're a very *special* friend, and I'm looking forward to seeing where this goes. I just don't want to move too fast and mess it all up."

"Like I've told you before, I'll wait as long as it takes." He looks down at his watch. "Are you about ready to go? I hate to take you home but I've got to get to work."

"Sure," I reply.

Chase moves to the cash register and pays our check while I browse the deli case. The pastrami looks amazing, so I order a pound to go. I add a bottle of wine, a block of smoked provolone, and a box of crackers at the register.

"This will be perfect for girl's night," I tell Chase as the waitress bags my selections. I pay with my debit card, and Chase carries my bag to the car.

"I'm going to miss you in the kitchen tonight," Chase tells me as he pulls the car away from the curb.

"Not as much as I miss you when you're not there," I assure him. "I doubt that Paul gives you the same looks he gives me. I'm much more comfortable when we work together."

"Kiara, do you want me to say something to him? I mean, we are in a relationship now. Granted, it may be the slowest-moving relationship in history, but I'd be completely within my rights if I told him to cut out his shit."

"But then you'll just be in the same position I am," I remind him. "We don't need Paul pissed at all three of us. Not to mention, he could mess with your standing at the college if he wants. He does grade you, after all."

"I forgot that point," Chase admits. "I'll play nice for now, but if he crosses any farther over the line, I'm going to say something. I'll be smart about it and report him to the college first. I know you filed a complaint about him the first time you left Fission. If I do the same, there's no way they'll take his word over mine."

His every thought is about protecting and taking care of me. Is it really possible that this man is for real? Is this what love is supposed to look like?

"If he says anything else, I'll let you know," I promise. "And I'll think about your offer to call Madison again, though I'm pretty sure it's best if I just leave the college thing alone until fall."

"Just let me know," he says as he pulls into our parking lot.

"Jenny must not be back yet," I observe, looking at the vacant spot my new used Honda usually occupies. "I hope everything's going okay at the doctor's office."

"You know how it is, if you're appointment is scheduled at ten, you can expect to see the doctor around one-thirty," Chase says as we get out of the car. He takes my hand again and we make our way to our floor.

"Thank you for breakfast," I tell him as I unlock my door. Chase follows me in to the apartment and sets my groceries on the kitchen counter.

"You're more than welcome." He smiles. "One of these days, I'm going to make you breakfast in bed."

"I like the sound of that," I tell him.

He puts his hands on my hips and looks me deep in the eyes. "So, you let me hold your hand today."

"I did."

"I don't want to push my luck, but what would happen if I lean down and kiss you right now?"

"Why don't you try it and find out?"

Chase pulls me close, leans down, and plants a soft, sweet kiss on my lips. I lean against his chest as he lifts his head and tightens his arms around me.

"I hope you know how much I care about you, Chase, and how much I appreciate everything you've done for Jenny and me."

"I know," he assures me. "I care about you, too, more than I ever thought was possible. That's why I'm happy to do things for you and Jenny. I know that you haven't felt safe or protected since you were a very young girl. But things are different now, you don't have to handle everything on your own."

I squeeze him tightly and pull away. "I know you need to get changed. Stop by when you get home?"

"Nothing could keep me away." He kisses me again and reluctantly leaves the apartment. I walk to my bedroom, open the closet door, and climb onto a stepstool.

I know it's back here somewhere.

I grope around on the top shelf. My hands finally fall on a small box; I pull it off of the shelf, climb down from the stool, and settle down on my bed. I pull the last note my parents ever left me out of its hiding place and tear it in to pieces.

They said that leaving was the best thing they could do for me. They said it was because they love me. But that's not what love is. Love is never giving up, facing whatever may come together. Love is what I have with Chase and with Jenny. They're my family now.

I toss the scraps of worn paper in to the wastebasket. For the first time since I was sixteen years old, I don't feel like an orphan.

Chapter Eight

Chase changes into his Fission uniform quickly and leaves his apartment twenty minutes early. He has a phone call to make, and he needs to eliminate any chance of Kiara overhearing it. Once he reaches his car, he pulls his cell phone from his pocket and dials his sister's number.

"Hey, little bro," she answers on the first ring. "How's life?"

"Life is good, Madison, how are you?"

"I can't complain. I wish I could see you more often, but I know that you've got a busy schedule. I met some new people at a karaoke bar last week, so I'm not as lonely as I was."

"I'm sorry I haven't been able to make more time for you. Do you have plans on Sunday? We do a great brunch at the restaurant. You and your friends should come in. If we're lucky, I'll be able to break out of the kitchen for a few minutes to say hi."

"I can probably do that. So why are you really calling? I know it's not to inquire about my weekend dining plans."

"I was hoping that you could put in a good word for Kiara. Weston has kept her pretty busy in the kitchen, and she hasn't been able to make it to any of the meetings she scheduled with the Admin Board. They've refused to reschedule again, but do you think you could change their minds?"

"I'm not sure it's my place to ask, Chase," Madison replies. "I know they've already rescheduled for her more than they've ever done for any other student. I put my neck out for her the first time I talked to them, and I don't mind telling you that I caught some shit when she no showed. I think it would be best if she just waits them out. Have her reapply in the fall and maybe I'll be able to convince them that she's changed."

"Kiara isn't a bad person, Madison. She's just overwhelmed."

"I'm sure that's true. But all the board cares about is her attendance. They don't care about how she's handling her personal life."

"Is that why they revoked her scholarship, her attendance?"

"I don't know, I just assumed that was the case," Madison replies. "Did they not give her a reason for pulling her aid?"

"No, they told her it would all be discussed at the hearing."

"Well, then she should have made it to the hearing. I don't know what else to tell you."

"Madison, there's a chance that Robbs Martin was the reason they pulled her aid. If that's the case, then Kiara has every right to know about it. The police do, too, for that matter. Could you dig around and see if you can find out the exact reason she lost the scholarship?”

“I’ll see what I can do,” Madison agrees. “You’re going to an awful lot of trouble for this girl. Are you sure that she’s worth it?”

“I’m positive. Kiara’s the one, Madison. You’ll understand when you meet her.”

“Will she be gracing us with her presence on Sunday?”

“I doubt Paul will let us out of the kitchen together. He and Kiara have a history together so we try not to flaunt our relationship in his face.”

“Like I said, little bro, sounds like an awful lot of trouble to go through for a woman.”

“You let me worry about how much trouble I can handle. Just try to find me some answers. And don’t share any of these opinions of yours with Dad. I don’t need both of you lecturing me.”

“My lips are sealed. And on the subject of keeping things from Dad, I’d rather you didn’t mention my brunch date to him. You know how he feels about tats, and Lewis is covered in them.”

“Deal,” Chase agrees. “Call me as soon as you find out anything. And Madison? Thank you.”

“No problem, little bro, talk to you soon.”

Chase ends the call as he pulls into the Fission parking lot. He knows that Kiara will be pissed when she finds out he brought Madison into things again, but he hopes that knowing the reason behind losing the scholarship will make her fight harder to get it back.

"I know it was Robbs," he says to no one. "I just hope that I can prove it."

<<<>>>

"That steak smells amazing, Chef Sands," Chase calls out from across the kitchen.

"Thank you, Chef," I call back with a smile. We're at work and dinner service is busy, but we're on top of things. Paul is away from Fission for the night and the entire kitchen staff is in a good mood. Jenny's in the dining room, but she pops in periodically since Paul is gone.

Chase slides a plate into the service window and joins me at my station. "That really does smell amazing. We should go to the diner for steak and eggs in the morning."

"I don't know," I reply in a teasing voice. "I was thinking that breakfast in bed sounds good for tomorrow."

A wide smile spreads across his face. "Well, you won't hear me argue with that." His expression changes, and he pulls his phone from his back pocket. "I've got to take this, I'll be right back."

Chase leaves through the back door, and I turn my attention back to the grill. I feel refreshed after spending last night at home with Jenny, and I'm actually happy to be back in the kitchen.

If Paul could just stay away all of the time, everything would be perfect.

I pull a rare filet off of the grill and set it on a sizzling cast iron plate. I arrange mashed potatoes and roasted carrots on a separate plate and gently place everything onto a wooden serving platter. I carry the platter to the front of the kitchen, slide it into the service window, and turn back to my station just as Chase walks back through the door.

Oh my God, why does he look like that? This can't be good.

Chase walks toward me but can't seem to look me in the eye. I takes me by the arm and leads me out into the dining room.

"What are you doing? Service isn't over yet. Has something else happened? Who was on the phone?"

"Sit down," Chase insists softly.

I slide into a booth but continue badgering him with questions. "Was it the super? Is the apartment okay?"

He slides in across from me and takes a deep breath. "There's no easy way to say this, Kiara. I thought that it was important to know why you lost your scholarship. No one's given you a straight answer so I asked Madison to look in to it. Before you get mad, I want you to remember that I promised not to ask her to talk to the board. I didn't say anything about detective work."

"What did she find out? It was Robbs, wasn't it?"

"She emailed me your file. I've forwarded it to you, and I think you need to go home to look at it."

"I can't go home. Service isn't over," I remind him again.

"It's almost over, and the rest of us can handle it."

"Why are you telling me now instead of waiting until we get home?"

He's silent for a moment, and I realize the answer.

"You've already looked at the file, and it's bad, right? So bad that you can't look at me. You couldn't spend the rest of the night in the kitchen pretending not to know whatever it is you now know."

"It's not that bad," he assures me. "I just thought you'd want to know as soon as possible. I'll make sure that Jenny gets home tonight. Promise me that you won't open the email until you get to the apartment."

"I take it none of this is up for discussion?"

"It's not. I'll call Paul if I have to and make up a reason for him to send you home."

"I don't like being told what to do."

"No one does, but sometimes you need to listen to reason."

"Fine," I reply, standing up abruptly. "Am I at least allowed to get my purse?"

"Don't be snarky, sweetheart, just trust me and go home. I'll come over when I get off."

"Don't bother." I don't want to make a scene in front of the diners so I calmly return to the kitchen and gather my things. Once I'm in my car, I break my promise to Chase and open the email on my phone. There are several files attached and I open the one labeled "Video".

Holy shit, no wonder they kicked me out. That only happened once! And it was my first day at The Madden Crowd. How in the hell did Robbs get a camera in that walk in?

There's no audio to the video, which makes the scene look worse than it actually was. Instead of hearing me push off James's advances, anyone watching this would think that we were carrying on a torrid affair. I've seen enough. I toss my phone onto the passenger's seat and drive to my apartment in a daze.

Chapter Nine

"Kiara, I know that you're in there. Jenny just dropped me off. She's going back to Fission to help with inventory. I'm not going away so you may as well let me in," Chase tells me from the hallway.

It's been three hours since I got home. The moment I arrived, I collapsed on the couch to pour over my file, and I've been here ever since. Aside from the video, it contained several statements from Paul, James, and an assortment of male chefs I've had classes with. All of the statements are basically the same, accusing me of making inappropriate sexual advances and making my peers uncomfortable. Not a damn thing in the file is true, but I'm humiliated that Chase and Madison have read the lies. I reluctantly swing open the front door and let Chase into the apartment.

"I know that the video looks bad, but if you could just *hear* what happened, you'd know that I didn't do anything wrong. James came on to me in that cooler, and I shoved him off. And none of those statements are true. Aside from James and Paul, I don't even know those men."

"I believe you," Chase answers simply.

"You do? Why?"

He shrugs. "I just do. I know that Robbs is behind all of this. I had Madison look in to it because I was hoping to find definitive proof. I think that we should ask Paul if he really made that statement."

"I've already called and left him a message. I called James, too. He answered, but he didn't give me a chance to say anything. He just called me a slut and hung up the phone, so that statement from him might be authentic," I say with tears in my eyes.

"It's okay, Kiara." Chase wraps an arm around my shoulder and pulls me close. "You're not a slut. I told Madison that none of those statements are true and that you're not the type of girl who sleeps her way to the top. You may have made some mistakes with Paul, but I knew you'd never go for a slime bag like O'Toole."

My heart fills with guilt. *But I did go for that slime bag. I'm lucky I never had sex with him in my apartment. My student file would be filled with porn.*

"You've put too much faith in me," I tell him sadly.

His shoulders sag as he realizes what I'm saying. "You mean…"

"I got involved with James while I was in the city. I could say that he manipulated me or that I got caught up in the excitement of my new life, but the truth is that I knew better and I did it anyway."

"You made a mistake. It doesn't change the way I feel about you," he insists.

"How can you say that?"

"Kiara, if it weren't for Robbs, I'd never have known this and that would have been fine. We didn't make any commitments to each other before you moved to New York. You were completely free to do whatever you wanted. I've made plenty of mistakes of my own. I was a college football player, remember? I'd hate for you to hold my past against me, I'm not going to do that to you. All that matters to me is our future."

"You really don't think any differently of me?"

"Kiara, I love you. *All* of you, the good and the bad. No statement or video is going to change that."

"I love you, too, Chase."

"I'm going to kiss you now." He smiles. "And then I'm going to carry you into the bedroom and have my way with you."

I wrap my arms around his neck as he lowers his face to mine. He kisses me softly, sweetly, and I melt into his body. He lifts me from the ground, and I wrap my legs around his waist. He walks toward the bedroom, moving his lips down my face and neck. I lean away from him and lift my shirt over my head, tossing it to the floor.

"You are so beautiful." He lowers us on to the bed. "I'm going to lick every inch of you."

He plants soft kisses on my belly as he unbuttons my jeans. He slides them down my legs as I kick off my shoes. Chase throws my pants aside and takes my left foot into his hands. He kisses my arch and runs his tongue up the side of my leg and behind my knee. I want him to continue higher, but instead he moves to my right leg and blazes the same path.

"Your skin is so soft… you taste so good." He groans and raises his lips back to mine. I squirm beneath him, reaching for his waistband.

"Be patient," he tells me as he pulls my hands away. "I've waited so long for this. I want to enjoy every last moment."

I relax my hands and rest them on the mattress. Chase rolls me gently onto my side, unhooks my bra, and lays me back. He dives his face into my breasts, licking and sucking wildly.

"Chase, I need you now," I beg. "I've wanted this for so long, too… please don't make me wait any longer."

He jumps off of the bed, quickly strips out of his clothes, and climbs back on top of me. His firm, chiseled body feels amazing against my bare skin. I part my legs and reach down to guide him into my aching hole.

His thick, hard cock is dripping in anticipation, and l long to feel it inside of me. Chase pushes in the first inch and stops for a moment.

"You're so tight, Kiara. You feel so amazing."

"I need you," I beg again. I wrap my arms around his waist and grab his rock hard ass cheeks, pushing him farther inside of me.

"I'm afraid I'm going to crush you." He breathes heavily.

"Well, I know how to fix that." I put one hand on his shoulder and push him onto his back, moving with him so we remain connected. He pulls himself up and rests his back against the headboard as I lower myself down into his lap. I plant my feet on the mattress and slowly start bouncing up and down. Chase's throbbing cock strokes every inch of me, and I know I won't be able to hold myself back very long. I lose my balance mid-bounce and come down at an odd angle. I feel the tip of Chase's cock grind against my G-spot and lose all control, letting my most basic instincts take over. I grab Chase by the shoulders and repeat the movement over and over, harder each time, until I feel my body explode in release.

Chase wraps his arms around me and rolls me onto my back while I'm still in the throes of my orgasm. He thrusts into me urgently and cries out in his own satisfaction. We roll onto our sides, still connected, to regain our breath.

"Don't think for a second that I'm done with you tonight," Chase warns, kissing me again. "I may never be able to get enough."

"That's fine with me, baby." I smile. "I'm going to go grab a bottle of water. I'll be right back."

He reluctantly lets me leave the bed. I set off for the kitchen but decide to stop in the bathroom first. I push open the door and immediately realize that something's not right.

I don't remember leaving my tablet in here.

I look around the room and notice that several things are out of place.

Maybe Jenny rearranged earlier, and I didn't notice it.

I decide to inspect the apartment before I say anything to Chase.

The easiest place to start will be the kitchen. I'll know instantly if anything's out of place. Jenny knows I have everything just how I like it in there.

I flip on the kitchen lights and feel frozen with panic. The countertop appliances have been completely rearranged and our grocery list has been wiped off our refrigerator marker board. In its place is a single message written in red.

I'M STILL WATCHING. AND I'M STILL COMING FOR YOU.

Jenny shuffles into the kitchen just after the sun comes up. "Oh my God, Kiara, have you been up all night?"

"Yes, and I'm nowhere near finished. I'm going to call in to work, I can't stand to leave this place the way Robbs left it."

"I'll call in, too, and help you. What have you done so far?"

"Just the kitchen," I reply. "I washed all of the dishes and disinfected every inch of the room. I've been washing all of my clothes, too, and I think that we should do yours. There's no telling what that psycho may have left behind. Chase is going to replace the locks again as soon as the hardware store opens. The cops left around three; they didn't find any prints."

"That's what all that black smudgy stuff in the bathroom is!"

"Yeah, they made a hell of a mess and didn't find anything. You'd think that they'd at least clean up after themselves."

"Kiara, maybe we should take Officer Marquez's advice and leave town for a while. We could rent a car and disappear until they track him down."

"He'll track us, Jenny. And we'll be away from everyone we know who could help us. Besides, Robbs has been evading the cops for months now. Do you really want to be on the run that long? How would we even afford it?"

"All right, points taken," she gives in. "But could we at least have Chase stay here from now on?"

"Yes," I say with a blush. "I don't think that that will be a problem. In fact, he's in my bed right now."

"Kiara! You finally did it! It took you long enough," she teases.

"I know, and I realized that the bathroom was rearranged right after. Talk about killing the moment."

"So the sex happened before I got home, and Chase never left after I went to bed."

"Right."

"God, that is terrible timing. But I'm glad that he was here when you realized what had happened."

"Me, too. I'm sorry that I forgot to call you. I know how stressful it is to pull into the parking lot and see the blue lights."

"It's okay, I did the same thing to you. It's crazy how much you forget about during chaos. I just wish that one of us had been here when he broke in."

"What are you talking about, Jenny? He could have killed us."

She shakes her head. "He proved that he can get in here, if he'd wanted to kill us, he could have. He's trying to scare us, and I refuse to let him. I'm not going to live in fear anymore. If I do, he wins. I hope I'm here when he shows up again. I'll put my pepper spray and self-defense training to good use, I promise you that."

She really has been getting a lot out of those meetings.

"I just want him caught, I don't care how it happens," I tell her.

"My sentiments exactly," Chase says as he steps into the kitchen. "I guess I'm not the only one who couldn't sleep? I noticed that you never came to bed last night."

"I won't be able to sleep until I get the Robbs off of everything. Jenny and I are both going to call in to work."

"I'm going to do the same. I'll make the call and explain what happened last night. It's Paul's restaurant. He can handle it without us for one day."

Jenny opens the refrigerator door, and I brace myself for her reaction. "Kiara, did you throw out all of our food?"

"Yes, I bagged it up and tossed it down the trash shoot after Chase went to bed. We have to assume that he did something to it, better safe than sorry."

"I'm actually surprised that the police didn't think of that," Jenny replies.

"I'll run to the corner store and buy some coffee," Chase offers. "I'd go across the hall and get mine, but something tells me you're going to make me do this at my place, too."

"Better safe than sorry," I say again.

Chase shrugs. "I don't have much over there anyway. I'll pick up some breakfast while I'm out, and I'll call Paul."

"Thank you, baby," I tell him with a hug.

"You're welcome. I'll be back soon."

Chase grabs his keys from the kitchen counter and leaves the apartment.

"You two are so cute together." Jenny smiles. "So what finally made you trust him?"

I tell her about what we found in my student file.

"That bastard! It had to be Robbs! Let me see the file."

"That's really not necessary, the fewer people who read those lies the better."

"I don't want to read the statements. I just want to look at the file types."

"What does that matter?" I ask as I pass her my phone.

"It might not, just give me a second." Jenny taps the screen a couple of times and then turns the phone back toward me.

"The statements are all attached individually. If we can find someone who's halfway decent at hacking, we can have each file traced back to its source. And I bet that every last damn one of them will trace back to Robbs."

"If we could prove that, the board would have no choice but to reinstate my scholarship."

"Exactly."

"That's brilliant. How do you know about this kind of stuff? You've never talked about computers before."

Her smile disappears, and I know that I've hit a nerve. "My father is a computer programmer," she finally answers. "I guess I could try to call him, see if he can trace the files."

"You don't have to do that," I tell her quickly. "I'm sure that Chase knows someone from his old university who can help us out."

She breathes a long sigh of relief. "That would probably be better."

"Jenny, have you called your parents and told them about what happened in New York?"

"No," she admits. "I've been tempted to a couple of times, but I just can't make the call. I know exactly what they'll say. My father will tell me that it was God's will, because babies out of wedlock are an abomination. Then my mother will insist that it's for the best, because it's impossible for a single mother to find a good husband. That was the worst night of my life, and they'll see it as redemption. I can't take that right now."

"It's okay, Jenny, if that's how they feel then you're better off without them."

"Most people don't understand how a person can feel that way about their parents," she says with a sad smile.

"I know, but we're not most people." As I move to hug her, I hear my phone ring in the living room. "That might be Chase, I better get it."

"Of course, go ahead."

I grab my phone and see Paul's cell number on the screen.

Damn it, doesn't he understand that I don't have time for this right now?

"Hello?" I answer impatiently.

"Chef Sands, as I'm sure you're aware, it's Fission policy that an employee calls in for themselves when they're not going to be able to make it to work," Paul says hatefully. "As you and Jenny have both broken that policy, I have no choice but to terminate your positions."

"Are you fucking kidding me?" I hiss. "I know Chase explained the situation to you. How can you be this heartless?"

"It's not my job to worry about what happens to you outside of the kitchen. I have a business to run, and I need staff that I can count on."

"I see. And what reason are you giving for getting rid of Chase?"

"Mr. Abbott overstepped the boundaries of his apprenticeship by fraternizing with you. I intend to file a report about his actions with the ethics board of *Le Cordon Bleu*."

"You do that. And while you're busy patting yourself on the back for being a horse's ass, I'll round up all of the women from Fission *you've* fraternized with over the years. I bet the Better Business Bureau and the Austin Chamber of Commerce would be interested in that information as well. Not to mention the local papers. What's the name of that female food critic at *The Post* who likes you so much? I wonder if she'd keep singing your praises if she knew what kind of person you really are."

"You do whatever you have to do, and I'll do the same. And don't bother bringing your jacket back this time. The fucking thing is cursed; I don't want it in my restaurant."

A few moments of silence pass, and I realize that Paul has ended the call. I toss my phone onto the sofa and let out a long laugh.

"What's so funny? It sounded like we just got fired," Jenny says with a frown.

"We did," I tell her. "And I've never felt better in my life."

Chapter Ten

We spend the next six hours cleaning, and I finally feel like the apartment is Robbs free. To my relief, neither Jenny nor Chase seem too upset that we're all suddenly unemployed. Chase leaves to buy new locks for our door, and Jenny sits down at the couch with my laptop.

"You don't mind if I use this, do you? I want to look at the job postings."

"Go ahead," I tell her. "But I think I have an idea about where we could all work."

"Really? That was fast. I'm surprised at how well you're handling this. For weeks you've been saying that we were stuck at Fission because we need the money. Suddenly we've both been fired, and you don't seem concerned at all."

"An idea came to me when I was talking to Paul. When I mentioned rounding up all of the female employees he's screwed, it dawned on me that I'd be able to find most of them at the same place."

"Which is…?" Jenny asks, still confused.

"Patrick's new restaurant," I answer simply. "He's set to open in two weeks, and I'm sure he's still building his staff. And he and I always got along well in the kitchen. He's the one who gave me my spot in the apprenticeship competition."

"Me, too!" Jenny smiles. "I don't want to work in the kitchen again, but I wouldn't mind waiting tables. And I bet tips will be even better there. Kiara, this is a brilliant idea. Do you think he'll give Chase an apprenticeship?"

"I don't know if Chase would even be interested in one. He mentioned something about focusing on school for the rest of the semester. But if Patrick is shorthanded in the kitchen, I guess it's possible. I'll call Patrick tomorrow and see if he has any openings."

"I'm going to hold off on this until after you talk to him," Jenny says, shutting the laptop. She lets out a long yawn. "I bet I didn't get two hours of sleep last night. I'm going to take a nap."

"Okay, I think I'm going to run to the market and replace our groceries. Is there anything in particular you'd like me to pick up?"

"Don't forget Diet Coke."

"It's the first thing on my list. Chase should be back with the new locks soon. Do you want me to stay until he gets here?"

"No need," she insists. "I really meant what I said earlier. I'm not afraid of Robbs anymore."

"All right, well I'll have my cell on me if you need anything. I shouldn't be gone more than an hour or so."

Jenny laughs. "I've been to Whole Foods with you before, remember? You're going to get mesmerized by all of their fancy products, and I won't see you until nightfall."

"I'll try to stay focused." I laugh. "I'll see you soon." I send Chase a quick text explaining my plans and toss my phone into my purse. I grab my keys and leave the apartment just as Jenny's going back to bed.

Maybe I should stay… I hate leaving her alone. But I'm starving, she must be starving, and the police promised to drive by the building every fifteen minutes. Jenny will be fine.

I have an overwhelming feeling that we haven't seen the last of Robbs but I convince myself that Jenny is right. We can't live in fear and limbo, basing our every move around what Robbs may or may not do.

I won't be gone more than two hours, and Chase should be back any time. Jenny will be fine.

I drive two miles and pull in to the Whole Foods parking lot. Once inside, I try to ignore the organic, free-range offerings in front of me and focus on our necessities. I load my basket with Diet Coke, cereal, and coffee beans before making my way to the proteins. As I round the corner, my eyes fall on Chase. He's on the other end of the store but I'd recognize his broad shoulders anywhere.

He must have gotten my text and decided to join me. He's so sweet. But I wish he'd have gone straight back to the apartment to stay with Jenny.

I take three steps in his direction and stop dead in my tracks. A beautiful thin brunette joins Chase, and he casually wraps an arm around her shoulders.

Who the FUCK is that? And what is he doing with her? DAMNIT how is this happening to me again? Why can't one fucking man in my life be worthy of trust?

Chase and the woman turn and he spots me standing in the aisle. He looks from me to the woman at his side and a look of panic crosses his face. I push my basket up to him and give him a cold stare.

"Kiara, this is…"

"I don't care who this is," I snap.

The woman blushes. "I know how this must look to you, but…"

"I'm sorry," I interrupt her. "But this is between me and Chase. He'll be all yours in just a minute." I turn back to him.

"Don't bother with the new locks, I'll call the super. I need to speak with him anyway and give notice on our month-to-month lease. Jenny and I will be out of the building in a week. I'd appreciate it if you'd steer clear of us until then."

I leave my basket in the aisle and stomp toward the front of the store.

"Kiara, wait!" Chase calls after me.

"Chase, just let her go," the woman tells him.

I can't fucking believe this. He's been so helpful, so caring. I thought I'd finally found a man who loves me. But he's worse than the rest of them combined. At least Paul admits that he's an asshole, and James would be the first to call himself a man whore. Chase prances around like a well-mannered Southern gentleman but he's really just a snake.

I drive around aimlessly for over an hour, ignoring my cell phone. It rings every five minutes, but I know that Chase is on the other line and I have nothing to say to him. I finally pull into a convenience store and load up on soda and junk food before I go home.

We'll just order dinner in tonight. I haven't had Thai Palace since we moved home, and they'll deliver.

I pull into the parking lot and stack the twelve packs of Diet Coke in my arms.

I'll come back for the rest of this...

I walk through the entrance and into the elevator. The sodas are heavy in my arms but I barely notice. The elevator carries me to the third floor, and I try to decide how to tell Jenny that Chase is an ass and we have to move again. The doors slide open; the moment I step into the hallway, I know that I have bigger problems to worry about.

The front door of our apartment is splintered and barely hanging from its hinges. I drop the twelve packs and rush into the living room.

"Jenny!" I cry out in panic. All of the furniture has been overturned and the television screen is busted.

Glass shards are scattered throughout the carpet, and Jenny is nowhere to be seen. I rush into her bedroom and find her laying in the middle of the floor.

"Jenny!" I say again, shaking her lightly. She stirs and groans but doesn't open her eyes.

Fucking mother fuckers. That son of a bitch was here again, and the man who was supposed to be protecting us was too busy screwing around on me. Well, fuck this. From now on, I'll do everything myself.

I grab my cell phone from my purse and call 911 as I cradle Jenny's head in my lap.

"Emergency dispatch, how may I help you?"

I give the woman my name and address and explain that my roommate has been attacked. "The cops have been looking for Robbs Martin for months, but he always makes it past them. We've mainly been dealing with Officers Jones and Marquez."

"Yes, Ms. Sands, they're patrolling your area now. I've dispatched them to your apartment, along with an ambulance. Would you like me to stay on the line until they get there?"

Jenny stirs in my lap and tries to open her eyes. I hold her for what seems like hours but she never completely wakes up. Finally, I hear a knock from the living room.

"Ms. Sands? It's Officer Marquez."

"They're here now, thank you," I tell the dispatcher.

"You're welcome, Ms. Sands. The ambulance should be there shortly."

"We're in the first bedroom," I call out to Marquez as I end the call.

He rushes into the room. "Kiara, what happened?"

"I wasn't here but I think it's pretty obvious that Robbs came back. I just went to the market to get groceries. I tossed everything out last night, I was afraid that he might have poisoned it when he broke in. I came back to this. Jenny's moved a bit and made noise, but she won't wake up," I sob.

Another knock comes from the living room; Officer Marquez disappears and returns a moment later with a paramedic.

"Ms. Sands, I'm Eric Parker. I understand that you found Ms. Foster like this?"

"Yes, I came home about fifteen minutes ago. I tried to wake her. She moaned and stirred, but she hasn't opened her eyes."

Deep purple bruises had already popped up around Jenny's eyes. Her blonde hair is matted with congealed blood, but I can't see its source. Eric pulls out a handheld radio and calls down to his partner for a gurney.

"We'll call ahead to the hospital and order a head CT." He takes Jenny's blood pressure. "Her vitals are good, but the head trauma is definitely concerning and it looks like she's lost quite a bit of blood. Have you called her family?"

"I'm her family."

"Do you know her blood type?"

"O positive, the same as mine," I answer, remembering from the first time Robbs put Jenny in the hospital. "If she needs blood, you can take it from me."

"That's the most common blood type, so I'm sure that we have plenty on hand. But if you'd like to make a donation at the hospital's blood bank, it would be much appreciated."

"Whatever she needs, I'll do it. Do you see anything that suggests how long ago this happened?" All I can think about is the hour I wasted when I left Whole Foods. I'd been upset for selfish reasons and while I was busy sulking, my best friend had been attacked in our home.

"Judging by how dry the blood is, I'd say at least an hour," Eric answers. "That's just my guess though. The ER doctors will be able to give you a more definite answer."

I turn to Officer Marquez. "Robbs must have been watching the apartment all day. He waited until Jenny was all alone. How could he have done that? I thought you were keeping a close eye on the building. And I know he didn't plant cameras in here, I searched the entire apartment while I was cleaning."

"I'm sorry, but our resources are limited. We had officers patrolling the area, but we don't have the man power to post full-time guards."

Yet another knock sounds from the living room and two paramedics walk in with a gurney.

"Okay, Kiara," Eric announces. "We're going to load Jenny now and take her to the hospital. Would you like to ride with her, or follow in your own car?"

I look back at Marquez. "Can I leave now, or do you need me to give another statement?"

"You go on ahead with Jenny. Jones is downstairs, he's calling your super about getting that door replaced. I'll file the new reports and meet up with you at the hospital."

The paramedics gingerly place Jenny on the gurney, and she finally opens her eyes. "Kiara?" she asks softly.

"I'm here, Jenny," I tell her, taking her hand. "The paramedics are loading you in the ambulance. The doctors in the ER are going to take great care of you, and I'm won't leave your side."

"Where's Robbs?" she asks.

"I'm sorry, Jenny, he got away again."

She's agitated and struggles to sit up. "That's not possible, I got him."

"Jenny, what do you mean you got him?" Officer Marquez delicately presses. "What can you tell us about what happened here this afternoon?"

"I was sleeping and a loud noise woke me up. I'd brought one of Kiara's knives in here with me. I had it under my pillow. I took it out and hid it under my blanket. I pretended to be asleep, and I heard my door open. I didn't open my eyes until after he landed the first punch. Robbs had an evil look in his eyes, and he just kept hitting me in the head. He didn't realize I was awake until I jumped up with the knife. I caught him off guard and stabbed him in the stomach. I know I got him, I felt the knife hit bone. That's the last thing that I remember."

Not all of this blood is hers, I realize with relief.

"You've done great, Jenny," Officer Marquez tells her in a soothing voice. "You just rest now. I'll alert the area hospitals and clinics to be on the lookout for an abdominal stab wound."

"Jenny, I'm Eric," the paramedic chimes in. "These are my partners, Rocco and Sean. We're going to get you to the hospital now. Can you tell me if anything hurts?"

"Everything hurts," she replies with a frown. "But my head is the worst of it."

"You took several hard blows. You probably have a concussion, but it's a good sign that you're awake and talking."

"Kiara, where's Chase?" Jenny asks.

"Don't worry about that right now," I tell her. "I'll call and tell him what happened once we hear what the doctors have to say."

"I'll post an officer here until the apartment is secure. We'll also need to have the tech team go through the place again, but I doubt we'll find anything," Officer Marquez tells us. "I'll talk to you soon."

"We're going to move you now, Jenny," Eric warns. "Don't worry if you start feeling a little dizzy, that's completely normal."

They lift the gurney, and its wheeled legs drop to the floor. I grab my purse and Jenny's and follow them out the door. When the elevator opens on the ground floor, we're met by Chase.

"Kiara, what happened?" he asks.

"What do you think happened?" I snapped. "While you were off with your little tramp, Robbs paid another visit."

His face turns bright red. "Kiara, that little tramp was Madison. Paul filed an ethics report against me at the college, and she's trying to help me out of it. We both tried to explain it to you…"

Fuck, I forgot all about his sister. Of course that's who he was with!

I'm ashamed of my mistake but I don't have time to make it right. "Chase, we've got to get to the hospital, I don't have time to do this with you right now. I'm sorry I jumped to conclusions."

"Are you riding in the ambulance?"

"Yes, I don't want to leave her," I tell him. Jenny's eyes are closed again, and I'm not sure if she's passed back out or if she's trying to give Chase and me a moment of privacy.

"I'll follow you in my car," he offers quickly.

"No, he broke down our front door and completely trashed the apartment again. Officer Jones has already called the super. Can you stay here until someone puts a new door on?"

"Whatever you need, Kiara."

"There's also quite a bit of blood in Jenny's bedroom. I don't want her to see it when we get back. I don't know if it can be cleaned, but could you at least find a way to cover it up?"

"I'll take care of everything. Please call me the moment the doctors know something. If Robbs shows his face again, I'll put him out of his misery."

"Jenny stabbed him in the gut. With any luck, he's bled out in a ditch somewhere and we'll never have to see him again."

"Good for her," Chase says, obviously impressed. "I'm sorry for the misunderstanding, Kiara."

"Ms. Sands, we really should be going. Would you like to follow in your own car?" Eric asks impatiently.

"No, I'm sorry. I'm ready now."

They load Jenny into the ambulance; I climb in behind them and take a seat at her side.

Jenny opens her eyes. "The moment my head stops pounding, you're going to have to explain to me what you and Chase were just talking about."

"The moment your head stops pounding, I'll do anything you want. Are you sure that you're okay? Emotionally, I mean. Do you want me to call someone from your support group?"

"I'll call them myself as soon as the doctors are done with me. And yes, emotionally I'm fine. I hate to say it, but stabbing Robbs felt better than anything I've done in a long time." She smiles.

"I can only imagine. Maybe he'll show up one last time and I can take my turn." I smile back at her, and we ride to the hospital in silence.

Chapter Eleven

"So what's the verdict, Doc?" Jenny asks Dr. Fields parts her curtain. We've been at the emergency room for three hours, and Jenny has had every test imaginable.

"You've got a pretty severe concussion, but no lasting damage," the doctor announces.

"Thank God," I say with a sigh of relief. "So I can take her home?"

"Not just yet. Jenny, I'd like to admit you overnight for observation. We'll run a new CT in the morning and if the swelling in your head has gone down, I'll discharge you then. The pain meds will also be more effective if we administer them through your I.V. instead of orally."

"That sounds good to me," Jenny quickly agrees. She's been on a morphine drip since we arrived, and I can't remember the last time I saw her so giddy.

"Dr. Fields," Jenny continues. "Have you treated anyone with a stab wound today?"

"I can't disclose information on my other patients," he answers patiently. "I understand that you gave better than you got this afternoon, and I admire that. But I can't tell you if he is here. If it makes you feel any better, if Mr. Martin were to show up here for care, I'd be legally required to call the police."

"I talked to Marquez ten minutes ago, Jenny," I chime in. "They haven't found him yet."

"I don't know if that's good or bad," she says after a long pause. "I wanted to stop him, but I never wanted to kill him… I'm not sure how I'll feel if he's found dead somewhere."

"Jenny, as your doctor, I can tell you that two more blows to the head would have ended your life. You saved yourself today, and that's nothing to be ashamed of, no matter what's happened to Robbs Martin," Dr. Fields says softly. "I'm going to have you moved to your regular room now. I'll check in on you in a few hours."

"Thank you, Dr. Fields."

The doctor steps back through the curtains, and Jenny turns to me.

"So what happened with you and Chase this afternoon?"

"Jenny, we don't have to talk about that now. You need to rest and it was nothing important."

"But I'm *dying* to know," she pleads. "It will make me feel better, take my mind off of things."

"It's a long, stupid story. I made an assumption and basically made an ass of myself. Chase's sister will probably never speak to me again, and if I'd just acted like a reasonable person, I would have gotten home to you a lot sooner.”

“Kiara, don’t start blaming yourself again. I’m not upset that this happened, I finally got to defend myself. I’ve worked so hard to not be afraid of Robbs and when he was standing over me, I really *wasn’t* afraid of him. I was pissed off and my instincts just took over. I didn’t even know I *had* instincts.”

“I’m proud of you, Jenny. I just wish that I’d been there.”

“Which brings us back to my question, what assumption did you jump to? And what does Chase’s sister have to do with it?”

“I saw them together at Whole Foods. They looked so relaxed and comfortable with each other, so I assumed…”

“Oh, Kiara! You accused him of cheating on you with his sister?” Jenny stifles a laugh.

“I did, in the middle of the grocery store. I really told him off, too, insisted that we were moving and I never wanted to see him again. They both tried to explain themselves but I didn’t give them a chance.”

“I’m sure Madison will understand. Chase had to have told her that the apartment had been broken in to last night and that we’d all just lost our jobs. Anyone would be cranky after all of that.”

“I hope you’re right. But she’s also read my student file and watched that video. She probably thinks that I’m a whore and Chase has lost his mind.”

"I don't think Chase is going anywhere, Kiara. You'll have plenty of time to show Madison who you really are."

My cell phone vibrates in my pocket. I retrieve it and see Officer Delco's number on the screen.

"Hi, Officer Delco, thanks for calling me back," I answer.

"Kiara, I just got off of the phone with the Austin PD They told me what happened; are you and Jenny all right?"

"We're fine. Jenny has a concussion, but the doctor says that she'll make a complete recovery."

"Marquez said they still haven't found Robbs. I hope that the bastard is bleeding out somewhere. Tell Jenny that I'm proud of her."

"I will, that's actually why I called you, Officer Delco. I have a question, and I don't know any of the Austin officers well enough to ask them."

"Go ahead."

"If Robbs does die from the stab wound, what will happen to Jenny?"

"Absolutely nothing," he quickly assures me. "This is a clear case of self-defense. You girls have done everything you were supposed to, you have police reports going back four months. At the most, his family could file a wrongful death suit in civil court but again, with the evidence we have, the judge would throw it out."

"Thank you, Officer Delco."

"You're more than welcome, Kiara. My niece loves all of your old furniture. Did your personal items arrive okay?"

"Yes, thank her for me again please. The nurse is here to move Jenny to her regular room so I need to hang up. I'll talk to you soon."

"Take care of yourself."

"What did he say?" Jenny asks nervously as she slides onto her new hospital bed.

"It was self-defense, plain and simple. You won't get in any trouble."

"He's sure?"

"He's positive."

"Kiara, will you go to the meeting tonight and let the girls know what happened? They'd want to know, but I'm not up for talking about it anymore."

"Of course, whatever you want."

The nurse steps out of the curtain and returns with two orderlies. "Okay, Jenny, we're going to take you upstairs now."

"I'll come with you and stay until it's time to leave for the meeting."

"No, Kiara, go home and make things right with Chase."

"Are you sure? I don't want to leave you."

"I'll be just fine, I promise. If I need anything, I'll call you."

"We're taking her to room 5138," the nurse tells me. "That's the fifth floor, first wing, room thirty-eight."

"Thank you, I'll check in as soon as the meeting is over."

"I'll see you then," Jenny says with a yawn. They wheel her down the hallway, and I make my way through the sliding emergency room doors. I suddenly realize that I don't have my car.

I can't ask Chase for any favors right now. Not until I apologize and make things right.

I take out my phone and call for a taxi. The dispatcher promises one will arrive in five minutes, so I take a seat on a bench and wait.

Chapter Twelve

I wake up on a cold concrete floor with a pounding in my head. The room I'm in is dark and damp, and I have no idea how I got here.

"Good morning," Robbs says hoarsely. "I was wondering how long you'd be out. I'm glad you finally woke up, I was getting impatient."

"What did you do to me?" My eyes adjust to the dark, and I see him slumped in a nearby folding chair. I don't need the lights on to see that Robbs is pale. The room smells like iron, and I know that he's still bleeding from his wound.

"The same thing I did to Jenny, I knocked you the fuck out. I don't know if you noticed, but I changed the game up a little bit. I don't want to kill you anymore. I want you and Jenny to both live long lives, so I have as much time as possible to make you suffer."

"We didn't get that memo, Robbs," I tell him sarcastically. "You should have left that on the marker board, maybe Jenny wouldn't have stabbed you. How are you feeling by the way? You don't look so good."

"That bitch barely left a scratch. I'll be just fine, and I'll make her pay for thinking she could hurt me. But first, you and I are going to have some fun."

He tries to get out of the chair but he loses his balance and falls to the floor.

"You're right, that was fun," I taunt him. "What are you going to do next?" I survey the situation as he struggles on the floor. My hands are tied behind my back, but the bindings feel soft, like twisted-up fabric instead of zip ties or rope. My head hurts and the right side of my scalp feels wet, so I know there's a good chance that I have a bleeding head wound. But my eyesight is fine, and I don't feel dizzy or nauseated.

There are no widows in the small room and one wall is lined with shelves of outdated medical equipment. I realize that I must be in the hospital basement.

I was on the bench before he knocked me out. How did no one see him? And how long have I been here? Chase doesn't know that I was on my way home, and Jenny isn't expecting to hear from me until after tonight's meeting. No one's coming to help me. I wonder if he took my phone.

I try to part my legs and realize that they're not bound.

That's one point in my favor. If I can get on my feet, I can make it out that door.

Robbs sits up and leans against the legs of the folding chair. It slides a little but he manages to pull himself to his feet. I brace myself for attack but he sits back down on the seat.

"Barely a scratch, huh?" I ask mockingly.

"It's nothing I couldn't stitch up myself. I'll be fine in a few days. You're going to need a little longer to recover." He pulls a short, thin knife from his pocket. "You see, I've made a decision, Kiara. From now on, whatever you girls do to me, I'm going to do twice as bad to you. Don't worry, I'll call in an anonymous tip in time for doctors to save you. But I'm going to carve an homage to Jenny's handiwork on both sides of your body."

"No, you're not," I tell him defiantly. "Because you can't get out of that chair. You're going to pass out soon. And when you do, I'm going to get out of here and call the police. Don't worry, I'll get the doctors here in time to save you… so you can rot in jail for the rest of your miserable goddamn life."

"You're in no position to threaten me, Kiara," he says, rising to his feet. "Maybe you're right, maybe I am about to pass out. That just means that I need to get to work."

As he stumbles toward me, the door to the storage room bursts open.

"Kiara!" Chase screams.

"Chase, he has a knife!" I warn. I tuck myself into a ball and roll to my right. Chase tackles him to the ground, and they land right where I'd been laying.

I look up and realize that a crowd of people have entered the room. Someone turns on the lights, and I see Officer Marquez, Doctor Fields, a nurse, and a pair of security guards enter the room.

"Kiara, are you all right?" Officer Marquez asks. I nod. "Let Dr. Fields take you into the hallway, he has a gurney waiting. I'll come find you after I've dealt with Robbs."

"Thank you, Officer Marquez," I tell him as he helps me to my feet and cuts my bindings.

He turns to Chase. "You can let him go, I'll take him now."

Chase reluctantly releases Robbs. He turns to me and breaks out in a cold sweat. "Oh my God, are you all right? You're bleeding! What did that bastard do to you?"

"I'm fine, Chase, I've just got a headache. Looks like I'm probably spending the night in the bed next to Jenny."

Chase leads me into the hallway with Dr. Fields and the nurse following closely behind. They help me on to the gurney; the nurse wraps a blood pressure cuff around my arm while Dr. Fields checks my eyes with a small flashlight.

"Do you have any idea how long you were knocked out?"

"What time is it?"

"Seven-fifteen."

"I left the emergency room at four, so three hours, I guess."

"Well, you definitely have a concussion. We'll get a CT and see how bad it is. We'll move Jenny into a double room and have a bed made up for you. I'll get you something for your pain as soon as the scans are finished."

Chase walks alongside my gurney as the nurse wheels me in to the radiology room.

"How did you know where to find me?"

"Delco, he tried to call you a couple of times and he got concerned when you didn't answer. He called Jenny in her hospital room, she called me, and we realized pretty quickly that you were missing. Delco called in some favors and we were able to get the GPS coordinates off your phone. I've been here with Jenny, I didn't want her to be alone with you missing. To be honest, I didn't really want to be alone myself."

"Thank you for being with her… and for saving me."

"Robbs is in pretty bad shape. I hope they save his sorry ass so he can face charges for what he's done."

"Okay, Mr. Abbott, we need you to step out now," the nurse announces.

"You'll wait for me right outside?" I ask him nervously.

He bends down and kisses the top of my forehead. "Like I said a long time ago, Kiara, I'm not going anywhere."

Epilogue

"Kiara, how long on the *Monte Cristo* rolls?" Patrick calls from across the kitchen.

"Four minutes, Patrick," I reply happily. I've been working as Patrick's kitchen manager for the last six weeks. He hadn't had a spot for me the first time I called, but that changed quickly after his soft opening. The man who'd held the position before me just couldn't keep up with Patrick's pace. He knew from experience that I could, and I've never been happier.

The name of the restaurant is *Sandwiched* and the menu is full of eclectic comfort food favorites from all around the world. The prep cook to my right is pickling vegetables for Vietnamese *Banh Mi*, while the line cook to my right pounds out veal parmesan. The menu is reasonably priced, the food is delicious, and the atmosphere is causal and down to earth. It's the complete opposite of everything I'm used to, and I never want to leave.

"What time does your party start?" he asks, checking his watch.

"They'll be here in an hour. Thanks for letting me take a few hours off. You're welcome to join us if you can get away from the kitchen."

"I'll stop by and say 'hi' to everyone. Do you have your new class schedule yet?"

"Yes, I left it on your desk. Classes don't start for another month… are you sure you can work around my schedule?"

"It's important that you finish your degree," he tells me. "Unlike Paul, I understand that. I know you won't want to work here forever. You *shouldn't* want to work here forever. You won't be happy until you have your own restaurant. I'm just happy to give you somewhere to hone your skills."

"Thank you, Patrick. You know, I never realized that you and Paul didn't get along. You were always friendly at Fission."

"I kept my mouth shut and kept my head down. I made a deal with my wife a long time ago; we agreed that I wouldn't open my own place until our house was paid for. We both wanted to make sure that no matter what, we'd be able to keep a roof over the kids' heads. Paul paid me well, so I kissed his ass."

"Have you heard from him lately?"

"No, but one of my produce suppliers told me that he's in major debt to everyone in town. His accounts are all frozen, and they have no idea where he's getting his food. I don't think that Fission will be open much longer. Which is a shame, I know how much it cost him to open it."

I hadn't spoken to Paul since the day he'd called and fired me. I heard through the grapevine that he'd started drinking pretty heavily again, and I knew it was just a matter of time before he lost his restaurant.

"Do you mind if I use some of the langoustines? I know they're expensive."

"Like I said, Kiara, use anything you'd like. All of your good news deserves one hell of a celebration."

Until two months ago, my life had been one disaster after another, usually two or three at a time. And then suddenly, everything changed. Good things started happening. I'm still trying to adjust to the shift.

Tonight, my friends and I are celebrating this week's great news. On Monday, Robbs Martin pled guilty to thirty-two counts of stalking and harassment, twenty-six counts of criminal mischief, eight counts of breaking and entering, four counts of attempted murder, and one count of manslaughter in the death of baby Maggie. The judge was horrified by the case file and sentenced him to a total of ninety-nine years in prison. He won't be eligible for parole until we're all in our late eighties.

On Tuesday, the good news continued. The Administration Board at *Le Cordon Bleu* voted to reinstate my scholarship. They also issued a formal apology for terminating my original scholarship without giving me a chance to defend myself against the charges.

If not for Chase, I'd still be trying to figure out how to pay next semester's tuition. In the aftermath of Robbs' capture, all I wanted to do was spend time with Chase and Jenny. I blocked everything else from my mind. I hadn't even thought about the college until Chase announced that Madison had gotten me another hearing. It was then that I learned that Jenny had told Chase about her idea to trace the files. He called a friend with computer skills and sure enough, all of the files traced back to Robb's I.P. address. Madison took the evidence to the Board, and they agreed to see me. I'm now a semester behind, but I'm grateful that I have a chance to finish.

Chase took classes over the summer, so we're now on track to graduate together. We were tempted to schedule classes together, but in the end we decided against it. He, Jenny, and I are about to move in to a house together, so we think it will be healthy to take some space at school.

I pull the langoustines from their shells and drop them in a lime-cilantro marinade. I'm trying to get all of my dishes prepped before everyone gets here. Landon, our line cook, will fire them so that everything's fresh when we eat.

"So what else is on your menu tonight?" Patrick asks.

"I prepped extra *Monte Cristo* rolls, I thought we'd start with those. I did plenty; you shouldn't have to roll anymore tonight. I'm also doing the langoustine sliders, pork *Banh Mi*, and a couple of the dip platters… unless that's too much. You really don't have to cover this, Patrick, I'd be happy to pay."

"For the last time, Kiara, I want to pay for it. I'm so happy for you, and I'm happy to have you here. Now, is that future sister-in-law coming tonight? I think we need to set her up with Landon."

"Yes, Madison is coming. But Chase and I still aren't engaged," I tell him.

Patrick has become like a big brother to me since I started working here, and he loves that Chase and I are together. If my mother was still around, I imagine she'd pester me about settling down with Chase exactly the way Patrick does. He's offered Chase a job a half-dozen times, but Chase is happy where he landed. He's currently working at Novu, an Indian Fusion restaurant near our new house.

Jenny is also happy with her new job. She's working as a teacher's assistant at one of Austin's private, art-centered elementary schools. The students have all of the usual classes like math and science, but almost half of their days are spent in the theater. Jenny's trying to decide between going back to school for her teaching degree and moving to the West Coast to pursue her own acting dreams.

My best friend has been a completely new person since she fought back against Robbs. She moves with a confidence I'd never seen in her before and I really believe she'll accomplish anything she sets her mind to. I'm so glad that I let my guard down, forgave her, and built the relationship we have today. I can't imagine my life without her.

And loving Jenny opened me up to the absolute best thing that's ever happened to me: falling in love with Chase. He loves me in ways I never realized were possible, and I still can't figure out what I ever did to deserve him. And with him, I've found something that's been missing from my life for a long time, a family. Chase's dad and sister have welcomed me with open arms. And despite the way I protest to Patrick, I'm looking forward to becoming an official part of the Abbott family. I'm in no hurry, of course, but knowing that that day is in my future is a comforting thought.

The kitchen door swings open and Margot, one of the waitresses, peeks her head in. "Kiara, your friends are here. I just sat them at table twelve, and Casey is mixing your first round of drinks."

"Go," Patrick insists. "I'll take care of the rest of this."

"Are you sure?"

"It's your party, Kiara, get out there." He smiles.

I wash my hands, pull off my apron, and check my reflection in the stainless steel sink.

"You look beautiful, go," Patrick says again.

I smooth my hair and join my family with a happy heart.

-The End-

If you enjoyed this series, I would appreciate your leaving a review of the book. Good reviews encourage an author to write as well as help books to sell. Good reviews can be just a few short sentences describing what you liked about the book without having a spoiler. If you could spend 30 seconds writing a review, I would appreciate it: you can review this title right now at your favorite retailer.

Here is a preview of **another story** from the series that follows the "Fifty Recipes For Disaster New Adult Romance Series".

Star Bright - Book 1

THE SUNLIGHT creeps into my room. I groan and turn my head the other direction, trying to sleep through it. The last thing I feel like doing is getting up this morning. I never want to get up again. Everything I've done for the last few months has been robotic.

The holiday season is usually my favorite time of year. There is nothing I love more than browsing around the shops, looking for the best things to buy for my parents and friends.

That was before everything in my life went to hell. Now the thought of seeing anyone or even shopping makes me want to go back to sleep for the rest of the day.

Maggie… my daughter…

This would have been her first Christmas.

The thought comes to me quickly, before I can attempt to stop it. I try to stop all thoughts of her. Yet all it does is drive me into the pit of despair even faster. If I start thinking about her now, I will never get out of bed. I tell myself I will handle this morning the way I handle every other morning – with baby steps.

Open my eyes. It sounds ridiculous to make that a step but when I tell myself baby steps, I truly mean baby steps. If I think of what to do all at once – get up, shower, make coffee – it is all so overwhelming that I don't want to leave my bed.

The baby steps continue. Get out of bed. Walk to the bathroom. Brush my teeth. Open the shower door.

Depression makes even the thought of getting in the shower to wash, only to do it all over again tomorrow, seem idiotic.

After my shower, I decide to go grocery shopping. I remember coming home last night and not finding anything substantial to eat. Instead I ate three slices of bread and went to bed. My stomach is growling loudly at me, demanding something decent to eat.

I slip on an oversized long-sleeved T-shirt and a pair of baggy jeans. Gone are the times when I cared about what I looked like. I don't want anyone to notice me ever again. It is safe to be by myself. I tell myself I can handle being alone.

Before I leave, I check my bank account on my phone. My savings are dwindling. I need to get a job. This can't last forever. When I quit my job, I figured something else would fall into my lap. But it's hard to have things fall in your lap when you never leave your bed. *I'm becoming pathetic.* I grab my purse and head out into the chilly morning.

A thin layer of snow covers the ground. The sun has now retreated behind a mass of gray clouds. They threaten a heavy snowfall. I wouldn't mind if it snowed everyone in. Sadly, Netflix is my new best friend.

The grocery store is brimming with families with their kids in tow, out of school for the holidays. I curse myself for not thinking of this before I left my apartment this morning. I wander around blindly, my list in hand, as my gaze falls on the kids around me. My heart beats quickly in my chest and my skin feels numb. All I want is to take Maggie's hand and walk through the store with her. I would kill to see her try to grab something off the shelf or plead with me to get her a doll in the small toy section.

Instead I am alone, a panic attack blooming on the brink. What is my trigger exactly? Happy kids? Couples who look down at their children and beam? I feel stupid as I park my basket in a random aisle and bolt into the restroom, which is thankfully empty. I go into one of the stalls then close my eyes tightly.

I can't live like this forever. Every time I decide to leave the house, I find myself overwhelmed by people or past memories. Everything seems to be trying to get my attention, telling me that my old dreams have died and I am letting life pass me by.

I have done things in my life that I am not proud of. I have terrible taste in men. I have a habit of only being attracted to assholes or drunks and I have had no issues cheating on people to be with someone else.

My skin feels hot and itchy as I try to avoid the panic attack that will knock me over. I focus on my breathing.

I am here. I am here. I am here.

I am nowhere else. What I have done in the past is in the past. I can't get Maggie back. I won't get Paul back after what I've done to him. I even feel like I deserve what Robbs has done to me.

Focusing on my breathing and repeating my mantra helps slow my heart rate down. I am glad no one else has come into the bathroom. The last thing I need is someone else thinking I am crazy.

After ten minutes, I am able to leave the stall. I splash some water on my face and look in the mirror. I hardly recognize myself. I have let myself go. I have to get a handle on my life but I have no idea how to do so. I have been hoping a sign will come to let me know what to do next. But what if that is just an excuse to give myself a pass on my shitty behavior? What if this is the sign – almost having a panic attack in a supermarket over happy children?

I leave the restroom, ready to get my grocery shopping done without further incident. By the time I leave the supermarket, I am feeling grounded again. Sometimes my head gets the best of me. I decide I'll brush it from my mind and go get a coffee. I haven't bought anything frozen, so I don't need to get home right away. My inner chef refuses to die, so the thought of making a frozen meal still does not appeal to me, even with how depressed I am.

It has been a while since I have treated myself to an overpriced iced coffee. But today is quickly becoming a day that is unlike the others so I head into the coffee shop, trying to ignore the small crowd standing in line to wait. I find myself lost in thought at the menu, which seems to have doubled in items since the last time I was here.

Someone taps on my shoulder, and I nearly jump out of my skin. I take a deep breath and turn around, fearing who it will be.

If you enjoyed this sample then look for **Star Bright - Book 1**.

Here is a preview of **another story** you may also

enjoy:

Devil's Advocate: A BBW MC New Adult Romance Series - Book 1

KRISTIE LOOKED at the sky as she pulled up in front of the casino. The air was chilly and the clouds were dark and threatening snow, which was the last thing Kristie felt like dealing with. She had been in her car for over ten hours, driving home from college for the holidays. Her back was sore and her legs needed to be stretched out. She wanted a hot bath in a Jacuzzi tub. She'd settle for a hot tub. But who was she kidding? There was no hot tub to be found at her parents' house and trying to have a hot bath without being interrupted was almost impossible.

Kristie had approached the holidays with an ever-growing sense of dread. It wasn't that she didn't want to see her mother, but every time she came home, it was like being suffocated. Her hometown had held more appeal for her when she was younger, back when her father was alive. Since he'd died and her mother had gotten remarried last year, Kristie had delayed going home at all. She had only met her step-father in passing and hadn't met his nephew, who he tried to raise on his own.

Kristie had saved up to stay at a hotel the entire break. It had made the most sense to her. It would cause the least amount of stress during her stay and give her space when she needed it. But when she had mentioned this to her mother, there was no way to mistake the sadness in her mother's voice for anything else. Knowing she was upsetting her mother by refusing to stay at home with her new family, Kristie had cancelled the reservation and agreed to stay at her mother's house instead.

She looked up at the casino where her mother had worked the last five years. Her mother worked in the back offices, far away from the lights from the slot machines and the sounds of people winning money. The casino was a little run down but brought in a steady stream of people who could afford the middle-level slots and risks it provided in a town that was mostly quiet.

The stale smell of cigarettes and alcohol hit Kristie in the face as she stepped inside. She looked around, seeing if anything had changed since the last time she had been here. Nothing jumped out of her. A few of the slots seemed to have been upgraded, but the carpet was still worn down and dirty and the place had an air of despair that made Kristie's skin crawl. She had never been to Las Vegas, but she imagined that the casinos there weren't as depressing.

Kristie made her way to the back and asked for her mother through the grate where an attendant was standing, looking at her cellphone. The woman went off to find her mother, and Kristie was soon ushered into the back offices. The casino décor quickly ended back here. Her mother's small office was near the back, shoved in a corner. The door was ajar, and Kristie peeked her head in.

Her mother was looking at the computer, squinting through her glasses to whatever was on the screen. When Kristie knocked on the door gently, her mother looked up and smiled. Kristie was startled to see she was going gray. The last time she had seen her mother, she had been a brunette. It was odd to see age creeping up on her. She came over to her and hugged her tightly.

"It's so nice to see you again."

"You, too, Mom."

Her mom urged her to sit down as she sat across from her at her desk. It made Kristie feel odd, as if she was interviewing to be her mother's daughter. Her mom didn't seem to notice, however, and smiled again. They made small talk for a while, mostly talking about Kristie's experiences at college. Kristie felt tired. She knew her mom meant well, but she really wanted to go home and nap. She was only here to get the address to her mom's new place.

"How are things with Lionel?" Kristie finally asked, feeling as if she didn't bring up her mom's new husband, she would never get out of the tiny office.

Her mom seemed to relax now that Kristie had brought him up, "He's great. Really, we're just wonderful. There are some issues, though…"

"Like what?"

"Well, it's actually one of the reasons that we wanted you to stay with us instead of a hotel. See, Lionel's nephew, Gray, is a bit of a handful. Lionel still feels responsible for him since he became his legal guardian when Gray was just a little boy."

Kristie wasn't following, "Okay…"

"He tends to run on the wrong side of the law, and we thought it'd be so great if you two could meet and maybe hang out."

The words hung in the air. Kristie felt a twinge of annoyance. She had thought her mother wanted her at the house because she had missed her, not because she wanted her to play nice with her new step-father's nephew. They weren't in grade school anymore. Trying to change someone set in their ways by sticking them with a goody-goody was a useless attempt.

Kristie took a deep breath and held it for a few seconds, letting the air out slowly. Her mother watched, a worried expression on her face.

"What do you want me to do with him?" Kristie finally asked.

Her mom, taking the fact that Kristie hadn't said no as a good sign, started to ramble. "Well, maybe just hang out with him. Show him what you do for fun. Maybe you two can go to the movies or something."

Kristie raised an eyebrow, "Go to the movies? What does this guy do for fun anyway that has you two so stressed out?"

Her mom avoided her stare and sighed, looking tired. "He runs with a bad crowd and doesn't like to listen. He's a good kid though. He's just lost."

"And you think I can fix him?"

"It wouldn't hurt to try, would it, Kristie? For me?"

Kristie sighed and nodded in agreement. How could she say no to her mother? She would always wish that her mother hadn't gotten remarried, but she didn't want her mom to be unhappy either. Her mom got up and walked over to her, hugging her tightly. Her mother's hugs had always reminded Kristie of being a little kid, outside playing till the sun set and running back inside for dinner. Back when her father was alive. Kristie shut her eyes tightly, willing the memories to leave her. She didn't want to think about her father right now.

Her mom finally pulled away and looked at her, smiling, "We'll have to really talk, you know, all about college and everything."

"Yeah, of course."

Her mom's eyes swept down her quickly, so fast that if Kristie wasn't used to it, she never would have picked up on it. She steeled herself.

"Maybe you and Gray can go to the gym. It'd get him out of the house and you could lose a few pounds at the same time," her mom said cheerfully.

Kristie mumbled in agreement and gave her mother one last hug before leaving the office. She should have known that there wasn't going to be any way in hell that her mother would have let an entire conversation go without making some sort of remark to her about her weight.

As she trudged through the casino, her mood lowered with every step. She regretted coming here for the holidays. Before her, they spread out in a bleak landscape. Dealing with her mother's 'helpful advice' in regards to her weight, and trying to show her loser relative by marriage around town. At the very least, she should have kept the hotel reservation.

Kristie dragged out the drive toward Lionel's house. Her mother had given her the address and it was close to the casino. A ten-minute drive didn't seem like enough time to prepare for whatever she was going to walk into. As she turned down the street where her mom's new house was, she found herself taking a deep breath. The first time, she just drove past the house. It was non-descript and had nothing of worth showing that made Kristie even notice it. Her mom had stopped gardening after her father died, and the front yard of this house was plain and dull.

Kristie pulled into the driveway. The garage door was open and a man was underneath a truck, working on it. She could only see his feet. Kristie got out of her car, grabbing her bags, and looked inside the garage. The man didn't look up when she shut the door of her car.

"Hello?" Kristie called out toward the man under the truck.

He didn't answer. Heavy metal was blasting out of a stereo nearby, but it was such an old stereo that the music sounded tinny. Kristie called out again, but the man still didn't answer. She knew that he heard her because he stopped working at one point and went still before resuming. She hoped this wasn't Lionel, because the guy was an asshole. *Probably his fantastic nephew.* Kristie trudged toward the front door, leaving the other guy behind. What a fantastic trip this was going to be.

If you enjoyed this sample then look for **Devil's Advocate: A BBW MC New Adult Romance Series - Book 1**.

Here is a preview of **another story** you may also enjoy:

Torrid Exposure - Book 1

"I THINK it looks nice."

"Are you crazy? It isn't even at all."

"Well, you do it then, April."

I sigh and take a step forward, looking at the photo that Emily had hung up in the living room. It looks crooked to me. Okay, maybe just a little off center. I lean forward and nudge it slightly with my finger. It slides just over enough to look perfectly center to me and I look back at her.

Emily is wearing an amused expression on her face. "Oh, yeah, massive difference."

I know she is teasing me. I roll my eyes and look back at the photo. I hear Emily leaving the room to go finish unpacking in her own bedroom. I look around the living room. The big things seemed to be unpacked. I sit down on the couch and sink into it, relaxing my feet for a moment.

Moving felt as if it had taken ages. I am glad to see that the big things are all unpacked. Now I can try to relax for the night. Even though it is hot outside, part of me wants to bundle up underneath a pile of blankets and go to sleep.

But I get up and make myself walk to my own bedroom. *My own bedroom.* It sounds foreign to me. Not that I haven't ever *had* my own bedroom. Of course, I had my own bedroom when I lived at home. But I shared a dorm room in college so I wasn't exactly dealing with the utmost of privacy.

Now, however, I have a space all to myself. The only other person in this apartment is Emily, my best friend since I was little. Finally, it feels as if life is falling into place.

I sit down on the floor and start going through one of the boxes. I have always been terrible at packing. I usually end up shoving everything in boxes without any sort of organization at all. I never learn, apparently, because this current box has everything from clothes to my laptop. At the bottom, I yank something out. It is a photo album. This is weird… I didn't put this in here.

I flip it open to a random photo and see myself at age six. My skinny arms are wrapped around my sister, who is beaming at the camera. Behind her is a water slide. We must have been at some water park.

I scowl. My sister, Spencer, must have slipped this in the box. It was most likely a last ditch attempt at getting me to reach out to her.

"It isn't going to work," I say out loud and shove the photo album back in the box.

Emily sticks her head in inquiring, "Did you say something?"

"Yeah. Not to you though. Just…" I bite my bottom lip, "… just that Spencer shoved this stupid photo album in one of the boxes. I didn't notice it until now."

Emily is staring at me, clearly trying to figure out what to say next. She, of all people, knows the relationship I have with my family and that it isn't the best. But I don't want to ruin our day of getting our own place with mention of them so I quickly shake my head.

"No, it's cool, really. I'm just going to finish unpacking in here."

"Okay," she replies and turns around to leave before hesitating. "Listen, April. You know if you need to talk about them, you can. You don't have to lock it all up inside."

"I know. Thanks."

Emily nods at me and leaves me alone in my bedroom again. My earlier zest at having my own space is now slightly dulled. I sit on the floor and run my fingers over the cover of the photo album. I don't know when Spencer would have snuck this in. Did she really think this would do anything? Knowing her, she probably thought I would see it and decide to move back home.

Well, she is wrong. I stand up and decide to go through another box. If I find another surprise from her in any of these boxes, I am going to lose it on her. But I then think quickly, maybe that is what she wants me to do.

I decide I'll unpack something I like. The big box holding my photography equipment is stacked up against the wall. I yank it over and sit down on the floor again, opening it up and slowly pulling everything out.

Once I am holding my camera, I feel myself calm down a bit. It is state of the art. All my equipment is expensive – and I had purchased it all by myself. No hand-outs from Mommy and Daddy, no matter what anyone may think. I go through the box and organize everything. I was itching to take photos of my room and I took some spontaneous shots. I want to start a photo album of my life beginning with moving out on my own and continue on as I get my career going.

After I finish taking some photos of my room, I grab clean clothes and head into the bathroom for a quick shower. I can hear Emily talking to someone quietly on her phone in the kitchen. It is probably her boyfriend. Ever since Matt and I broke up, she is worried that if I hear her talking to her boyfriend, I might start crying over my failed relationship.

Maybe I would have a couple of months ago. But I am working every day to get over Matt and everything we went through. I tell myself that what we had was just a college romance. Of course it was going to end after graduation. That was what I told everyone after we broke up. I downplayed how serious we were. I felt like a fool for not seeing it before it happened.

Only Emily knew how hard the break-up hit me. Better not to think about Matt now. I have other things that I need to focus on. Whatever I went through with Matt is in the past now.

I step into the shower to clear my mind. I have things to get arranged. No use in thinking about the past.

If you enjoyed this sample then look for **Torrid Exposure - Book 1**.

Here is a preview of **another story** you may also enjoy:

Alpha Packed: A BBW Paranormal Shifter Romance - Book 1 by Darla Dunbar.

THIS WAS a huge mistake. Darlene should have known better, but in utter and total desperation, she agreed to this date. Now the guy in front of her—what was his name again? Steve? Mike? She couldn't even remember now—had been talking non-stop about pro wrestling. But not even actual real wrestling. The stuff that was fake and basically just soap operas with some terrible phony fights thrown in.

"So then the Ice Cube challenged The Man to a battle!"

"Wow, really?" Darlene replied, feigning interest on every possible level.

This was her mistake. She had been spending way too much time at home lately, curled up on the couch, binge watching reality television shows because they made her feel better about her boring life. Darlene would leave for work in the mornings, do eight hours at a boring local bookstore, come home, eat and watch TV. She also stayed up far later than any normal human should, which resulted in limited forms of social communication.

That was how Darlene ended up on some free dating website. She deleted most of the messages she got. They were mostly from guys who seemed to think of her as a sexual fetish instead of an actual human being. Getting messages from guys who were into her being overweight made her feel uncomfortable. Darlene either got disgusted looks or sexual lust over her size. Both sucked. She had been about to delete her page for good

when a guy who appeared to be normal messaged her.
He hadn't made any gross comments about her size and
even made her laugh once or twice with his messages. It
had been eight months since her last relationship blew
up in her face. *Why not try something different?* She
decided to accept his date.

The guy was so boring that Darlene wished the
restaurant would go up in flames so she could flee. She
was flipping through her options on how to end the date
early when he finally pushed his plate away.

"That was delicious," he said.

"Oh yeah. It was great," Darlene lied, thinking the
potatoes were too dry for her liking.

The check came and the guy—what was his
name!—made an effort to search for his wallet. *Oh here
we go...*

"Oh man. I forgot my wallet at home!" he said with
fake surprise.

"Yeah, yeah, I got it," she mumbled, slamming her
debit card on the table.

It didn't take a genius to figure out this asshole had
asked her out to throw her what he thought was a "pity
date" and get a free meal out of her. He would probably
go home to all his idiot friends and talk about how he
gave the fat girl a date because he was just so nice.
Darlene felt like punching him in the face.

She paid, and they walked out of the restaurant in
silence. He escorted her to her car and then glanced

around, as if checking so that no one could see him, before he tried to kiss her.

"Yeah," Darlene lifted up her hand to block him, "I don't think so. Thanks for nothing though, seriously."

The man scowled and before he could say something back, Darlene got into her car. She pulled out of the parking lot as quickly as she could, wanting to forget the entire terrible date.

What a mistake. What an absolute mistake. Not even just the date. The last couple years of her life had been a huge mistake. She wished she could travel back in time and re-do everything. The first thing she'd do would be to say a resounding *no* when Austin proposed to her.

Darlene pulled into her apartment complex five minutes later. She had picked a nearby restaurant so she could make a quick escape home if needed. She walked up to the second floor. The couple by the stairwell was fighting again. They were constantly screaming at each other over everything. Some nights, Darlene wanted to yell back at them to just break up. Other times, she wanted to tell them to make it work, because being alone was terrible.

She opened the front door of her apartment and glanced around. Her computer was on in one corner, and a few blankets were thrown on the couch for maximum comfort for those times when she drowned herself in ice cream and terrible reality shows. Everything else was clean though. Darlene couldn't stand her apartment being messy or dirty. She wanted it to be perfect, as if she could make her apartment look like how she didn't feel.

Darlene yanked off her high heels and plopped down in front of her computer. She deleted the online dating profile and stared out the window. That was it — she was going to become a hermit. Well, as much of a hermit as one can be if they still had to go to work and grocery shop and run errands…but other than that she was totally going to be a hermit from now on. People were not her thing. People were just terrible all around. And she'd had enough of terrible people.

She moved to the couch, wrapping herself up in a blanket. Darlene mused over what she would watch. Terrible shows about being tricked into online dating seemed like a good end to the night. It'd make her feel better at the very least.

Her cellphone rang loudly. Darlene jolted awake, startled. She wasn't used to her new ringtone. It used to be the theme song of an old cartoon she liked, but after everything went to hell she changed it to a normal ring in an effort to seem more adult. Now the ring was bleating loudly and annoying her. She looked at the front of the screen… her boss.

"Hello?"

"Hey, sorry, did I wake you?"

"No, Maria," Darlene lied. "What's up?"

"I had to fire Jacob. Can you cover his shift? You'd be working till three."

Darlene glanced at the clock to see it was a little past eight in the morning. "That's fine. I'll leave now."

She hopped in the shower, letting the warm water rush over her. She wasn't surprised that Maria had to fire Jacob. He was constantly late and unable to help any of the customers who came into the shop. The bookstore was small and dealt with books that couldn't be found at any of the chains. Business was slow, but the books were rare enough that Maria only needed to sell a few each month to keep the business going. Darlene liked how quiet it was and the fact that human interaction was minimal. She knew she needed to get over this slump she was in, but felt no desire to. Almost everything Darlene did as of late seemed to feed into it — her lifestyle, her job, even the stupid things she spent time watching and looking up online.

The bookstore was only a ten-minute drive to downtown and located between a coffee shop and a cheesy massage parlor. Maria hated the massage parlor. She thought it was tacky and ruined the charm of the street. Darlene usually liked to watch to see how many guys went in there. She swore it was a front for some hookers.

Darlene parked her car and headed toward the bookshop. She could already tell no one was in the store. She walked inside and waved to Maria.

"Oh, I am so glad you are here!" Maria exclaimed when she saw Darlene. "I'll have to hire someone right away, but you and I will have to work extra in the meantime."

"No problem," Darlene replied, shoving her purse under the front counter.

Darlene worked here for almost four years. Maria was a good boss. She always treated Darlene with respect and even gave her an entire month off after her father passed away three years ago. She was an older Native American woman with a bushy head of white hair that she barely cared enough to run a comb through. She wore large glasses that looked like they were from the seventies. Her fashion left a lot to be desired. Maria seemed to put on whatever she grabbed first and didn't look twice in the mirror afterward. For instance, today she had on a blue shirt with an off-color green skirt and black shoes. Her earrings were painted octopuses she had probably made herself — she liked making crazy jewelry.

"So," Darlene asked. "What happened with Jacob?"

Maria scowled. "He comes into work high as a kite, stinking of weed. Starts rambling to me about how he was in the woods last night and *like, totally felt something, like, man*," Maria said, mimicking Jacob's slow tone. "He was an hour late on top of it. I can't have someone late, stinking of weed and scaring off the few customers I get each month… especially after the last incident."

"Yeah, that was a mess." Jacob had hit on one of their regular clients in such a crass manner that she had threatened never to return again.

"Anyway, thank you so much for covering. I'm going to head off now. One of the grandkids is having a birthday party. You'll be okay?"

Darlene cast a sarcastic glance around the empty bookstore. "Wow, I hope I can handle it."

Maria laughed and grabbed her purse, heading to the door before stopping. "Hey, how was your date?"

Darlene frowned. "A total mess."

"Sorry, love. Hang in there, okay?" Maria said before leaving.

Hang in there. Darlene sighed. She has been hanging in there for way too long. When was she going to get a grip on her own life again? She walked around the shop to make sure everything was in its proper place. Darlene knew it would be, of course. It wasn't as if they had a ton of customers come through.

Maria had the marketable books up front, which brought in some tourist traffic during the summer. The farther back in the store one went, the stranger the books became. Darlene ended up in the back again, like she always did. Maria kept the supernatural books back here — books about ghosts, werewolves, mermaids and all sorts of paranormal creatures. Darlene always felt drawn to these; she never knew why. As a kid, she liked to pretend to be a ghost hunter. Nowadays, she liked to watch terrible B-movies about ghosts.

She trailed her fingers along the spines, letting the musty old-book smell wash over her. Darlene stopped in front of one book about ghosts, pulling it off the shelf. She had just flipped it open to a random page when the tiny bell on the door jingled. Surprised, Darlene looked up.

A tall man in amazing shape walked in. He had brown eyes, a beard and scruffy hair and wore a leather jacket. Darlene found herself gawking at him. He was so handsome her knees turned to jelly.

"Hi!" she said, but her voice sounded too high pitched, like she was eleven. "Hi, sorry, back here." She walked up front to him.

"Hello," he said in a deep voice that sent shivers down her back.

"Hi," Darlene repeated and then tried to get a hold of herself. "How can I help you?"

"I'm lost. I'm trying to find Roman's Tavern."

Her eyes widened. "I don't know if it's open yet."

Was this guy a hardcore alcoholic? It was still early in the morning, and he wanted to find a bar. Roman's Tavern was the only bar in town that Darlene hadn't ever gone to. It brought in a wild crowd that made her uneasy. Any time she drove past it and saw the crazy partying in there, she realized how much she wanted to go and that scared her. She was never much of a partier. The fact that such an overwhelming urge to go when she drove by made her nervous. What if she went and lost her head?

The cops were there often, breaking up fights. Bike gangs were always seen there. Sometimes, if she left work at closing time, she'd drive by it and hear the thumping music and smell the cigarette smoke. She thought about going in every time. What would happen? Would she get hurt? What if she was missing out on something?

To Darlene, Roman's Tavern represented a life she could jump into if only she wasn't afraid. But she *was* too afraid. Life as a hermit was too comforting.

"Do you know where I can find it anyway?" he asked.

"It's down the street. On the corner, kind of pushed back a bit. It has this rundown broken sign that you might see if you drive by it."

"Thanks a lot, Miss…"

"Darlene." She held out her hand.

He stared at it for a second and then shook it. "Idris. Thanks for the help. You guys sell books about ghosts?" He pointed to the book she was holding when he came in.

His hand was so warm that Darlene had to snap herself back to the conversation. Was he sick? Shouldn't he be resting instead of going to some bar?

"Yes," she managed to respond. "We have a supernatural section in the back. Ghosts, vampires, werewolves…the usual."

"Werewolves, huh?" he replied. "Okay, well, nice to meet you."

Before Darlene could say anything else, he was gone.

She stood there, clutching her book to her chest, thinking about the feeling of warmth from his hand. What in the world was that about?

If you enjoyed this sample then look for **Alpha Packed: A BBW Paranormal Shifter Romance - Book 1 by Darla Dunbar**.

Other Books by Carla Coxwell

- Star Bright New Adult Romance Series (This series follows "Fifty Recipes For Disaster New Adult Romance Series")

- Torrid Exposure New Adult Romance Series

- Devil's Advocate BBW MC New Adult Romance Series

- Obsessed Bounty Hunter Romance Series

Get the latest update on new releases from the author at:

https://www.carlacoxwell.com/newsletter

About the Author - Carla Coxwell

Carla has always been a fan of romance novels. To augment what she made waiting on tables to help her way through college, Carla also did some freelance work in the romance genre.

Now she enjoys living vicariously through her characters in her New Adult Romance books.

Connect with Carla Coxwell

I really appreciate you reading my book! Here are my social media coordinates:

Friend me on Facebook:
https://www.facebook.com/CarlaCoxwell/

Follow me on Twitter: https://twitter.com/carlacoxwell

Check me out on Goodreads:
https://www.goodreads.com/author/show/10691544.Car la_Coxwell

Subscribe to my newsletter:
https://www.carlacoxwell.com/newsletter/

Visit my website: https://www.carlacoxwell.com/